I0589298

the red bekisar

Ahmad Tohari
Translated from the Indonesian by
Nurhayat Indriyatno Mohamed

Dalang Publishing

The Red Bekisar
Originally published as *Bekisar Merah* in 2011 by Penerbit PT Gramedia Pustaka Utama, Jakarta, Indonesia (ISBN: 978-979-22-6632-0)
Copyright © 2011 Ahmad Tohari
Translation copyright © 2014 Nurhayat Indriyatno Mohamed

Publication of this book is subsidized by the Center for Research and Development, Office of Research and Development, Ministry of Education and Culture of the Republic of Indonesia, and in collaboration with Penerbit PT Gramedia Pustaka Utama.

Cover design: Herfitrisna Yulianti Asnar
Book design: Son Do
Editor: Sal Glynn
Indonesian literary advisors: Manneke Budiman and Julia Eka Rini

Dalang Publishing LLC
San Mateo, CA
www.dalangpublishing.com
dalangpublishing@gmail.com

ISBN: 978-0-9836273-2-6
Library of Congress number: 2014955502

THE RED BEKISAR

Translator's Note

"Handle with care, because this is my baby," Lian Gouw, publisher extraordinaire, told me before I began translating *The Red Bekisar.*

It's easy to see why she was so concerned this novel be done right. Ahmad Tohari has put out fewer than ten books since 1980, yet has won scores of accolades for his prose. *The Red Bekisar* shows Tohari at his best, from the opening description of a rain-lashed valley to the desolate truck ride from Karangsoga to Jakarta.

I had a harder time translating this book than any I'd done before. It was more than the language, the little-known birds and plants, and frequent lapses from Indonesian to Javanese; I also had to keep up with the constant shifts in tempo that make reading this book a truly immersive experience.

The timing was also a problem. I began translating just as Indonesia was in the middle of an election campaign that seemed poised to hand the presidency to a former scion of the Suharto clan—an ex-general accused of human rights abuses. The political horse-trading and smear campaigns of the present mirrored the themes of abuse of power and moral turpitude described so vividly in *The Red Bekisar.* I was struck by how a story set more than forty years ago carried a message that rang as true for today's world. Tohari's novel is a moral indictment of the government as it was then—and remains.

As the campaigning grew uglier, and my deadlines to the patient Ms. Gouw came and went, I saw that *The Red Bekisar* was more than a story of two lovers overcoming difficulties to end up in each other's arms. It was a love story with a happy ending, certainly, but a love story in the same vein as *Anna Karenina*—exquisitely tragic.

For all their optimism, Lasi and Kanjat are tragic figures caught up in life's vagaries, exploited by the likes of Mrs. Lanting—a caricature of the many people who inhabit the overlap between politics, business, and vice—and powerless to resist.

The world that Ahmad Tohari presents is one of heart-rending beauty and unspeakable ugliness.

To translate this book, then, meant plumbing those depths and touching those heights. If the English version of *Bekisar Merah* spans those extremes, I will be proud to have done it justice.

Nurhayat Indriyatno Mohamed
September 2014

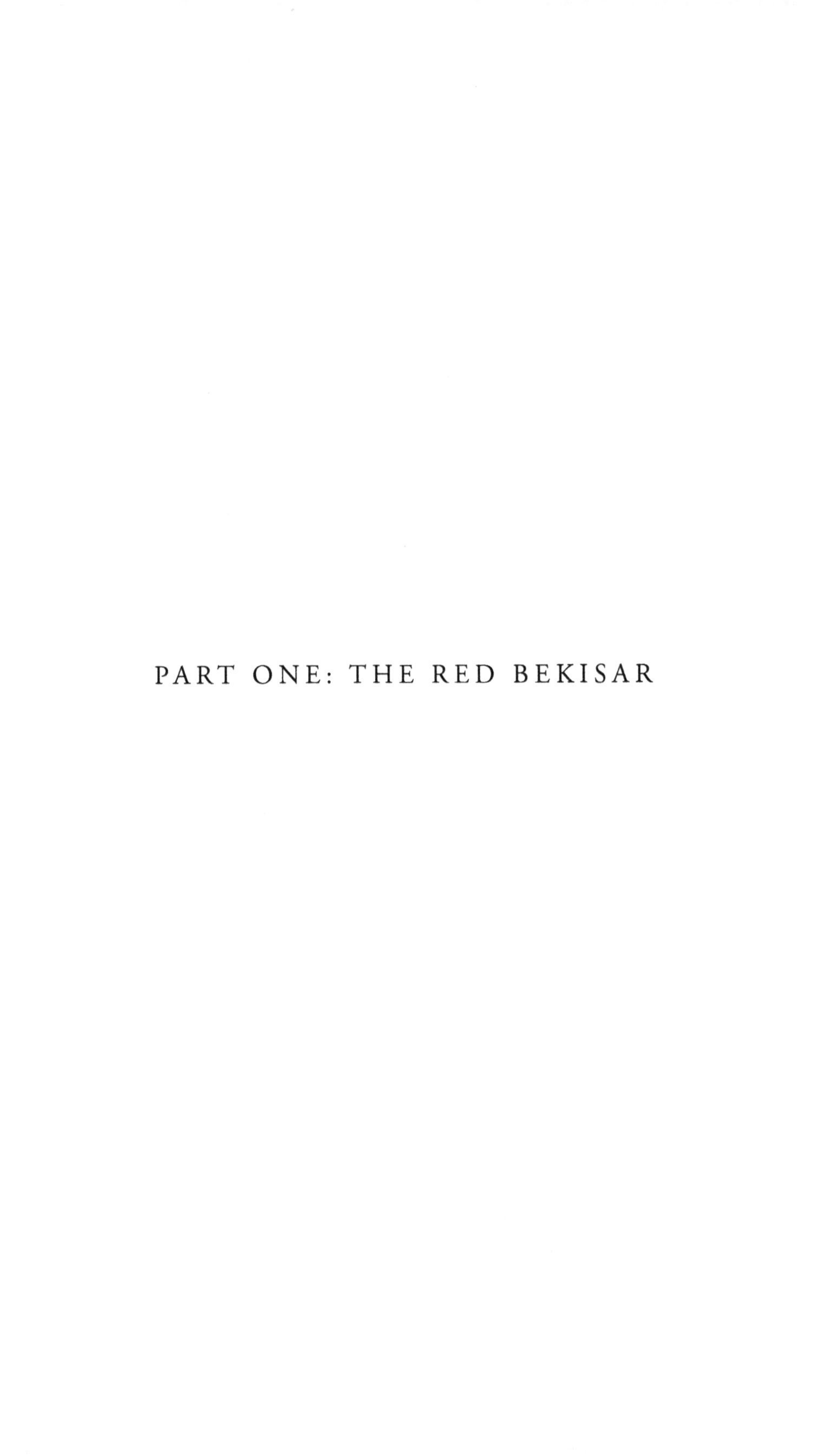

PART ONE: THE RED BEKISAR

Chapter 1

Behind the curtain of afternoon rain, the coconut palms across the valley looked like bathing virgins, full of vigor and life. Willowy trunks swayed in the wind like slim bodies swinging with ease and charm, and wet fronds hung like hair between their shoulder blades. The wind suddenly picked up and the fronds swayed in the same direction, like the arms of a dancer following the rhythm of the rain, like girls playfully lined up beneath a spout of falling water.

The palms grew on a slope among a lush grove, the tilt of the slope making it look like a classical Balinese painting hung on a wall of sky. Beside the palms that imparted softness were *sengon* trees that grew straight and thin in strong white lines. Young sugar palm leaves unfurled yellow and vibrant. A reddish-brown dogfruit tree and a crepe myrtle with giant purple flowers stood close to a flame tree with vivid red blossoms. The branches of *jambe rowe*, a kind of areca palm with its round, large fruit, gave the scene an aged look.

Sweeping rain darkened the panorama across the valley, but weather during the transition between seasons could change in an instant. The rain kept falling and the wind blew harder until the clouds parted and the sun shone from the west. It lit the large painting across the valley, bringing brighter colors and more depth. Pearls shimmered where the sunlight reflected at just the right angle off the wet, swaying leaves.

A rainbow arched in the gray-blue sky behind the hill. Nature had swaddled its virgin children after their bath in a mist of colorful light.

The sun disappeared and everything went dark again. Rain fell harder as thunder echoed against the valley walls. A strong wind seemed intent on uprooting the coconut palms.

Darsa's heartbeat quickened. He looked at the coconut palms across the valley for a long time, almost in despair. The rain and wind had to stop soon or he could not go out and tap the trees.

He was a tapper of *nira*, and accustomed to climbing more than a dozen palms in the rain to collect *pongkors* full of nira and replace them with empty ones. Today wind and thunder accompanied the rain. No tapper would go out in this kind of weather, even when he knew the consequences of not collecting the pongkors in time: the nira would turn sour and be useless for making palm sugar. All he could make out of sour nira was *gemblung* sugar, a pasty concoction that sold for very little. Failing to produce palm sugar meant a loss of what little income a tapper made. During those times, he had to put his meals on credit at the local food stall.

From beneath the eaves of his bamboo house, Darsa stared to the east across the valley where the rain drenched the coconut palms. He felt restless, as though his livelihood as a tapper was being challenged.

For Darsa, as for all tappers, the coconut palms were a hope and challenge, a source that gave him the desire and reason to live. But as long as the rain and wind refused to let up, Darsa was powerless to go near the palms that seemed to beckon him with their fronds.

Thunder echoed again and the rain poured down even harder. Darsa's heart shrank inside him. He had to resign himself to seeing his precious nira turn into a sour brew because he couldn't get to it in time. He was desperate. The pongkors called to him, spearing his heart with pleas to collect them. When the rain let up, Darsa had new hope, but when it began falling heavily again and thunder rang out, all hope disappeared.

The drum at Grandfather Mus' *surau* called the *azar* prayer time, faint against the noise of the rain. It was late afternoon and almost dusk. The weather would not change any time soon and Darsa's chance to collect nira had vanished.

His shoulders drooped from near hopelessness as he turned and went inside his house. He stood in the middle room and watched his wife, Lasi, hang a wet sheet on the clothesline beneath the eaves on the west. She had just bathed. Her hair was loose and wet. It fell behind her right ear, curled to the front, and, Darsa imagined, splayed across her chest.

Darsa thought of the coconut palms in the rain. Lasi faced away from him and he admired her bare back and neck. The contrast between her dark hair and fair skin created a strange attraction. Lasi's skin was fairer than that of any other woman he had seen. He felt eternally lucky to have a wife with a special kind of beauty, especially those features close to her hair, like her neck and her cheeks. When Lasi laughed, a pretty dimple appeared in her left cheek.

The charm and sense of life Darsa had witnessed moments before in the coconut palms across the valley transposed themselves perfectly to Lasi. Just as the palms challenged him to tap them, Lasi, too, had a tempting promise and vitality. In Lasi, he had a receptacle to manifest himself as a man and a nira tapper. Darsa found a haven of trusting loyalty in his wife. Even more than in the coconut palms that never stopped giving, he saw in Lasi the very value and purpose of his life, even though they had been married three years without her having given him any children.

Lasi finished hanging the wet sheets. As she turned to go into the house, her eyes locked on her husband. He surprised her, even though she no longer found how he looked at her as strange. She sometimes stole a glance at him and studied his body from behind: the muscled and balanced body of a young man; the body of a tapper who twice a day climbed a dozen or more coconut palms. Climbing up and down the palm trunk exercised every muscle, especially those in his legs, arms, and back. The result was a lean body with wiry and toned muscles. If there were a disadvantage to a tapper's body, it would be the slight hunch from constantly gripping the trunk to climb and descend.

Lasi and Darsa smiled. Outside, it still rained heavily. The small bamboo house felt cold and lonely. The only sounds came from the rain and the wind whistling through the bamboo poles stacked out back, and the occasional clucking of a mother hen and her chicks on the back porch. No sign of life came from the house of Lasi's parents, the only one nearby. Lasi and Darsa kept looking at each other and smiling.

"Las, do you think I should go out?"

"It's still raining."

"What if I go anyway?"

"That's up to you, but it doesn't feel right for you to work in this kind of weather."

"Do we still have rice?"

"Yes, and I have a little money. We have enough to eat tomorrow even if we can't process today's nira."

"It seems such a shame to let the pongkors hang there waiting for the nira to curdle. It'll rot."

"But it's raining hard."

"The rain is heavy, right, Las?"

"Yes."

Lasi left her thought unfinished when the mood changed. Darsa looked at her with gleaming eyes. They both smiled. Darsa always trembled when he looked into his wife's coal black eyes. Just like her skin, Lasi's eyes were special: her eyelids were heavy, without creases. The people in the village said Lasi had almond-shaped eyes. Her eyebrows were prominent and turned up at the ends, like that of a Chinese woman.

Darsa wanted to say something, but Lasi felt cold and darted into their bedroom to get her *kebaya*. He followed her and closed the door. They stayed together inside.

A male frog crept through a gap in the bamboo wall, and hopped through the rain toward a female frog in a puddle. They tussled and mated in the water while croaking deep and hoarse. The mother hen on the back porch gathered her chicks to the warmth beneath her wing. It was indeed very cold.

Darsa had almost fallen asleep next to his wife when the rain stopped and bright sunlight broke through the dark clouds. The spirit of the true tapper woke him. He got up and left the bedroom.

Lasi understood. Her husband was called away by his work, his sense of life. Any tapper seized the first chance he had to collect his pongkors.

While Darsa went to bathe at the well, Lasi prepared his tools: a sickle, pongkors, harness, and bamboo hat. She joined him at the well and bathed again, even though her hair was still wet from earlier.

Lasi let Darsa go without a word. She listened to the hollow clanking of the pongkors as they hit against each other hanging from the harness around Darsa's shoulder. The young tapper walked over the muddy ground, his legs lean and strong, to the far slope of the valley. Rainwater dripped from the leaves and fell on his hat. Water trickled through a ditch covered with ferns, wet and bright green. Darsa stepped on the footbridge made from two bamboo trunks.

He was halfway across when he saw the yellow branch of an areca palm bend, then snap from the tree and float to the ground. It settled on a clump of wild pineapple. From where the branch had broken, Darsa saw the half-sheathed white heart of the palm tree. He felt as if he had just witnessed the death of a palm branch and the birth of the palm heart.

Beyond the footbridge, Darsa followed a path carved into the rocky sides of the valley. He descended again and crossed another footbridge until the field that formed the valley floor was in front of him. At the end of the valley was a slope. That was his land, where he grew his coconut palms.

Darsa lowered the harness from his shoulder and detached two pongkors. Rainwater still poured down the palm trunk he planned to climb. As he took his first step, he attached the pongkors to the hooks hanging from the back of his belt. He climbed higher and the pongkors swung like tails below him, one on the left and the other on the right, with the sickle tucked into his waistband. Water droplets fell from the top of the palm with every move he made. Darsa kept climbing with the spirit only a tapper possessed.

To always think of God was most important for any tapper working high in the coconut palms. Darsa never forgot. Like all tappers, he knew the outcome of being negligent on the job. Falling from a treetop had dire consequences, and few tappers lived through such a tragedy. Darsa understood he always had to have his wits about him wherever he was and whatever he did. He also needed to be aware of his surroundings. He had to be attentive. Generations of tappers had taught each other how to attain and hold a high level of awareness by declaring with one's tongue and heart that the work being done was in the name of the Almighty Protector.

As he squatted on top of the palm branches and cut grooves into the trunk, Darsa was unable to focus completely on what he was doing. He had a hard time forgetting his good fortune at home. Strangely enough, he found it difficult to convince himself the source of his fortune to be Lasi, his wife who was nothing short of perfect. Darsa believed in the sanctity of marriage and never doubted her faithfulness. Yet the idle chatter that Lasi, with her fair skin and distinctive eyes and cheekbones, was more suited to be the wife of a village chief than of a nira tapper fueled his doubts. Darsa also heard that his small bamboo house was a dilapidated shed unworthy of a woman as beautiful as Lasi. He saw how other men's eyes lit up when they saw her.

He made his way down from the first palm. The pongkors hanging from his belt were full of nira. Before his feet touched the ground, he already unhooked the pongkors and lowered them gently to the ground. He took two empty pongkors and prepared to climb the next palm.

For no particular reason he enjoyed tapping the second palm, perhaps because it offered an unobstructed view to the west. From high up, Darsa saw his house and even vaguely saw his wife when she went outside. The palm grew right next to an areca palm, and its leaves fell below his eyes as he hunched in the branches. In the crook of one of the branches was a starling nest. The chicks, their eyes still shut, chirped for food with every movement they heard. The inside of their mouths was red. They looked very weak, but charming. The adults flitted around looking for food. Darsa could watch them for hours. The chicks made Darsa wonder when Lasi would have a baby. There was beauty in how a mother starling fed her chicks, and he imagined the beauty of a mother breast-feeding her baby, especially if the mother was Lasi.

They had been married for three years without children. This was a sore point with Darsa. A friend once joked that Darsa was not up to the task because he had yet to get Lasi pregnant after so long. The joke hurt him. He had a more urgent and fundamental realization: a child would be the embodiment of his very being, and the knot binding him to Lasi. A marriage certificate could always be hidden under a mat. But a child? When Lasi cradled a baby, Darsa knew the idle chatter would end. His dominion over Lasi would be unquestionable. No one would ever say the mother of his child was more suited to be the wife of a village chief.

The adult starlings returned, each with a grasshopper in its beak. They stayed away from their nest while Darsa remained in the palm. The chicks chirped hearing their parents. Darsa paused what he was doing and looked at the leaves of the areca. The chicks opened their beaks wide, their mouths bright red inside. Darsa saw a baby tossing guilelessly in its cradle. He drew a deep breath.

At the house, Lasi prepared the fire and the pot to cook the nira her husband was collecting. It grew dark outside. She took a batch of firewood from the pile behind the stove and prepared the bamboo sieve to strain the nira. During the rainy season, Lasi often bemoaned the lack of dry firewood. Cooking nira over damp firewood was torture. If they were very unfortunate, they would be unable to make palm sugar.

One time they had no dry firewood to finish the job and Lasi had to strip the straw from their bed to feed into the stove. The nira was on the verge of caramelizing. When it reached that stage, the fire had to be kept going, and the straw was the closest thing she had for fuel. Even so, Lasi was wracked by dread that her husband would be angry for ruining their one and only bed.

Fortunately, Lasi's mother had great advice for such a situation: bathe, comb your hair, and redden your lips by chewing on betel leaves. Dress in your best kebaya and greet your husband at the door.

It was indeed powerful advice. Darsa ignored the news that the straw stuffing had been stripped from his bed. His focus was on his wife. That night the lamp in Darsa's home went dark earlier than usual, and the couple slept on a mat on the dirt floor.

The prayer drum sounded again from Grandfather Mus' surau at sunset. For Lasi that meant one thing: the low bellowing of her husband blowing into an empty pongkor from the top of a coconut palm. He did that to signal he was coming home soon.

Darsa put the pongkor up to his mouth. When he had the right position, he sent out a call to be heard at the house. All the tappers had their own ways of blowing so their wives would recognize their calls.

Lasi blew on the fire in the stove to be certain it kept burning. The heat from the stove turned her pale cheeks red. Sparks flew and Lasi looked up when she heard the bellow. Her tense face relaxed, but only for a moment. The sound was from another man. She knew Darsa's call like she knew all the items needed to cook the nira.

She squatted in front of the stove. The empty pot was hot. It should be filled with the nira by now but Darsa had yet to return. It was already dark outside. Lasi got up, feeling the need to do something.

An oil lamp hung on a post. The night had truly fallen. She took down the lamp and brought it to the stove. A wan light washed over the room as Lasi replaced the lamp. She heard the heavy footsteps of a man carrying a bulky load over wet ground. Lasi prepared to welcome her husband, help him take off the harness, and pour the nira from the pongkors into the hot pot.

She stopped in the doorway and looked out into the fading light. A man approached in a hurry. He carried a load on his back instead of his shoulders, and instead of a harness of pongkors, he had a limp body. As they came into the lamplight, the picture became clearer: the man carrying the load was Mukri, another tapper. Darsa lay against his back. A groan and a trickle of blood escaped his mouth.

Lasi froze. Her whole universe went into a tailspin, buzzed, and filled with shooting stars. She felt her consciousness float away and make somersaults.

"There's a frog jumping," Mukri said, panting beneath the weight he carried. "Don't say anything else. There's a frog jumping."

Lasi opened her mouth with no sound coming out. She stood, turning and gawking as Mukri went into the house and put Darsa down on the bamboo bench in the middle room. Darsa collapsed and let out a long moan. Lasi snapped out of her daze and rushed to her husband, but Mukri grabbed her by the shoulder.

"Calm down, Las. Don't say anything other than, there's a frog jumping."

A whole range of emotions appeared on Lasi's face. Her lips trembled. Tears streamed from her eyes. Her nostrils flared. She flailed her arms. She felt her throat catch and was unable to speak. She broke out crying.

"Surely we belong to God. Is there a frog jumping?"

"Yes, it's okay, it's just a jumping frog," Mukri said, soothing.

Lasi screamed and fell unconscious, collapsing on the bench and the floor. Darsa groaned again.

Wiryaji and his wife rushed over when they heard Lasi scream. Wiryaji was Lasi's stepfather and Darsa's uncle. Neighbors who lived further away soon followed. Grandfather Mus, the most venerated man in the village, was fetched from his home near the surau. Someone was sent to notify Darsa's parents in the next village. Everyone who gathered knew what had happened, yet only said there was a frog jumping. The word "fell" was never uttered among the community of tappers. They refused to accept the negative by invoking the positive.

The women tended to Darsa and Lasi. They carefully took off Darsa's wet shorts. One woman forced him to gulp a raw egg. They were relieved when they saw he had barely been wounded, just a few cuts and scratches on his arms and back. But there was a stinging smell of urine. They covered Darsa from his feet to his neck with a sheet.

Lasi awoke after one of the women blew in her ear. Crying, Lasi curled up near Darsa's feet. He looked pale. The woman told her to make a cup of hot tea to warm her husband.

Darsa moaned on occasion as he lay still. Mukri told the others what happened. He was tapping a coconut palm nearby when disaster struck.

"I knew what I had to do. When I saw the frog jump, I climbed down immediately. I stripped naked and danced like a monkey circling the jumping frog."

"What about the smell of piss?"

"Yah, I pissed all over his body until he was soaked."

"Mukri did right," Wiryaji said. "That's what you do to help a jumping frog. A tapper never forgets that.

"It's lucky you were nearby when it happened. Someone else might have shouted and done the wrong thing. Mukri, thank you for your help and taking care of things correctly."

"Sure. Anyway, I have to go. I still have work."

"It's late. How are you going to keep climbing?"

Mukri disappeared into the dark night, his footsteps audible for a few moments after he had gone. The men and women turned their full attention to Darsa. Lasi kept crying. The others tried to get Darsa to pray and invoke the name of the All Merciful.

From Mukri's story, it was clear Darsa had fallen from a tall palm. As for how he managed to escape serious injury, like impale himself on his scythe, and even, as Mukri claimed, remained conscious through it all—everyone had his or her own ideas.

Wiryaji was convinced that his nephew and stepson-in-law still lived because Mukri had done what every tapper knew to be right in helping Darsa, and the impact of hitting the ground was lessened by the branches he struck on the way down. Grandfather Mus declared with full conviction that God Himself had saved Darsa. If not, he would have died like every tapper who fell from the top of a coconut palm, or at least been badly injured.

Lasi's home was full of people on that cold, wet night. While an old woman tended to Darsa, Wiryaji consulted with the neighbors on what to do next. One said that he appeared well enough to be cared for at home. Another said he should be taken to a hospital right away. He said tappers had been known to come away unscathed after a fall, only to get worse and die.

"Wiryaji," Grandfather Mus said, "the decision is in your hands. I agree Darsa should go to a hospital. We have to do our best for him."

Everyone fell silent, including Wiryaji. Lasi cried instead. Darsa groaned again.

"Grandfather Mus, we don't have the money," Wiryaji said after a long pause. Everyone was silent. Grandfather Mus leaned back on a bamboo bench until it creaked. The mood changed from concern for a friend who had been struck by disaster, to confusion because there was no money to treat him. For the tappers, they had faced this experience before.

"Las," Wiryaji said in a low voice. "Do you have anything to sell?"

All eyes turned to Lasi. She shook her head as tears welled up again.

"What if you pawn the coconut palms?"

"Don't," Grandfather Mus cut in. "What will they live on?"

Mbok Wiryaji, Lasi's mother, paced the small room.

"In this situation," she said, "We must go to *Pak* Tir. Lasi always sells him sugar."

Everyone in the house fell silent. They agreed Lasi had no other choice, but also knew what it meant to borrow money from Pak Tir. She would only be allowed to sell her sugar to him and no other broker, and for a low price. For a tapper's wife, the bitterness of this choice was sweeter than letting her husband lay there weak and moaning.

Wiryaji set off for Pak Tir's house to represent Lasi. Pak Tir usually refused to lend money at night, but the fate that had befallen Darsa was unusual.

While Wiryaji was gone, the others tended to Darsa. They washed him with warm water to clean off the mud and the smell of urine. Darsa screamed when the water touched his wounds.

The men fashioned a makeshift stretcher and two torches from bamboo.

***

The village of Karangsoga sat at the foot of a volcanic range. Signs of past volcanic activity were still seen on the steep slopes, with ravines and crevices covered with ferns. The dark and heavy soil stored enough water to keep the little stony rivers and creeks bubbling all year round. Because of its many creeks, Karangsoga had an abundance of footbridges linking its dirt paths. The villagers crafted pipes from bamboo to channel the water from higher elevations to their fish ponds, bathing pools, and rice paddies. The soil never turned acidic because of the constant supply of running water that could be easily drained. When it rained, the ground absorbed the water quickly. There were never any puddles, and the water in the creeks stayed crystal clear.

Except for on the sliver of rice paddies and fields, sunlight seldom reached the ground in Karangsoga. The fertile volcanic soil kept all the vegetation green and lush. Bamboo grew in tight clumps and snake-fruit trees bordered the fields. Strangely, coconut palms grew poorly there. Karangsoga was too high, which made the air too cold for palms to grow. But it was also said Karangsoga was too fertile, so there was little chance for the coconut palms to grow properly. The branches on the ones that did manage to grow never opened fully or produced much fruit. Because of this, the first generation of Karangsoga villagers chose to tap their palms for nira rather than wait for a disappointing coconut harvest. Besides, the squirrels that thrived in the dense bamboo thickets and fed on the young coconuts were always difficult to get rid of.

Before they knew how to make coconut palm sugar, the people of Karangsoga tapped the areca palm. Its sap had long been used to make palm wine. After they were advised against drinking palm wine, the people of Karangsoga started processing areca sap into sugar for their own use. They soon sold it, and tried to make sugar from coconut palms. Coconut tapping took off quickly. Karangsoga had fertile soil and abundant water, but little flat land for rice or other crops to feed the growing population.

That night, a group of villagers set out from Karangsoga carrying a stretcher. A torch lit their way, followed by a man and two women. Another torch brought up the rear of the procession. They hiked a dirt path through a passage carved in a rocky hill, down again and across a footbridge made of areca trunks, before disappearing into a thick grove of trees. They emerged on a small road edged by a sheer rock face, crossed a second bridge, and cut through a field of snake-fruit trees. Smoke from their torches billowed gray and tailed off. The further they went, the dimmer the light, until they were swallowed by the night. A bat flew into the circle of light, then turned back abruptly and vanished. A green grasshopper flung itself into the flame of one of the torches. Its gossamer wings scorched instantly and the unfortunate insect fell to the ground. The trees swayed in the wind and water from the earlier rain drizzled through the leaves.

The five people in the procession barely spoke. There was the occasional groan from Darsa, lying on the stretcher covered with a cloth, or Lasi sobbing as she walked beside the stretcher. The silence was only broken by the sound of footsteps, the hum of insects, a green frog croaking in the undergrowth of a steep ravine, and the hiss of the torches as they swayed with the steps of the people carrying them.

After crossing the third footbridge, they came to the final climb before making their descent into a wider and rockier valley. Men and women appeared from the houses that dotted the sides of the valley; most had already heard about the accident. They stood with their arms folded across their chests, muttering prayers for the recovery of one of their own who had met disaster. The same fate could befall their husbands, sons, or brothers.

The night had grown colder by the time the procession reached the main road. They turned west to the clinic in the county's capital five kilometers away. They picked up their pace. There were signs that it would rain again. Lightning ripped the sky with increasing frequency. During the brief lightning strikes, dark clouds gathered.

Lasi sobbed when an owl hooted in the distance. The people of Karangsoga associated an owl's hoot with death. Fortunately, Darsa groaned loudly. At least he was alive. Lasi quickly fell in step with the others who raced to beat the rain and save Darsa.

***

News of a tapper being hospitalized after a fall was common for the people of Karangsoga. Dozens had ended up worse than Darsa and many had died. One broke his neck, and another had the scythe tucked in his waistband disembowel him. A tapper was squatting when he fell and impaled himself on a bamboo staff. It took several men to remove his body. Lightning struck Pulan when had reached the top of a palm, and his body flung into a *pandan* thicket. The people of Karangsoga were used to such incidents, and soon forgot about them.

This was different with Darsa. They spoke about his fall with keen interest and curiosity. Darsa was not important to them, but Lasi would be a widow if he died. The people of Karangsoga predicted the village would heat up with whispers, rumors, and speculation, as it did before she married. Lasi would again be the talk of the village, among the women as much as the men.

The stories of Lasi's birth and how her mother had been raped would flare up, along with those about her father, who had endowed his daughter with such unique features she was the beauty of Karangsoga.

***

(1961) At one in the afternoon, the school bell rang and the children bid goodbye to their teacher. More than a dozen boys and girls spilled out of the sixth grade classroom. Once out the door, they scattered across the yard into the sunshine. The boys ran, bolting like young goats out of a pen. Behind them, three girls walked together chatting.

They wore their hair in ponytails and were barefoot. Each carried books and wooden rulers.

They left the schoolyard and turned on a rocky path, going up and down steep inclines to a path covered over with thick foliage and bamboo. One girl left when they reached a crossroad, and Lasi and her other friend continued on their way. A short distance later, her friend left the path and turned into her front yard. She pinched Lasi's cheek as they parted. "No wonder the teacher likes you. You're so pretty." She ran off, leaving Lasi frowning and bemused. *Really? Am I pretty?*

Lasi was alone. She quickened her pace, even while crossing a footbridge. The second bridge made her stop. She often paused to look down while crossing that particular bridge. The water was so clear rock crabs could be seen crawling at the bottom of the creek. The eight-legged creatures gathered there because small children defecated from the bridge. The crabs were so accustomed to feces hitting the water that they came out of hiding whenever anything made a splash.

Lasi dropped a clump of dirt into the water. Just as she expected, five crabs large and small came out at once. Lasi was especially pleased to see one of the creatures. Her favorite crab had incredibly strong pincers almost the same size as the rest of its body. The crabs honed in on the source of the splash, but Iron Pincer swept everyone aside. Lasi pinched her fingers open and shut, and almost unconsciously mouthed, "Grab and squeeze until it crumbles."

Nothing was caught or crumbled yet Lasi was pleased when the crabs retreated to their hiding place.

She wanted an encore of the show when footsteps at the other end of the bridge made her raise her head. Four boys her age approached, giggling. Three of them were classmates and the youngest one, the runt of the pack, was Kanjat, Pak Tir's son.

The boys liked to harass Lasi, especially out of the classroom. She looked at them wide-eyed, her cheeks turning red.

Tension settled over the footbridge made from a single areca trunk. Kanjat, who tagged along, looked worried. The others started chuckling and mocked Lasi as they usually did.

"Lasi-pang, Lasi the Jap kid," one of them said, pouting his lips and pointing at Lasi. Another boy stuck his tongue out at her.

"Your mom was raped by a Jap. It's no wonder you've got slanted Jap eyes."

"You've got Chink eyebrows. Yeah, you're half-Chink."

"My name's Lasiyah, not Lasi-pang," Lasi shouted back at them.

"Lasi-pang."

"Lasiyah."

"Lasi-pang, Lasi-pang, Lasi-pang. Lasi the Jap kid."

"Your mom was raped by a Jap. Your mom was raped."

Lasi whipped her ruler from under her arm and ran to the end of the bridge, ready to take on her tormentors. Deep down, she felt like the rock crab with the giant pincers. She had no qualms about snipping the boys' heads clean off their necks, but she only had a wooden ruler.

Two of the boys ran, while the third stood there and let Lasi hit him on the back with the ruler. He laughed, wincing, and Lasi broke out crying.

Pleased their teasing had made her cry, the boys fled, but Kanjat remained. He stared at Lasi with wide, clear eyes while she cried and soon he too cried.

"Las, I didn't tease you," said Kanjat, who was two years younger and smaller than Lasi. "You're not mad at me, are you?"

Lasi shook her head and tried to smile. Even if Kanjat had remained quiet, she knew he had no part in the tormenting. He was a cute, chubby little boy with round and sharp eyes. He wore a nice shirt and pants and was the best-dressed child in Karangsoga. Pak Tir, his father, was a broker of palm sugar and the wealthiest man in the village.

With her eyes still damp, Lasi resumed her journey home. Kanjat followed her and turned into a side street after she sent him a feeble smile.

Lasi walked with her head bowed. Fallen decayed bamboo leaves rustled beneath her feet. Branches seemed like they moved to brush against her body. She crossed the last bridge and climbed a path carved into a rock. Finally, she arrived at a bamboo house with a yard hedged by snake-fruit trees.

Lasi went straight to her room and stayed there. She ignored her mother calling her for dinner.

She stared at the walls, still upset by the earlier teasing. Even though they mocked her nearly every day, Lasi could never get over it easily. The teasing always stirred questions in herself: *Why do none of the other girls have to go through the same thing? Why do they always call me Lasi-pang? And what is a Jap?* Her most important question was, *what does rape mean? My mother was raped? Why do people look at me so strangely, as though there is something wrong with me? Is it because I'm the daughter of a woman who has been raped?*

These questions had multiplied since she was a young child. She heard other things people said that were no less distressing: Wiryaji was her stepfather; her real father was a Japanese man who had abandoned her mother before Lasi was born. She knew the talk about her mother being raped, making her the bastard child of that rape. *But what was rape?*

The questions burned in Lasi's heart. She wanted was to be an alpha crab with powerful pincers to snip off the heads of everyone in Karangsoga—including her mother for never explaining any of the things that gnawed at her.

The door to her room opened and her mother entered. Mbok Wiryaji's face fell when she saw Lasi brooding with a blank expression and glassy eyes. She had seen her child like this before, but the shadows in Lasi's face were darker this time.

Mbok Wiryaji saw rage and disappointment in Lasi's eyes. She was stunned. She wanted to speak, but the words stuck in her throat. She swallowed and turned to leave when Lasi called out to her. Mother and daughter exchanged glances.

Mbok Wiryaja waited for her child to speak. Lasi stared at her, then bowed her head and began choking, her short breaths a sign of the turmoil inside.

"Are the other kids bothering you again?"

"Always," Lasi snapped. Anger flared in her eyes. There was a sharp indictment in her voice when she said, "Why do I have to face the scorn of others every day?"

Mbok Wiryaja heard Lasi almost scream, "Because of you, I always have to face this torment." She sighed and folded her arms over her chest. She lived with the pain that constantly ate at Lasi. Her daughter's pain was the extension of her own, and had throbbed in her soul for years.

She was determined to bear the pain alone. No one, especially not Lasi, should suffer too. But the people of Karangsoga loved to gossip, and so Lasi heard the secret her mother had tried to conceal.

The stories that reached Lasi tended to be embellished for the satisfaction of whoever told them. Mbok Wiryaji never understood why the people of Karangsoga kept bringing up the shameful tale that happened so long ago. *Is this what the ancestors meant when they spoke of an age of brotherhood without compassion? Do they not want my child and me to live in peace? Does Lasi's beauty make them jealous?*

Mbok Wiryaji sat beside Lasi and sadly looked at her. She was proud of her child. Lasi had a flawless skin, thick, flowing black hair, and was taller than the other children her age. She had long, shapely legs. Lasi would grow to be a beautiful woman. *Why must she be the object of people's scorn?*

Lasi looked up and Mbok Wiryaji felt a sharp jab in her heart. Yes, she knew her child demanded an explanation for the things that made children and adults taunt her. She no longer had any need to keep the secret. She wanted to reveal everything. She was about to speak when she was gripped by doubt. *Lasi is only thirteen years old. Is it appropriate for a child this age to hear about the shame of unwonted lust?* The thought stopped her. *When Lasi is older, I will tell her the truth.*

Lasi grew anxious waiting for her mother to speak. "Is it true that Wiryaji isn't my father?" she asked without looking up.

Mbok Wiryaja quickly straightened. "Yes, Las. He's not your biological father," she said haltingly.

"Who is my real father? Is it a Japanese man?"

"Yes." Mbok Wiryaji swallowed. "There used to be many Japanese here. They were soldiers."

"People say you were raped by a Japanese man. What does that mean?"

Mbok Wiryaji swallowed again. Her lips trembled. She fiddled with her hands. Her eyes and her nose began to water. She startled when Lasi, in the same flat voice, repeated her question.

She stuttered, "Raped means forced."

"Forced how?" Lasi went on.

"Oh, Las, I was forced to submit. Do you understand?"

Lasi's eyes widened. She knew what her mother meant. Anger flared across her fair face. Her lips moved as though she was about to speak, but she just gaped. When she managed to get a word out, it was her mother's turn to stare.

"Was it because you were raped that you became pregnant with me?"

"Oh no, child. No."

"Are you lying?"

"Oh, Las, Mother's not lying. Listen to me. You were born three years after that despicable incident. By that time, the Japanese man had come back in Karangsoga with a band of guerrillas. Your father trained them. Those young men and Grandfather Mus asked me to forgive him. They even asked me to accept his proposal."

"Did you want to?"

"At first, Las, I agreed because I couldn't say no to the men and Grandfather Mus. In the end I realized your father was a good man."

Her brow knitted, Lasi fell silent for a moment.

"Las, I agreed to marry your father, and you came along after that. When I was five months pregnant with you, your father left with the guerillas. He never returned. The word was that he died in captivity of the Dutch."

Lasi sat frozen and frowning, but slowly her tension began to ebb.

"Oh yes, Las," Mbok Wiryaji went on, "your father did look Chinese, and he looked funny when he wore a sarong and a prayer cap. People said his real name was Miyaki or Misaki. Grandfather Mus gave him a new name, Marjuki."

"My father was Marjuki?"

"Yes. And he looked Chinese."

"He looked Chinese?"

"That's right. The Japanese resemble the Chinese."

"Mother, why does everyone say I'm a bastard?"

Mbok Wiryaji was silent. Her eyes reddened again.

"Las, they know very well who you are. I don't know why they make up stories, maybe to hurt us. Never mind, Las, let them be. We'll turn the other cheek. It's said that those who turn the other cheek are respected in the end."

The only sound in the room was a long sigh from Mbok Wiryaji. A heavy burden that weighed on her for years had been lifted from her shoulders. She tried to read her daughter's reaction to her confession.

Lasi seemed unmoved. She stared at the ground. Her fingers picked at the corner of the pandan mat. Without looking at her mother, she stood and left her room.

Mbok Wiryaji was relieved when Lasi headed for the dining table. She believed that one could only eat when one's heart was at peace.

At fourteen, Lasi graduated from the village school. Four of her classmates immediately married. Lasi also expected to get married if her parents accepted the proposal from Pak Sambeng, her teacher. They refused because Pak Sambeng already had a wife. For the next six years, Lasi did not find a husband. This was highly unusual by Karangsoga standards, especially since she was so attractive. Yet everyone knew why Lasi remained single.

The people of Karangsoga were very particular about heritage when it came to picking a wife or a daughter-in-law. Everyone knew Lasi's father was a foreigner who had appeared in Karangsoga for a few months. He died several years later and was buried who knew where. A woman from a broken family was undesirable in Karangsoga. The rape served to further tarnish her reputation. Lasi was branded a bastard, even though the term was unduly cruel and unjustified.

Some said that Lasi was different from the other Karangsoga girls. This made the local youths reluctant to propose to her. A wife should not easily catch the eyes of other men, they said. Strangely, they still enjoyed making Lasi the object of their conversation.

Lasi remained unmarried until she was nearly twenty years old. In Karangsoga, only a mute girl would be single at that age. She was the most beautiful woman of her generation in the village. This generated so much gossip it made her reluctant to leave the house.

She passed her days as an unmarried daughter in the Wiryaji family, one of many families of tappers in Karangsoga. In the mornings, she prepared the stove and the large pot. Later, she poured the nira out of the pongkors through a bamboo sieve and into the pot. The filtered dregs ranged from slivers of bark to dead bees and horned beetles trapped in the pongkors. During bad weather, the nira had thick, white foam. Lasi shuddered when she found a drowned lizard or mouse.

She enjoyed watching the nira bubble in the pot. Its fragrance and bubbling stirred the senses. The thick steam rising in swirls stirred her imagination of the manly tapper. When the nira caramelized, it turned brown or a dark red. Small bubbles appeared on the surface and burst with a soft pop. At this point the boiling mixture was nearly at its prime, and Lasi took the pot off the stove. Waiting for it to cool, she stirred the stringy caramel and ladled it into molds made from bamboo sections each about four fingers tall.

Lasi seldom spoke except to her mother, but when Wiryaji, who was getting old, fell ill, she found a new friend. Wiryaji's nephew, Darsa, took over tapping his palms. He was quiet and Lasi liked him. Quiet people appealed to her. They talked little and stayed away from gossip unlike most of the villagers. Darsa was good looking. His body was well balanced, with muscles knotted in the classic way of tappers. Besides, he was only a few years older than Lasi.

Occasionally, he slipped a ripe snake fruit or mango between the pongkors filled with nira. Whenever Lasi asked, "Is this for me?" Darsa smiled and his eyes shined. He turned shy when Lasi's mother caught him exchanging glances with her daughter.

Mbok Wiryaji was well aware of their mutual attraction. It inspired her to pair them off. If that could be arranged, it would end the taunts that tormented her. A girl, especially a beautiful one, remained the object of the neighbors' small talk until she married, settled down, and had children. After that, people only paid attention to how she walked. But the talk about Lasi, about her mother being raped and her father leaving, was still heard after she married Darsa.

***

The valley and hills around Karangsoga appeared hazy in the thin morning mist. The mist also gave depth to the scenery, distinguishing the closer features from the more distant ones. In the east, the sun peeped from behind a peak and painted the treetops red-yellow. The view to the south was of a broad expanse of low-lying flat land. From this high vantage point, villagers could watch the egrets fly below the horizon. When they bowed their heads a little, a carpet of rice paddies and farmland unfolded. The county's capital was also visible in its entirety, and the coastline of the South Sea met the horizon.

Lasi set out to visit Darsa at the small hospital in the county's capital. She took a short cut to avoid meeting anyone going to market. The villagers were curious and Lasi was tired of their questions. In the dim early morning light, the coconut palms swayed as the tappers climbed. Dewdrops fell from the leaves, causing drizzles. The pongkors clattered as they struck one another while the tapper climbed a palm.

Crossing a footbridge, Lasi wondered why she had spent so much time looking at the crabs in the water below. A kingfisher flew overhead. It followed the top of the ravine and tweeted before dropping among the snake-fruit trees. The call of a *tokay* gecko from inside a hole in a tree trunk broke the silence of the dew-spangled morning. A fantail bird chirped cheerily before bolting after a fly. Its tiny body was a blur as it hopped from one branch to another in the thick vegetation. Beetles buzzed from one crepe myrtle flower to another. Two lizards chased each other on the footpath in front of Lasi, and the chirp of cicadas roused the day from its stillness.

Lasi walked quickly, looking straight ahead of her. When she reached the road out of the village, she stepped into a horse-drawn buggy with several other passengers already seated. They were from Karangsoga and Lasi only said as much as she needed; her heart was already with Darsa at the hospital. He had been there a week and his superficial wounds had started to heal. The young tapper possessed the ability to recover quickly. Darsa also regained his appetite.

After asking the nurses how much she had to pay, Lasi calculated that the money she borrowed from Pak Tir was only enough to keep Darsa in the hospital for ten days. Lasi heard the nurses whisper about Darsa needing further care at a bigger hospital because there was still something wrong: he had lost control over his bladder. The nurses also spoke about the possibility of neurosurgery.

Neurosurgery? What is that? Lasi grew dizzy just thinking about it. She worried that kind of treatment might kill her husband. *How much will it cost?* Lasi was given the answers to her questions when the head doctor of the clinic called her in to explain Darsa's condition.

"Your husband is out of danger, but he needs to go to a bigger hospital so he can be treated properly," the young doctor said. "You know, don't you, that your husband keeps wetting his clothes? He's incontinent."

Concern spread across Lasi's face. "Will he need expensive treatment?" she asked with trembling lips.

"I believe so. It might cost tens, maybe hundreds of thousands."

Lasi swallowed, and swallowed again. A sheer wall had gone up in front of her, blocking her vision. Her face reflected helplessness instead of concern. "I'll talk with my parents," she said after a long silence, and left the doctor.

In Darsa's room, she tried to hide her worries. She sat by the edge of his bed and forced a smile while massaging his arm. She noticed a stinging smell and changed Darsa's sarong. Lasi brought out the food she had carried from home. But Darsa showed no interest in the rice cakes and salted duck eggs she had brought.

Lasi wanted to tell him what the doctor had said until she saw how pale and stricken he looked. She tried to find something else to talk about to lighten the mood. She said, "The house feels empty at night. I sleep at my mother's place."

Darsa only raised his eyebrows.

"Mukri's tapping our palms," she went on, "just until you're well again."

"What's the price of palm sugar?" Darsa's voice was hoarse.

"Six rupiah, not enough for a kilo of rice."

Darsa raised his eyebrows again, but he had expected the low number. Tappers had hopes that remained hopes, like for the price of sugar to be the same as the price of rice. This humble hope rarely came true. They asked about the price of sugar every day, and always dreaded the answer. The price of palm sugar never took into account the great risk that tappers had to face. The husband might fall out of a coconut palm and the wife might slip into a vat of bubbling caramel. Lives were at stake in both instances, but the sugar rarely fetched the same price as rice.

"I have to go home and wash your clothes. I'll be back tomorrow."

Darsa nodded. He watched Lasi pack his soiled clothes with their burning stench. As she turned to leave, he caught a glimpse of the back of her neck. Darsa's eyes lit up and a fire ignited in his heart. His imagination was about to run wild until cut short by the knowledge that he was weak and incontinent. Ever since his accident a week ago, Darsa experienced the one symptom hated by all men: impotence.

Lasi went straight to her parents' house as soon as she returned to Karangsoga. She cried as she stepped over the threshold.

Wiryaji and his wife thought Darsa's condition had worsened, and met Lasi.

"How is he?" Mbok Wiryaji asked.

"Still the same, Mother." Lasi wiped away a tear. "The doctor says he needs to go to a bigger hospital because he keeps wetting himself. Mother, it's very expensive. It can cost hundreds of thousands."

Lasi sobbed while her parents sat dumbfounded. They were startled when she asked, "What shall we do, Mother?"

For a long time, the short question remained unanswered. Hundreds of thousands? They had never dreamed of having that much money. Never.

"What shall we do?" Lasi asked again.

Wiryaji coughed. His wife sighed. Seeing them at such a loss, Lasi cried harder. Her thoughts were scattered and she was very sad. The mood in the room remained morbid and tense. Neither Lasi nor her parents had anything to say. The silence dissipated when Mukri, Grandfather Mus, and several of the neighbors came in. They wanted to know how Darsa was doing, and the news from Lasi left them in shock.

"We can only get that kind of money if we sell Lasi's house and land," Wiryaji said in a resigned tone. "Should we do it? If so, who'll buy it quickly?"

"Pak Tir can buy it," his wife said. "The problem is, where will my daughter live? Darsa might recover, but if he doesn't, this costly wager is for nothing."

"Mother, I feel sorry for poor Darsa," Lasi said. "I want him to be taken care of until he's well. Can't we sell my palm grove?"

"Don't, Las," Mbok Wiryaji cut in. "That land is the source of your livelihood and your children's safety in the future. No matter how small, land secures your future and that of your children. I won't let you play with it."

"But Mother, I need to help poor Darsa," Lasi repeated.

"Las, everyone feels for Darsa, but we don't have any money. We have to accept things as they are."

Lasi started to cry again. Grandfather Mus coughed, and Mbok Wiryaji took a deep breath.

Grandfather Mus scraped his throat. He was the one man everyone turned to for advice, and he wanted to speak, but the memory of a similar accident about a year ago stiffened his tongue. At that time, Parja had fallen while tapping a coconut palm. Seeing how badly hurt he was, his family refused to take him to a hospital. They decided against going into debt to pay for his treatment, because they believed it would only be a waste of money. Grandfather Mus had pleaded with Parja's parents to take him to a hospital, even if they had to borrow the money.

In the end, Parja died and his family was left with a debt that was still unpaid. Parja's wife also fell ill, making a double suffering for the family. Grandfather Mus always felt guilty when he met one of Parja's children, who were orphaned and uncared for. Grandfather Mus coughed for a third time, but the words stayed in his throat. He was silent when Wiryaji asked him directly for advice.

The only sounds that penetrated the deep silence draping the room were long sighs and the chirping of the birds in the trees outside. Birds never grieved. From far in the distance came the thump of a woman stirring caramel to pour into bamboo molds. The fragrance permeated the entire village. The scent was the hallmark of Karangsoga, the village of palm sugar producers.

Wiryaji broke the silence. "We've done all we can. We have a debt that will be hard to pay back. We can't do anything more. If our efforts aren't enough to heal Darsa, so be it. We have to accept things as they are."

"Yes," Mbok Wiryaja said. "We must accept. Tomorrow we'll bring Darsa home and take care of him here. He might get well once he's home. Allah has no shortage of ways to show His compassion. Isn't that right, Grandfather Mus?"

Grandfather Mus smiled and nodded as a resentful expression crossed his face.

Lasi walked to the well. She washed Darsa's clothes that reeked of urine, crying.

Mukri and the neighbors left with their heads bowed.

The sun had almost reached the top of its arc, and the coconut palms in Karangsoga swayed in the soft breeze.

Chapter 2

The wet season passed and the dry season had arrived. Karangsoga turned cold and fog often blanketed the night. On the volcanic terrain, trees stayed green because the rich soil retained plenty of moisture. The sound of water running through the rocky creeks and the fern-covered valley floor was always present. Karangsoga's dry season meant a lack of rain for a month or two.

Nature had lavished the village with an abundance of water and fertile soil. Yet, the coconut tappers of Karangsoga were poor—a situation that was never mentioned or questioned.

Life in Karangsoga moved like the water in the rivers. People drifted by, collided, and sometimes drowned or rotted at the bottom. No one complained or felt compelled to find another line of work, less high-risk and higher paying than tapping coconut palms. No one thought to form a tappers' association to stabilize the whims of the free market that manipulated the price of their sugar.

The village remained calm as though the poverty of the tappers was a prepackaged reality everyone had to accept.

On a regular quiet night in Karangsoga, the near-full moon dominated the sky, with only a few clouds drifting in the west. Grandfather Mus left his small surau after several other old men. Beneath the eaves of the hut, he lifted his face upward. The moonlight lit his face and warmed his heart. His sandals squeaked with the rhythm of his footsteps as he walked home. The squeaking stopped when he stepped inside his house.

The door creaked when he opened it. His wife had placed a cup of hot tea and his box of tobacco on the table in the front room. They often sat together for hours, waiting to get drowsy. In the evenings, there was little to do for a couple whose four children had long left and started families of their own.

Grandfather Mus wanted to do more than sit in silence tonight. The moon he had glimpsed from the surau had lighted his way home. In his front room, he kept a *gambang* older than Grandfather Mus himself. He was known as a student of antiques, and played the gambang to accompany the mystical verses he sang in the rhythm of *sinom* or *dhandhanggula*.

For Grandfather Mus, the mysticism channeled through the rhythm of the gambang was the cry of longing from a subject for his Master, the cry of the wanderer seeking to unite his origins with his final destination. When immersed in his mysticism, Grandfather Mus was oblivious to everything around him. Entranced, his body drenched in sweat and tears streaming down his face, his voice pierced the night and penetrated the sky. This was even more so when he sung chosen verses.

> *A special man achieved true enlightenment*
> *The view from his heart became clear the moment he faced God*
> *Crushed and melted were all the curtains of the world*
> *His view dissolved in the greatness of God*
> *He never stopped calling His name*
> *For him there was only Allah*
>
> *His every move became homage*
> *The prayer of his soul stood the test of time*
> *Even when his body was in an unholy state*
> *The eye of his heart never stopped looking at Allah*
> *The truth for him was the oneness of being*
> *Both in prayer and outside*
> *He aligned his human desires with the will of the Almighty*

Everything stopped once Grandfather Mus, through the prayer of his own humanity, came to in the ordinary world.

No one in Karangsoga, not even his wife, understood how far the old man's soul traveled when he sat cross-legged with his gambang. When he shut his eyes, his heart saw the world in a truer light. People understood the superficial meaning of his gambang playing, the rhythm that greeted the heart and touched the soul such that they were content to listen. In the middle of the night, when the moonlight cast shadows of the trees on the ground and the air of the dry season was bitingly cold, the people of Karangsoga melted into the soft sound of the gambang that drifted to every corner of the village and bounced off the hillsides before disappearing into the valley.

After several stanzas, Grandfather Mus shifted over to a bench. He rolled a cigarette as his wife cleaned her lips after chewing a wad of betel leaves. A woman called out a greeting and they recognized her voice. It was Mbok Wiryaji.

"Are you alone?" Grandfather Mus opened the door.

"It's just me."

"Where's your husband?"

"At home."

Mbok Wiryaji looked somber beneath the hanging oil lamp. She always came to see Grandfather Mus and his wife when she had a problem at home.

"Have a seat. You look gloomy. Did you have another fight?"

"The usual. Maybe that's how it's supposed to be, my husband and I always fighting."

"You're gray now but you haven't changed."

"We were talking about Lasi and wound up arguing. Rather than make a fuss at home, I decided to escape here."

"Bring some warm rice and silver barb fish stew once in a while, and we will welcome you happily. Don't just come to unload your headaches. What's the matter this time?"

"It's Lasi. I mean, it's her husband, Darsa. We've been taking care of him at home for four months, and there's been no change."

"Is he still wetting himself?"

"Yes, but his behavior is different. He gets angry easily and he's cranky all day long. Yesterday he smashed a plate because Lasi was gone too long to the store. I feel sorry for Lasi. Her husband is like a paralyzed goat. Every day she has to wash his smelly clothes, and yet he is always mad at her."

"Who gathers the firewood?"

"That's it, you see. Lasi's been cooking nira since she was little, but as for finding firewood? I can't bear to see Lasi struggle every day to gather firewood from the forest. What worries me is that her suffering might never end. What happens if Darsa doesn't recover?"

"Don't think like that."

"Grandfather Mus, Lasi is still young. Must she spend the rest of her life serving a husband who can only wet himself?" Mbok Wiryaji asked with a sour smile.

"Hush."

"I'm not joking, Grandfather Mus. How long can Lasi last in a situation like this? Should I just be quiet?"

"If I'm not mistaken, I sense a certain meaning in your words. You no longer want Darsa to be your son-in-law?"

Mbok Wiryaji was startled.

Grandfather Mus smiled. He had guessed correctly.

"Don't be in a rush. Darsa was a good husband before the accident. Now he's weak because of factors beyond his control. Do you have the heart to cut him loose?"

"I've a question too," Grandfather Mus' wife said. "Does Lasi no longer treat Darsa as her husband?"

"Not really. Despite his stench, she stays by him faithfully, and that makes me pity her more. Will she have to suffer for the rest of her life?"

"Before you take off on a tangent like that, have you done all you can for Darsa?"

"He wants for nothing, Grandfather Mus. After he didn't get well in the hospital, we've tried all kinds of herbal medicines. We've also said prayers for him."

"Keep trying the best you can. And pray too. You said yourself, if Allah chooses to show compassion, he has many ways of doing so. Why despair now? Do you no longer believe that Allah receives all prayers?"

"I believe all that, Grandfather Mus. It's just…" Mbok Wiryaji hesitated.

"Go on, why did you stop?"

"I'll just come straight out and say it. Yesterday I received a message from Pak Sambeng, Lasi's old teacher. When Lasi was younger, he wanted to marry her but we refused him because he already had a wife. She's gone and he still wants Lasi. He says that if he can't have her as a virgin, he'll take her as another man's former wife."

"Enough. So, this is the real reason you came here. It seems you want to have a teacher as your son-in-law. You should have refused the moment you heard Pak Sambeng's message. One thing you should never forget is, never suggest anyone to divorce. Darsa is your husband's nephew. If you make a wrong decision, you and your husband might get in trouble. I can't support your thinking along these lines. I'm only on your side when you keep trying and praying for Darsa's recovery."

"Grandfather Mus, believe me, we're still trying. Currently, Darsa is being treated by Bunek, a masseuse."

"Bunek the midwife?"

"Yes, I know she is a midwife, but many people say that her massage has helped men whose thing has died."

"Did you call Bunek?"

"No. Lasi wanted her husband treated by her."

"That's sound thinking. I will sincerely pray for those efforts to work."

Mbok Wiryaji nodded. She leaned back in her seat, still dissatisfied.

"You can rest here, but don't spend the night. It's not good to leave your husband at home alone." Grandfather Mus reached for his tobacco box. A moment later, his lighter flared and he exhaled a breath of smoke. The still of the night crept into the house.

When Grandfather Mus' wife told Mbok Wiryaji to go home, she only responded with a deep breath. She was sound asleep.

***

Bunek's most distinctive feature was her quick gait. She took long strides and swung her arms far because she was always rushing to women on the verge of giving birth. Bunek also had other features no less distinctive. She stood the tallest in any group of women. She had a hearty laugh and was talkative. When she spoke, she said the most vulgar things. She talked about intimate subjects as casually as she chewed betel leaves. She had an oval face and everyone believed she was beautiful when younger. Her skin had retained its smoothness, even though she had several grandchildren. Her thick hair was beginning to gray, but Bunek routinely combed it to look neat and tight.

Many women used her services, and her massage technique was known to be soft yet powerful. She mastered a skill no other masseuse could compete against. More than her massages, most villagers enjoyed the light and cheer she brought with her wherever she went. For Bunek, all problems could be tackled with laughter, even with vulgar talk. The stabbing pains in a woman's stomach when she was in labor were a minor inconvenience as far as Bunek was concerned. "I've given birth too. The pain when the baby is about to come out is enough to make you want to squeeze your husband into crumbs. But I kept having kids. I had another, and another. I was addicted. Don't you feel the same? No? Hahaha."

One time a woman about to give birth swore to heaven and earth that she would never get pregnant again. No more. Bunek listened to her, smiling. "Last year you swore to heaven and earth, but I knew you'd be pregnant the next year. What are you going to swear to now? Come on, I want to hear you swear, hahaha."

The only reason a woman in labor refused to call for Bunek was her outspoken ways. She was known to tell the husband to get a mistress if he was impatient for his wife to recover from the labor.

When confronted for giving out advice like that, Bunek brushed it off. "It's normal for men to have a pressing need. If they can control themselves, more praise to them. But what happens to those who can't? What are they supposed to do, look for a crab hole? Hahaha."

When she tended to Darsa, Bunek had the same cheeriness she was known for. At first, this irritated Darsa. He felt Bunek belittled his suffering, but, in time, he enjoyed the unfettered ranting of the midwife. On why his bladder kept leaking, Bunek only said, "Oh, that's nothing. It's just water dripping. Like the nira you tap, your bladder will stop leaking when the time comes." Bunek's comment on his inability to get an erection was: "That's also nothing. It's like a sleeping snake. It'll get the urge to move once the weather turns warm."

Bunek's repeated statement, "that's nothing," coupled with her ready smile helped boost Darsa's morale. He believed his physical disability was a temporary problem Bunek would help him overcome.

Darsa accepted Bunek, and resigned himself to a massage from his feet to his head. She always paid special attention to his belly and groin.

"It's no wonder your little boy is dead. The joints around your groin are as cold as leaky faucets," Bunek said. "You have to move so your joints don't freeze up."

Darsa only moaned.

"Are you drinking herbal medicines?"

Darsa moaned again.

"Yes, even though they're bitter you have to drink them. The ingredients are blade grass root, the tip of the areca root, and cloves. Do you know why there's blade grass root?"

"No."

"Blade grass root is clever and has strong penetrating powers. It can even penetrate rocky ground."

Darsa grimaced.

"Do you know what the cloves are for?"

Darsa grimaced again.

"Cloves create warmth. That's right, because everything starts from warmth."

For the first week, Bunek came to the house to treat Darsa every day. After that, she asked Darsa to come to her house at night. "During the daytime, I have a lot of work," she said, and added, "Besides, you should walk to revive the muscles in your groin."

Darsa happily obliged to Bunek's request. Going out at night meant he was unlikely to meet anyone. He reeked and people pinched their nose when they passed him. Lasi often went with him to Bunek's house. Only when she was exhausted did she let him go alone.

The first rain fell, marking the end of the dry season, after nearly five months. The shrubs that had wilted along the walls of the valley turned green again as new shoots and buds sprang up. The *puyengan* that covered the unfarmed land began to flower and appeared like a yellow sprinkling everywhere. New crevices showed in the stretch of ferns along the slopes of the ravines.

When the sun rose, thousands of butterflies of all kinds and colors fluttered around the wild flowers or chased after mates. Later in the day thousands of moths emerged. The swarms invited birds and predatory insects. Swallows, pigeons, and fantails flaunted their agility in pouncing on their prey. The dragonfly was satisfied with one moth in its mouth.

The few moths that survived found a mate quickly. After the male moth bit the female on her bottom, they fluttered to the ground and lost their wings. They then crawled to a secluded spot and dug a hole to start building a new colony.

Darsa collected dry branches for firewood in a heavily wooded area. He had been doing light work for the past few days. Half a year of bed rest had weakened his muscles, so he had to postpone tapping palms just yet. Even so, he appeared to have changed for the better. His face was brighter and his movements stronger.

Lasi also noticed another change: Darsa stopped getting angry as often. He was also more talkative. Sometimes, he laughed and joked with Mukri. He usually pulled a face when Mukri brought the nira, especially if Lasi appeared too eager about helping unstrap the harness from his back. Mukri did indeed like to make eyes at Lasi and sometimes threw her a flirtatious smile. Lasi had gone without a man's touch for months and found herself surprised by Mukri's advances. Only surprised, nothing more.

There was another, more meaningful change. One day Darsa came up to Lasi as she squatted in front of the stove. Looking happy, Darsa whispered, "Las, the pants I've worn since morning are still dry."

Lasi looked at her husband with gleaming eyes. She broke into a smile. "Thank goodness. That's why there've been fewer clothes to wash."

"Are you happy, Las?"

Lasi looked down. Her face reddened.

"How about you? Are you happy or not?"

Lasi and Darsa looked at each other. Lasi's heartbeat quickened. She blushed and bowed her head.

"We should have a celebration to give thanks."

"Yes, once I've fully recovered and back to how I was before."

"Yes."

Lasi resumed tending the stove. The nira in the pot bubbled like the joy that bloomed in her heart. Smoke curled into the air. The scent of the nira as it turned red was fragrant. *Oh, truly Allah never slept*, Lasi whispered to herself. Darsa was finally healed thanks to His compassion. Those who called her the miserable widow could finally shut their mouths. Her mother, who constantly mentioned Pak Sambeng, could also shut her mouth. Lasi let out a breath of relief. Tears welled up in her eyes.

The rain that begun the previous mid-afternoon let up with the beating of the drum at Grandfather Mus' surau for the pre-dawn prayer. Parts of the dirt floor in Lasi's house were wet because of a few broken roof tiles. The air was very cold as Lasi and Darsa bathed together by the well. They reveled in the outpouring of joy that had been bottled up and played, splashing each other with water. Above them, a fantail chirped and fluttered, moving quickly as though representing the spirit blossoming in the hearts of the young couple. Darsa was back doing his job that throughout his convalescence had been entrusted to his neighbor, Mukri.

Despite his bad experience of dropping to the ground from a treetop, Darsa was eager to climb, and not the least bit concerned he might fall a second time. Never had a tapper in Karangsoga been cowed from climbing again after surviving a fall. Rakam fell three times and only died on his fourth fall. He would still be collecting the nira if he had survived that last fall. Even so, Lasi stood for a long time at the front door after seeing Darsa off. She mouthed a prayer. *Go safely, return safely*, she whispered. Heaven forbid it turned out like the last time, when he went safely and returned a broken man in Mukri's arms.

The sun dipped to the horizon by the time Lasi had finished cooking the nira. The palm sugar was ready, packed in a basket and covered with dried hibiscus leaves to absorb any moisture. She strapped the basket to her back with an old sheet, the knot digging between her breasts. She never realized this made her breasts look more prominent and drew stares from men.

The basket of sugar on her back, Lasi walked quickly to Pak Tir's house. She felt much better selling the sugar from the nira her husband had collected, instead of that collected by another man. The sun shone in her face, forcing her to squint. Many butterflies still fluttered around. Crepe myrtle flowers at the start of the rainy season blossomed in clumps of purple with their yellow pistils on beds of shiny green leaves. Several beetles with yellow backs flitted between the fresh flowers and shed their old sheaths. A pair of finches hopped between branches. The male let out a shrill and clear chirp. The sounds of the cicadas made the day seem more alive.

Lasi kept walking. She crossed the areca-palm footbridge, smiling as she remembered spending much time there, and climbed to the straight alley that led to Pak Tir's house.

Several other women had already gathered to sell their sugar. Lasi waited her turn. She felt the mood grow silent and awkward, as though there was a chasm between her and the other women. They seemed aloof. Keeping to themselves, they smiled oddly and winked at each other.

Three men carrying crates of sugar from the warehouse to the back of a truck parked in the yard also smiled and exchanged glances when they noticed Lasi.

Pak Tir was busy with his scales. A fat man with a round, balding head, he moved quickly and mechanically. He operated the scales expertly, catching the lever at the moment the copper stem began to rise. His sleight-of-hand gave him an extra fraction of an ounce of palm sugar at each weighing. He became irritated whenever anyone paid too close attention to how he weighed the sugar, and paid the women with indifference.

"The price of sugar's gone down again. I'm just following the rules from the buyers. When they raise the price, so do I. When they lower it, I must too."

The wives of the tappers were used to hearing bad news. All they could do was accept it. Most of them owed him money, and what they sold on a given day was what they needed to live on that very same day. For them, the price of the sugar was a terrifying condition they had to accept regardless.

Pak Tir always had an explanation for the lower price. It was the fruit season, he said, so demand for sweet food had gone down. Or, the sweet soy sauce factory in Jakarta that usually bought palm sugar had burned down, and the buyers were left with unused stock in the warehouse. Or the price of diesel had gone up because the government had cut the fuel subsidy. The buyers were forced to lower the price of sugar to cover the increase in freight costs.

The tappers' wives always listened to Pak Tir diligently. They nodded when he was done, but didn't understand the connection between the drop in the price of palm sugar and the fruit season, or the burning of a sweet soy sauce factory, or the increase in the cost of diesel fuel. They nodded because it was all they could do. Nodding was a sign of their helplessness.

When at last it was Lasi's turn, Pak Tir looked at her for a moment while clicking his tongue and shaking his head. Like the women around her, he smiled oddly. His voice was full of sympathy. "Oh,

Las, how unfortunate you've been. But you have to be patient. Bear with it, Las, perhaps it's your fate."

"Pak Tir, what do you mean?" Lasi stammered, confusion written across her face.

"What, you don't know?"

"What should I know, sir? What's going on?" Lasi grew more agitated. Her lips trembled.

Pak Tir went back to shaking his head.

"Las, I don't want to say anything until you find out for yourself. It really is strange, Las, very strange. Everyone in the village knows, but you haven't noticed anything."

Lasi took the money he gave her for the sugar, her hand shaking with anxiety. She headed home without counting the money. The women continued looking at her. Lasi felt as though she was gored in the chest with a sharp claw. The back of her head felt hot from the stares as she walked with long brisk strides to get home as quickly as possible. She ignored the millipede that crawled out in front of her, even though looking at the slow, disgusting creature made her shiver.

Lasi was about to enter the front yard when her mother appeared.

Mbok Wiryaji hiked up her sarong as she walked with a profound rage on her flushed face. "Oh, Lasi, my child. How unlucky can you be?"

"What is it, mother? What's going on?"

"Darsa, that no-good husband of yours, is a jerk. He has no scruples. Sipah is demanding he marry her. Don't go back to that house. You must demand a divorce."

Lasi listened to her mother's explosion of sharp, biting words. She watched her mother move about in her impassioned state as she stood frozen, her eyes fixed in a stare, her mouth agape as if she was about to speak.

Lasi floated into a strange world where she clearly saw everyone. The trees and the birds smirked and taunted her. The sun was a dirty yellow, and the water at the bottom of the ravine guffawed.

Bunek appeared topless, her breasts hanging down to her navel, grinning and showing off her missing and rotten teeth. Her natty hair was a clump of filthy fibers. She cackled and brayed for the longest time. The terrible, ear-splitting sound rang out, and echoed off the valley walls.

Lasi's world continued to turn and tumble. Everything floated and scattered amid a million fireflies, a million stars, and a million fireworks going off at once. A striped snake curled ready to strike, and a scorpion. The tinkle of something shattering sounded in her ear. Then everything went silent. The topsy-turvy slowly righted itself. That which scattered assembled, and that which congealed melted. Everything cloudy became clear. Lasi slowly returned to the real world.

In her feeble perception, Lasi saw Sipah, the old maid and Bunek's youngest daughter. The painfully shy girl with a deformed leg demanded that Darsa marry her. The moment she understood, Lasi dropped her basket and the money. The metal coins clattered on the rocky ground. Lasi clenched her fists. She was hurled back into her fantasy world, where she became a giant rock crab with pincers made of iron. She was ready to snip off Bunek's head first, then Darsa's, and everyone else's. But there never was a giant crab, or pincers made of iron.

Lasi had been thrown off the stage where she once belonged. She stood in the middle of nowhere, without a screen or mirror to see her reflection. She had nothing to prove that she existed. Nothingness hammered inside her chest.

Swaying like a banana leaf in the wind, Lasi started to walk. She had a dead expression in her unblinking eyes and moved like a creature barely conscious.

Mbok Wiryaja followed her home, still cursing and condemning Darsa. When she reached the doorway of her house Mbok Wiryaji saw her own husband sitting quietly like an empty pongkor. She grew angrier than ever.

"Darsa, that nephew of yours is a rotten pile of filth. He doesn't know how good he had it. For half a year, he was the paralyzed goat we had to tend, and now he humiliates my daughter. Do you know how quickly she could have a new husband if she wasn't still married? Her next husband will be a gentleman, a teacher, someone with a salary, not a stupid tapper who reeks of rancid nira. He stinks. Do you know how many men are waiting for Lasi to be single again?"

"Wait a minute," Wiryaji said patiently.

"No. Your nephew is dishonest. I regret I ever agreed to let him marry my daughter. I regret it."

Mbok Wiryaji gasped for air as she ran out of words.

Lasi sat quietly on the bench. A silence descended that was soon broken by the sound of approaching footsteps.

Grandfather Mus appeared and stood at the door for a moment. Several neighbors also showed up.

"What is going on, Wiryaji? I can hear the shouting all the way to my house."

"It's Darsa. My nephew is a bad boy. Sipah, Bunek's daughter, is demanding he marry her. Darsa has brought shame to his family," Wiryaji said in a tired voice.

"There, Grandfather Mus," Mbok Wiryaji suddenly lashed out. "I was the one who wanted Lasi to ask for a divorce, but you didn't agree. Now it has come to this. You have to take your share of the responsibility and tell Lasi to get a divorce."

"Patience. I've shared your pain from the very beginning. Now I also blame Darsa. You have every right to be angry, but you can't act as you please. Darsa is clearly in the wrong. I only ask that you not talk about divorce just yet."

"Why wait any longer? Do only men have the right to demand a divorce?"

"That's not what I meant. You need to wait until everyone has calmed down. It's not good to make decisions in anger and confusion. Besides, whatever you want to do about Darsa, it's still Lasi's right to decide. Believe me, your daughter has her rights. Only a faithful husband deserves a faithful wife."

The neighbors tried to calm Mbok Wiryaji. One man reminded her of the belief among the Karangsoga people that everything is predestined. "Man can't explain why things happen," he said.

Lasi looked like a firecracker about to explode, but she remained silent. She held herself stiff and tense, but quiet.

Grandfather Mus had intended to call Darsa, but thought better of it. Bringing Darsa before Lasi and her mother when the mood was so heated would be like dangling a cat in front of a rabid dog. "I'm going home. I ask you remain patient through this ordeal. And you, Las, come with me so you can calm yourself at my house. Okay?"

Much to everyone's surprise, Lasi followed Grandfather Mus. They watched her with pity. Lasi and Grandfather Mus weaved through the vegetation on their way down the hill, and vanished from sight after they turned south.

***

Karangsoga was once again gripped by gossip. The story spread in every direction, embellished by whoever told it. Most people believed Darsa's folly was Bunek's fault. Sipah was crippled and shy, and hardly the kind of woman to flirt with Darsa. One woman said in all earnestness, Bunek would be the first person to know when Darsa was healed. Darsa had to test his recovery on another woman before going to his wife. A healer like Bunek had likely imposed such a condition.

"Maybe Bunek wanted to offer herself as the test subject for Darsa's recovery. Who knows? She might have felt ashamed because she was gray and had grandchildren, so she passed Darsa on to Sipah."

The speaker smiled smugly at the conclusion of the story and was greeted with guffaws from those listening.

Another man had no less audacious a story, as though he knew precisely what went on between Darsa, Bunek, and Bunek's virgin daughter. According to him, Bunek asked Sipah to massage Darsa in her place, but Sipah refused. Finally, afraid of making her mother angry, Sipah agreed, and Bunek left the two of them alone. "Even though she has a deformed leg, she's still a woman, right?" There was another burst of laughter.

The stories about Darsa and Sipah grew more complex and twisted by the day. Bunek initially responded by laughing, but soon needed to set the record straight. In that same folksy way of hers, she told everyone. "Darsa? Oh, that's nothing, just a matter of live and let live. I helped restore his manhood and in return, I asked for his help. It was a very simple request, and enjoyable too: Marry Sipah. It's tedious waiting for a man to propose to her. None of you wants to marry my crippled daughter, right? Hahaha."

"But you set up Darsa and used Sipah as the bait, isn't that right?" Bunek cackled.

"With that kind of arrangement there's no need for setups or bait. It's a simple issue. Darsa is a man and Sipah is a woman. It's between a man and a woman. Sipah may be crippled, but only one leg is useless." Bunek laughed again. She had won everyone over and made them smile, even laugh.

***

Karangsoga rang with the stories of Darsa and Sipah as a truck pulled out of Pak Tir's front yard after sunset. Pardi sat at the wheel, with his assistant, Sapon, next to him. He carried four tons of sugar, so Pardi had to be very careful how he drove the old truck. The road through the village, though paved with flat stones, was narrow and full of steep inclines and descents. Before he could get to the main road five kilometers away, he had to go around uphill and downhill corners, and cross old narrow bridges. In a few spots, he had to drive along the edge of the ravine or the foot of a rock face. Pardi never forgot how the previous year, the driver he replaced had rolled over with a cargo of sugar and was smashed to bits at the bottom of the ravine.

Pardi was relieved as he rounded the final bend. The truck's headlights reached far ahead when the descending road was straight. Pardi lit a cigarette and Sapon eased back. A bat fluttered into the glare of the headlights, weaving erratically as it chased an insect. Up ahead, the headlights caught a wildcat or weasel by the side of the road. The blue light reflecting from its eyes was clearly visible before it ran into the undergrowth.

The road leveled off on the approach to the main road and Pardi released the brake pedal, but suddenly stomped down on it.

A woman darted from behind a tree. Every driver knew this was how prostitutes attracted men's attention, especially drivers. Pardi stepped on the brakes because the woman had deliberately blocked the road.

The heavily laden truck lurched to a halt and the engine cut off while still in gear. Pardi and Sapon cursed before they both exclaimed, "Lasi? What's she doing here?"

Pardi and Sapon got out. To their surprise, Lasi jumped into the cab of the truck and sat down. "I'm going with you," she said, staring straight ahead. Her face was cold and stiff, like a wall of stone that never yielded.

"What? We're driving to Jakarta."

Lasi stared ahead.

"Don't, Las. We know you have problems. But people will say I'm meddling in your affairs," Pardi said.

"Besides, we'd feel bad for your husband and parents, and Grandfather Mus. They might think we took you away. That could get messy," Sapon said.

Lasi remained in her seat. Pardi dropped his cigarette and ground it out under his sandal. Sapon walked in a circle. In the strained and awkward atmosphere, the truck's engine started again.

"Las, where do you really want to go?" Pardi asked.

"Wherever the truck is going."

"I told you, Jakarta."

"Then it's Jakarta."

Pardi scratched his head. Sapon walked away and slumped at the side of the road.

"What do you think, Pon?"

"Up to you, Pardi. I'm fine as long as no one accuses us of anything."

"Pardi," Lasi said, "heaven and earth are my witnesses that I'm leaving of my own accord. If you object, I'll get out and sit in front of the wheels. Well?"

Pardi scratched his head again and climbed into the cab. Sapon followed. Lasi sat between them. The engine roared and the truck picked up speed.

As he changed gears, Pardi muttered, "As long as you've sworn on heaven and earth, I'll swear that I have nothing to do with your running away."

When they reached the main road Pardi stopped the truck. "I want to buy some cigarettes," he said, and jumped out. He did buy cigarettes, but also left a message with the storekeeper for Lasi's parents. He wanted to avoid any blame for Lasi leaving Karangsoga.

They turned west onto the main road, joining the stream of cars from the east. The truck moved smoothly on the asphalt road and the engine growled evenly. Pardi lit another cigarette and the cabin filled with light. Sapon looked to his right and saw tears in Lasi's eyes.

Crying, Lasi knew what she had done: she had run away from Karangsoga, the land of her birth, where she had lived for twenty-four years of her life. She ran from the home where she first came into the world, a home with a role that had meaning. Lasi left her stove and her pot in which the fragrant caramel bubbled. She had run away from her problems toward uncertainty in a new world where she would have to grope her way, an unknown world that didn't know her.

Lasi was wracked by doubt and fear. The pain from what Darsa had done and being made to feel worthless to her husband strengthened her resolve. Freeing herself of her bonds was the only way to fight back. She had to keep running, even without a direction.

During the hour's drive along the main road, Pardi scratched his head and lit a new cigarette the moment he finished the old one. Sapon tried to sing, but his voice was hoarse and strained. He tried whistling, and that was just as unpleasant. They rode in silence until Pardi pulled up in front of a restaurant. Sapon got out and jammed a wedge beneath the wheel to keep the truck from rolling.

"Las, I'm hungry. I usually eat at this place. You haven't eaten either, have you?"

"No, but I'm not hungry."

"Whether you're hungry or not, you have to eat. We have a ways to go, and it's not good to travel with an empty stomach. You could get sick."

"That's right, Las," Sapon said. "Let's eat first."

"I've never eaten away from home. I'm ashamed."

"Here's your chance to try. Besides, you came with us, you have to adapt to our ways. We don't want you getting sick because of an empty stomach and become a nuisance."

"Are we far from Karangsoga?"

"Yes. No one will know you here. Come on, get down."

"I don't have any money. Lend me some, okay?"

"Don't be like that. You're with us, so we're responsible for your meals. Unless you plan to embarrass us."

Lasi followed Pardi and Sapon into the restaurant. Lasi and Sapon took a seat as Pardi headed for the back.

A young woman served Pardi, handing him a bar of soap and a towel. Pardi seemed to know her well. They looked like a couple. Sapon noticed Lasi's surprise. "That's how it is, Las. People say that if a truck driver wants to rest, he visits. That's why he has a lot of girlfriends."

Lasi tried to understand this novel experience. She had never seen anything like it in Karangsoga.

The white light of the pressurized paraffin lamp fell on Lasi. Her kebaya was wrinkled. She had put up her hair in a simple knot, like a woman going to work in a rice paddy. Her oily face showed it had been a long time since her last bath. She was barefoot and her lips were pale. Sapon heard her stomach rumble.

A bit clumsy at first, Lasi wolfed down her food and drank a large glass of sweet tea. She would never eat so ravenously if she had not been hungry for so long.

Sapon remembered villagers had said that Lasi refused to eat or sleep after finding out her husband's deception. If that was true, she had gone two days without eating, and likely without sleeping.

He shook his head and smiled. Even in her distress, he saw what made her special: the contrast between her black hair and fair skin was striking. Her eyes and her eyebrows were like no other, and made her stand out easily. She was tall like her mother, who was taller than most women in Karangsoga. Sapon smiled again. This time he thought of Darsa. Everything Lasi's mother said about him was true. Darsa had never known how lucky he was to have a wife as beautiful as Lasi, who, according to the villagers, was more suitable for a village chief.

Pardi came out of the back room after changing his clothes. Lasi was again surprised, but Pardi just smiled at her and called for his food. The same young woman served him as she would a husband.

Lasi thought of Pardi's wife back in Karangsoga. It was true what people said, all men were lechers.

The young woman with the curly hair and hoops in her ears looked hard at Lasi. She felt affronted and her heart beat faster. Lasi wanted so much to explain that she was a married woman and never seduced another man. She was just hitching a ride in a truck to escape, and Pardi happened to be the driver. The words never left her tongue. All she did was swallow and the words died inside her chest.

After whispering to his girlfriend, Pardi turned to Sapon and Lasi and said, "It's time to head out." The hour hand on the old clock hanging on the wall of the restaurant pointed to eight. The night air was bitingly cold. The truck engine rumbled and they resumed the final four hundred kilometers of their journey.

Pardi smoked one cigarette after another. When his lighter flared, Sapon glanced to his right. Lasi looked calmer. The third time he looked, her eyes were closed. Emotionally drained by her husband's folly, sated from dinner, and lulled by the truck's movement, Lasi quickly became drowsy. Now she was asleep. Her head leaned to the left and came to rest on Sapon's shoulder. Her breathing was soft and even.

"Pardi," Sapon whispered.

"What?"

"Lasi's asleep."

"Let her sleep. Should I pull over?"

"That's not what I meant. I feel sorry for her."

"You're not the only one. I'm confused about her plans. Is she leaving Karangsoga permanently or what? Will she return with us tomorrow?"

"I think she will."

"And if she doesn't?"

"I'm not thinking about whether Lasi will go back or not."

"Then what?"

"I'm thinking that in this truck right now there's a beautiful woman, more beautiful than your girlfriend, Pardi. Aren't you—"

"Hush, you idiot. Don't try anything. We truck drivers may be dirtbags, but we have rules. We never mess with married women. That's just not done. It's a big taboo and jinxes the journey."

"You're right. What's going to happen once Lasi is no longer married? It's going to be a circus."

"Circus or not, I'll be the first to propose. You don't believe me?"

"Lasi wouldn't marry you because she knows you have a wife and girlfriends along the highway. She'll pick me because I'm single."

"You idiot. I'd give up anything to have Lasi, get it?"

Sapon and Pardi almost laughed until they remembered Lasi sitting between them.

She stirred, stretched, and leaned more heavily onto Sapon's shoulder. Lasi was sound asleep.

The sugar truck entered Tegal at eleven o'clock that night and stopped to refuel. Pardi told Sapon to get under the tarp in the truck bed. He wanted Lasi to have more room to sleep in the cab. With her legs folded, Lasi slept more comfortably next to Pardi. She slept through the journey, unaware of the stops in Indramayu and Pamanukan. In Indramayu, Pardi slept for a couple of hours in the back room of a restaurant. Sapon knew Pardi had a girlfriend there too.

They reached the outskirts of Jakarta toward dawn. Pardi stopped outside a restaurant lit by two paraffin lamps. He woke Sapon to keep watch, because he wanted to rest until eight o'clock, when the big buyer would be ready to receive their load.

A woman with a cigarette in her hand served Pardi a glass of coffee. Her colorful makeup belied the softness of the early day. Lasi slept inside the cab of the truck, and Pardi stretched out on a bench beneath the awning of the restaurant. He fell asleep, the glass of hot coffee only a few fingers' width from his head.

Lasi woke to traffic noise. She looked outside and was shocked to see the sun already up. She had no idea where she was. What about Pardi and Sapon? She saw Pardi sleeping beneath the awning. Lasi wanted to get out of the truck but had trouble opening the door.

Sapon appeared beside the truck. "Ah, you're awake."

"Where are we, Pon?"

"This is Jakarta." Sapon opened the truck door.

Lasi stepped out. "I need to go to the bathroom. Is there a well around here?"

"I'll take you."

Sapon led Lasi inside the restaurant and walked to the back. The paraffin lamps still burned, even though it was daylight. Three women slept jammed against each other on a long bench, traces of makeup visible on their faces. They wore bright colored clothes. Two other women sat and talked while smoking. Both looked up when Lasi and Sapon entered. One woman grabbed Sapon by the hand after Lasi entered the bathroom.

"Is she new?" asked the woman with the large earrings.

"One of Pardi's, is she? Has he brought new stock?" asked a woman with chafed calves.

"Why do you want to know?" Sapon snorted.

"Hey, we were just wondering."

"Don't talk nonsense. She's my neighbor from back in the village, a decent woman with a husband."

"I didn't ask if she had a husband," the woman with large earrings said. "Our friend here," she pointed to the woman with chafed calves, "she has a husband. I'm asking if she's new stock."

"No."

"If not, what's she doing with you guys?" Both women laughed.

Sapon ignored them.

Lasi came out of the bathroom and joined Sapon and Pardi, who had woken up and was talking with *Ibu* Koneng, the owner. She wore her hair in a huge bun and looked Lasi up and down, like a cattle trader examining a fat cow.

"Have a seat, Las," Pardi said after introducing them. "Sapon and I have to unload the sugar in a bit. Stay with Ibu Koneng; take a shower and rest. We'll be back in the afternoon or evening."

Lasi nodded slowly.

"Besides, it's not fitting for women to deliver merchandise to a warehouse," Ibu Koneng added in a friendly tone. "Wait with me for a while. You'll have lots of company. What's your name again?"

"Lasi, bu."

"Lasiyah," Pardi said.

Ibu Koneng gave Lasi another look.

"I apologize for asking, but is your mother or father Chinese?"

Embarrassed, Lasi bowed her head. She turned to Pardi and he understood.

Pardi told Ibu Koneng a long, convoluted story about Lasi having problems at home and needing to get away for a bit.

As he spoke, Ibu Koneng appraised Lasi with bright and curious eyes.

"Oh, so that's it?" she asked Lasi.

Lasi nodded again and smiled flatly. Her heart fell when she realized how far she was from Karangsoga, without money or a change of clothes. Her eyes glazed over as she wondered, *what am I doing in this strange and crowded place?*

Before he took his seat behind the steering wheel, Pardi went to Lasi and handed her some money.

Lasi froze. She had only accepted money from her husband or for selling palm sugar. It was hard to accept money from others because she knew that money was a tool of trade. Anyone receiving money had to be ready to lose something in exchange.

"This is just to tide you over, Las. You might want a drink while I'm gone," Pardi said.

"Thank you, Pardi. I'll accept this as a loan. Some day I'll repay you."

"Don't worry about it, Las. We're both far from home. We have to help each other."

"You're right, Pardi, but I don't want to be a burden. I insist on treating this money as a loan."

"Fine, do what you need to do. I certainly don't consider you in my debt."

Lasi watched the truck that had spirited her far from home pull away from Ibu Koneng's restaurant. She was hit by how odd everything felt the moment the truck and its two occupants vanished from sight. Lasi turned and walked toward the wooden bench beneath the awning.

"Pardi said you didn't bring a change of clothes?" asked Ibu Koneng.

Lasi nodded and blushed.

"In that case, wear these for now. Would you like to bathe first?"

Lasi agreed and Ibu Koneng called for a towel.

The woman with chafed calves brought the towel and handed it to Lasi with feigned friendliness.

Lasi showered and changed into the sarong and bright blue kebaya. She felt refreshed. The bright color of the clothes accentuated her complexion. She combed her hair and knotted it in as neat a bun as she could. Ibu Koneng offered her breakfast in the back of the main room. Being fussed over made Lasi feel uncomfortable, but she accepted Ibu Koneng's kindness. The woman with large earrings and the one with chafed calves kept staring at her. The three younger women who had been sleeping together were awake, and regarded Lasi as a competitor.

Lasi recognized the women as prostitutes, the same as the girls Pardi met at each restaurant along the highway. As far as she knew, Karangsoga had no such women. She had heard stories and now saw them with her own eyes. She was among them. *Would that make Ibu Koneng their pimp, as people say? Did she use the restaurant as a cover for her other business?*

"Las, Pardi said you were having problems," Ibu Koneng said without looking at her.

Lasi nodded, uncertain.

"Tell me, is it money, in-laws, or husband?"

"Husband, bu," Lasi said softly.

"Is your husband miserly, too amorous, or the kind that strays?"

"The kind that strays."

Ibu Koneng nodded. There was no hint of surprise on her face.

"Yes, that's how it usually is. A husband like that deserves to be taught a lesson. He'll know what it feels like if you get back at him by going astray too."

Lasi rolled her eyes.

"I mean, many wives get back at their husbands by doing the same thing. You're not like that, are you?"

"Ibu Koneng, I'm a village girl. All I could do was run away when I learned what my husband had done."

"You didn't ask for a divorce?"

"No, bu. In my village, the word divorcée isn't a nice label to wear. Too many eyes scrutinize your every move and too many ears listen to what you say. People are ready to judge every step you take and every word you speak."

"That's true. I know about that sort of thing. So then, what are your plans?"

"I don't know," Lasi shook her head.

"Stay with me for one or two weeks until you've calmed down. After that, you can decide where to go next."

"Won't that inconvenience you?" Lasi asked after a long silence.

"Many of the drivers' wives come to visit and stay with me."

"The drivers' wives?"

"Well, their wives or girlfriends. As you can see for yourself, a lot of women stay here."

Lasi frowned. She felt uneasy. Why did Ibu Koneng talk about the women with her? *Am I the same as those two with the large earrings and chafed calves?* Lasi swallowed.

Koneng sensed that Lasi was offended.

"There are many women at my restaurant. I'm sure you understand their jobs. As for you, Las, there's no need to do the same. I know you're proper and not like them. You can manage the restaurant or work in the kitchen."

"I don't know, bu. I'm afraid I'd be too shy to manage the restaurant. Perhaps I can help in the kitchen."

Ibu Koneng smiled.

"Las, it's not my intention to treat you like a servant. I just want to give you a chance to forget your troubles. I really pity you. Do you understand?"

Lasi had found a friend who understood and was willing to be a vessel into which she could pour her feelings.

With a nod and smile, Ibu Koneng cunningly positioned herself as a safe haven for Lasi who felt uprooted from her own world. To Lasi, Ibu Koneng had handed her an umbrella and a drink of fresh water while she wandered in a barren desert with the sun beating down on her. Lasi felt cared for.

The sense of being safe compelled her to agree when Ibu Koneng asked her to come along to the market. They rode in a pedicab, weaving through the noisy, boisterous streets very different from the quiet pathways of Karangsoga.

Ibu Koneng watched as Lasi gawked at the crowded surroundings and pretended not to notice. They stepped out of the pedicab and Ibu Koneng led Lasi across the street. Lasi scrutinized the shabby, crowded, and incredibly filthy market. She was no stranger to the mud of the rice paddies, but the mud at markets disgusted her. It was only because she wanted to avoid offending her hostess that she followed Ibu Koneng wherever she went. She filled a large basket with the vegetables, tofu, fish, and eggs Ibu Koneng paid for.

At two in the afternoon, Lasi and Ibu Koneng sat chatting beneath the front awning of the restaurant when Sapon showed up alone. Lasi asked for Pardi, and Sapon told her he was arranging the transport of a load to Tegal.

"Las, Pardi said to get ready right away. He'll be here any moment and we'll leave immediately."

"Leave for where?" Ibu Koneng asked.

"Where else but home?"

"Yes, I know. But Lasi wants to stay here. If you don't believe me, ask her yourself."

Lasi looked from Sapon to Ibu Koneng and back again. Several times, she was on the verge of speaking, but no words came out.

"Don't make things hard for us, Las. You have to come. If you don't, Pardi and I will get into trouble. People will ask us all kinds of questions."

"Pon, don't pressure Lasi when she's heartbroken. Let her do as she chooses, which is to stay here and find herself again."

"Really, Las," Sapon said brusquely. "You have to come home. If you want to return here later, that's your business, but you left with us so you have to come home with us too. You can be angry with your husband, but what about your mother? You left without telling anyone."

Lasi was flushed. The image of her house flashed before her. She saw every inch of the small house she had lived in for three years. Her heart fluttered when she imagined the bed with its bamboo frame and the woven mat turned glossy from wear. She remembered every step of the path she walked along whenever she went to Pak Tir's house to sell her palm sugar. The footbridge made of the single areca palm, the sound of the pongkors knocking against each other, and the popping of the caramel bubbles as she stirred the palm sugar. Her memory brought back the quiet nights filled with the sound of Grandfather Mus' gambang and singing. And then there was her mother. She was an only child. Her mother must miss her tremendously.

Lasi almost agreed to go with Sapon when she had a vision of Bunek, Sipah, and Darsa and the rest of the Karangsoga villagers sneering at her. Her ears rang with the crying of the baby inside Sipah's womb. Fireworks went off inside her eyeballs. A dry clinking sound pierced her ears. Lasi gasped for air. She tried to swallow several times, but spit stuck in her throat.

"Las, don't lose your mind," Sapon said, breaking the silence. "Are you coming home or not?"

Lasi was shocked. She looked at Ibu Koneng, absent-minded.

Ibu Koneng smiled and tried to appear calm.

"Let's try this," she said gently. "You transport sugar to this area once a week, right?"

Sapon nodded.

"Leave Lasi with me. If she wants, you can take her home next week. If she doesn't, you can't force her. How about that, Las?"

"Yes," she said in a hoarse voice. "Next week."

Sapon fell silent and bowed his head. Stumped, he had nothing else to say that might persuade Lasi to return home.

"Trust Lasi to me," Ibu Koneng said.

Sapon looked at her and frowned.

"I know what you're worried about, and it won't happen. Lasi is different from the other women here. I won't treat her like them."

A truck honked several times. Sapon ran out to meet Pardi, who wanted to stay on the road. Their conversation left Pardi dissatisfied and he got out of the truck. He walked to Lasi who stood near Ibu Koneng. Like Sapon, Pardi tried to persuade Lasi. She was determined to stay. She repeated the words she had spoken the day before: heaven and earth were her witnesses that Pardi and Sapon were absolved of any fault for her leaving. She took full responsibility for her actions.

Pardi resigned himself to the situation and wanted reassurance. "We trust Lasi to your care, Bu Koneng,"

"Good. I won't betray the trust of people I've known for so long. Believe me, Lasi will be safe."

Disappointed, Pardi and Sapon sauntered back to the truck. They waved as they pulled away.

Lasi felt something move away from her heart. Whatever stabbed her in the chest now pierced her soul. Tears filled her eyes and her vision blurred. Pak Tir's truck faded into the distance, along with the stream of other vehicles heading east.

Chapter 3

The Kalirong River sprang from the web of creeks on the slopes of the mountain north of Karangsoga. Upstream, it resembled a long chasm with a flow of clear water, and ferns covered the bottom. The trickling was only audible in certain spots, but downstream the Kalirong supplied water to the rice paddies and fields to its left and right. Large boulders, some of them exceptionally so, stood in the riverbed, like eternal guards immersed in the clear water of the Kalirong for all time. The water gushed through this section, whipping up peaks of white foam visible between shiny black rocks. Water skaters skimmed over the surface of the water. For these long-legged weightless insects, the water's surface was a place to slide about, catch prey, and mate.

All kinds of trees grew along the banks of the Kalirong: purple coral trees studded with thorns, and yellow flowers that sprang up in the spaces between the rocks. The *logondang*, whose strands of fruit sprouted straight from the branches, spread far over the surface of the river to more easily scatter their seeds through the flowing water. Jambe rowe palms grew narrow and straight along the banks of the Kalirong. The curve of its leaves set in a neat pattern and its large round fruit made it look prehistoric. Pandan grass meandered in an almost unbroken line along the riverbank, and served as a hiding place for weasels. Those fish-eating creatures came out of hiding when it was quiet and gathered on top of a rock, only to flee when they spotted a human.

Another large logondang tree grew by a bend in the river. All kinds of birds frolicked in the dense foliage, knocking its small round fruit into the water below. A small splash broke the silence each time a fruit hit the water. When a gust of wind knocked many fruits out of the branches at once, they made a series of soft plops.

A tiny red bird perched on a branch hanging out over the water, almost touching it, and shook off the moss growing there. Several fruit fell into the water and again the sound of splashing was heard.

A dry leaf drifted on the water surface and floated for a moment before being swept behind a black rock. A swaying reed whistled each time its tip touched the moving water. A frog jumped into the water trying to find safety, but the snake chasing it was faster. The frog croaked in the snake's mouth. The sound grew weaker and stopped when the frog entered the snake's stomach.

Darsa let out a long breath. He watched the snake slither away, weighed down by the frog inside him. For the past few days, he had shunned company and the mossy rock hidden beneath the leaves of the banyan tree, offered a secluded place that welcomed his restless heart.

Nearby, a large, flat-topped boulder stood the middle of the river. Frequent touching by human hands had smoothed its surface. Many tappers bathed next to it, before climbing on the flat surface and praying while only wrapped in a sarong. It was a striking sight: a man dressed as simply as could be, assuming the *sujud* position to pray on top of a large rock in the middle of a river. It was quiet except for the gurgling of the water, the chirps of the tiny sunbirds, and the series of splashes as the wind knocked the fruit from the banyan tree.

The sun had almost set and left the western sky edged by golden-red clouds. The silence deepened as the birds stopped chirping and the wind died down.

Darsa stood and sighed. There was no joy in his movements as he stepped into the calf-deep water and began his ablutions. Jumping from boulder to boulder, he reached the top of the large flat rock.

He prayed, the wilderness his silent witness. Darsa performed sujud for an audience with the Highest Consciousness to understand the constant upheaval buffeting his soul. He wanted to understand what he had done and brought him face-to-face with the worst experience in his life: Lasi had left him and caused a commotion through the village. It was bad enough he had to accept her decision, but he also had to marry Sipah, a woman he never imagined as his wife.

Trying to understand his wrong doings was like standing in front of a steep rock face. He remembered the night at Bunek's house. It started out no different from previous nights, with Bunek massaging him.

Darsa had improved over the past few days, and believed he was completely healed. His body reacted, as it should have when Bunek stimulated him with her touch as well as her words.

"What did I tell you?" Bunek laughed. "Any snake will rise when it gets enough warmth."

She told Darsa to lie still while she stepped out.

Darsa heard her talking with Sipah. He couldn't make out what they were saying until Sipah refused to do something her mother asked.

"Don't be stupid. I'm asking you to get rid of the bad fortune stuck to you, the same bad fortune that has left you an old maid."

"Is it my deformed leg, Mother?" Sipah cried.

"No. Other women are deformed worse than you, and they're married because they're not cursed with a bad fortune."

"What if I get pregnant?"

"You dimwit. Getting pregnant makes this better. I'll ask Darsa to marry you. It'll be great if it lasts. If it doesn't, no problem. All that matters is that you lose your bad fortune. At the very least you will be a divorced woman, which is better than being an old maid. Do you understand?"

Bunek returned to the room after persuading Sipah. Darsa pretended not to have heard anything. Bunek asked him to sit up and told him what she wanted in her casual, easygoing patter, even laughing occasionally.

Darsa was torn. Part of him feared hurting Lasi. She was too kind to betray. Lasi was the mirror in which Darsa saw his reflection. It would be stupid to shatter such a valuable mirror. He was also reluctant to disappoint Bunek after she had patiently tended to him for so long and finally succeeded. And there was desire. Even blinded by desire, Darsa could see the consequences his actions would have.

Darsa considered which choice to make: not hurt Lasi or please Bunek and sate his desire. He felt a strong push to give up that chance, to abandon all reflection. The crucial moment bore down on him, and he was swept away, dissolved, maybe even ceased to exist.

He was no more; this man was someone else. This Darsa had forgotten Lasi, and the Highest Consciousness.

He lost who he was. Darsa faltered when he tried to recover his old self. He felt like a stranger. He groaned and sighed to clear his confusion. This had the opposite effect and caused greater confusion.

The drum from Grandfather Mus' surau sounded the sunset prayer. It grew dark as Darsa remained on the rock. He repeated the sujud position and ignored the swarming mosquitos eager to suck the blood from his body. The croaking of a bullfrog came from behind the large boulders on the riverbank. Flying foxes squabbled over the nira spilled from the pongkors left hanging in the coconut palms. Darsa heard the splashes of a weasel hunting for his evening meal of fish.

Night had fallen. Darsa brooded on top of the rock, not knowing what he should do. Return to a home that was empty and cold since Lasi had left? He wanted to stay away from facing the house, his loneliness, and Lasi's absence.

At the peak of his misery, he pictured himself hanging lifeless from the branch of the logondang tree that stretched above the Kalirong. That would convince Lasi he was truly sorry. Darsa knew better than to take his own life. To leave Karangsoga was the only solution.

Darsa stood in a daze. A gentle wind sprinkled the leaves with a fine mist and dropped banyan fruit in the water. A soft, rhythmic sound came from the direction of Grandfather Mus' house. The sound of the gambang reminded Darsa of him.

Darsa had avoided speaking to anyone. Grandfather Mus might offer guidance, or at least be willing to listen. Perhaps the old man would give him a solution that would bring Lasi back.

From bank of the Kalirong, Darsa walked down a path used by tappers until he reached his darkened house. The creaking door sounded eerie in the dark. Darsa lit a lamp, and the light illuminated the void inside the house. It was silent and empty. The small house had lost its soul. Darsa paused and felt a stabbing pain in his chest. He stared at the stove and the pot Lasi had used to cook the nira. He felt another stab in his heart when he saw her kebaya hanging on the line.

For a moment, Darsa stayed lost in his thoughts. He sighed before closing the door and walked to Grandfather Mus' house. He heard the sound of the gambang. As he got closer, he heard the old man chanting. Although hoarse, the voice was in harmony with the notes of gambang flowing from his fingers.

Darsa stayed on the front porch until Grandfather Mus returned from the spiritual journey the sounds of the gambang had carried him.

He concluded a *dhandhanggula* verse and rested his arms lightly across the gambang. His head was bowed, for in his heart still lingered in an intimacy with the All Peaceful. When Grandfather Mus got up shakily, Darsa cleared his throat.

"Who's out there?"

"It's me, Grandfather."

The door opened and Darsa entered. Grandfather Mus motioned him to take a seat on the wooden chair across the table. Darsa smiled, but was unable to hide his anxiety. Grandfather Mus smiled broadly, his expression perfectly clear.

"You're looking thin and shabby. Hard times?"

Darsa grimaced as Grandfather Mus laughed.

"Everyone knows you're paying penance for your sins. That's not an easy burden to bear."

"I'm lost." Darsa listlessly hung his head.

"You have trouble with the consequences of your actions. You've probably asked yourself, what happened that turned your life upside down and confused you so much you've become this skinny. Am I right?"

"That's why I came here. I want you to help me find a measure of peace. Grandfather Mus, I'm really lost."

The old man coughed and smiled.

"That can wait. Have you eaten yet?"

"Thank you, Grandfather. But I don't want to eat."

"How about a cup of coffee?"

Darsa nodded and Grandfather Mus asked his wife to prepare the beverage.

The heartbroken tapper shifted uneasily in his seat. He looked around him at nothing in particular. He sighed several times.

"Grandfather…"

"Yes?"

"I've made a big mistake and regret it. Will Lasi will accept my apologies?"

"I also believe you've made a mistake. You've hurt your wife, and ignored the rules the Almighty set for good conduct. Don't despair too much, because your sins against the Almighty are easily forgiven. The Almighty's mercy knows no bounds. You will receive His mercy if you truly seek it. The Almighty is too great to be bothered by the sins of mortals, no matter how grievous they may be."

Darsa nodded. A glimmer of hope swept across his face.

"What's more difficult," Grandfather Mus went on, "is to receive your wife's forgiveness. Your sin against her is very serious. She's only human, like the rest of us, and not a source of mercy like the Almighty."

"I don't want my marriage to fall apart, Grandfather. I don't want to lose her."

"Having a wife as beautiful as Lasi is a real blessing, and losing her can cause great suffering. I know, everyone knows, yet it all comes down to Lasi. What if she refuses to return to you? Seeking divorce is a man's right and he can do as he pleases, but don't forget, a wife like Lasi can also leave. That's been proven, hasn't it?"

Darsa bowed his head. His suffering was visible in his sunken and lifeless eyes.

"What should I do, Grandfather?"

The old man fell silent. He rolled his tobacco, slowly and mechanically. The flame from his lighter lit up his face before it was shrouded in smoke a moment later.

"Darsa," he said in a ponderous tone.

"Yes, Grandfather?"

"The first thing you need to do is to have the courage to accept yourself, including that you made a mistake. If you can't muster that courage, you're going to have a difficult time."

Darsa lifted his head with great effort.

Grandfather Mus smiled.

"When you did what you did with Sipah, did you realize that there would be consequences?"

"Yes, Grandfather. I already guessed what might happen."

"Well, in that case it is all on you. You knew from the start what you were doing, so you must bear the consequences. You can't avoid it. You have to harvest the fruit of your own toil, and that goes for everyone."

Darsa swallowed and froze in his seat. After a long pause he said, "Grandfather Mus..."

"Yes?"

"From the very beginning I didn't want to make this mistake. Honestly, it's like I said, I knew the result. Still I did what I did. I ask you, how could this happen?"

"What do you mean?"

"Is it true that humans only do what is preordained?"

The old man, piqued by Darsa's question, straightened in his seat. He exhaled a cloud of smoke and closed his eyes. A snatch of mystical verse came to him, a teaching from Sunan Bonang, one of the *wali*.

> *To me, the perfection of God covers everything*
> *Man has no will or purpose*
> *Man is deaf, dumb, and empty*
> *All will comes from Allah*

Grandfather Mus swallowed and nodded. He decided to keep from Darsa what had just flashed through his mind. The shabby young man would never understand Sunan Bonang's teaching about the origin of will. He needed a simpler explanation.

Darsa cleared his throat.

"Now listen, young man. People are granted power by the Almighty to overcome the desires and wants they know have bad consequences. They are also granted a clear heart that reminds them to be ever mindful. When you go against the voice in your heart, you're being unmindful and forgetting the purity that constantly strives for your own good. When you ignore this goodness, you get the opposite, which is badness. Now, that's easy to understand, isn't it?"

Darsa frowned. "Do you mean humans know what they do?" His eyes filled with earnestness.

Grandfather Mus chuckled. "You knew the consequence of what you did with Sipah. The awareness means you had a choice. What you did to Sipah was your decision."

Darsa looked baffled. He struggled for the meaning of what Grandfather Mus had said.

"Don't be too hard on yourself, you're not alone. Many people like you have made mistakes they never meant to, because they ignored the purity in their own hearts. Very few people can faithfully heed the voice of purity."

"What should I do?" Darsa asked after a long silence.

Grandfather Mus rolled another cigarette. His wife came into the room with two glasses of hot coffee.

"Accept the fact you made a mistake. That's how you can lift the weight from your shoulders and find a solution. Leave it up to Lasi whether she stays with you or not."

That last sentence pierced Darsa's chest, and he turned miserable. He muttered as he shook his head, as though trying to shake off the terrible certainty facing him.

"Must I marry Sipah even though I don't want to?"

"Yes. You have to accept the village elders' verdict, and besides, you must pick the fruit of your toil. It's said that *suweng ireng digadhekna, wis kadhung mateng dikapakna.* Do you understand?"

Darsa shook his head.

"It's too late to be looking for a solution when the damage has been done."

Darsa smiled an aggrieved smile.

"The more reluctant you are to accept the consequences, the heavier the burden on your heart. If I were you, I would accept everything fully and seek absolution. Trying to fight it, even in your heart, will only lead to more suffering."

Darsa bowed his head lower. His gaze fixed on the tabletop. On the surface, he envisioned Lasi returning from the well, her body sheathed in a batik wrap. Her wet hair clung to the back of her neck and snaked around and over her shoulder, falling between her breasts. He heard her footsteps and smelled her hair. When he realized it was just his imagination, he felt a stabbing pain in his heart that coursed through his veins. No longer caring that Grandfather Mus looked at him, Darsa began to sob.

"Grandfather…"

"What?"

"I told you it's hard for me to lose Lasi, even though I've admitted my mistake. How can I get Lasi to return?"

Grandfather Mus laughed.

"Why do you ask? It's easy: go find her in Jakarta and bring her home."

"I mean, what can I do within? There's no way I can go to Jakarta to look for her."

"Oh."

The old man laughed again, and Darsa kept his head down.

"All good things come from the Almighty, as all bad things come from yourself; it's only the Almighty you can ask for help. Repent first, and then pray and pray. If you are meant to be with her, you won't lose Lasi. Believe me."

Darsa heaved a long sigh. A smile appeared on his tired face. Grandfather Mus' last words held a glint of hope, no matter how faint and distant.

A night bird flew over the house chirping as Darsa stepped outside. Grandfather Mus looked on as he stood in the shadows of the starlit night. Darsa was unsure where to go. Back home to a painful emptiness or to the rock in the middle of the Kalirong to pray?

He turned past Grandfather Mus' house, wet his feet in the rock-lined pool, and climbed to the surau. He had spent every night of his childhood in the same hut. Darsa now came back, not to pray, but to grapple with the problems that impeded his life.

From the sound of splashing water and the door opening, Grandfather Mus knew Darsa was in the surau and likely to spend the night there. He shook his head and took a deep breath. He was deeply concerned for the young man.

***

When he chose the lives of palm tappers as the subject of his final-year paper, Kanjat only thought in practical terms. The tapper community was the world that surrounded him. It was more than just a world that he experienced and understood. He had grown up among the tappers. Through his father, Pak Tir, who bought their palm sugar, Kanjat was close to nearly all the tappers and their families in Karangsoga; he knew their pains and joys, their dreams and dreads.

He enjoyed his childhood alongside the children of the tappers. He drank raw nira straight from the pongkor with them, played tag in the shade of the trees, and trapped dragonflies using sticky jackfruit sap. On full moon nights, Karangsoga rang with the sound of the tappers' children chasing fireflies or playing tag. Kanjat was always among them. He spoke the truth when he said he knew, was familiar with, and had lived the life of tappers, from tears to laughter.

When he began working on his paper for his bachelor's degree in agricultural engineering at Jenderal Sudirman University in

64

Purwokerto, Kanjat faced a soul-piercing fact: researching the palm tappers' lives was less practical than it originally seemed. A latent awareness from his subconscious demanded his attention. His affinity and concern for the tapping community had piqued his subconscious and demanded he make them the subject of his paper. The tappers' lives were more than just fond childhood memories. They had taught him about resentment and disappointment, and these had shaped his character.

His friends had often deprived themselves of the joy of playing tops or marbles to help their parents collect firewood, and most had dropped out of grade school before finishing. He knew boys who were left fatherless after their father died by falling from a palm; Kanjat never forgot how they cried. Some had mothers who had burned their arms in a cauldron of boiling nira; their wails still rang in his ear. Cimeng's father went to jail for five months after he was caught taking pine branches from the edge of the forest to use as firewood, the scraps left behind by the real thieves who were allowed to log by the head ranger. Kanjat had lost his playmates when the price of the palm sugar dropped. With less food in their stomachs, the children had no energy to play marbles or tag.

Kanjat's concern for the tappers developed naturally, and increased when he went to high school. At that age, he could read the faces of the tappers' wives who came each day to sell their sugar to his father. Kanjat saw the worry in their eyes as their sugar was weighed; there was helplessness when they were told the price of sugar was down, and one of joy mixed with fear when they heard it had risen slightly.

The tapper community's suffering transformed into numbers and data as Kanjat did the research for his paper. What seemed like an odd symptom that weighed on the tappers' lives became tangible proof that could be counted and analyzed. The price of sugar, for instance; Kanjat found the tappers received a disproportionately small share of the final price the consumer paid, especially in the big cities.

From his research, Kanjat also found that with prices so low, the tappers' hard work had no real economic value. What they were doing was best described as a desperate effort to sustain themselves, their wives, and children. Only the brokers who bought from the tappers, wholesale buyers in the big cities, and retail vendors profited from the palm sugar trade.

Also profiting were the food, drug, and other industries that used palm sugar as an ingredient. They created the market mechanism, and their influence on the price of the sugar was significant, even absolute.

It always flabbergasted Kanjat that the tappers living in misery essentially subsidized those more prosperous. They risked their lives in the treetops, facing the danger of falling at any moment, and made a large contribution to the wealth of others while their own stomachs stayed empty.

A tapper was made to believe that poverty was his destiny. He hung his hopes on one simple thing: the willingness to sweat and risk his life could be traded for a kilogram of salted rice. This small hope was often dashed when the price of sugar fell below the price of rice. Kanjat had data that showed it was common for a kilogram of sugar to be worth no more than half a kilogram of rice.

Because of their low earnings, the tappers had trouble getting enough firewood, especially in the rainy season. What little money they had couldn't be spent on firewood and they shifted the fuel cost to the ability of the pine and teak forest to replenish itself.

They stole from the forest, at the risk of being caught by the forest ranger. More than a few had seen the inside of a jail.

No matter how Kanjat calculated, he arrived at the conclusion that because of the production costs and risks, the economic value of palm sugar should be higher than rice. What this revealed was a stark injustice: the price of grain was protected by a minimum retail price. A minimum should be in place for palm sugar as well, and its lack meant the tappers had no guarantee of a fair price.

Kanjat found in his research an attempt to improve the tappers' lives by setting up cooperatives in villages like Karangsoga. The tappers paid dues to be members of the co-op. In return, they received discounts on batik wraps, soap, cheap rice, kerosene, and free health care if they were injured in a fall.

Trust in the co-op was brief. Discounts ended before the tappers had gotten their dues' worth. The palm sugar co-op transformed into an institution that practiced trade monopoly and put pressure on its members. Prices fell further because the supply chain was longer. The co-op had to sell to the buyers who stockpiled the sugar and controlled its distribution and sales. The heads of the co-op, all of them village elders, had to be paid. Eventually, the co-op collapsed from lack of trust by its members. The people of Karangsoga wanted no part of any co-op again.

The revelations Kanjat found through his research fueled the concern he always had for the tappers. He wanted the paper to be subjective, but anyone reading it later might say it was more political than scientific. Kanjat sought out the opinion of Dr. Jirem, the supervisor for his paper before the evaluation.

"I've read your proposal and I agree. Why have any doubts?" Dr. Jirem asked.

"I'm worried people will laugh at me."

"What?"

"Any critic is bound to say the bias in the paper is from a moralizer. An attitude like that in this context is considered out of place in the scientific world."

Dr. Jirem laughed and patted Kanjat on the shoulder.

"I see it the other way. If anything, your bias toward the object of your research will give the paper more weight. I don't believe the scientific world should be sterile. I'm bored of papers that are mute and gelded when it comes to the real problems around us. I see in yours an affinity with a community that has long been marginalized. That's why you have to keep going."

"Won't my paper be seen as a socialist slogan?"

"Perhaps, but I'll defend you as best as I can because I like your spirit. Your affinity for the tappers' community shows your indebtedness and gratitude to them for having provided your livelihood for so long. This is not a scientific sin. Far too many scholars lose their sense of gratitude to the 'mother' who raised them. They choose to be carried away by pragmatism. From certain aspects, pragmatism becomes amoral, and they become amoral because they're afraid of being called moralizers.

"Many scholars forget, or pretend to forget, the teachers who educated them from grade school all the way to university are paid by the public. The taxpayer also pays for the educational facilities they use, from school buildings to laboratories. They forget the status of their degrees has almost no social function. They think it's a personal achievement, and because of that only has an individual function.

"Jat, many scholars like us lose their importance in the eyes of the community that raised us. Many academics are unmotivated to give thanks and give back. It's not surprising the public has lost a lot of trust and hope in us."

Kanjat scratched his head.

"Have you ever heard the saying that a stupid person is a clever person's meal? That's the refrain of the general public, which considers itself stupid, what they mean by clever people are scholars. If someone were to say that many scholars eat their own 'mother,' how could we deny it?

"Young man," Dr. Jirem went on. "I see in your paper a spirit of rebellion against the tendencies I've described. That's why I say keep going. Bravo."

Once again, Dr. Jirem patted Kanjat on the shoulder.

For Kanjat, that soft tap had a deep meaning and fired up his enthusiasm. His doubts evaporated. The struggle inside his heart over his paper's subjectivity ended. At the same time, waves of shame and guilt surrounded his soul: the livelihood of his family and himself had been paid for by the sugar broker's profit he knew was unfair.

As though discovering a grenade ready to explode, Kanjat had to admit he had been one of those people whose lives were subsidized by the tappers' misery. The cruel thought cut into his soul, pierced his mind, and shook the foundations of his dignity. He had never thought he would live at the expense of others, especially those who suffered.

Kanjat grew increasingly angry. His education from grade school to university was paid for by sugar-trading profits. In his reveries, he often saw chemical equations in the trunks of the coconut palms, and graphs in the palm fronds that swayed in the wind. The new Vespa scooter his father had bought him looked like a set of scales to weigh the sugar, and he became reluctant to ride it.

The scales. Kanjat knew how much of an ogre that brass measuring-instrument was to the tappers. The man who controlled it was said to be the friend of a ghost that played with the weight discs. Every mark not counted was an ounce of sugar manipulated for the profit of the broker. And the broker was none other than Pak Tir, his own father. Kanjat gulped.

To ease his guilt, Kanjat brooded by himself beneath a tree in the campus yard. He tried to share his guilt with the other students. Surely, from among those who came to the campus each day, one was in the same situation. They might be the son or daughter of a broker who took advantage of his business partners, like his father. Or a government official who earned much more than his salary. Or a contractor who built village schools that only lasted three years because he had skimped on the quality and quantity of the construction material.

Did such students share his guilt, or did they think the questions came from a crazy person, and were not to be asked? The only answers he received were the clickety-clack of horse hooves from the carts that passed the campus, sounding flat and bearing secrets.

The unique gratitude Kanjat had toward the tappers was sincere and preyed on his soul. His indebtness flowed through every vein, whispering to be cleared, at least morally. Kanjat felt he was constantly being pursued.

He tried to find justification based on commerce: profit was the fundamental aim, and everything else was less or not important. This meant sugar brokers like his father were not at fault, and the profits they made were valid and reasonable. His father was only one end of a network that created a dependency so absolute that the tappers had no choice but to rely on them. Without the hated trading network, the tappers' lives would be worse. This reasoning tormented Kanjat further. Guilt swallowed him, even when he saw he was only being naïve.

In this state, Kanjat returned to Karangsoga. He was unsure why he was going back. He might have had a few days off, or needed more pocket money, or to please his mother, who always asked him, her youngest child, not to stay away too long. He wanted to quell the anxiety that ate at him every day, yet it increased when he reached Karangsoga.

The moment he set foot in the village, he heard about Lasi, the suffering wife of a tapper, who had run away a month earlier to Jakarta. At first, Kanjat ignored the news and the stories about Darsa's misdeed that led to Lasi leaving. But after letting the rumors sink in, Kanjat felt a twitch from the archives of his past.

Lasi. Her name had a special meaning for Kanjat. Even though he rarely visited Karangsoga, Lasi's name had stayed with him even after she became Darsa's wife. She was the beautiful white rabbit often taunted by the boys. As a little boy, he tried to defend her, and never could. Lasi was his companion when they played hide-and-seek on full moon nights. When they hid together, he pressed himself against her. He remembered the scent of her hair. When they played, Lasi acted like the big sister. "Jat, I always wanted a younger brother," she often said, and affectionately pinched his chubby arm. He never forgot how white her arm was when they played rock-paper-scissors.

When he entered junior high, Kanjat no longer played with Lasi. He barely saw her because he boarded at a school in town, but every time he returned home, he waited for Lasi to sell her mother's palm sugar. Kanjat was happy just to talk to her, or exchange a shy smile. She had a dimple in her left cheek. Why did that small fold have such an attraction, and why did he like it so much? Was it because it came with the unique shape of Lasi's eyes and her strong eyebrows, or because of the contrast with her long, jet-black hair? Kanjat never knew the answer. Since they were kids, Lasi had been different. She was fair, she had unique eyes, and the dimple in her cheek was exquisite.

Kanjat wanted to be friends with Lasi when he was in his teens, but she avoided him. Although in Karangsoga no young man and woman dared be close in public, Kanjat felt there was another reason why Lasi pulled away. He learned from a third party that she was embarrassed to be close to someone from a rich family while she was poor. When he finished high school, Kanjat had changed. He was well built, handsome, educated, and rode a motorcycle, a lavish gift from his mother. In every respect, he was no longer Lasi's younger brother.

Kanjat's sweet illusions of continuing their childhood closeness ended once he went to university. Lasi still represented his beautiful childhood spent playing on moonlit nights, but her name also reminded Kanjat of the hard lives of his neighbors, the tappers.

Even though he rarely saw Lasi, Kanjat often pictured the tappers' lives through her face, even her dimple. Lasi was like a leaf. On its upper surface were the childhood memories and her dimple. The other side held the difficult life of the tapper. Both sides often tugged at his soul.

Now, the leaf representing the tappers' world had vanished. The woman he always hoped to see when home on holiday had fled from Karangsoga. All Kanjat could do was accept it as there was nothing he could offer Lasi, as an individual or a representative of the tappers.

Kanjat wanted to know more about what happened to Lasi. He looked for Pardi, who tinkered under the hood of the truck in the yard.

"Ah, the young master. When did you get home?" Pardi greeted him.

"This morning. Is something broken?"

"No, the air filter needs to be cleaned. I can take care of it myself."

"Finish up and meet me later at the fish pond behind the house."

"Why do we have to meet in a secluded place if you're going to give me a present?"

"Hush."

Pardi went to the well to wash his hands before walking to the back of the house.

At the fishpond, Kanjat fed the giant *gouramis* caladium leaves. "I heard Lasi went with you to Jakarta. How long ago?" he said casually. Without looking at Pardi, he continued to feed the fish.

Pardi was surprised. He never expected the son of his employer to ask him about Lasi. He fumbled for a cigarette in his pocket, lit up, and exhaled the smoke. "Maybe a month ago."

"Do you know how she's doing now?"

"I just got back from Jakarta again last night. After unloading I went to see Lasi."

"Wait. Where's she staying? With whom?"

"You've been with me on a sugar run to Jakarta before."

"Yes."

"Do you remember stopping at a restaurant run by Ibu Koneng in the Klender area?"

"Yes. You left Lasi in that kind of a place?" Kanjat asked, agitated.

"That's what she wanted. Sapon and I tried to make her return with us the same day we went to Jakarta, but Lasi insisted on staying. When I saw her yesterday, I asked her again. She said she doesn't want to come back."

"Is it because her husband married Sipah?"

"I doubt it. She doesn't know he's married again. I wanted to tell her yesterday, but I didn't have the heart."

Kanjat was silent. He crushed the last caladium leaf in his hand and squatted by the pond. His gaze fell on the surface of the water, but he didn't notice the fish vying for food. Instead, he relived his childhood days with Lasi, running across a footbridge during the dry season on a night crowned by the moon.

Pardi slipped away. It seemed his employer's son had suddenly lost his tongue. Pardi shrugged his shoulders.

***

A Chevrolet pulled up in front of Ibu Koneng's restaurant. Mrs. Lanting stepped out of the car. Her bulk made her look like she waddled to the doors. A man wearing dark glasses, who was either her driver or lover, followed her. Mrs. Lanting was over fifty and the man who never took off his dark glasses was twenty years younger. The pair often showed up at the restaurant, and were close friends with Ibu Koneng.

"I'm sorry I couldn't come sooner," Mrs. Lanting said when Ibu Koneng appeared.

"I've been waiting for a few days. I thought you weren't interested in pursuing your luck."

They went to the back room. The man grabbed a beer and asked for a glass and ice as he took a seat beside Mrs. Lanting. The woman with chafed calves served him.

"This one's special," Ibu Koneng said after looking around. "You'll make a big profit and must promise me a handsome cut."

"Ibu Koneng, we'll get to that later. I came because you said you had new merchandise. Is it an antique lamp, a copper pot, a rare dagger, or…"

Ibu Koneng laughed. Mrs. Lanting traded in various goods. She sold anything from antiques and precious stones, to daggers and talismans, and young girls. For girls, she catered to a special market that only served the upper class. The trade was inspired by a geisha who arrived in the 1960s at the State Palace, and became First Lady a few years later.

The beauty of that Japanese girl, who often appeared at the side of the Great Leader wearing a Javanese-style kebaya, captured the hearts of many people. Because the Great Leader was her patron, lesser leaders from a small, closed circle, followed his example and looked for new wives from Japan or China. If they had problems making the Japanese girls legitimate wives, they kept them as mistresses. All that mattered was to mimic the actions of the Great Leader. It was a guarantee for not falling off the revolutionary rails, a political slogan the Great Leader had popularized.

The smaller leaders had difficulties in obtaining Japanese girls, but their desire to follow the Great Leader was part of their never-say-die revolutionary spirit. If they were unable to find a genuine Japanese girl, they made due with a half-breed. Many Japanese soldiers had left children behind in areas such as Kuningan in West Java.

The hunt for girls with Japanese fathers began. In many cases, the smaller leaders ignored the fact that the girl was already married. It was another business opportunity for the middleman. From scouring the hinterlands for antique lamps and talismans to give peace of mind to officials, politicians, or community leaders, they now also looked for girls fathered by the Japanese.

Mrs. Lanting served as a link in the girl trade, and had supplied the market's demands on several occasions.

"Her father was full-blooded Japanese, not Chinese like the one who cheated you," Ibu Koneng said.

"Oh, so the goods you're talking about is a half-Japanese girl?"

"Shh. Not so loud. She's in the kitchen. She's not a girl, but you'll see for yourself. Polish her up a bit and she'll look like the real thing. I'll have her serve tea."

Ibu Koneng went behind the curtain that served as a room divider. Her guests listened to her telling someone to prepare drinks and snacks.

"I didn't do anything to her because I've nothing to hide," Ibu Koneng said, when she returned. "Later, you'll understand how busy I've been turning down all the men who want a taste of this Japanese morsel. They only back down when I tell them that she's not on the menu, she's my cousin and her husband is a soldier."

Ibu Koneng had more to say, but Lasi appeared carrying a tray with three glasses of tea and a plate of cookies.

Mrs. Lanting examined her subtly while her companion took off his dark glasses, something he rarely did. Ibu Koneng smiled when she saw the twinkle in Mrs. Lanting's eye.

After putting the glasses and plate on the table, Lasi turned to leave, but Mrs. Lanting stopped her. "Just a minute, young lady. What's your name?"

"Lasi, bu. Lasiyah." She smiled awkwardly, but it was enough to produce the sweet dimple in her left cheek.

"Do you enjoy staying here?" Mrs. Lanting's eyes shone brighter.

Lasi smiled again. It was a difficult question to answer. After a while, Lasi answered with a perfunctory yes.

"That's right, you have to enjoy living in the city. A woman as beautiful as you shouldn't be rolling around in the muddy rice fields of a village. The best of everything is found in the city." Mrs. Lanting spoke as if she addressed her own daughter.

Lasi returned her smile and the dimple became more prominent.

The man grinned and stared at Lasi slack-jawed, showing his yellow and black teeth.

"She'll definitely do," Mrs. Lanting whispered after Lasi left. "You've outdone yourself this time. Where did you find her?"

"To find someone like her, you need to send out dozens of scouts and wait for months before finding out whether you have succeeded or failed. I was lucky. I didn't have to look for her anywhere because she came to me." Ibu Koneng smiled proudly, and told everything she knew about Lasi.

Mrs. Lanting was elated and had to keep her excitement about having found a piece of valuable merchandise well hidden. She worried that her enthusiasm would make Ibu Koneng ask for a high price.

"Okay, Lasi is mine now." Mrs. Lanting opened her handbag. "Here's your money. I'll leave her with you until I'm ready."

"Not now, I don't need money this time."

"You don't need money?"

Ibu Koneng smiled confidently. "Let me see your ring. Now that's what I like."

"Don't be putting on airs."

"I'm serious."

Mrs. Lanting looked at the diamond ring on her finger. "Ibu Koneng wants this expensive ring," she stammered.

"Give it to her," the man ordered.

Mrs. Lanting straightened and sent him a look of protest before she took off the ring and reluctantly handed it to Ibu Koneng.

A burst of light flashed from the diamond as Ibu Koneng slipped the ring on her finger. She broke into a broad smile.

Ibu Koneng went into the kitchen after her two guests left. "Las, look at this. Nice, isn't it?" She showed Lasi the new ring and looked as happy as a little girl with a new pair of shoes.

"It's very nice. In my village only the chief or Pak Tir's wife would ever have a ring like that." Lasi stared in admiration. "How much did it cost, bu?"

"Maybe a few hundred thousand, maybe a million. Mrs. Lanting gave it to me as a gift. She's very rich and kind."

Lasi stared at Ibu Koneng's hand. "She also spoke with me. She must be kind."

"That's right. Tomorrow or the day after she's going to give you a present too, or take you out for a ride. For someone like Mrs. Lanting, wealth isn't that important. Her four children are all well off."

"The man who sat next to her, is he one of her children?"

"Hush. He's her husband."

Lasi was shocked. A look of regret swept across her face.

"That's Mrs. Lanting for you. She always marries a man who is young enough to be her son. It's great, isn't it, Las?"

"Always?"

"Yes. Mrs. Lanting often changes husbands or partners or whatever, and she always finds a younger man."

Lasi smiled. She was smiling even after Ibu Koneng had gone to her room.

Mrs. Lanting and her husband were back at the restaurant the next day. In addition to her handbag, Mrs. Lanting carried a package under her arm. Her husband walked behind her with a magazine. They entered without waiting for Ibu Koneng to meet them at the door. The man again took a beer and asked for a glass with ice. The woman with large earrings served him this time. The visitors took seats in the middle room and called out for Ibu Koneng. She was still in bed, but bolted awake when she recognized the voices.

"Sleeping this late in the day?"

"Sorry. I was up until late last night talking with Lasi. Besides, what are you doing here so early? Don't you know that my business is open at night? You shouldn't have come so early."

"Lazybones, it's ten and you say it's early? No wonder this place doesn't get anywhere, the owner's lazy. Never mind. Where's Lasi?"

"She's around somewhere. Where can she go? She doesn't even dare go out alone."

"That's good. I want to see her wear something other than a kebaya and a sarong. Try getting her to put this on."

Ibu Koneng took the package Mrs. Lanting held out and opened it. Inside were outer garments and underwear, all of good quality. "I hope Lasi doesn't refuse to wear these clothes because they're so nice," she said.

"Don't underestimate Lasi. She may be from the village, but she's a woman like the rest of us. Have you ever heard of a woman turning down fine clothes?"

Lasi was doing the dishes in the kitchen. She quickly dried her hands when Ibu Koneng called for her.

"See, I was right, Las. Mrs. Lanting is kind, isn't she? Look, this time she brought a present for you. Here, try these clothes."

For a moment, Lasi looked speechless at the clothes Ibu Koneng held out to her.

"Ibu, I'm not used to wearing clothes like that. I usually just wear a kebaya and a sarong."

"When you live in the village, it's okay to dress like that. But you're in Jakarta, Las. Look around you. Few women your age wear a kebaya and sarong."

Lasi looked doubtful, but her eyes shone when she looked at the clothes again. She hesitated. Finally, she reached for the clothes.

"Come on, don't think about it too much. Go on and change out of your shabby sarong and kebaya."

Lasi submitted, laughing.

Ibu Koneng smiled. In her heart, she praised Mrs. Lanting: indeed, a woman had never been known to refuse fine clothes.

Alone in her small room, Lasi hesitated again. She held the folded new clothes. Her mother had told her many times that nothing was ever given without something being expected in return. Even from Lasi, her mother said, she demanded obedience, in exchange for having given birth to her and feeding her.

Lasi had seen plenty of examples of the truth in her mother's words. There was a time she received money from Pak Tir every day in exchange for her sugar. Pak Tir never paid her more than her sugar was worth. When she received vegetables from her neighbors, she repaid them in kind. Grandfather Mus said, "Only the gifts from the Almighty are truly free, because He needs nothing from outside Himself, not even the praise or testimony of men."

Lasi's doubt grew. She believed what her mother had said. Mrs. Lanting, a woman she barely knew, had given her the clothes. Ibu Koneng, who was kind enough to offer her a place to stay, she repaid with her work. What could the woman who had given her these clothes possibly want from her?

The door opened and Ibu Koneng came in. She seemed surprised that Lasi had yet to change. "Don't you know how to put on these clothes? Here, let me help," she said cheerfully.

Lasi reluctantly submitted.

Ibu Koneng shook her head in admiration and envy when Lasi's body emerged from the wrinkled kebaya. Her youth was radiant. Her fair skin was even fairer on her back, and the contrast made her hair look blacker. How would it look once she had shampooed? What if she brushed her teeth and painted her lips more regularly?

"They fit just right. How nice," Ibu Koneng said. "Come on, Las. Let's show Mrs. Lanting how you look."

Lasi walked awkwardly as Ibu Koneng led her out. She became more bashful when she stood in front of Mrs. Lanting and her husband.

"I think… I think the skirt is too short," Lasi stammered.

"Says who? You have nice legs, there's no need to hide them." Mrs. Lanting smiled. Her eyes swept over Lasi's body. She told Lasi to sit down and asked Ibu Koneng for a comb. Standing behind Lasi, she slowly undid her bun.

Lasi felt awkward, but pleased. The attention showered on her made her feel spoiled. She liked the fragrance of Mrs. Lanting's perfume.

"Las," Mrs. Lanting combed Lasi's hair.

"Yes, ibu?"

"Ibu Koneng tells me you ran away to find peace of mind, is that right?"

"Yes."

"And have you found peace living in a restaurant full of people? Do you like living among loose women? I mean, heaven forbid people think you're like them."

Lasi swallowed and looked down.

"You shouldn't stay here. Come with me. I have a big house with an extra room. What do you say?"

Lasi was lost in thought. She saw her home in Karangsoga and heard the nira bubbling in the pot, and smelled it caramelizing. An image of Darsa flashed before her. Her heart beat faster. A sense of anger and disgust choked her. She heard her mother calling her home.

Lasi's eyes filled with tears and she sobbed. Living at the restaurant was uncomfortable, and sometimes stifling. It was unpleasant to live under the same roof as the woman with large earrings and the one with chafed calves. They put themselves on display before they went off with men who paid for them. Lasi knew they sometimes served men in the back room. Yet, she hesitated to accept Mrs. Lanting's offer. The woman who combed her hair was a stranger.

"Why are you crying? I'm not forcing you, Las. It's up to you if you prefer to stay in your small, stuffy room."

"It's not that, bu. Won't Ibu Koneng mind? Who will help her cook and clean the dishes?"

"Don't worry about me. If you want to go with Mrs. Lanting, you should. I can find someone else to help. Let me put it this way, Las: it's better for you to go with Mrs. Lanting. Trust me. You don't deserve to live in a place like this. You remember when one of the men flirted with you?"

Lasi nodded.

"Then accept Mrs. Lanting's offer. You'll like staying with her."

"What if Pardi comes tomorrow or the day after?"

"I'll tell him you've gone to live with Mrs. Lanting. If he wants, I'll bring him to you. It's that easy."

Lasi wiped her eyes with the back of her hand. Mrs. Lanting finished combing her hair. She tied it off into a ponytail instead of putting it back up into a bun and smiled with satisfaction. She ignored Lasi drying her eyes.

"There, you see? You really are beautiful. People will say you look like Haruko… Haruko what?" Mrs. Lanting turned to her husband.

"Haruko Wanibuchi," he said.

"Yes, that's right, Haruko Wanibuchi. It's a shame your teeth are so Javanese. Now that you look so pretty, do you want to stay here or come with me?"

Lasi wanted to shake her head, but she already wore the clothes Mrs. Lanting had given her. In her simple reasoning, Lasi felt beholden to Mrs. Lanting. The least she could do to reciprocate was accept her offer.

"Las, I need an answer from you."

"Yes, bu. I'll come with you. I can do the dishes."

"Don't think like that. I know you want to get over the heartache of your husband cheating on you. You come with me and rest at my house. This place is not good for you. That's it."

"Yes, bu." Lasi started to cry again.

***

Mrs. Lanting told the truth when she said her house was big, and had an extra room for Lasi. When she entered the big house, Lasi felt so out of place she wanted to return to Ibu Koneng's restaurant. The large, bright room, with its teak bed and thick mattress made her uncomfortable. She never had owned a wardrobe, a dressing table, or any of the other pieces of furniture.

Lasi couldn't fall asleep on her first night. Her room in the village had a bamboo bed, with a straw mattrass with a woven pandan mat on top. The bedding was so familiar that the foam of her new mattress, even though very soft, felt uncomfortable. Lasi was also plagued by a sense of exile. She felt she had been marooned into another world.

With her eyes wide open, she brooded about what she was going through. Why had the place of her birth treated her with hostility since she was little? What had she done wrong to turn her marriage into such a hot stove she had to leave? Why was she now staying in a big house with a woman who was neither friend nor family? What would happen next in this strange place?

Lasi was certain of one thing: she wanted to stay away from Karangsoga, and especially Darsa. She had enough of the unfriendliness of the villagers, and plenty hurt by Darsa's cheating. She wanted to escape from the place of her birth, even though there were people she loved: her mother, Grandfather Mus, and even Wiryaji, Darsa's uncle. Lasi felt incredibly lucky that, amid her uncertainty in Jakarta, she met someone as kind as Mrs. Lanting, who gave her clothes and shelter.

Lasi wanted to contribute, and one day joined the two maids in the kitchen. Mrs. Lanting stopped her and insisted she gave her dirty clothes to the laundress.

"Las, in this house you're my child," Mrs. Lanting said. "If you want to work, come with me when I go out. That will be your job. You also can help me take care of the rose bushes in the back yard."

It was easy, but also puzzled Lasi. How could anyone be that kind? Besides not allowing her to do any work, Mrs. Lanting bought her clothes, slippers, and makeup. The items were of good quality.

One day, Mrs. Lanting took Lasi to a salon and had her hair washed, trimmed, and styled. Her face was brushed with a mixture of paste and water, while Mrs. Lanting and the stylist studied the picture of a woman in a magazine. Lasi sensed she was being made up to look like that woman. Mrs. Lanting referred several times to Haruko Wanibuchi. Was that a name? If so, it was certainly the strangest one Lasi had ever heard.

After being made up, Lasi was dressed in foreign clothes. Mrs. Lanting called the dress a kimono. Next, she was taken to a photo studio.

When the picture was printed, Lasi saw a very different version of herself. Lasi's heartbeat quickened when she looked at her picture. She felt unsettled and pleased, proud and odd.

"There, what did I say? You're very beautiful and not a village girl anymore. Your father was Japanese; now you look as you're supposed to, like a beautiful Japanese girl," Mrs. Lanting said.

Lasi laughed. Her eyes shined and her heart soared as if she were dreaming.

"Las."

"Yes, bu?"

"It's nice to be beautiful. A young woman with your beauty can have everything."

"I don't understand, bu. Am I really beautiful?"

"Look at the photo. It's more appropriate to call you a Japanese girl than a girl from… er, where is it you're from?"

"Karangsoga, bu."

"Let me ask you, Las; now that you know you're beautiful, don't you regret being the wife of a tapper? It's one thing if he was faithful, but your husband hurt and betrayed you."

Lasi forced a smile and sighed.

"You're still young and attractive. Will you go back to your husband?"

Lasi shook her head. Tears welled up in her eyes.

"You're right. Why go back to a jerk? The fact you don't want to go back to him tells me you're capable of loving yourself. What if one day a man wants you? Believe me, you'll find a new husband very quickly. Who knows, he might be a rich man. It's not unlikely, Las. You deserve to have a rich husband."

"I'm not thinking about a husband."

"I understand. You're still upset. Eventually you'll need a companion, and I'm sure he won't be a tapper. You're too beautiful for any man in Karangsoga."

Lasi was often shocked by the way her appearance had changed. Even without the makeup, she looked different. The heat from the stove hadn't singed her skin for the past two months. Her hands were soft because she no longer wielded an axe to chop firewood, and she no longer walked barefoot. Mrs. Lanting taught her to sit at the dressing table and apply the various paints and powders. At times, her lips flared red.

Lasi felt awkward using cosmetics at first. Mrs. Lanting kept encouraging her, and when Lasi noticed the cosmetics made her more beautiful, she happily, even excitedly, applied her own makeup. She was also motivated by Mrs. Lanting's question, "You're beautiful. Don't you regret being the wife of a tapper?"

Being a tapper's wife meant more than sweltering in the heat from the stove and working hard, it also meant she was poor for life. There were never any fine clothes to drape around her body, or jewels or makeup. Lasi remembered how hard it was to cook the nira whenever it rained. The nira would be watered down and the firewood damp. Several times, she had to burn the stuffing from her mattress when she had run out of dry firewood. In bad weather the nira went sour, and produced sugar as hard as asphalt, reddish black in color and not fit for sale. When that happened, there was no money for food because Lasi's household, like every family of tappers, never had any savings.

Even so, Lasi had no regrets about being a tapper's wife, because the hardships were nothing out of the ordinary for womenfolk. Darsa's infidelity had made her question the validity of those circumstances. The comfort of living with Mrs. Lanting contributed to the scrutiny of her life as a tapper's wife.

Living with Mrs. Lanting, she never had to break a sweat, yet all her needs were met. She wore good clothes, earrings, a watch, and shoes she never imagined owning. Her life had become far removed from that of a tapper's wife. Back then, when she wanted to buy a cheap sarong she'd have to save for months, and even then had to skimp on meals. Owning an eighteen-karat gold ring weighing two grams only happened in her dreams.

Still, she kept asking herself how Mrs. Lanting could be so kind. Was it because, as she had said, she considered Lasi her own child? Mrs. Lanting told her that she was lonely. Her children had left home and never came to see her. She said, quite candidly, that her children were angry because of her relationship with the man wearing dark glasses. Lasi, too, disliked him from the first time she saw him. She was scared of him. Luckily, it turned out he lived away from the house. Ibu Koneng was right when she said it wasn't clear whether he was Mrs. Lanting's driver, lover, or husband.

Mrs. Lanting, again in her own words, wanted to help Lasi find her father, or at least his side of the family. She had several friends who had served in the Japanese army and now managed big factories in Jakarta. "The Japanese are orderly. They kept records of all their compatriots who were lost during the war. Those records can help find your family in Japan. Las, you have a chance to meet your father's family."

The idea throbbed in Lasi's chest. It stemmed from the uncertainty she had grown up with. Was it possible? Could she ever meet her father, or at least his family? Lasi had told herself that it was almost impossible, although she believed otherwise. Anything was possible when the Almighty willed it.

When she thought about meeting her father, Lasi became excited and scared. She sat in front of the mirror and made herself look good for the moment she met him.

Yet the more she imagined her father, the more she was reminded of her mother and her home in Karangsoga. In the middle of the rainy season, the villagers were probably busy with the rice harvest. The corn harvest had come before.

Lasi wanted to sit beneath the logondang tree by the Kalirong river and play the *serunai*. She smelled the rice stalks on the breeze and heard the shrill voices of Karangsoga girls as they shooed the pigeons pecking at the rice. She thought of the rice stalks turning yellow, carpeting the fields edged by coconut palms being tapped.

Lasi saw herself walk the narrow path cutting through the fields. She passed a clump of winged-bean plants, their blue flowers surrounded by beetles. She parted the heavy rice stalks in her path. The early morning dew wet her feet even though the sun was already high. The rice stalks scratched her legs. A wood grasshopper with dark red wings took flight. A dragonfly buzzed by, making a tinny sound. A wren-warbler chirped as it circled above the cut stalks. The clear water of the Kalirong gurgled as it trickled between the rocks. A bee flew straight at her face and Lasi jolted, snapping back into the present.

She dropped the photograph she held. Lasi looked around, but Mrs. Lanting was nowhere to be seen. Lasi bent over to pick up the photograph. She sat back down and stared at the white wall.

The wall turned into a screen and showed her empty house in Karangsoga. From behind the front door, every Karangsoga villager emerged. Darsa and Sipah were among them. They gathered in the front yard and stuck their tongues out at her. Lasi closed her eyes and imagined changing into a giant crab that went about snipping off heads.

"Las…" Mrs. Lanting's voice startled her.

"Yes, bu?" Lasi stammered.

"Go fetch the pesticide. There are ants on my roses."

Chapter 4

If not for Handarbeni, Mrs. Lanting would never have heard of Haruko Wanibuchi. The former military officer now chief director of the Bagi-Bagi Niaga Company, a foreign-owned firm that had been nationalized, often brought up her name. Mrs. Lanting learned Haruko was a Japanese movie star whose pictures adorned glossy magazines and calendars. For Handarbeni, Haruko was a romantic fantasy, the most beautiful erotic dream. Her beauty, Handarbeni said, surpassed that of Naoko Nemoto, the geisha who graced the State Palace in Jakarta.

"Get her from Japan. Can't you arrange to have Haruko considered a reparation?" Mrs. Lanting joked with Handarbeni. "The cost shouldn't be a problem for someone who's the head of Bagi-Bagi Niaga."

"It doesn't work like that. To get a taste of a Japanese girl is easy. I have money. Bringing one home means overcoming a political hurdle, protocol, or something like that."

"What do you mean?"

"We're Javanese, and Naoko Nemoto is already at the palace. If I brought a Japanese girl like Haruko, I would be stepping on toes, eclipsing the sun. We Javanese don't dare do anything that copies the personal accomplishments of the Great Leader. That's asking for trouble."

"Are you, a former soldier and fighter, scared?"

"You could say so. More to the point, I don't want any trouble."

"Be honest. You don't want to lose your position at Bagi-Bagi Niaga, right?"

"Oh, enough of that. My new house in Slipi is empty and I need to fill it quickly. Not with a Haruko, but with something in high demand these days."

"I know, I know."

"My friends who already have one say they're great."

"Have you seen any of the girls left behind by the Japanese soldiers and are in high demand?"

"A friend showed me his. He really made me jealous, and told me you were the supplier."

"Rare goods are always appealing, like antiques or a prized *bekisar*. You're asking me to find such a thing."

"Rare or not, antique or not, I'm not joking."

"I know you're not joking. You need a bekisar to adorn your new palace. You're looking for one, correct?"

"What do you mean by bekisar?"

"A showbird that's a cross-breed between wild and domestic chickens and used as decoration by the wealthy. Pak Han, children from interracial marriages are often very attractive. They evoke romantic and lusty illusions, fantasies of pleasure. Oops, I'm getting a bit coarse."

"All that matters is I want to have fun."

"You're fortunate to have the means to obtain anything you want for your pleasure."

"It's fate. I've always had good fortune since I was young. During the days of the revolution, I left the gambling table to join the battle. I just wanted to be part of the ruckus and show off. I was happy when we engaged in a gunfight. It was like playing with firecrackers. I always enjoyed the sound more than what people called the revolution. I did my shooting, bang-bang-bang, and then ran. Young women like reckless and brutal men. Many of my friends died, but I wasn't even wounded. In fact, I was promoted to lieutenant. And now…"

"You're in the chief director's seat."

"It's fate, my dear."

Three months later, Mrs. Lanting sent the man wearing dark glasses to Handarbeni with photographs of Lasi. In a note, she wrote that if he liked what he was offered, he must agree to the following stipulations: Handarbeni had to give Mrs. Lanting his brand-new Mercedes and reimburse her several million rupiah for expenses to find the object. If he didn't, she would offer Lasi to an executive of Pertamina, the state oil company.

In his office, Handarbeni studied the three pictures he had received. One was of her full body, another showed her upper half and face, and the third was a close-up of her face. The sixty-one-year-old glowed with anticipation. He smiled and walked to the mirror, where he combed his thinning but slicked hair. He straightened his collar and went back to his desk to take another look at Lasi's photos.

The woman in the picture gave every impression of being a Japanese girl. Even her eyebrows and hair looked like that of Haruko Wanibuchi. The red of her kimono was the same shade that Haruko had worn in a calendar picture. Lasi's appeal was the same, perhaps even stronger.

Innocence or shyness gave the woman in the photos a glow of naivety. Handarbeni was full of experience. Encountering a woman past her bloom was often annoying. The woman in the photos seemed to be hiding something behind a half-contrived smile. Was this the image of a country ingénue? Handarbeni recalled a friend wondering, "Why does a country chicken taste better than a broiler hen? Could it be because the country chicken eats worms and insects while the broiler eats food made in a factory?"

Perhaps, Handarbeni found the woman in the photos beautiful because he was desperate for a Japanese girl. He picked up the telephone and dialed Mrs. Lanting's number, then waited impatiently for her to answer.

"I've seen the pictures. I like to meet her. Where? Your place?"

"Wait, easy does it. Take a real close look. Even though her father was pure Japanese, she's certainly no Haruko."

"She sure looks like her."

"Even so, she's still not Haruko."

"It doesn't matter. The point is, she's very impressive. What's her name?"

"Las, Lasi... I've forgotten her full name. She's twenty-four and has a husband."

"I don't care. What I want to know is, where is she? When can I meet her?"

"Pak Han, I've told you to be patient. Your bekisar is safe; she's not used to Jakarta yet. She has yet to be tamed. I must be very careful with how I handle her. One wrong move can frighten her back to the jungle."

"I just want to see her."

"That can be arranged. At this initial stage, Pak Han, I only want to let you know I've found the bekisar you ordered. It seems you're interested. Is that correct?"

"Yes, yes."

"Thank you. Oh, and remember your promise."

"Sure, sure. When should I send it, or will you come to get it?"

"I'm only reminding you. I'll take everything once the bekisar is in your hands."

Mrs. Lanting hung up. She smiled and let out a deep breath. Her complicated transaction would turn out to be very profitable. Handarbeni had deep pockets and seemed enamored by the bekisar from Karangsoga, but Mrs. Lanting knew her work was far from finished. If anything, it was at a delicate stage. She knew there was a possibility the bekisar couldn't be tamed, that she would reject the man who desired her. Mrs. Lanting knew wealth was effective bait for taming a bekisar that came from an impoverished background.

Mrs. Lanting took Lasi out more often. They ate in restaurants, shopped at Pasaraya, visited one of her friends, and attended wedding receptions in lavish banquet halls. Lasi grew more accustomed to wearing shoes and watches, talked on the telephone, and turned on the television. Mrs. Lanting watched her closely and was convinced the bekisar enjoyed all of it.

The change in the bekisar made Mrs. Lanting smile. Lasi's fair skin appeared more radiant. Her hair shone and when she smiled, her teeth were white and beautiful. Her heels, once flat and cracked, were as round and as smooth as an egg. Lasi's old awkwardness was only visible when she met someone for the first time. Mrs. Lanting listened to her sing along with a musician on television, and said to herself, "My bekisar has been tamed and is content in the city."

Handarbeni called Mrs. Lanting repeatedly asking to meet Lasi. She had postponed the meeting out of concern that Lasi wasn't ready yet, but now the situation was ripe. The time had come for Handarbeni to meet the bekisar he wanted to purchase. Mrs. Lanting picked up the telephone and told Handarbeni he could meet Lasi later that afternoon at her house.

"All this time the bekisar has been at your house?"

"Yes. Why?"

"If I had known, I would have come from the beginning, with or without your permission."

"Never mind. You'll meet her later this afternoon. Please, Pak Han, be gentle in how you approach her."

"What do you mean?

"Well, don't be crude. I haven't told Lasi anything. I haven't mentioned your name or given her any idea about you."

"What should I do?"

"Come over and visit like a regular friend at five in the afternoon."

"Why does it have to be in the afternoon? How about now?"

"I understand your impatience, Pak Han, but not now. We're not ready."

"Fine, this afternoon it is. Do I need to bring any gifts?"

"If you want to bring me something, that's fine. As for Lasi, it's not appropriate for your first meeting. Besides, you need to make sure this bekisar is worthy of occupying your new house. You've only seen her photos."

The appointment was at five in the afternoon. Before three, Mrs. Lanting asked Lasi to bathe. Lasi thought they were going out, as so often happened lately. She noticed Mrs. Lanting getting dressed up.

She became weary when Mrs. Lanting told her to put on a kimono. "Where are we going? Why do I have to wear a kimono?" She had never gone out dressed like that.

"Nowhere, Las. I'm expecting a guest who wants to see what a traditional Japanese dress looks like."

"Is it a friend of yours?"

"Yes, a man. Why are you so surprised? Las, I have more men friends than women friends, and the one who's coming is a good man. He's very rich. He has four or five houses. He's really very rich. You'll notice all my friends are like that."

Lasi thought, *A man like that wants to see me in a kimono?* She stayed quiet until Mrs. Lanting told her to go to her room and get dressed.

Mrs. Lanting helped Lasi apply her makeup and arrange her hair. She became more animated once it was time for Lasi to put on the red kimono.

"Las, I never get tired of saying that you truly are a Japanese girl."

"Really?"

"Yes. It's true."

Lasi straightened her clothes and walked to the mirror.

"Las, what if a man wants to be with you? Like I said, you're still very young and attractive. It wouldn't be unusual for any man, maybe even a rich one, to desire you."

Lasi waited to answer. "I'm not thinking about getting another husband. I ran away because of my husband, remember?"

"It's your own fault for being so beautiful. Your body entices men. Look, I'll help you choose a man who's worthy of being your husband."

"I'm not even divorced yet."

Mrs. Lanting laughed.

"For a man with money, divorce is no problem. You can get one anytime you want."

Lasi tried to divert the conversation. "Am I done?"

"Yes, you are, and it's not even four. I need to run out. You stay here and wait for the guest."

"Go out? But..."

"I won't be long. Honestly, I'll be back before the guest arrives. If I'm late, welcome him and wait for me."

"I'm shy, bu."

"You've been with me for a long time; why are you still shy when meeting people? Besides, you're my child and you're beautiful."

Lasi wanted to object more but Mrs. Lanting had already turned away. Lasi watched as she took her bag from the table and waddled off like a Manila duck, out the yard and to the street, where she flagged a taxi. Lasi heard brakes squeal, a door open and shut, and the roar of the car engine as it faded into the distance.

Alone in her room, a tremendous turmoil swept through Lasi. She was afraid of standing in for Mrs. Lanting to welcome the guest, and face a man she had never met. Who was he? She sat down in front of the large mirror and looked at her reflection. Lasi choked with fear. *What if Mrs. Lanting is right and I am beautiful? Any moment a man is coming over to see me wearing a kimono.* She grew agitated.

The ringing doorbell jolted her out of her thoughts. *Good heavens, he's arrived and it's only four-thirty.* Lasi hurried to the front room, took a moment to compose herself, and turned the doorknob.

She stared at the man standing before her. He was as surprised as Lasi. They looked at each other long and deep, as though in a standoff.

Lasi's lips trembled. She saw herself as a child running through a moonlit night. A chubby boy tried to hide with her in a game of hide-and-seek. She laughed at how close he pressed himself against her.

As the childhood memory played out before her eyes, the man let out a deep breath. He had recovered from his initial surprise. "Las," he said. His voice was hoarse.

"Kanjat? Oh my God, I didn't recognize you." Lasi reached to clasp him by the shoulder but stopped short. Still, she let her hand rest in his grip for an unusually long time.

"I didn't recognize you either."

"How did you know I'm here?"

"Ibu Koneng gave me the address. I came with Pardi on one of his sugar runs. He usually stops to rest at her restaurant. We argued with her earlier. She refused to tell us where you were until Pardi threatened to call the police."

Lasi's breathing was ragged. Her hand slipped out of Kanjat's grasp and fluttered aimlessly. "Oh, I'm happy you came. You're so grown up and handsome. Do you know how my mother is doing?"

Kanjat felt awkward and embarrassed. Though he knew Lasi, he had a hard time believing the woman in the red kimono was her.

When Ibu Koneng told him that Lasi was living with a rich woman, he thought she worked as a maid. The woman before him looked nothing like a maid. Dressed and made up, Lasi made his heart race. Her dimple, which had always attracted him, was even more beautiful. Lasi was like a piece of wood that had been varnished: the grain was still visible, but everything looked more polished. Kanjat swallowed.

"Where are my manners? Please come in. You're a guest here. Consider me your hostess because the owner of the house just went out."

Kanjat smiled. His gaze took in her whole body.

Lasi became uncomfortable. "Jat, excuse me, do I really look that different? Strange? Funny?"

Kanjat looked down as he met Lasi's shining eyes. "You look fit to be the mistress of this house," he gulped.

"Don't say that, Jat. You embarrass me." Lasi blushed. "Come on in. Or would you rather sit on the terrace?"

Kanjat pulled up a rattan chair. Lasi took the seat across from him, a small oval table between them.

"Jat, you haven't answered my question. How's my mother?"

"She's fine. I saw her yesterday when she came to sell her sugar. From what she said, I gather she's had difficulties since you left."

Lasi swallowed. "Does she know you were coming here?"

Kanjat shook his head.

"You came here without any messages for me?"

Kanjat nodded. He fidgeted, unnerved by how Lasi looked at him with her Oriental eyes.

If one child in Karangsoga never made fun of her, it was Kanjat. If one child stood up for her against the taunts, it was he. And if there was a cute, chubby child she thought of as a little brother, it was Kanjat. She had never felt ashamed in his company for coming from a poor family, and if she had not been embarrassed by her poverty, she'd always want to be sweet to him.

"Las, I just wanted to see you."

Lasi quietly listened to Kanjat speak with his head down and looking nervous.

"Now that I'm here, I know the answer," Kanjat continued, "I want you to come back to Karangsoga. In the end, it's your choice. Your husband has married Sipah. Please forgive me, I didn't mean to be the bearer of bad news."

Lasi frowned. Her uneven breathing spoke of the storm raging inside her. Tears sprung in her eyes as the old wound opened.

"Las, how did you end up living here?"

"Ibu Koneng didn't tell you?"

"All she told us was that you followed Mrs. Lanting."

"That's what happened. Mrs. Lanting treats me like her own daughter. I don't do any work here, except accompany her when she goes out and take care of the flowers."

Kanjat was silent though his heart skipped a beat.

"Are you happy?"

"How do I put it? I just feel better here than back home. It would be difficult to live in the same village as *them*. Why do you ask, Jat?"

Kanjat bowed his head. He suspected there was something behind Mrs. Lanting's kindness toward Lasi, but he kept those thoughts to himself. He said, "All I can say is, I want you to come back to Karangsoga. Go home to your mother if you don't want to see your husband."

Lasi shook her head vigorously and wiped the flood of tears with her hands.

"Why not?"

"What would I go home to? My marriage is destroyed. I no longer trust my husband. My family is poor; I've suffered since I was little. If

I go back, everyone in Karangsoga will treat me like they did before or even worse: they'll enjoy hurting me."

"Las, you shouldn't say that. I'm from Karangsoga too."

"I'm sorry. You're the only one…"

Lasi stopped. Her vision blurred as she rested her eyes on Kanjat. She longed for her childhood and Kanjat's protection against the bullies. A scene from her past came back vividly: she was on her way home from school, about to cross an areca-palm footbridge. At the other end, three boys blocked the path. A fourth boy, smaller than the others, stood by looking confused. She shooed the other boys away, hitting them with her ruler. The little boy wanted to help her, but was powerless. Little Kanjat hoped she knew he wasn't one of the bullies. He was much smaller back then; now he was a strapping man with a mustache and hairy arms.

"Jat, how's school going?"

"I'm almost done, Las. I'll be an engineer soon."

"That's great. Your family's rich and you're going to be an engineer, so why go to this trouble to find me, someone who has always been scorned by the people of Karangsoga?"

"Las."

She started to cry again. Her fair cheeks turned red.

Kanjat was stymied by her question and grasped for words. "Do you want to come back?"

Lasi shook her head. Her red eyes fixed on Kanjat's face, looking for any sign to explain why he kept asking her to go home. Slowly, she saw what she was looking for in Kanjat's smile and eyes. Her heart thumped in her chest. *Oh, can what I'm feeling be true? Did I catch a genuine sign in Kanjat's eyes? Perhaps not. I'm just an abandoned wife, poor and two years older. He's single, educated, and the son of the richest man in Karangsoga. There's no way he sees anything in me. He can easily find a girl who is younger and more worthy. No.*

"Well, Las?"

"Jat, I'm thrilled you came here for me, but I don't want to return. Let me stay here to find peace."

"What about your mother? She's suffering."

Lasi bowed her head.

"Is there anything I can say to sway you?"

She shook her head.

Kanjat leaned back in his seat. "Okay, Las. If you don't want to, I respect your wish. Even so, may I visit from time to time?"

"Oh, my God, I'd like it if you didn't forget me. Come as often as you want. I don't want to forget you either. You're not angry, are you?"

Kanjat produced a wan smile. He stood and held out his hand.

"Are you leaving?" Lasi asked, surprised.

"Yes, I should get going. Poor Pardi has been waiting for me."

"But you're not angry, right?"

"Right." Kanjat forced a smile.

"Wait a moment…" Lasi dashed into the house and returned with a photograph in her hand. "Please give this to my mother, and tell her I'm doing well."

Kanjat looked at the photo of Lasi in her red kimono. He had never thought of Lasi being so attractive. He bit his lip.

"Sorry, Las, may I keep this photo?"

Lasi parted her lips but no sound came from her mouth.

"Do you like it?"

Kanjat nodded.

His smile made Lasi blush. "If you like, you may keep it, but don't destroy it, okay? Do you want to give me your photo too?"

Kanjat was taken aback. "Unfortunately I didn't bring one. Oh, wait."

He reached for his wallet in his back pocket and opened it hurriedly. He smiled when he found a passport photo of himself wearing a white shirt and black tie.

Lasi's eyes sparkled as she studied his picture.

Kanjat smiled and put Lasi's photo into his shirt pocket, looked at her, and excused himself.

She was at a loss for the words to tell Kanjat goodbye. They looked at each other and smiled. Her hand was moist with perspiration when she shook Kanjat's. Her eyes followed him as he left.

Kanjat walked away without looking back. When he fell from her view behind the fence, Lasi shut her eyes tight.

As she sat down, Lasi regretted not insisting that Kanjat explain why he, Pak Tir's son, had come. *There was no way he came here from Karangsoga without a good reason. Why did he not speak plainly? Besides, he knows very well I'm still Darsa's wife.* Lasi also regretted rejecting Kanjat's offer so quickly. Going back with him would allow her to see her mother, and settle with Darsa.

She was jolted out of her reveries when a blue car drove up to the house. It was a few minutes to five. The expected guest had arrived. She hurried inside before he stepped out of the car. She wiped away the traces of her crying, fixed her makeup, and opened the front door.

The guest already waited on the terrace. The first thing that caught Lasi's eye was the massive gold ring with a blue stone on his finger. His wristwatch was also gold. He was rotund, had a nonexistent waist, and protruding belly. His round face had a fat and oily nose. He had a thick neck and chin. Lasi smelled his cologne.

She sensed him looking her over from head to toe but it only lasted a moment. A second later he smiled like an old teacher praising a clever and pretty student. His smile put Lasi at ease.

"Good afternoon. I'm Pak Han," Handarbeni's smile broadened.

"Good afternoon, pak. Please come in."

"Thank you, but let me first say, Mrs. Lanting is very fortunate. She told me she adopted a very beautiful young woman. Are you the one?"

Lasi was taken aback by the unexpected question. She blushed and nodded stiffly. She could tell from the way Handarbeni looked at her that he was the man who wanted to see her dressed in a kimono.

As Lasi grew more nervous, Handarbeni became more pleased. He enjoyed the nervousness of the young woman in front of him. "I also know your name. Lasi?"

Lasi fiddled with her fingers and their bright red nails. This gave Handarbeni a greater opportunity to look at the bekisar he was about to purchase.

Handarbeni derived a strange pleasure from feeling like a tomcat staring at a dumb, blind mouse. He relished the sensation because he so often had to deal with experienced mice that wanted to be caught. He had often felt like he was being handed a banana that had already been peeled; not a square inch had been left unexplored, and nothing of that womanly secret was left intact. Overripe bananas were terribly vexing.

"That kimono suits you very well. I heard your father was Japanese."

Lasi smiled cautiously, which made her dimple more attractive. In Karangsoga, it made her uncomfortable, annoyed even, to be called part Japanese, but Handarbeni made his reference sound refreshing. Mrs. Lanting and Handarbeni used as a compliment what the people of Karangsoga used as an insult.

"Please come in, pak," Lasi said to ward off any more questions.

"Okay. Where's the mistress?"

"She stepped out for a moment, and asked me to stand in for her until she returned."

Handarbeni smiled and nodded understandingly. That old Mrs. Lanting really was slick, and for once Handarbeni was thankful. His expression grew more cheerful.

"In that case, come sit with me. I'm so used to coming here that I feel like your adopted mother's brother. Relax, you're a Jakartan now. You can't be shy and Jakartan as well. You enjoy living in the city, don't you?"

Lasi smiled and nodded. She assumed her guest expected that answer. Her thoughts drifted to Kanjat. *Where would he be on his way home?*

Handarbeni lit a cigarette. "A lot of people from the country come to the city because life back there is hard. You're more suited to city life."

"Do you think so? I'm simple and uneducated."

"Uneducated?"

"I only completed the village school."

"Even so, you're more suited to be a city person. Do you know why?"

Lasi shook her head.

Handarbeni's laughter eased the tension, and Lasi relaxed.

"It's because you shouldn't work in fields under the hot sun, or carry a basket on your back. You're worthy of being a mistress, living in a nice house, and have a car."

"That's right," Mrs. Lanting cut in. She had stood behind the door for some time. "That's right, no one can deny that Lasi deserves to be a mistress. Pak Han, do you have a suitor for her?"

"When we look for such a man, we'll certainly find one. As educated people say, the finest things are always spoken for. Isn't that right?"

"That's right, Pak Han. The finest goods always sell quickly."

Handarbeni and Mrs. Lanting laughed.

Lasi felt uncomfortable being praised so excessively as if she were an item for sale. "I'm sorry, bu, I haven't prepared any drinks. Pak Han kept me here in the living room."

"Any man would want to spend time alone with you. Go on, then, fetch the drinks."

It was quiet for a moment. Handarbeni took a drag of his cigarette and blew out the smoke. He leaned back in his seat, completely at ease. "I like your bekisar. She almost looks Japanese, except she's taller. I'm convinced that when it comes to acquiring rare goods, you really are very good."

"When you're pleased, the compliments fly out of your mouth like moths in the rainy season."

"That's right. Thumbs up to you. How did you ever find such a fine bekisar?"

"There's no need to mention the obvious. I'm not sure it's a one hundred percent success. Your bekisar, Pak Han, walks like a country girl, all hurried and stiff. She's very far from elegant. That's something I'm working on."

"Yes, I noticed, but you must understand I don't want her to turn entirely into a city girl. I'd like her to retain a bit of country color."

"You're bored of the artificial look so many women in the city have. You want to indulge in her innocence."

Handarbeni smiled. He stretched his legs and leaned his head back against the seat cushion.

"If only I could bring my bekisar home with me right now." He laughed without changing his position.

"Don't be like a little child with a new toy. We have a long way to go, Pak Han. I know Lasi very much wants to separate from her husband, but she isn't divorced. That's one problem. Second, we have to convince her to be your bekisar. That's the most difficult part."

"I'm aware of that. I'm also aware the human heart can be unpredictable. Clearly the whole business could get messy if the bekisar doesn't want to go into the cage I've prepared in Slipi."

"That's why you need to be patient and wise. Patience is the key. I'll also ask you to…"

Lasi returned with drinks and snacks, and her presence immediately ended the conversation. From the look on her face, Lasi was unaware that she was the subject.

"I ask for you not to be too pushy," Mrs. Lanting resumed once Lasi had left the room again.

"I'm over sixty."

"I know you have a lot of experience. What I mean is you should act passive but sweet. I'll do the rest and herd the bekisar into your cage, and make sure she goes in willingly. To ensure a satisfactory outcome, Pak Han, you have to wait for two or three months. I have my doubts you'll be able to comply with my request."

Handarbeni chuckled and smiled.

"Don't smile just yet. I have something else. From now on I expect you to take care of all the expenses of caring for the bekisar."

"There's no need to mention this because she's already mine. Even before you asked, I was prepared to bear those costs. All that matters is a guarantee that you'll succeed."

"You trust me, don't you?"

"You've proven yourself trustworthy so far."

"Thank you. Just so you know, I already have the bekisar accustomed to everything from brushing her teeth to repairing her broken fingernails. She knows the names of her makeup items, and foods and dishes. But I haven't succeeded in convincing her that she's no longer a country girl married to a tapper. She has low self-confidence and doesn't quite believe in the advantages of her looks. Fortunately, the bekisar is smart. She catches on quickly to what I teach her."

"Very well, Mrs. Lanting. I'll leave her with you because I trust you. Call her so I can see her once more before I leave."

"You're leaving now?"

"I have business with a friend later this afternoon."

Lasi entered the room in her red kimono. She blushed as Handarbeni flashed her a compliment in the form of a thumbs up and held out his hand.

"I'm glad you're content living with Mrs. Lanting. What have you seen since you've been in Jakarta?"

Lasi bowed her head and twiddled her fingers.

"We haven't seen all that much," Mrs. Lanting said.

"Next time we'll go out together. Would you like to see Ancol Beach or watch a movie at Hotel Indonesia?"

Lasi blushed.

"Pak Han, why don't you invite us to your house for a visit?" Mrs. Lanting said.

"Oh, you're right. I'd like it very much. Pick a time when I can expect you."

"Certainly, we'll let you know. Which house should we visit? I'm sure you want us to visit you at the new one you've just built in Slipi."

Handarbeni laughed in agreement. His eyes twinkled as he nodded and smiled at Lasi.

***

Kanjat kept thinking about Lasi after he left Mrs. Lanting's house. All kinds of emotions filled his heart. Lasi's physical appearance was far from what he had expected. She had become so attractive. Kanjat's heart beat faster each time he pictured her. It was about more than the way she looked. He felt uneasy finding out she lived in a rich stranger's house. He questioned Mrs. Lanting's purpose for taking in Lasi. Through the news and by word of mouth, he had heard about country girls who were coerced into prostitution in the big cities. Kanjat hoped nothing like that would happen to Lasi. There was something wrong about Lasi being in that big house in the Cikini neighborhood. At the very least, she was there against her will. Ibu Koneng had reassured them that Mrs. Lanting had no ill intentions. She refused to say more, and Kanjat refused to believe her.

"Did you see her?" Pardi asked Kanjat as he stepped out of the taxi in front of Ibu Koneng's restaurant.

Kanjat waited for the right answer to come to him.

Pardi saw his dark expression, and his only response was a nod of the head.

"Are we going straight home?" he asked as Kanjat climbed up into the truck's cabin.

"Have you loaded up? Where's Sapon?"

"There's a cargo of junk headed for Purwokerto. Sapon's sleeping in the back."

"In that case, let's go."

Pardi turned on the ignition when Kanjat tapped him on the shoulder.

"Hold on, Di. I want to talk for a bit."

"Talk about what? Lasi?"

Kanjat pulled Lasi's picture out of his shirt pocket.

Pardi stared. "*Mas* Kanjat, is that Lasi, Wiryaji's daughter?"

"You don't recognize her?"

"Just a few months away from the village and Lasi's already so different. She's incredibly beautiful, mas. You would be proud if she was your girlfriend. Even though she's only the daughter of Mbok Wiryaji and no longer a virgin, Lasi would make a very suitable wife for an engineer."

"Don't talk nonsense."

"Do you think I don't know that you like Lasi?"

Kanjat, realizing he'd been found out, smiled stiffly. He took the photo from Pardi and put it back into his pocket.

"What do you think is going to happen if she stays with Mrs. Lanting?" Kanjat looked away.

"Do you have a bad feeling about it?"

"Honestly, yes. I'm sorry for her and very worried Mrs. Lanting is going to turn Lasi into a prostitute. Do you think I'm overreacting?"

"No. I more or less agree. Supposing we're right, what should we do?"

"Lasi's no longer a child, and besides, she has a husband. The only thing I could do was ask her to come home. I tried and failed. Lasi enjoys living with the rich woman. She looks pampered. Di, when I went there, Lasi wore the same clothes as in the photo."

"Beautiful?"

"Don't ask."

"Of course she was. I'm sure Mrs. Lanting took Lasi in because of her looks. Mas Kanjat, I don't think this is going to end well. I agree that you should get Lasi away from Mrs. Lanting. I feel sorry for her, mas."

"It's not that easy, Di. Besides, like I told you, she's a married woman. It wouldn't be right to take care of someone else's wife. What would the people back in Karangsoga say if later it turns out... Oh, never mind."

Pardi laughed.

"Mas Kanjat, there's nothing wrong with thinking like that. As much of a cad as I am, I don't mess with married women, not when there are so many single women around. But when it comes to Lasi, who would be in a better position to help than you?"

"I've tried as far as it is proper."

"Lasi might have come home if you promised to look after her."

"I see what you're getting at. I should marry her once she divorces her husband?"

"Sorry, that's just an idea. I know it's not easy for an engineer and Pak Tir's youngest son. Karangsoga will be in uproar if a rich and educated single man married a poor divorced woman older than him.

Your parents might not agree to your marrying her. But if I were you, Mas Kanjat, just supposing…"

"Well?"

"I wouldn't care what the people in Karangsoga said. If I loved Lasi, the first thing I would do is be honest with myself, and to hell with other people's gossip. Lasi is a good woman, and more beautiful than ever. The most important thing is to be honest."

Kanjat sighed.

Pardi offered him a cigarette, and he turned it down. The cab of the truck filled with smoke as Pardi lit his own.

"Di," Kanjat said, breaking the silence.

"Yes?"

"I would be embarrassed if the people in Karangsoga knew I liked Lasi. Please don't say anything. Hold your tongue as long as Lasi remains married."

"Okay, I promise. You have my word. Besides, I'm obliged to help you. Call it loyalty to my boss. What's more important is finding a way to help Lasi. Really, Mas Kanjat, you must save Lasi."

"Unfortunately, I can't do anything for the next week or two."

"Why not?"

"I have to prepare for my exams. The soonest I can come back to see Lasi is next month."

"That's too long, mas."

"I also want to move as quickly as possible, but what can I do? Should I put off the chance to finish university?"

"I understand, but anything can happen in a month."

"You're not the only one who's worried, Di. Let's get moving."

Pardi threw his cigarette out of the window and started the truck. The engine roared to life and the wheels turned. Pardi shifted to third gear, then fourth, and the truck from Karangsoga hurtled to the east.

Beside him, Kanjat leaned back in his seat. In his faraway gaze was a cheek so fair and translucent that the network of veins beneath the skin was visible. A flurry of hands played paper-scissors-rock, and one of them stood out for its fairness. It was Lasi's hand.

Chapter 5

The light in Lasi's room was off, except for a small lamp with a blue shade that glowed in a corner of the room. The night was still. Lasi had gone to bed earlier, but she remained awake. She heard the ginger drink vendor clanging his bowls in the distance. The clock chimed two. Lasi grew more agitated and turned off the lamp. As the darkness swallowed the room around her, Lasi tried to still her heart and lay down to wait for sleep to come. But her anxiety only increased.

Against the backdrop of the dark night, she saw the figure of Kanjat, who had come to see her the week before. Pak Tir's son had grown big and handsome. His smile and the light in his eyes belonged to a grown man, and made her heart beat faster. She needed to forget him. The previous evening Mrs. Lanting had taken her to visit Handarbeni at his home in the Slipi area. It was a new, solid building.

Lasi was used to seeing large houses in Jakarta. Handarbeni's house had floors whiter than the dinner plates they used back in Karangsoga. The rooms were large, the kitchen shiny, and the living room had a fishpond. The furniture was made of teak, with thick, soft cushions. Every bedroom had its own luxurious bathroom.

Her heart thumped hard when she saw the large portrait hanging in a silver frame in the living room. It was a picture of her in the red kimono.

107

Lasi wanted to ask why her picture hung there. She was reluctant to ask Handarbeni, despite his being friendly and sweet as he showed the house.

Mrs. Lanting sensed Lasi's confusion. "Las, I gave your photo to Pak Han. I told you that he likes women in kimonos. He hung it there."

"What do you think? Very fitting, isn't it?" Handarbeni asked.

"Very fitting indeed," Mrs. Lanting said.

Embarrased, Lasi bowed her head.

"It would be even more fitting if Lasi decorated this new house. Pak Han, what do you say?"

"I worked hard to build this house. Who do you think it's for?"

"You're not joking?" Mrs. Lanting asked.

"I'm not a child. Why would I joke?"

Handarbeni and Mrs. Lanting laughed, both of them trying to read Lasi's expression.

Lasi blushed deep red and smiled shyly. Her chest felt tight and she was hot and sweaty. She wanted to leave immediately. Fortunately, Handarbeni had invited them out for dinner.

Worry blunted any appetite Lasi might have had. It showed on her face, even after he showed them around Pasaraya above the restaurant, and bought her clothes and an expensive handbag.

The next day Mrs. Lanting asked Lasi to join her on the terrace. As she busied herself tatting, she brought up the matter of Handarbeni's house. "Las, do you not know why Pak Han hung your picture in his new house?" Mrs. Lanting asked without looking at her.

Lasi looked down and shook her head. She knew she was about to hear something surprising.

"Las, Pak Han thinks a lot of you. He likes you and wants you to be his wife. He's very serious."

Lasi stared at Mrs. Lanting. For a moment, she had trouble breathing. The shock caused the blood to drain from her face. She frowned.

Mrs. Lanting continued. "If you want, Pak Han's house can be yours. I would be pleased if you became Mrs. Handarbeni. You're so beautiful, you can make someone as rich as Pak Han fall in love with you. What do you say, Las, will you accept the offer?"

Lasi kept her head bowed. Her hands trembled as she wiped away her tears.

"Las, accept his proposal as a stroke of fortune. Granted, he's not young anymore and he already has one or two wives, but he can give you anything you desire."

Mrs. Lanting paused to pick up the ball of yarn on the floor. "You know what it's like to be a hard-working wife fully dedicated to her husband. What came of that? You couldn't even afford a gold chain the thickness of a hair. In fact, your husband betrayed you. Your clothes were wrinkled and your body was broken. Now you can change your destiny. Don't squander this chance, because you're perfectly suited to being a rich man's wife." Mrs. Lanting paused again, this time because she was thirsty. She took a sip of sweet tea the maid had served, and went back to her tatting.

Lasi stopped crying.

"Well, Las?"

"Ibu, the truth is," Lasi stuttered, "I haven't thought about being another man's wife. I still have a husband." She paused and her lips trembled. "My heart is not at peace from the hardship I brought with me from the village. Besides, does Pak Han want me? I'm a poor country girl who only finished the village school. What does he expect from me?"

Mrs. Lanting chuckled. She continued her sermon, peppering it with an occasional laugh.

"Oh, you simple country girl. You have what all men want: a beautiful face and a nice body. Women who are too smart, especially those with a higher education, repulse men. For a man, a woman can be uneducated or poor as long as she's beautiful. They like compliant women even more. Men are bastards. Do you hear me? Now you know why Pak Han likes you. He sees in you a doll to decorate his house and his bedroom. Believe me, you will always be pampered and catered to, as long as you remain a doll." Mrs. Lanting broke out into laughter.

Lasi did not understand and the lines in her forehead grew deeper. "Ibu, it doesn't feel right talking about another man without a divorce certificate in my hand."

"Oh, that's easy," Mrs. Lanting cut her off, her voice cold and flat. "Very easy. If you want, you can get the certificate without having to go back to your village. It just takes money, Las. With Pak Han's money, or whoever else's, you can get anything, let alone a divorce certificate."

"Yes, but I haven't given any thought to marrying again." Lasi's tears gushed and her tongue felt numb while an image of Kanjat flashed before her.

Mrs. Lanting remained composed, and engaged with her needles and yarn. "I've told you, accept Pak Han. It'll be to your advantage. Besides, why pine over a husband who betrayed you? A certificate of divorce is easily arranged."

Lasi frowned.

"Can I think about it, bu? This is a very important matter, isn't it?"

"It's not just important; it's also incredibly good fortune for you."

"You said Pak Han already has one or two wives."

"That's right. He's also too old for you. What does that matter if he can give you a big house with the finest trappings, good clothes, and money in the bank or a car? Las, I'm a woman, just like you. I have plenty of life experience.

"I used to think like you. I was unwilling to share my husband because I wanted to remain loyal. Whether we had enough to eat was never an issue, just as long as we were happy. I wanted a husband who was handsome and compatible. Now I know that prosperity is the most important. What's the use of being an only wife and having a young husband if you live in a shack, can't look after yourself, and constantly want more? Las, we only live once; why stay poor? You can change your destiny. Don't let this opportunity pass; you might not get a second chance."

Lasi bit her lip. Mrs. Lanting had left Lasi tongue-tied.

"Yes, but I'd like to have time to think about it."

"The issue is clear. All right, fine. You may think it over. My advice is, don't disappoint those who are trying to do good by you. Give me an answer tomorrow because Pak Han is waiting. Don't disappoint me and Pak Han. If you refuse this opportunity, you're an ignorant fool and ungrateful for all I've done." Mrs. Lanting stood, looking irritated.

In her room, Lasi startled when the clock struck three in the morning. She tossed and turned. *I have to give an answer in the morning. What can I say?*

She had only one of two answers to give: Yes or no. It was difficult to settle on either one. Each was concealed in a jungle of uncertainty, doubt, and ignorance. Being confronted by the two choices startled Lasi.

Did she have two choices? Oh, no. There was only one choice. It was impossible for her to say "no." She recalled the gifts she had been given and shuddered.

Mrs. Lanting had provided her with shelter and clothes, food and drink, money and jewelery. In addition were the gifts from Handarbeni. Lasi felt trapped and caged by it all. She had violated the rule she had always known to be true: nothing was given without something else expected in return. The person who received should be prepared to give. *I've buried myself in this debt, this moral duty, or whatever it's called. If I have any dignity left, I should give Mrs. Lanting what she's asking to pay off the debt. I must accept Pak Han.*

Lasi started to sob. Her heart felt heavy. She thought of her encounter with Kanjat. Once again, she wondered why Kanjat had not been forthcoming and promised to live with her, and taken her away. Lasi sighed. Beneath the tangle of anxiety, Lasi recognized the truth in Mrs. Lanting's words: life as a tapper's wife held little hope. She knew the daily meal was paid for by the work done the same day. Often things were worse, like when the price of the palm sugar hit a low, or the sugar was too moist and not setting right. The tappers were stuck with this way of life and accustomed to sorrow. For as long as she had been with Darsa, Lasi had never thought of escape. Like everyone else in Karangsoga, she had never questioned the hardship and poverty because no one could see a way out. Hardship and poverty were accepted as part of their daily lives.

She still managed to find flashes of joy, such as the pleasure in having the nira she cooked set into a hard and golden form. Bathing at the well sheltered by a bamboo screen was rejuvenating after a long day in front of the stove. And how satisfying was a bowl of rice with *sayur bening* and *sambal trasi* after a hard day's work. She no longer had those moments. None of them could be replaced by Mrs. Lanting's pampering as part of living in Jakarta.

There was also the satisfaction when she received payment for the sugar she sold to Pak Tir. It was never very much, but she was always happy holding the money that came from the sweat of Darsa and herself. Making money from labor never weighed on the conscience. It was different when Lasi received money from Mrs. Lanting, who often said it came from Handarbeni. On those occasions, Lasi felt as though she was being sold. It upset her terribly to learn she had lost the ability to refuse such gifts.

The clock chimed three-thirty. Lasi tried to make out the ceiling in the dark as her mind's eye produced the people of Karangsoga who had belittled her. She shut her eyes as she remembered Darsa's betrayal. *I won't go back to Karangsoga, even though I'd be glad to be a tapper's wife with any man except Darsa.*

Then what? The question kept coming up. Lasi felt cornered. She thought of Kanjat and weighed the possibility of leaving to join him. Lasi was too cowardly to leave Mrs. Lanting's house. Besides, how could she find Kanjat? She was also afraid of being the trap that chased the fish, and Kanjat had never told her about his true intentions.

No. I won't run to Kanjat.

Lasi grew more agitated. She lost count of how often she turned. She tried to sleep on her left side, her right, on her back, and face down. The storm in her heart raged wilder. She arrived at a dead end and knew she had no choice but to become Handarbeni's wife. *Can I? Is it true what Mrs. Lanting said, that it's nice to be a rich man's wife?*

She had never experienced wealth or thought about it. Like every tapper's wife, the world of the wealthy was not hers. It was alien.

In Karangsoga, she saw that world in Pak Tir. Even though he lived and mingled among dozens of tappers, he remained an alien. Pak Tir spoke plainly without being apologetic when he announced the price of sugar had dropped. Since childhood, Lasi knew that wealth was for people like Pak Tir, who never faced hardship or cared about the tappers.

In her village, Pak Talab had the help of a relative who was said to be an important man. He became a supplier of construction material and was always awarded government contracts. Pak Talab grew rich almost overnight. Lasi knew the villagers were riled by how he carried on. Where Pak Tir used his wealth for his own enjoyment, it was different with Pak Talab. He and his family liked to draw attention and recognition for their wealth.

Pak Talab associated less and less with his neighbors. He worried about being regarded as one of them. When he received any acknowledgement, usually a compliment, he became as excited as a spoiled child. But when no acknowledgement was forthcoming, he was unpredictable: he sulked or got angry, or was ostentatious and stuck-up. Most villagers were uncomfortable, even ashamed, of Pak Talab's antics.

What should I do as Pak Han's wife? Do I avoid the kind of behavior Pak Talab indulged in so I don't rub other people the wrong way?

Or?

Or?

Or should I do like Pak Talab and show Darsa I didn't deserve the way he treated me and everyone in Karangsoga that I seized an opportunity for revenge for how they always tormented me?

Lasi sat cross-legged on her bed in the dark room. She smiled in the quiet and got up to turn on the lamp. She squinted as the room flooded with light. She sat down in front of her mirror and stared at her reflection. The woman and her reflection cast stares at one another that cut to the heart. A sudden understanding pushed the two into conversation.

Las, maybe Mrs. Lanting is right; marrying a rich man would be nice. I'm confused.

You must accept Pak Han's offer. What will happen if you go against Mrs. Lanting?

That's the trouble.

Enough already, Las. No need to think too much. Let things happen how they are supposed to happen. It's your fate. Why did you end up here if that were not the case?

Okay, I will.

Make the most of the opportunity. You've experienced the hardship of being a tapper's wife. Soon you'll have prosperity at your fingertips. You've suffered enough from the spiteful gossip of Karangsoga's people. Show them who you really are and what you can do to them.

Can I?

You can.

Lasi went to bed weary. *I have to surrender to whatever will happen,* she told herself, and lay down. The pressure in her chest eased with each long sigh, and the visions that tumbled before her settled and faded. Her eyelids felt heavy. Her large universe shrank into a smaller universe. Lasi stretched and took a deep breath before floating off to sleep.

She dreamed she still lived in Karangsoga and saw Darsa fall from a coconut palm. He was badly injured from impaling himself with the scythe tucked in his waistband. Darsa died in a pool of blood. Lasi woke gasping when she heard the clock chime six.

At breakfast, Mrs. Lanting demanded Lasi's answer.

"Have you made a decision?"

"Bu, the truth is I can't decide. I'll do as I'm told and leave you to decide what's best. I'll submit. But I'm scared."

"Scared? Why?"

"I'm just a country girl. Am I the right woman to be Pak Han's wife?"

"Las, you've grown into a city woman. No one would believe you came from the country. Get rid of any doubts about accepting Pak Han's offer. You've never been married to a rich man. It's easy, Las. You'll see, everything is easy and ordinary."

Lasi fidgeted with her spoon.

"Ibu, what about the divorce certificate? Without the certificate from my husband, I can't possibly marry again."

Mrs. Lanting turned cold. "Don't worry about Pak Han's abilities. Like I said, you can get the certificate here. In Jakarta everything can be arranged, Las. Your divorce certificate, even your certificate of domicile can be obtained with money. Pak Han can make things happen quickly. All you have to do is wait. Convenient, isn't it?"

Lasi frowned. "I want a genuine divorce certificate from my current husband. I also want my parents' blessings."

"I see. You want to go back home first."

"Yes."

Mrs. Lanting considered the possibility that Lasi would stay once she was back in Karangsoga but dismissed the thought. This bekisar was too naïve. Lasi could be trusted.

"Okay, Las. Go ahead. Arrange for your divorce and while you're doing so, ask for a letter of change of domicile. You probably miss your mother.

"Pak Han will want to see you about the marriage before you go. Like it or not, you have to talk with him first. Now you can go on dates. Won't that be fun?"

Mrs. Lanting's laugh rang out.

Lasi bowed her head.

"Come on, Las, dating is important to have fun in life. Even though I'm not young anymore, I still like to date." Mrs. Lanting laughed again.

Lasi bowed her head lower.

***

Handarbeni arrived at Mrs. Lanting's house at seven in the evening. He looked dapper in his crème shirt and dark green pants. He had a crisp smile and his eyes were filled with happiness. His thinning hair was neatly combed and dyed black from the pomade he used. From his telephone conversation with Mrs. Lanting that afternoon,

115

Handarbeni knew the bekisar had agreed, or at least not refused, to be his. He had come to talk to her in person.

Mrs. Lanting welcomed him on the terrace. "You look sharp, Pak Han."

"Thank you. It's the way I like to look."

"When the heart is on fire, everything changes. You're clean-shaven, well dressed, and all smiles. I'm sure you're happy tonight. Who wouldn't be after obtaining such a beautiful and young bekisar?"

Handarbeni smiled and sat before his hostess offered him a seat. He took a cigarette from his shirt pocket and lit it. He was obviously nervous.

Mrs. Lanting chuckled. Funny, even a grandfather was jumpy when waiting for his date to come out of her room. Mrs. Lanting went inside to tell Lasi her guest had arrived.

Lasi nodded when Mrs. Lanting told her to fix her makeup before going outside to meet Handarbeni.

"Pak Han, your bekisar has been tamed and you can put her into the cage you already prepared. Be smart about keeping her content. Your bekisar is going to encounter many things she has never imagined, not in the least her marriage to you. She has a lot of adjusting to do, and if you fail her, even the best nest won't make her content. You have to take very good care of her."

"I'm no longer a young man. I'm used to being patient."

"I know what you're like. I still must remind you. Now, do you want to visit with her here or some other place?"

"You know what I want."

"You want to go out with her. Go ahead. I have my own appointment tonight."

"So you have a date as well?"

Mrs. Lanting grinned.

Handarbeni almost joined her laughter but held back when Lasi appeared.

Mrs. Lanting arranged for Lasi to sit in the chair closest to Handarbeni. An awkward silence fell until Mrs. Lanting cleared the air.

"What else can I offer other than congratulations? Pak Han and Lasi, enjoy your first heart-to-heart talk. Unlike the last time, I won't be the third wheel between you two."

A car turned into the driveway. The man wearing dark glasses stepped out after blowing the horn.

"My ride is here. Pak Han, Lasi, use your time as you see fit. I'm off. Congratulations." Mrs. Lanting hurried away like a duck waddling to a pond.

Handarbeni watched her, amused. Even a grandmother could be as skittish as a young virgin when she was on a date.

Left alone, Handarbeni and Lasi fell into a silence. She had difficulty looking up. Anxiety gnawed at her heart for submitting to ownership by another man. Her vision blurred and she saw the bedroom in her house in Karangsoga. Darsa's sarong fluttered on the clothesline inside the room. She thought she had breathed his scent, when, in fact, it was Handarbeni's cologne.

"Las." Handarbeni's soft voice startled her. "Mrs. Lanting told you about my intentions, hasn't she?"

Lasi merely looked at him. Her expression was like the surface of a still pond, without the slightest ripple, but a heavy burden was visible in her empty gaze.

"Well, Las?"

Lasi frowned and nodded slightly.

"Mrs. Lanting says you have accepted my offer. Is that right?"

Lasi stiffened. Doubt and worry appeared on her face.

"Well? Please, speak, Las."

"I'm doing what I'm told," Lasi said softly, her head still bowed.

Handarbeni let out a sigh of relief. He kept his gaze fixed on Lasi and hid a smile.

"We have much to talk about, but not here. Let's go out and have dinner. You'd like that, wouldn't you?"

"I'm shy." Lasi fidgeted.

"There's no need, Las. You've been a Jakartan long enough as Mrs. Lanting's daughter. To live in this city, you mustn't be shy. Let's go."

Lasi nodded. She had no choice.

Handarbeni's eyes sparkled. "Las, I'd like to hear your voice."

"Yes, pak." Her voice was soft after being silent for so long.

"I may be old, but I'd prefer you call me *mas*. Are you okay with that?"

"Yes, pak. I mean, yes, mas." Lasi sounded almost forced.

"That's better. Now put on something warm. It's a bit cold outside."

Like a puppet in the hands of a puppet master, Lasi started toward the door when Handarbeni stopped her.

"Just a minute, Las. I almost forgot. I have something for you."

Handarbeni rummaged in his pants' pocket and handed Lasi a small package. "Open it in your room, and if you like what you see, wear it."

Lasi held out her hand stiffly and mumbled barely audible thanks. In her room, she took a jacket from a hanger. The wrapped package in her hand held something round and heavy. When she unwrapped it, she gasped. The bracelet was not very big, but studded with many gems. She slipped it on her left wrist without thinking. The gems reflected a bluish-white light. Lasi's heart pounded.

She knew nothing about jewels or diamonds. Lasi felt as though sorcery was at work to make her smile. The spell whispered that any girl would be happy and proud to have such a bracelet on her wrist. An incantation told her she would be foolish to refuse such a gift from Handarbeni. Lasi's smile broadened and still lingered when she rejoined Handarbeni in the living room. The smile emphasized her dimple, and reminded him of Haruko Wanibuchi, even though he only knew the Japanese film star from the pages of entertainment magazines.

"Are you ready, Las?" Handarbeni's tone of voice was like that of a little girl talking to her doll.

"I'm ready, Pak Han."

"Mas."

"Oh, yes. I'm ready, mas."

Handarbeni took Lasi by the arm as they walked—an elderly gentleman escorting his young girlfriend—and gallantly opened the door on the left side of the car. He circled to the right side, and a moment later, the engine purred into life.

Lasi froze. She felt as though she should never be alone with any man, no matter whom.

"What would you like? Fried chicken, *rendang Padang,* or Chinese food?" Handarbeni asked as the car drove down Cikini Street.

"Um, whatever. I'll just go along."

"I'd much prefer if you had a request."

"I have no requests."

"How about *ayam kalasan* at the Arya Duta?"

"Whatever."

"I forgot. You're half-Japanese. Have you ever tried sukiyaki or tempura?"

"What are those?"

"Dishes from your father's country, Japan."

"I've never even heard of them before."

"Would you like to try?"

"Pak… I mean, Mas Han, I'd actually prefer rice with sambal trassi and vegetables."

Lasi was shocked at her frankness. She wished she could take back her words.

Handarbeni almost burst out laughing when he remembered that laughing at the honesty of a girlfriend was hardly considered gentlemanly. "I'll take you with pleasure, Las. In Jakarta, everything is available. Trust me, we'll find a meal of white rice, sambal trassi, and vegetables. Do you want sayur bening and salted fish too?"

Lasi laughed softly and bowed her head. "Those are dishes for country people like myself, Mas Han. Do you like them as well?"

"Yes, I like them."

"You're not pretending?"

"When the matter of food doesn't get mixed up with trying to show off, everything is simple. What matters is staying healthy. It's nutrition that counts, not the food or the price or where it's from."

"You really like sambal trassi?"

"Hmm, yes. Even more so if you prepare it."

Lasi blushed. The ambience turned intimate and Handarbeni reached to stroke Lasi's chin. Shocked, she jerked her head back.

At a Sundanese restaurant, Lasi found the dishes she had missed for so long. Her palate and digestive system were accustomed to simple meals, and she thoroughly enjoyed her dinner. The spiciness of the sambal trassi and tang of the salted fish whet her appetite. She finished off a full plate of rice, and only being embarrassed for Handarbeni stopped her from asking for seconds.

Handerbeni noticed how Lasi's cheeks flushed red from the heat of the chili, and the radiance in her half-Japanese face. His heart swelled when he realized that she was his. "Las, where do you want to go after dinner? How about a movie?"

"I don't want to go anywhere."

"In that case, let's go back home to Slipi. We can talk in our own house, and be much more comfortable. You'd like that, won't you?"

"I can't stay out too late."

"Are you afraid of Mrs. Lanting?"

"Not afraid, I just wouldn't feel right."

"Call Mrs. Lanting if you need. We'll soon be husband and wife, won't we?"

Lasi was taken aback. She suddenly realized he had plenty of reasons for saying that.

On the drive to Slipi, Lasi only answered Handarbeni's questions. She had yet to understand the role she was supposed to play. Her feelings were in turmoil, but she was certain she should not be in her situation. The feeling became stronger once she entered Handarbeni's new house.

"Las, this is not just a house, it's our house. You're the mistress here."

"No, Mas Han," Lasi interrupted.

"All right. It would be more accurate to say you're the mistress-to-be of this house. Even so, I consider you the rightful mistress. Don't feel out of place. You know your way around if you need anything to eat or drink. There's a wardrobe filled with clothes for you. Please forgive me, I still need to find the right maid. All I have here now are Min, the driver, and Ujang, the security guard."

Lasi stopped listening. She was tired and the meal she had enjoyed made her drowsy.

Handarbeni asked her to move to the sofa and took a seat close to her.

Lasi wished she weren't in this situation, even more when Handarbeni put his arm around her shoulder. He made her uncomfortable, but she didn't dare do anything to hurt his feelings.

"Las…"

"Yes, mas?"

"The house is fully stocked. If you're tired, you can sleep here. There are many rooms; you only have to pick one. It's all right, Las. Really."

Lasi twiddled her fingers and shook her head.

"Surely it's better here than at Mrs. Lanting's. Her house will never be ours, will it?"

Lasi shook her head again. She no longer wanted to be alone with Handarbeni, much less sleep under the same roof—especially in the same room.

Handarbeni was at a loss. He fetched two canned drinks from the refrigerator and came back to the sofa to find Lasi dozing. He put the drinks down on the small table next to the sofa and sat down. Lasi startled him when she asked to be taken home to Mrs. Lanting's.

Handarbeni slapped his forehead. He had an idea. "Hold on, Las."

He walked out of the room and returned with a small film projector. He placed it on the table and pointed it at the wall. After setting up a reel of film, he unspooled the power cable and plugged it in. The projector lit up. Handarbeni fiddled with the lens. When he found the right focus, he dimmed the lights and started the movie.

Lasi jolted awake when the lights went off and the movie played on the wall before her. Handarbeni sat down beside her and put his arm around her shoulder.

"Don't fall asleep, Las. Let's watch."

Lasi's eyelids felt heavy, but she followed the scene playing out before her. It was prehistoric times. A nearly naked man with long hair prowled along a riverbank. He was burly and young, and armed with a large bone. Insects and small birds scattered as he made his way through the brush.

Lasi enjoyed the scene. It reminded her of collecting firewood in the forest, the flying insects, the crackle of twigs snapping underfoot, and trickle of water at the bottom of the ravine. She smelled the moss growing on the cliff face and heard the crowing of a wild rooster. A spider web sparkled like a silk net. Lasi was frightened when a crocodile appeared on the screen and attacked the prehistoric man. He fought it off with his bone, and she was relieved when he defeated it.

Her gaze fixed on the living pictures projected on the wall, she barely noticed Handarbeni's arm move down to encircle her waist.

The prehistoric man walked until he reached the edge of a valley, where he spotted a pair of wild goats rutting. The billy goat was big and rough, even brutal, and the nanny goat seemed to barely be able to stand up.

After watching the goats, the man entered a forest of giant trees. On a large branch growing parallel to the ground, a pair of monkeys mated. It was primitive, bestial, and clinical.

Lasi turned her face away and closed her eyes, giggling. Engrossed in the movie, she didn't pay attention to Handarbeni as he moved closer.

The prehistoric man captivated Lasi, especially when he turned and ran, going back the same way he came. Small birds scattered as before. Insects fluttered everywhere as he ran through shrubbery, open fields, along the edge of a cliff, until he reached a riverbank dotted with caves. He entered one of the caves and emerged a moment later pulling out a woman. When he forced her to drop the suckling baby, Lasi held her breath.

Next to her, Handarbeni laughed. He had played this pornographic movie more than a dozen times before, and had a reason for showing it to Lasi.

She froze when the prehistoric man forced himself on the woman. He was as brutal as the billy goat. Primitive, bestial, and clinical, like the monkeys. To Lasi, the scene between them was wild, unnatural, savage, immoral, disgusting, and more than she had words for. She felt nauseous. Her heart thumped and she was dizzy. Drenched in a cold sweat, she shivered. She sighed and shut her eyes. She could no longer watch the scene that struck her as obscene. It was worse than any perversion she had ever heard about. One image made her hair stand on end: her husband had never so much as made her suck his thumb. Yet, what she saw was ten times more perverted.

The movie was over. Lasi was glad not to have watched it to the end. Even so, she felt dizzy and on the verge of vomiting. When Handarbeni turned on the lights, she was pale and stricken.

Lasi rushed to the bathroom. The rice, sambal trassi, and vegetables she had enjoyed earlier gushed out.

Handarbeni paced while waiting for Lasi. He shook his head. Something had gone wrong. He had put on the pornographic movie to arouse Lasi. Once she was on fire, he planned to take her to his heart's content. Instead, she threw up. Handarbeni was puzzled, and concerned that Lasi might be ill. He tried to compose himself when Lasi came out of the bathroom. "Las, are you sick?"

"No." She was pale and her lips looked ashen.

"Why did you throw up?"

"I felt sick. But it's gone now," she sat down gingerly.

"I have medicine for that. Let me get it."

"Don't put yourself out, Mas Han. I'm better now. I don't need medicine," Lasi lied. Her head throbbed and she felt queasy.

"In that case, I'll make you sweet tea."

Sitting alone, Lasi felt as though she had returned from a strange place. The movie she had seen made her shudder. Inconceivable, impossible. An act that for her was personal and secret, and the beauty of which lay in its privacy, had been ravaged.

The nausea and dizziness returned. Something in her soul had been trampled. The obscenity she witnessed gave rise to a piercing question: *Why do I feel so offended watching perverted behavior?* Lasi had the simplest of answers: *Because I'm not a goat, and I'm not a monkey.*

She wondered if being a country girl made such behavior hard to stomach. Being poor, uneducated, and inexperienced had made her backward. Being backward caused her repulsion at the shameless scenes. Those who drew enjoyment from watching such obscenities, like Handarbeni, were in the right and ahead of the times. That's why they didn't compare themselves to goats and monkeys.

Handarbeni wasn't the only one. Back at Ibu Koneng's restaurant, Lasi had seen something she thought was not quite right. Many of the men who paid for the woman with big earrings or the one with chafed calves appeared to have just met her, yet they went into a room together with barely an introduction. Lasi wondered: *What kind of intimacy can two people share without a connection of heart and soul? Is it just a physical union, copulating, not the joining of two souls?*

What she had done with Darsa always began with a spark in her soul. Desire started from the heart. What united them was more than their bodies. "Copulation" was far from an accurate description.

Lasi shook her head. Her mind wandered. She thought of the smutty movie, but this time went over the scenes with a lighter heart. She saw the characters from a different point of view.

The brutal and forceful manner of the billy goat was scary, but the monkeys? Lasi smiled. Those human-looking creatures looked so ridiculous in their mating scene. They had dumb, comical expressions. Lasi had to smile when she thought about them. She was giggling when Handarbeni came in with the tea.

"Are you laughing, Las?"

"It's funny. Apparently monkeys are just as raunchy as people." She burst out guffawing and leaned over the table, holding her stomach that hurt from holding her laughter.

Bemused, Handarbeni laughed with her. He was taken by how Lasi had worded her statement. Mating monkeys imitated the raunchiness of humans. Who knew?

Their laughter created a much warmer mood. Lasi felt like a giant crepe-myrtle leaf floating on the surface of the Kalirong: drifting, floating, and following the whim of the wind.

Handarbeni thought he had half-succeeded. True, he had failed to ignite Lasi's passion but the coziness left him free to talk intimately with her. He raved about the beauty of her eyes and the dimple in her cheek, and called her Haruko. When he felt they had grown closer, Handarbeni again asked Lasi to stay the night. She immediately withdrew into herself like a snail seeking shelter in its shell. Handarbeni repeated his question and Lasi shook her head.

He fell silent. Faced with Lasi's strong will, Handarbeni was prodded in a moral direction he had long ignored. Yet, he smiled. He sensed a defense in the artlessness of the country girl, one that required a struggle to break through, and a challenge to yield a nugget of pleasure. Handarbeni smiled with his heart in turmoil. It felt more acute when Lasi looked at him with a smile adorned by a dimple.

"What will it be, Las?" he sighed.

"I want to go home."

"Very well. I'll be happy to take you."

"Isn't it enough to just send Min?"

"No. Unless you don't want me to drive you."

Handarbeni escorted Lasi outside. Again, she had the feeling she should be anywhere but in the company of this man.

***

The fasting month rarely fell during the dry season. When this happened, the tappers relished it. The price of sugar climbed and sometimes hit a peak. The tappers never understood why the price rose, particularly in the ten days before the month-long holiday of *Lebaran*. All they had was years of experience of the price going up, even spiking toward the end of the month. Brokers like Pak Tir knew the price increase came from the increase in consumption of palm sugar in the big cities. Many city people consumed sweet dishes during the fasting month.

The combination of a high price for palm sugar and the abundance of firewood brightened the tappers' lives for a short time. Their work was much easier. Besides the availability of firewood, the dry season meant the coconut palms were less slippery to climb. Richer nira filled the pongkors. These were the days when the tappers smiled and laughed.

They had enough to eat and put aside a bit of money to buy new clothes for their children. With their hearts lighter, they often sang as they chopped the firewood or whistled in the treetops. Their children's cheeks and legs filled out. They were happy and sang together in the moonlight. One folk song they liked was about their hopes as children without enough clothes or food.

> *On Lebaran we complete our fast*
> *We celebrate, happy in soul and body*
> *We wear new clothes and eat fluffy rice*
> *What a joy to eat until our stomachs are full*

As the children ran around and sang beneath the moonlight, some of the men gathered at Grandfather Mus' surau. When life was good and had meaning, and the stomach was full, the tappers thought about what stayed in their souls but was often forgotten when they were hungry. The tappers invoked Allah to keep them safe, but often neglected to go to the surau when they were unable to decide which to take care of first, *oman* or *iman.* The oman symbolized the needs of the stomach. The question of oman and iman was a confusing one for the tappers. They often asked, "How can we worship properly when we worry about not having enough to eat the next day?"

As the worry subsided, the tappers were eager to prove they were God-fearing people, and knew they were in the constant presence of the Almighty. They fasted, and when their stomachs were safe, they no longer said, "What's the point of fasting if our stomachs are always empty?" Only in the surau could they manifest the relationship between their souls and the Almighty. They prayed together at night and recited the *slawatan,* or sometimes the *suluk sisiringan,* where one man recited and the others echoed.

Often, after tiring of the slawatan and the suluk, they talked about the law, and turned to Grandfather Mus as a source of reference.

This night there was a particular question, one that was always left hanging in the air because Grandfather Mus avoided answering it. Mukri had asked the question during the fasting month the previous year: Was a tapper like Mukri obliged to fast, even though he had to climb forty palms a day?

"Grandfather Mus, tonight I need a clear answer. I can't stand being in the dark any longer. When I don't fast, I'm scared I'm doing wrong, but when I do, my legs tremble as I climb the palms. And it's worse in the rain."

"That's right, Grandfather," San Kardi chimed in. "All these years you've refused to address this question. Now we're asking for an answer."

The night had turned quiet. Grandfather Mus bowed his head until his entire skullcap was visible. He coughed and raised his head. An honest smile graced his weathered face. "Ah, you never tire of that question. My children, the obligation to fast is for the faithful, and at its heart is sincerity and honesty. It's essentially a lesson in mastering temptation. Mukri, if you're strong enough to fast even when it makes your work harder, it's best you carry out the obligation."

"What if I'm not strong enough?" Mukri interrupted.

"Honesty is important. You know best if you can fast, and your work is indeed one that requires a lot of energy. If you truly feel unable, don't force yourself. You'll only be asking for trouble. In this case, you can make up for not fasting by giving alms or fasting at another time. It's that simple."

Mukri and San Kardi looked at each other. They were pleased to be free of a dilemma that had long weighed on them.

"Just to be clear, Grandfather, when I don't feel strong enough to fast because my work is hard, I can break my fast?"

The old man nodded and laughed, "As long as you're sincere and honest."

"Grandfather…"

"Hold on, I'm not done yet. You might think you have it easy, but don't forget that during the fasting month you're asked to control your desires and emotions. That's the lesson behind fasting."

"Your answer turned out to be so simple. Why did you wait years to give it?"

Grandfather Mus chuckled. The gaps of his missing teeth showed when he opened his mouth. "I try to refrain from talking about fasting. I know the work you do is very hard and dangerous, while all I do is look after a small fishpond. That's why I've been reluctant to say that your fasting should be the same as mine."

"And that's why you haven't been straight with us this whole time?" Mukri jibed. Everyone laughed, including Grandfather Mus.

A ripe moon was high when the men left the surau. The sound of the bamboo drum marked eleven o'clock. The children had long since gone indoors and slept in the embrace of the cool summer night. The only sounds came from a tokay gecko in the hole of an albizia tree, a chirping cricket, the flap of a bat's wing, and the tap of Grandfather Mus' wooden sandals as he walked home. The bamboo door creaked when it opened.

The moon had begun its descent in the west. A cat crossed the yard without a sound, its eyes glinting like a pair of blue lights. At the edge of the pond, a mouse squeaked. A pair of prowling foxes darted like shadows through the quiet night. Karangsoga slept in the cool air.

As Lebaran approached, and the price of palm sugar kept going up, the people of Karangsoga smiled wider and more often. At its peak, a kilogram of sugar was worth one and a half or two times as much as a kilogram of rice. This happened only for a few days every five years. During that time, the people of Karangsoga felt incredibly lucky for being nira tappers.

With a few kilograms of rice and a little money put aside, life was a joy and worth being thankful for. Happy to have the means to celebrate Lebaran, they went tapping through the cold morning mist with light hearts. They shared their happiness when they encountered one another by laughing or humming, even while in the treetops. They knew the current prices for palm sugar would soon fall. The knowledge compelled the tappers of Karangsoga to enjoy the rare and valuable moments of prosperity. They laughed while they could, even if only for a moment.

Karangsoga began its day with the drum from Grandfather Mus' surau just before dawn, followed by the call to prayer mingled with crowing roosters and chirping birds. Then came the sound of wooden sandals as a group of old men heeded the call to prayer. Water rippled in the pond next to the surau, where thousands of bees buzzed among the flowering trees, and the geese in Pak Tir's yard honked. The clanking of the tappers' pongkors was heard as the sky in the east brightened. Palms swayed as the tappers braved the cold mist to start their day's work of collecting nira.

The sunlight had yet to reach the tops of the palms when a sedan pulled off the main road and turned right, following the uphill path to Karangsoga. The tappers who saw the car thought it was one of Pak Tir's buyers, coming to the village with his family. Pak Tir had close relationships with his buyers and their families. After decades of doing business with them, they were almost like family.

Chickens scattered in front of the car as it crawled along the narrow, rocky road. A kid goat bleated and ran to its mother. A pair of geese stretched their necks, and the male let out a shrill and raspy honk. Village women emerged from their houses and chattered. It was unusually early for Pak Tir to have a guest. What kind of gift could he be expecting this time?

The car lumbered on and stopped at a footpath several dozen meters south of Pak Tir's house. After engine turned off, a thin man in his fifties wearing a *peci* stepped out of the car. From the other side appeared a young woman with an incredibly fair complexion and shoulder-length hair worn loose.

Two young boys ran to get a closer look, and a girl carrying her little brother on her back joined them. A tapper scoring a branch high up in a palm stopped what he was doing to watch what went on below. Who were the man and the woman by the car?

More children surrounded the car. One of the bigger boys was certain he had never seen the man before, but the woman looked familiar. Who was she? He remembered when Mbok Wiryaji came out of her house and ran down the path while she cried, "Las, Lasi, Lasiyah. Heavens, you're home, my child."

"Yes, Mother," Lasi showed no sign of overwhelming joy. The handshake she offered her mother was just as casual.

Mbok Wiryaji was lost for words. Her chest felt tight. She panted as tears welled in her eyes. She wanted to embrace her daughter, but a sudden reluctance held her back. The mother who had for months suppressed her longing for her daughter stood frozen. Something did not allow her to voice her yearning.

Lasi had changed. Her clothes, hair, slippers, her gestures and gaze, everything was very different. She looked like a rich and beautiful lady, the wife of a Chinese businessman or another important man. She seemed indifferent to their long separation. Why had she come in a car with a strange man?

"Mother, this is Pak Min, my driver," Lasi said.

Min bowed deeply, making Mbok Wiryaji very uncomfortable. She had never been treated that way. Min was exceedingly courteous to her daughter, as he might be to his employer.

Her mother knew her daughter had changed. Lasi, at the other hand, thought that much of her had remained the same. Her lungs were still sensitive to the fresh morning air in the village. Her sense of smell was strong enough to take pleasure from the ferns growing in the ditches around her. Her ears were in tune with the chirping of the fantail bird that darted acrobatically in the bamboo thicket. Lasi caught her breath when off in the distance, behind a veil of mist, she saw a palm sway. She saw the tapper descending the palm, two pongkors dangling from his waist. Lasi watched her old world pass before her eyes.

Her feelings in a jumble, Mbok Wiryaji led Lasi down the footpath. Min followed carrying a suitcase. The small procession made its way to the Wiryaji's house because Lasi did not want to stay in the one she had shared with Darsa.

Wiryaji, her stepfather and Darsa's uncle, met her at the front door. They exchanged greetings and a few clumsy pleasantries.

"Lasi came from Jakarta in a sedan," said the newest gossip spreading throughout Karangsoga. The story grew taller with each telling. Everyone in Karangsoga pieced together a story, as they wondered how Lasi had prospered in six months. Her striking looks separated her from the villagers and even her mother. They suspected

Lasi had prospered from her beauty. "If it wasn't for her beauty, Lasi would be just a maid in Jakarta," they said.

For the people of Karangsoga, the statement blunted their true accusation. None dare say they suspected Lasi of being a prostitute. How else could she get that car? Only the wives of the Pak Tir's business partners wore clothes and jewelry like hers.

Over the next few days, the gossip in Karangsoga grew. People no longer talked about how Lasi had obtained her wealth, they moved to a new topic: she wanted a divorce from Darsa.

Beyond anyone's expectation, the divorce process concluded quickly and smoothly. People said Lasi had a "sanctified letter" from a retired government officer in Jakarta that she showed to the Karangsoga village chief and the head of the local religious affairs office. Overwhelmed by the signature of the high ranking officer, the gossip-mongers went on, the village chief immediately brought Darsa before the religious affairs chief, and without Lasi being present, Darsa signed the divorce certificate.

***

Kanjat graduated as an engineer when he was close to twenty-five years old. At first, he was elated and proud, but the following days brought uncertainty. Kanjat was unable to answer his own question: *Now that I have my degree, what next?* Several of his fellow graduates had applied for jobs at the Ministry of Agriculture. Kanjat, for reasons he could not explain, refused to follow them. Applying for a government job meant facing an absurd bureaucracy and having to beg for pity from its machinations.

One friend suggested he apply at a plantation company exploring new land, primarily outside the island of Java. He could also work for a logging company. His friend said that applying for a job in the private sector was less complicated and the companies were professionally run. Even these ideas held no appeal for Kanjat, mainly because the logging companies and the regulations that spawned them played a major role in the destruction of forests in Kalimantan, Sumatra, Sulawesi, and Irian Jaya. Kanjat refused to be part of the cancer that ate away at nature.

Another offer came from Dr. Jirem: Kanjat could work at the university and become an assistant lecturer. At first Kanjat was uninterested. The pay for an assistant lecturer was low, and besides, Kanjat thought he lacked the diligence to be a teacher.

Dr. Jirem told him there were other opportunities to pursue on campus, and Kanjat began to warm to the idea. Dr. Jirem said he could join the research group he had been leading for the past year. Kanjat was surprised at how matter-of-factly Dr. Jirem broached the subject.

"Jat, have you forgotten about the thesis you submitted? I mean, do you still feel the same concern for the tappers?"

Kanjat only nodded.

"Ah, you young graduates. Only a few days ago you talked about your concern and solidarity, and now you've completely forgotten. Was it just a passing fad?"

Kanjat grimaced. He scratched his head. His face flushed and he caught his breath. The teacher's words pierced his heart.

Dr. Jirem noticed Kanjat took his words seriously and regretted his reprimand.

"Dr. Jirem," Kanjat said firmly, "I will always be a son of Karangsoga. I've always considered the tappers as members of my own family. Their hardship is something I'm concerned about, and it weighs heavily on my soul." Kanjat stopped, agitated.

"It's a burden?" Dr. Jirem asked, waiting for Kanjat to resume the conversation.

"Yes. While I can feel their hardship, I'm unable to do anything. Their prosperity is dictated by the free-market economy and there's not enough being done to support those who live in the margins. My obsession for helping the tappers might be in vain. Like I said before, I wouldn't be surprised if someone called me Don Quixote."

Dr. Jirem stuck his hands in his pockets and said, "I admit there's some truth in your words, yet there's also truth in the old saying: 'Better to do something, no matter how small, than nothing at all.'

Powerful forces with many interests have long dominated the sugar trade so on that front there's not much we can do. Still, isn't there any aspect of the tappers' lives where we can be of help?"

"There's a lot," Kanjat replied so quickly Dr. Jirem thought he'd been cut off. He smiled at Kanjat's enthusiasm.

Kanjat tallied the different aspects that could be the subject of research. He knew a big problem for the tappers was the short time the nira stayed fresh before turning rancid. Developing a cheap and easily available chemical preservative would help them immensely. They also needed an additive to make the sugar set. Kanjat was convinced both compounds could be developed with the help of several friends who understood chemistry. The tappers also needed to be taught the importance of fertilizing the palms, which they knew nothing about. When it came to the fuel the tappers needed, Kanjat found it hard to explain to Dr. Jirem.

"The tappers use wood and the chaff discarded by the rice mills. The stoves they use waste a tremendous amount of energy. My research showed that of the heat generated, only twenty percent is used."

"Only twenty percent?"

"Yes, and the firewood and chaff have to be bought. When the price of palm sugar drops, they can't cook the nira unless they steal wood from the forest, or cut down the palms they have."

"I know that from your thesis. The demand for fuel by the tappers is the biggest factor in the destruction of the forests around Karangsoga."

"They always sweep the forest floor clean of leaves during the dry season, so there's no opportunity for the topsoil to be replenished. One thing I left out of my thesis, the *soga* tree has almost vanished from Karangsoga. If the wasteful use of firewood doesn't end, my village will become a monoculture zone, because every tree except the coconut palms will be destined for the stoves."

"It seems there's a lot you want to do, Jat. What you need is the reassurance to erase any doubt and propel you into immediate action."

With the help of Dr. Jirem, Kanjat set up a team of researchers. Joko Adi was the chemistry expert, Topo Sumarso knew about agricultural production, and Hermiati prepared their findings for publication in the mass media. Kanjat addressed the environmental impact of the palm sugar production process.

The small team joined the research facility that Dr. Jirem had long overseen. Their office was a cramped room in a campus building, and when they did fieldwork, they often made Kanjat's family home in Karangsoga their base of operations. They frequently came together to discuss how far they had progressed in each of their tasks, and coordinate their activities.

Pak Tir shook his head when he saw the young people at work, especially his son. What was the use of developing an experimental stove that burned firewood more efficiently? Why list the various trees and shrubs they said were disappearing because the current stoves were voracious? What about the questions about the minutiae of the tappers' lives?

"If all he wanted to do was build a stove or hang out with the people in Karangsoga, why did I pay for his education to be an engineer?" Pak Tir asked his wife. "An engineer shouldn't do this kind of work. From what I know, they have good positions in offices in the city."

"He's still your son. Try talking with him and ask what he wants. If he chooses to work someplace far away, I'll be the one who suffers. Besides, he says he's a lecturer."

"A stove lecturer?"

"Don't hurt him. He's our youngest."

"That's just it. You always spoil him and that's why he does odd things. He's a university lecturer who wastes time making clay stoves. What kind of a lecturer does that? Instead of letting him do this and that, you should tell him to find a wife."

Pak Tir's wife knew her husband was disappointed in their son, but she avoided confronting Kanjat. The tension only worsened when they argued. She agreed with her husband. The difference was that she loved her son and feared he might move away from Karangsoga.

Kanjat's team had been working for a month. Kanjat, Joko, and Topo recorded many findings. Now it was up to Hermiati to summarize their notes in a press release. Kanjat was busy in Karangsoga, tweaking his efficient wood-burning stove that was a modified version of a model developed by the engineer Johanes. He was in his shop when Pardi appeared.

The driver's opening question was loaded with intrigue. "Mas Kanjat, have you heard? She's officially divorced."

"You mean Lasi?"

"Who else but her? Do you want to place a bet on who's going to be the first guy to go to Wiryaji's house and propose?"

Kanjat smiled.

"Have you seen her yet, Mas Kanjat?"

"Not yet. To be honest, Di, I'd really like to see her but it's awkward meeting in the village."

"I know, but now that she's divorced, there's no harm for a man to go see her, especially if he's single. Aren't you worried another man might get to her first?"

Kanjat smiled and motioned the driver to come closer. His expression kept changing as he talked with Pardi. They ended their conversation with vague smiles. Pardi laughed aloud.

That afternoon, Pardi went to Wiryaji's house to see Lasi. His step was light, his expression unburdened, and cigarette smoke billowed from his mouth. Pardi had a wealth of experience when it came to women, and looked calm as he took a seat across from Lasi. But the next moment had him flabbergasted.

Lasi placed several banknotes in front of him. "Di, I don't know your purpose for coming here, but please accept this money so my debt to you is repaid. Thank you for your kindness."

Pardi shook his head, dumbstruck. The only thing he could do was take the money he had loaned Lasi six months earlier.

"Now, Di, tell me what brings you here," Lasi said with a smile.

Pardi felt jittery. Her smile made his heart race and he could only swallow. "Las, I hope no one has come before me. I want to propose to you on your first day of being divorced. Will you accept?"

Lasi's eyes widened. "Creep. You're a typical man, a typical truck driver. Stupid. That's all you think about. Do you know how I've suffered? No."

"Las, I'm not joking. Hear me out first."

"No, no."

"Okay, but please don't shout like that. Honey, as beautiful as you are, you make as much noise as a gaggle of geese."

"You're a bastard, and rude."

Pardi laughed.

"Say what you want."

Pardi burst out laughing again and looked around, grinning.

"Where's your mother?"

"Inside."

Pardi reached into his shirt pocket and pulled out a letter he placed on the table.

As soon as she saw the sender's name, Lasi tensed and her lips trembled. The sound of Pardi striking a match was crisp in the silence filling the room. Lasi opened the letter and read the few sentences. She hid it when footsteps approached.

Mbok Wiryaji walked in. "Oh, it's you, Di."

"Yes. I thought I would propose to Lasi," Pardi said with a smile. "Who knows, maybe your daughter who now almost looks like a real Japanese will accept a bastard like me."

"Have you ever heard of any parent accepting a jerk as a son-in-law?" Mbok Wiryaji, cold as the lip of an earthenware water jar, left the room.

Pardi and Lasi laughed.

"Las, Mas Kanjat wants to see you. That's okay, isn't it?"

Strain returned to Las's face. Sighing, she bowed her head and reread the letter she held.

"How about it, Las? Why do you look so dazed?" Pardi asked.

Lasi frowned and narrowed her almond-shaped eyes.

Pardi watched her, enjoying himself. It was too bad Kanjat, his employer's son, had seen Lasi first. If only she favored him instead.

"Las, Mas Kanjat wrote in the letter that he wants to see you, right?"

"Yes, but I don't know why."

Pardi took a long drag of his cigarette.

Lasi bowed her head. Even if she didn't admit to being confused, it was apparent on her face and in her aimless gestures.

"Mas Kanjat only asked me to bring you the letter. Now that you have it, I'd better be going."

Lasi was startled.

Pardi thought she was about to give him a message for Kanjat. He waited and when no word came from her, Pardi turned and started to walk away.

"Wait, Di. Listen to me. I want to see Kanjat too, but I can't. It's best if we don't meet." Lasi bowed her head and sighed.

Pardi knew something was out of place. The look on Lasi's face and the words she spoke did not match. Pardi felt he was at a dead end. "Okay," he took another deep drag from his cigarette and said, "I'll give him the message."

Lasi remained silent. Strain returned to her face, she walked away and left Pardi to his own confusion.

***

As Lebaran approached, more people visited Grandfather Mus' surau. Men and women arrived shortly after breaking the fast. Mbok Wiryaji and her husband had left Lasi at home by herself. At first, she had wanted to go, but changed her mind when she remembered she had been a divorcée for only one day. Being in the middle of so many people and the object of their stares was too much for her.

Home alone, Lasi was torn by indecision. She sat in the front room determined to let everything pass without heed. She heard the drum at the surau, the sounds of children, and milky storks squabbling for nesting space in the bamboo thicket above her parents' house. Lasi ignored the butterfly flitting against the lamp hanging in front of her, but she did pay attention to the blurry figure she saw in the yard through the wooden railing. The figure came closer and grew clearer. It was a man heading for the front door.

Could it be Pardi? No, he'd just left and never wore a long-sleeved shirt. Kanjat? Impossible. She had sent word through Pardi of her refusal to see him. Lasi startled when she heard Kanjat's voice. Her chest rumbled with joy, anxiety, or uncertainty.

Kanjat stepped inside when Lasi opened the door. From the blush on her cheeks and the light in her eyes, Kanjat knew he was welcome. He smiled.

Lasi returned his smile.

They sat facing each other. Lasi stood to turn up the lamp and Kanjat tried to get there ahead of her. Their hands touched and they smiled again. Neither of them spoke.

Kanjat swallowed. "Las," he said, cutting through the uncomfortable silence. "Forgive me, I came even though Pardi said you didn't want to see me."

Lasi was overjoyed that Kanjat had ignored her message. She laughed, and her dimple was perfect.

It was Kanjat's turn to feel a rumbling in his chest. "Las, why are you quiet?"

"What must I say?"

"You're not angry?"

Lasi shook her head. She looked down. Her frown held a heavy burden.

"You look refreshed."

"Are you complimenting me?"

Kanjat smiled.

"I heard you finished university and are now a lecturer. That's great."

Kanjat blushed. "Las, I still have your picture. Do you know why?"

They looked at each other.

"I'd like to say something. You'll hear me out, won't you?"

Lasi looked up. A storm raged in her eyes and her face froze. Her intuition told her that Kanjat wanted to talk about her being a divorced woman. The glimmer in his eyes said as much. Lasi's heart shattered and was sucked into a vortex. She sputtered even before

Kanjat could open his mouth. Her breathing was ragged. In the middle of her turmoil, Lasi weighed whether she should stop Kanjat from what she was certain he would say. To let him speak would be to introduce another source of turmoil to set aside, no matter how difficult. Still, Lasi wanted to hear the young man say sweet things to her. She heaved a long sigh.

"Las…"

"What do you want, Jat?"

It was Kanjat's turn to be nervous. "There's a lot. Do I have to say it?"

"Jat, it's impossible. I'm a divorced woman and two years older than you. You're single, educated, and the son of a rich family. I'm not worthy of you. Many other girls are better suited to be your wife."

"Las…"

"We must have the courage to forget our desires, as strong as they may be, if we don't want regrets later."

"I stopped caring about that a long time ago."

"Don't forget, this is Karangsoga. Have you ever heard of a single man marrying a divorced woman here?"

"I haven't thought about that in ages."

"What about your parents?"

"Las, I'm an adult."

"Jat, I can't. You need to accept my decision." Lasi bowed her head, sobbing.

Kanjat sat shocked in the silence. The butterfly returned and circled the lamp again. He needed to heed Lasi's last words: "You need to accept my decision." He recalled his neighbors' gossip about the retired officer who had aided Lasi in the divorce process. "Las, do you have other plans?"

Lasi looked up. She wiped her eyes and sighed. In a heavy voice, she replied in the affirmative. It was quiet again. Lasi looked at Kanjat, trying to read his reaction.

A new energy revealed itself in his face. "Is it the retired officer, Las?"

"Yes. You already know."

"Everyone knows from the story that spread from the village hall."

"Yes. That's how it is, Jat. I have plans with another man."

Kanjat looked dazed. His voice trembled. "Are you serious? I mean, you won't consider me? Plans can be cancelled."

Lasi's eyes widened. "I can't go back on a promise. Jat, you can understand, can't you?"

Kanjat stayed silent for a long time. His Adam's apple bobbed up and down.

"Do you understand my feelings?" she asked. Kanjat looked into Lasi's eyes. An intense exchange between the two showed by the light in their eyes, and barely perceptible movements of their faces. Kanjat nodded again. His eyes were empty. "Las, I find it very hard to accept all this, but so be it."

Lasi fidgeted with the ring on her finger. The diamond gave off a bluish light.

Kanjat rubbed his palms on the tabletop. The butterfly still circled the lamp. Kanjat stood and held out his hand.

Startled, Lasi took the offered palm and fingers. They both felt a warm quiver in each other's grip. Lasi held on tighter to Kanjat. Tears welled in her eyes.

Kanjat walked quietly toward the door.

Lasi stopped him. "Jat, wait. I have a message for your parents. Please tell them I want to see them tomorrow morning."

"You'll come to our house?"

"Yes. I want to repay your father for the money I received when I pawned my coconut grove to him to pay for Darsa's, my, er, ex-husband's, medical treatment."

Thwack. The words stabbed Kanjat's heart. The irony hit him in the chest. He was back to observing the tappers' lives.

Lasi was prosperous and had no need to fret over palm sugar prices. Pawning one's coconut grove—the only source of livelihood for most people in Karangsoga—was only done when a tapper had real need, and always involved Pak Tir.

"Jat, what's the matter? Are you angry? You don't like me to visit your parents?"

Kanjat startled.

"Are you sick? Why are you so pale?"

"Oh, no, it's nothing. Come anytime you want. I'm sorry, I have to go." Kanjat grimaced, turned around, and stepped outside. As long as he stayed in reach of the light beams, he was a shadow moving further away. When he dropped out of sight, Lasi felt as if she were drowning in the vacuum of her heart. She closed her eyes and tried to ease the pain from the ringing in her ears.

Chapter 6

Lasi became Handarbeni's wife with a simple ceremony. The wedding took place at his house in Slipi. Officials from the religious affairs office were invited, and witnesses brought in from who knew where. The only guests were a few of Handarbeni's male friends, Ibu Koneng, Mrs. Lanting, and the man wearing dark glasses. Fortunately, the woman with chafed calves and the one with big earrings did not come.

Lasi was sad because none of her family or friends, not even her mother, was present at the Sunday ceremony, but her sadness soon dissipated in the easygoing, fluid, and playful atmosphere, where the presence of her mother seemed unnecessary. "Make believe" was the best description of how Lasi felt that day. She wondered why her heart and soul played no part in the marriage. In childhood, she often played a game of make-believe weddings with her friends. The game was funny and enjoyable, but unreal. Nothing was sincere.

Lasi tried to make sense of her own feelings. She could not forget Kanjat and this turned her marriage to Handarbeni into a farce. During the reciting of vows, Lasi's heart was filled with Kanjat. He was too far out of reach, or was it she who had made herself unavailable? Long before the wedding, she had agreed to be Handarbeni's wife. So why did she feel her marriage was merely a game?

Her heart told her that he had created the feeling. What took place on Sunday morning was meaningless. The plain wedding was opposite of the ceremony with Darsa, regardless that he had betrayed her.

The first days of being Mrs. Handarbeni were full of lessons for Lasi, particularly regarding husband-wife relations and man-woman relations. She had learned one lesson from Pardi when she ran away from Karangsoga. Pardi's girls at every restaurtant along the route to Jakarata served him without a sense of obligation, and served other men who came along without a sense of guilt. Pardi understood that his girls would go with any man who paid them. He seemed fine with the situation, not caring.

At Ibu Koneng's restaurant, Lasi learned that intimacy between a man and a woman had no rules. It was as easy and cheap as buying peanuts. Prostitutes like the woman with big earrings and the one with chafed calves were ordinary people. They chatted, went to the market, laughed on the sidewalk, and danced to music on the radio.

"This isn't Karangsoga," Mrs. Lanting had told her. "Life is what we make of it. If we consider it difficult, life becomes difficult. If we consider it enjoyable, life is enjoyable. Las, I always view life as good and comfortable, and enjoy every moment. You must do the same." Out of all the advice Mrs. Lanting had given her, the one that touched her heart was, "The time has come for you to fulfill your destiny as the wife of a rich man. Why question destiny?"

Lasi learned to delight in her new world. She assured herself that she was beautiful and worthy of being part of rich people's lives—destiny could never be refused.

She was genuinely happy when Handarbeni invited her to Bali. At his insistence, she swam in the pool of a fancy hotel, wearing a thin, very tight swimsuit. He stood laughing by the pool's edge as many men stared at her. Soon, Lasi reveled at being the center of attention.

After almost a year as Handarbeni's wife, Lasi was an integral part of Jakarta's elite. What she had only dreamed about before, Handarbeni made a reality. Mrs. Lanting was right when she said that as long as she remained a beautiful and pliant doll, she would get whatever she wanted. Handarbeni pampered Lasi the way a lover of birds cared for his bekisar.

During that year, Lasi learned more about Handarbeni. Again, Mrs. Lanting was right: he was already married to two other women before her. He only spent three nights a week at the house in Slipi; she was amply compensated to take care of any problems.

Handarbeni was nearly impotent. He only had erections with the aid of drugs. This weighed on Lasi, but she had retained the Karangsoga way of thinking—a wife must accept her husband with his flaws. Yet, she was deeply disappointed to find that her marriage lacked desire.

"Yes, Las. Pak Han needs you primarily for show and prestige," Mrs. Lanting said when Lasi visited her. He needs to uphold his manly image to his friends and associates. Remember, he's the chief director of a big company. Do you have trouble with this?"

"I can accept the situation even if I find it burdensome."

"What do you mean?"

"Mas Han is a good man, except he has asked for the one thing I can't live with."

"What is it?"

Lasi remembered the night she and Handarbeni were in the bedroom. Both were exasperated at Handarbeni's inability to perform, even after taking his medicine. To salve Lasi's disappointment at such times, he promised to buy her all kinds of things and fulfilled his promises the next day. That night, Handarbeni made an offer that left her feeling cornered and insulted.

"Las, I'm an old man. I can't keep you satisfied. If you want, you have my permission to find satisfaction with another man. I have only one condition: say nothing about it and continue to live here as my wife. If need be, I'll find a man for you myself."

Lasi cringed, remembering his words.

Mrs. Lanting smiled. "Las, you still haven't answered my question."

Lasi sighed and told Mrs. Lanting everything in broken sentences. She hoped for understanding, but instead Mrs. Lanting exploded with laughter and clapped her hands.

"Oh, Las, what did I tell you? Pak Han is an incredibly good man, isn't he? Oh, how great your destiny has turned out."

Stupefied, Lasi glared at Mrs. Lanting from the corner of her eyes. She was disgusted.

"Las, you can have fun with any man of your choosing, and with the blessing of your rich husband. Aren't you pleased? So what will you do?"

A vacuum filled Lasi's chest. She was trapped in its silence. She wanted to change the topic, but Mrs. Lanting kept pressing her.

"If only I were you, Las."

"I can't do what he asks, bu."

"This is Jakarta, Las. I'm sure, while many of the wives here are faithful there are many who aren't. Your husband's proposal is not strange. You'll get used to it after a while."

"I can't. I truly can't."

"Las, you're still very young. Surely, you need a man. Wait a minute. Is it because you can't find…"

"No, bu. No. I can't have another man."

"Don't be a prude. You have the chance for a pleasurable and comfortable situation, and you refuse. Don't you think that's stupid?"

Lasi bristled. Her face darkened.

"It's not a matter of prudishness. Even imagining this is very odd to me. That's all."

Mrs. Lanting laughed again, and then stopped. She wiped the tears streaming down her nose and cast a serious gaze at Lasi. Her tone was softer when she spoke. "I'll give you a piece of advice: ask for a divorce. Don't worry, I guarantee that you won't be single for very long. As for the new husband, you leave that up to me. That's easy. I'll find you a husband who's richer and, more importantly, younger. Trust me. What do you say?"

Lasi froze.

"I've never thought about it."

"What's the matter with you? Why did you come to me?"

Lasi had decided earlier to accept Handarbeni with his flaws, including impotency, and suppress her needs for the sake of the husband who pampered her with an abundance of riches.

She pitied Handerbeni. He tried to please her day and night, even though during the night he failed more often than not. It was difficult to live by her decision because Handarbeni kept bringing up the proposal he had made: "You can find satisfaction with another man, as long as you say nothing about it and continue to live here as my wife."

His reminder became a disgusting habit. Every time he failed to satisfy her, he mentioned it. He ignored her pleas to stop talking about it. She protested and sulked. She said she refused to listen to such a perverted offer again.

"Why do you keep saying that?"

"You're very young, and I don't mind as long as you don't talk about it or ask for a divorce. Is that clear?"

Lasi cried at her own husband saying such a thing. A very strange world had opened up and dragged her in. She protested, and asked to go back to Karangsoga for a few days. "I miss my mother," she said.

Handerbeni frowned, but then smiled and agreed to let her go.

***

The rain let up when Lasi arrived at Karangsoga in the afternoon. She came with Min in a new Mercedes. It was the first time she returned to her mother's house since she married Handarbeni. The moment she stepped from the car, she took in the fresh air. She smelled rain-drenched moss and ferns, the soil of her birth. Once again, she was the center of attention, but only a few children dared get close. They surrounded the car, their eyes bulging.

Mbok Wiryaji ran along the footpath. She knew who had come. The sound of her feet hitting the wet earth mingled with her outburst of joy. She stopped steps away from her daughter. They stayed distant until Lasi stepped forward and held out her hand stiff and proper, without any signs of longing. Mbok Wiryaji was relieved when Lasi smiled and asked about her health.

Lasi stood beside the car, looking at rain-drenched Karangsoga. On a rainy day, she was usually unable to make enough palm sugar to buy a kilogram of rice. The smell of caramelized nira sent her floating into her past. She saw the caramel bubble and the thick steam rise to the ceiling. The reminiscence ended abruptly when Darsa entered into the picture. Lasi blinked then followed her mother. Min had gone ahead and carried her luggage to the house.

Mukri and his wife came over after sunset. So did San Kardi's wife and several other neighbors. Lasi noticed how Mukri and the others carried themselves that evening. They kept their distance and waited until she asked a question before speaking. The expression on their faces and the light in their eyes were different too. Her bracelet captivated Mukri's wife. Lasi almost blurted out the price, but thought better of it. Mukri's wife would have been shocked. If Mukri sold his house, his land, and all his palms, he still would need more money to buy the small bracelet on Lasi's wrist. Pak Tir, the richest man in Karangsoga, learned from one of his buyers that Lasi's car was worth more than his entire fortune.

For the three days since she had been home, Lasi wandered around the village. She noticed how much the villagers' attitude toward her had changed. Everyone strived to be on good terms with her, and their faces glowed when she spoke to them. Their eyes spoke of regret at having looked down at her in the past. Lasi smiled; she was relieved an old malice had been removed. She remembered her mother's advice: never think of yourself as better than other people.

Lasi traced the footpaths she used to walk every day. Stepping on the areca palm footbridge made her happier than she had been in a while. Crickets chirped and a mother hen clucked as she led her brood of chicks.

At the end of her wandering Lasi stopped at a neighbor's fishpond. A shabby outhouse stood above the pond, and Lasi needed to defecate. Even though she had been married to a rich man for some time, she had never gotten used to the sit-down toilet in the house at Slipi. The outhouse stood in the shade of the trees. A breeze carried the smell away, and Lasi relished emptying her bowels.

On the fourth night, it rained again. Lasi reveled in another fond experience from the past: sleeping in the brisk air with the sound of the rain lashing the bamboo grove and trees behind the house. The chick of a milky stork in the grove called out plaintively for its mother. A bullfrog's croak echoed through the valley.

Lasi woke in the middle of the night from the leak above her bed. She was unable to sleep until she heard the drum from Grandfather Mus' surau for the pre-dawn prayer.

The leak gave Lasi the idea to renovate her parents' rundown house while in Karangsoga.

With a renewed sense of purpose, she asked Min to send word to Jakarta that she would stay in Karangsoga a little longer. Then she asked about Pak Talab. Was he still in the construction business? Mukri said he was.

When Lasi went to see Pak Talab, he came out to greet her. It was the first time she had been warmly welcomed by the contractor. After a brief and direct discussion, they reached an agreement. Pak Talab was to build a new house for Mbok Wiryaji.

When she returned home, Lasi told her mother about her plan.

Mbok Wiryaji stared at her. "Las, you're not joking, are you?"

"No, Mother."

"I never asked you to do this. I didn't…"

"Don't worry, Mother. I can see how old the house is. I'm going to have it rebuilt and you're not going to lift a finger. I don't want Mas Han to get rained on when he sleeps here."

Mbok Wiryaji was stunned. She had become small in light of her daughter's importance. She bowed her head and swallowed. She was a spectator of the prosperity her daughter enjoyed. The feeling grew and grew. Her presence was so trivial that she was not consulted on rebuilding her own house. Mbok Wiryaji swallowed again.

With a guaranteed payment plan, the work on the house would be done in two months. During that time, Lasi traveled between Jakarta and Karangsoga three times.

On one occasion, she came with Handarbeni. The villagers were surprised at her husband's age. He was certainly old enough to be her father. Handarbeni ended any reservations by being friendly from the beginning. He spoke with everyone and pledged money to fix several of the footbridges in the village.

Mukri came to see her. "Las, you should visit Grandfather Mus."

"Oh, my God. I'd almost forgotten about him. How is the old man doing, Mukri?"

"He's healthy. Did you hear his wife died?"

"May she rest in peace."

"Yes, but that's not why I came to talk to you. Grandfather Mus' surau is very old. You've rebuilt your parents' house. Would you donate toward rebuilding the surau?"

"I've never thought about it. I only remembered Grandfather Mus when you mentioned him."

"In that case, there's no harm in seeing him."

"You're right. I'll go to his house very soon."

Lasi visited the old man the next day. Mukri was right: the surau was decrepit, and so was the house, so much that Lasi had to be careful opening the front door.

Grandfather Mus lifted his head when he heard Lasi's voice but stayed in his seat. In the year since she had last seen him, he had grown skinnier and slower. He had bags under his eyes, protruding cheekbones, and his voice was deeper. The poor man. Lasi had learned from Mukri that Grandfather Mus lived alone. One of his children lived nearby and brought him his meals every day.

"Grandfather…"

"Is that you, Las?"

"Yes, Grandfather."

Lasi was overcome by compassion, and guilt for having been in Karangsoga for a while and only now coming to see him. She pulled a chair next to him. He looked more fragile up close.

"Do you still play?" Lasi asked as her gaze fell on the gambang in its usual place.

"No. My hands shake too much and my fingers tingle."

"Grandfather, Mukri says your surau needs to be renovated."

The old man was startled and fixed his cloudy eyes on Lasi.

"Is it true?" Lasi asked.

"No," he said firmly. "I'm guessing Mukri asked you to pay for the renovation. Do you want to?"

"Yes, I do."

"Do you have enough money?"

"I do, Grandfather."

"Ah, there's no need. The surau continues to provide peace of mind to whoever kneels before God in there. It unites the community, and fits the surroundings and people's habits."

"Wouldn't you rather have a prayer hall with tiled floors and brick walls? A surau with bamboo walls is old-fashioned," Lasi said after a moment of silence.

Grandfather Mus smiled.

"No, Las. Having a fancy prayer hall will alienate the people who live in homes made of bamboo and sleep on straw. A nice prayer hall makes people feel like they're in a strange place."

"What about loudspeakers for the surau? Mosques and prayer halls everywhere have loudspeakers, Grandfather."

"No, Las, thank you. The mosque at the village hall has a loudspeaker, and the call to prayer reaches as far as here. If we were to put a loudspeaker at the surau, it would be too much."

Grandfather Mus fell silent, uncomfortable at having turned down Lasi's kindness. "Las, if you want to be charitable, Kanjat could really use it right now."

"Pak Tir's son needs financial help?"

"He's working on an experiment to process nira on a large scale, like a palm sugar mill, so the tappers can save on fuel. Kanjat plans to use a large pump stove to process all the nira from the villagers, but he doesn't have enough money."

"What about his father?"

"The poor young man. Pak Tir has never approved of his son's experiments. He's very disappointed because Kanjat enjoys fighting for the tappers' interests, which Pak Tir thinks is inappropriate for an engineer and a lecturer."

"Hold on. Kanjat wants to buy the nira from all the villagers?"

"That's what I hear. If the experiment works, the tappers can sell their nira without having to process it themselves. They'll have more time for working in the fields and the gardens."

"So the tappers won't have to sell sugar anymore?"

"That's how it's supposed to be. But go see Kanjat. He can explain the process to you. I don't fully understand it, but I believe Kanjat is a good man, and what he wants to try is for a good cause. Go help him."

Lasi stared straight ahead and her mind's eye filled with Kanjat. He had been on her mind ever since she returned to Karangsoga. Where was he hiding? Did he hate her? His image always populated Lasi's fantasies: his thick eyebrows and sharp gaze, his simplicity, laconic demeanor, and protectiveness of her. Lasi's heart raced. Once she had a naughty thought: she compared the old Handarbeni to to the young Kanjat.

She had yet to make a decision about Kanjat when she left Grandfather Mus, but she called for Mukri's wife the moment she returned to her parents' house.

Lasi wanted to know the days Kanjat could be found in Karangsoga. Mukri's wife gave her spirited and detailed information, and threw in a few embellishments.

For instance, a young woman, Hermiati, was close to Kanjat. She wore tight blue trousers, had shoulder-length hair, and sat like a man when riding a motorcycle.

"Is she beautiful?"

"Not as beautiful as you. Besides, she only rides a motorcycle, and you ride in a car."

"But she's close to him, right?"

"Yes, especially when they ride together. They get very close. Wait a minute, you haven't said why you want to meet Kanjat."

Lasi felt the heat on her face. She tried to conceal her feelings, and quickly composed herself.

"I heard that Kanjat has all kinds of plans but not enough money. Grandfather Mus asked me to help him." Her answer seemed to satisfy Mukri's wife.

The entire time Lasi was in Karangsoga, she burned with curiosity because she never saw Kanjat. Mukri's wife said that Kanjat came to Karangsoga every Saturday afternoon, either by himself or with a few friends.

The next morning, Lasi saw Pardi talking with Min on the path outside her parents' house. Lasi called Pardi and he ambled toward her with smoke wafting from the cigarette in his mouth, and his lips fixed in a grin. He sat down and his first words had her on the defensive. "Ah, great lady, it seems you remember me."

"Don't be like that, Di. I've never forgotten you. If it were not for you, I would have never gotten to Jakarta."

"In that case, share some of your wealth."

"Really? Do you want to buy cigarettes?"

"No, I'm just kidding."

"You're not taking any sugar to Jakarta?"

"I just got back this morning."

"Still with Sapon?"

"Yes, but Pak Tir's son no longer comes with us. Why is that, Las?"

Lasi's face reddened. Pardi was the only one who knew about her and Kanjat. Her heart thumped. She found it hard to speak.

Pardi grinned. He enjoyed seeing Lasi squirm. He also enjoyed how beautiful she looked, especially her eyes.

"Di, I want to see Kanjat. Help me. Do you know how?"

Pardi laughed and the cigarette almost fell out of his mouth.

Lasi scowled.

"The world sure is an odd place, Las. First, he insisted on seeing you and now you whine about seeing him. This is the great thing: have you forgotten you have a husband? What do you want when you're already rich?"

"Come on, Di. I only want to see him. Is that so difficult?"

Pardi laughed again. He ignored Lasi's reason. "Don't be childish, Las. You need help to meet your boyfriend?"

"Bastard. Just pass a message to Kanjat, that's all."

"Really?"

Pardi's eyes lit up when Lasi's cheeks flushed. Lasi bowed her head. Her smile was awkward but telling.

"Careful, I could report you to your husband."

"That's enough, Di. I'm not joking."

"Okay, okay. It's true that a lover is hard to forget," he said, smiling.

Pardi left shaking his head, the smile still on his face. Lasi was rich and more beautiful than ever, and yet she desired Kanjat. Maybe she really did want to help him, but her eyes indicated she wanted to see Kanjat about more than just money. Pardi shook his head again. The smoke continued to waft from his mouth.

Lasi thought many times about seeing Kanjat again. In her fantasy, he came to Jakarta and met her in a very private place. She confessed that she had been caught in circumstances, and her marriage to Handarbeni was beyond her control.

"Jat, will you help me?"

Kanjat looked at her with doubt in his eyes.

"How? You're a married woman."

"Jat, my marriage might not last very long. I can ask for a divorce and be single again. Will you elope with me?"

"You mean, get married?"

"Yes. The truth is I'm ashamed. I should know better as a twice-divorced woman. I'm older, too. What should we do? Mrs. Lanting says I'm beautiful. Is that true, Jat? Am I beautiful?"

"Yes, Las. You've been beautiful since we were kids." A mischievous smile crossed his face.

Lasi jerked out of her reverie. She smiled wryly when no one was around, much less Kanjat.

At their meeting the next day, Lasi gazed at Kanjat with hopefulness, restraint, and shyness. Kanjat's calm demeanor made her feel small, but her heart raced whenever he looked at her. Her palms were sweaty.

"You called for me, Las?" Kanjat asked after sitting down.

"Yes. Thank you for coming. Where have you been?"

"I wanted to see you too. I don't know where time has gone."

"Jat, were you avoiding me?"

"Not really. What do you want to talk about? Pardi said you wanted to help me."

"Oh, Jat, why do you ask like that? Sit with me for a moment."

Kanjat was silent. He felt forced into a corner. Lasi caused a ripple in his heart and with the power of her eyes, seemed to make a demand of him.

"Jat, I want to tell you something. You'll listen, won't you?"

"Yes, I'll listen. Tell me everything you want."

Lasi swallowed several times.

"Jat, you know that I have a husband again."

"Of course, Las. Everyone knows."

"But did you know that I, um… that I'm in a play marriage? It's not real."

Kanjat frowned as he listened to Lasi. He was a professional with a university degree. He understood what she meant, even if he was less than one hundred percent right. He knew where the conversation went when a wife complained about her marriage. He sighed.

"Jat, do you know what I'm saying?"

"Yes."

"Now, let's change the subject. Grandfather Mus said you have a plan that requires money. Maybe I can help."

Kanjat smiled, but Lasi could read his doubts. He shook his head as if he was wrestling with a dilemma.

"How about it, Jat?"

"Thanks for your offer. The plan has turned out to be difficult to implement."

Kanjat tried to explain the results of his scientific research to Lasi, who, although rich, only had a primary school education.

"In our test we found that processing the nira in bulk with a modern stove encountered many problems. The tappers wouldn't sell us their nira because this was new to them. They have a hard time accepting change. Their income decreased, even with extra time to do other things. For tappers, processing the nira is all they know.

Unfortunately, the only way they can benefit is if they get free fuel. The environment, the forests around Karangsoga, will have to bear the cost."

"And so?"

"Las, my friends and I have tried to help the tappers for more than a year, and the results are nil. We've introduced a chemical preservative for the nira and a compound to get it to crystallize. We also developed a stove that uses less firewood. But like I said, the tappers aren't accustomed to change. Very few wanted to use our stove." Kanjat looked sullen.

His forced smile made Lasi tremble and bow her head. "Have you failed, Jat?"

"At least I tried. The enormous and complicated problems the tappers face can't be solved with small measures. Things like habit, level of knowledge, and culture are all factors. On the outside, the tappers work in a sugar trade that is unfair, and has nurtured a deep dependence. Only through big efforts, careful planning, political wisdom, and plenty of funding can the quality of the tappers' life be repaired. We don't have that kind of power."

"What was that? The tappers are dependent?"

Kanjat laughed. Lasi had either missed what he said, or had trouble following the train of thought of an engineer's mind. The mood turned jovial. Lasi finally smiled. Kanjat wanted to look away from the beautiful dimple in her cheek that captivated him. The more he looked at it, the wilder his heart beat. Lasi felt his gaze on her and answered with a half-formed smile. Kanjat took a deep breath and leaned back.

"Las, have you seen the red stakes in the ground by the side of the road and the footpaths?"

"Yes, what are they?"

"Power poles, Las. Karangsoga will soon have electricity."

"That's great. I'll ask Pak Talab to set up a connection to my parents' house."

"Yes. By God, we're certainly grateful. Electricity will make life easier for the people of the village. The problem is with the tappers again. Many palms are going to be cut down to enable the power lines to pass through."

"Oh, yes, I see. The lines will spread everywhere."

"Yes. The tappers have told me they have to give up their palms. Their source of livelihood will be cut down with no compensation. I can't do anything. Do you remember Darsa?"

"What about him?"

"He only has twelve palms, and ten grow along the edge of the valley."

"Those will be cut?"

"He came to see me yesterday and I had to tell him I couldn't do anything. I went to the village chief, and even he is powerless."

"Poor Darsa."

"It's not just him. In the villages where there's already electricity, tappers have fallen from the palms after being zapped.

"Since they're not going to get compensation, they refuse to let their palms be cut down. Besides, most have no other source of income. As long as there's no wind or rain, they're safe. But when any movement makes the palm branches touch the wires, it's a different story."

Kanjat knew he should not look at Lasi, but failed. Every time his eyes took in her beauty, he felt a quiver heating the blood coursing through his veins.

"So Darsa might get zapped?"

"No, his palms will be cut down. The lines will pass through that area."

"And then?"

"Darsa was asked to migrate to Kalimantan, but he doesn't want to because all he knows is how to tap nira. They say that where they plan to move him, there won't be any palms he can tap."

Kanjat shook his head. He lost his enthusiasm talking about the tappers' problems. Resignation was written on his face until he suddenly straightened.

"Las, they're going to start cutting the palms tomorrow morning. Do you want to see it?"

"What about Darsa? Are they going to cut his palms?"

"Yes. I don't have the heart to watch him lose his livelihood, but I should stay until tomorrow. That's enough for now. I must be going." Kanjat was about to get up.

Lasi glanced at him then looked away. "Jat, stay with me a little longer."

"Is there more you want to discuss?"

"I just want to chat. Will you stay?"

Kanjat raised his eyebrows and smiled. "I think we've chatted enough. If you'll excuse me, Las."

"I heard you have a girlfriend."

For a moment, Kanjat was taken aback, but then laughed. Hermiati was dark, independent, and straightforward. She was a smart student at the university and a good friend, but not his girlfriend.

"Okay, Las. I'll be honest, but only to you. I haven't been fortunate, so I don't bother to think about dating. First, you were Darsa's wife and now you're married to another man. I really am unfortunate."

"Jat, can you forgive me?" Lasi asked without looking up. Her cheeks flushed and her lips trembled.

"You haven't done anything wrong. Really, Las, you haven't done the least bit wrong by me."

"Jat, sooner or later my marriage is going to end. That's for certain. And I'll be single again. That's for certain too…"

Lasi left what she wanted to say incomplete. She wiped tears from her eyes.

Kanjat took a deep breath. He rested his chin in his hand as he listened to Lasi give a halting account of her true circumstances.

"My marriage is very odd. No one in their right mind would remain in one like mine for long."

Lasi talked about Mrs. Lanting and how she had offered to help Lasi find a lover.

Kanjat listened, frowning. Behind the veneer of lofty prosperity, Lasi bore an enormous burden because she wanted to retain her honesty.

"Jat, if I wanted to be with someone bad, it would be very easy. I have all the means to do that. And like I told you, my husband permits it. I'm still good, Jat. The problem is, with no one to take me out of this situation, how long can I be good? When I'm single again, what will become of me? Can you tell me, Jat?"

Kanjat leaned back and wiped his forehead. Her problem was serious and complicated. He felt a calling that grew more distinct. The object was inside a cage impossible to enter.

"Jat, I'm sorry. I shouldn't have told you. I'm ashamed." Lasi sobbed.

Kanjat stayed quiet. When he found the words to speak, his voice was hoarse.

"Las, you don't have to be sorry. You weren't wrong to tell me."

"Then you really know how I feel?"

"Yes, I know."

Kanjat nodded and smiled. That gesture meant a lot to Lasi, who let out a deep breath. She felt relieved. She smiled again, and this time just for Kanjat.

"I'll be going now. That's all, right?"

Lasi nodded. Her eyes glistened and her smile deepened.

Kanjat stood up and smiled as he shook her moist and trembling hand. For a moment, Lasi almost gave in to what she truly wanted but held herself back. Kanjat brusquely started toward the door.

She followed him and stood in the doorway to watch him walk away. Kanjat had left unfulfilled desire in her heart, and he was already far away and out of sight.

***

Darsa woke earlier than usual after a nearly sleepless night. He had no reason to collect nira that morning because ten of his twelve palms were to be chopped down. Squatting on his front stoop, he brooded on why his life had always been so hard. He had barely recovered from divorcing Lasi over a year ago, and now he was about to lose his only source of income. Should he go to Grandfather Mus and ask why he had to suffer through no fault of his own? Following the divorce, the old man had cited Javanese philosophy and said he reaped what he had sown. *Now I'm losing ten palms, who is at fault? Is this destiny? And if so, is it fair?*

Darsa was unable to answer the questions in his heart. He could only laugh angrily as he tried to convince himself that people, especially the poor like him, must follow another tenet of Javanese philosophy and only accept things as they were.

He had felt better in the past few months, and found happiness with Sipah, the woman he had to marry. She gave him a child, cute and fair, and his lame wife had this over Lasi. For Darsa, the child was proof of his manhood, the evidence of his being. The baby woke before dawn with innocent and charming babble. Darsa felt whole and purposeful with a baby in the house. That Sipah remained lame no longer bothered him.

Darsa was less inclined to take his crippled wife to weddings. He never worried about leaving her on her own, even when he went to a *wayang* performance that lasted all night. Darsa believed the saying that one could have many wives, but only one soul mate. For him, that was Sipah. Darsa also became more convinced that Allah was indeed just. By accepting his life, his new wife had given him a child. He had never experienced that sensation from a wife as pure and beautiful as Lasi.

That morning the calm in his life had evaporated. As the sun climbed in the sky, the men who were to cut down the palms in the path of the power lines began to arrive. They were young and had never been to Karangsoga before. The men were ruthless, caring little about the pain of the tappers. They set to work with their chainsaws: mechanical, unmoved, and arrogant.

The men worked amid the noise of their chainsaws. In less than two minutes, the first palm fell. Children cheered when the trunk hit the earth, unaware of the rancor in their parents' hearts. It was the first time they had seen a chainsaw, and its raw mechanical power amazed them.

Roars from the chainsaws drew a large crowd to watch the palms fall. The villagers were silent and resigned. Kanjat stood among them. He stayed quiet except for his deep breathing. Lasi stood by his side.

The crowd followed the path of the tree cutters. They shared the same worry: what would happen to Darsa's grove?

Darsa squatted on a mound of dirt. The palms he had tapped every day would soon come crashing down. He imagined his baby, Giman, jumping like a flying lizard from one coconut palm to another, and thought of his tools: pongkors, stove, pot for cooking the nira, and scythe. He saw himself fall from the top of a palm into the depths of a ravine until he was jolted out of his visions by the sound of the approaching chainsaws, which sliced through his heartstrings with a tremor that tore at his soul. Darsa clenched his jaw. Rage flashed across his face and replaced a moment later with the look of helplessness.

Mukri spoke to him, and Darsa stayed mute. Mukri had lost three of his palms, but twenty-two were left. He tried to cheer up Darsa. His eyes were open with no life in them, like the knots in a bamboo stem, unblinking, empty. Darsa's face turned chalky when the chainsaw's blade touched the first of his palms. The machine whined louder and the palm trembled, leaning over slowly until it touched the ground. The bushes and shrubs near the palm were ravaged as well. Insects scattered willy-nilly.

"Darsa, there's nothing we can do but accept. The palms will be cut down anyway. Instead of being sad and disappointed we should resign ourselves."

Darsa remained unmoved. Another palm fell. A hanging pongkor splashed its contents on the ground near him. It was like watching the corpses of his wife and daughter lying on the dirt.

Mukri patted him on the shoulder. "Really, Darsa, it's pointless to be sad or fight against a power we can't possibly resist. Try to make a living from the two palms you have left."

The third palm quivered, swayed, and swept down before Darsa. It crashed to the ground, and the jolt rocked his chest.

Flickers of pain exploded in Darsa's heart. Giman leaped between the palms still standing. The baby cried, and Darsa almost cried too.

Soon the fourth, fifth, and sixth palms were felled. With the trunks of his palms crisscrossed on the ground, Darsa's grove looked like it had been ravaged by a storm. He began to sway as he squatted and Mukri grabbed him by the shoulder when he thought Darsa was about to fall over. Darsa stood as the chainsaw cut through his tenth palm and walked home, devoid of life. Kanjat followed him. Darsa walked an incline away from the cacophony of the palms being felled and the chainsaws whining, to drop from sight at the end of the climb.

Kanjat sighed and kept his head bowed until Lasi startled him back into the present.

"Let's go to Darsa's house."

She took him by the hand and they followed the same path Darsa had taken in silence.

Lasi and Kanjat expected to find Darsa sitting with a vacant stare after having lost his grove, but when they reached his house, he was calmly smoking a cigarette.

His carefree expression and clear voice welcomed them. Sipah stood next to him carrying the baby, and limped inside when she saw Lasi and Kanjat approach.

Lasi stood before her former husband. Her eyes were wet. Darsa looked down. Lasi saw the empty pongkors piled up on the side stoop, and the cold and dead stove. The woven bamboo walls were frail and full of holes. Kanjat, Lasi, and Darsa tried to smile. Each waited to see who would speak first.

"You've come to visit my wretched home. Thank you, but we have no chairs," Darsa said. "Is there something you need?"

"We just came to see you," Lasi said.

"You're not here to persuade me to go to Kalimantan?"

"No."

"Thank goodness. You should be like Mukri, who tells me to be patient and resign myself. He's right. I should be resigned."

Darsa smiled. He took a deep drag from his hand-rolled cigarette and exhaled. A shadow of relief appeared on his face.

Kanjat was silent. The tremendous irony weighed on him.

"Like Grandfather Mus said," Darsa went on. "The palms were cut down because it was predestined. It was destiny. Accept your destiny willingly, he said. Well, he's right. If I refuse to accept what I can't change, what should a tapper like me do?" Darsa smiled again. He even chuckled.

Kanjat stood still as Darsa's words and simplicity pressed on his spirit.

"You only have two palms left." Lasi said.

"With twelve palms, I harvested three kilograms of sugar. With only two, I get half a kilogram. How in the world can a tapper make a living with only two palms?" Darsa burst out laughing.

Kanjat and Lasi knew that half a kilogram of palm sugar was worth less than half a kilogram of rice.

"Maybe I'll sell firewood," Darsa said, in a jovial tone.

"The forest patrols are tighter. You might get caught and punished."

"If that's predestined, what can I do? Besides, how am I supposed to eat if I don't make a living from the forest? If that means getting arrested, I should resign myself." Darsa laughed.

Kanjat grimaced, the harshest grimace of his life. Darsa's words were like a tentacle of the octopus sucking dry Darsa and thousands of other tappers like him. The tentacles were so tough that a weak and demoralized man like Darsa could only say it was destiny. *If I don't accept this, what can I do? Go on?*

Kanjat let his anguish rage in his heart, but Lasi was different. She heard Darsa's laughter as the most tragic weeping, the kind that could only be heard when couched in laughter. She wiped her tears and felt the strength to push forward. She walked into the small, shabby house and found Sipah sitting and weeping. Lasi was thrown back to her past. She felt the pain in the broken heart of the tapper's wife when the stove no longer burned because there were no more palms to tap.

Lasi sat next to Sipah as she wept. She reached for her pocketbook and pulled out several crisp notes. "Give this money to Darsa. That's enough for your family to eat for a year if you rent coconut palms. There, stop crying."

Lasi pinched the baby's cheek and left.

Kanjat followed her. He could do nothing for Darsa, who had given up his livelihood for the power lines, but would never be one of those with electricity.

Lasi and Kanjat had nothing to say on the way back. They heard the chainsaws still at work, along with the chirping of birds and crickets. As they entered a footpath covered by trees, a pair of fantail birds chased one another in front of them. Kanjat and Lasi had chased each other down the same path when they were children. Lasi recalled how Kanjat always pressed his body close to hers whenever it was their turn to hide in a game of hide-and-seek.

The air was hushed.

"Jat, I'm going back to Jakarta tomorrow or the day after. You'll follow me, won't you?" Lasi asked.

Kanjat perked up and gulped. He was unready for Lasi's question, his heart still at Darsa's house.

"I'm a civil servant, Las. It's not easy for me to leave whenever I want."

"I still have your picture. Do you have mine?"

Kanjat tried hard to pull his thoughts from Darsa's house. He did have the photo of Lasi in the red kimono. He could never give it up, not even to Lasi.

He smiled and nodded.

Lasi laughed.

Oh, her smile, the hollow in her cheek, and the captivating power of her eyes. Kanjat looked away. He wanted his heart to be tranquil.

They stopped beneath the shade of a tree. Sunlight peered through the leaves and cast a white patch on Lasi's neck. They both felt awkward and continued their journey. The afternoon was quiet except for the chainsaws in the distance. Most of the villagers watched the coconut palms being cut down. The sunlight made playful patterns on their backs. They listened to the crackle of the leaves underfoot. Both found it hard to speak.

After they crested the incline, Kanjat took his leave at a crossroads. Lasi had a charm that made his heart flutter. She also had a husband. Lasi made him think of Darsa and Sipah and Giman. The baby's eyes had clenched his soul, like an indictment for his failure to lighten the tappers' burden.

Kanjat walked on as his thoughts shuttled between Lasi and Darsa. Lasi's admission that she was trapped in an absurd situation had invigorated his long-held attraction to her. He wanted Lasi be in a good marriage regardless of which man was her husband. To leave her in the indecent life she had been dragged into was wrong. Kanjat mustered the courage to admit that Lasi had always been the hope and dream in his soul. If he could find a proper and honorable way, marrying Lasi would be his first thought.

Darsa represented the world of the tappers, who called for Kanjat's support. The richer members of society, himself included, owed the tappers a very large debt. However, a large parasite in the form of an invisible structure had turned that debt into a fantasy no one spoke of. To Kanjat, society's debt to the tappers was very real, and he had failed to pay his share. Their hardship would be an everlasting debt.

PART TWO: ORION

Chapter 7

The temperature in Handarbeni's office was set at sixty-five degrees, yet he felt hot and arid. He had hung up the telephone a few minutes earlier, but the conversation reverberated clearly, stinging his ear and his heart. Bambung, that ogre of a man wanted to borrow Lasi.

Handarbeni's Adam's apple bobbed; he swallowed several times and clenched his jaw. Bambung, known among the elite in the capital as a high-level lobbyist, had spoken in his style full of intrigue, metaphor, and subtlety. Slippery, twisty, and entrapping. The way he spoke held everyone captive. The strength of his intrigue was evident, even when couched as a joke.

He's actually great, Handarbeni thought. No wonder Bambung had managed to become such an important lobbyist, political and power broker, or whatever else he was called. He used words and language as weapons to leave others vulnerable, paralyzed. More than that, he left them defeated and bent to his will.

While Bambung had spoken in veiled sentences, his meaning was clear: he wanted to borrow Lasi, Handarbeni's beautiful red bekisar, for the weekend.

Handarbeni envisioned the fit-looking man with a head of thick graying hair, oval face, and powerful gaze. He suppressed his envy of the man's virility, for Bambung appeared to still have it, even though he was in his sixties too.

169

It was more than his virility; Bambung was truly accomplished. In privileged circles at the highest levels of power, people speculated about his background and the strength of his lobbying.

Some said he worked as an agent for a consortium of foreign oil companies. It was he, they said, who skulked behind the intrigues and conspiracies that allowed the petro dollars to flow into Jakarta after Sukarno was cast aside. The large amounts of petrodollars made it imperative the government adopted a production sharing system for the oil industry that benefited the foreign entities immensely.

This position gave Bambung tremendous influence over policy makers in the government, in particular those who decided on economic policy. When the economy became the focus of the new government, they once again relied on Bambung. He was like an octopus, with tentacles grabbing everything around him, an invincible influence that continued to grow.

Others said Bambung worked as a broker for international financial institutes. He had managed to win the trust of the international loan sharks with eye-catching logos, and paved the way for foreign investors. No wonder Bambung's lobbying carried so much weight; foreign funds would always be the backbone of the domestic economy. This was truer than ever now that oil, once the prime commodity of exports, had lost its sheen because the market system continued to be controlled by the big countries, and the wells were running dry.

Another rumor cast Bambung as a shaman. Supernatural power lay behind his contemporary, incredibly wealthy, and pragmatic lifestyle. Only a shaman could be an agent for the oil consortium or a broker of the financial institutions. Foreigners trying to do business in Jakarta understood the need to consider the influence of shamanism.

Bambung's powers also gave rise to plenty of rumors in political circles. Anyone looking for a seat in parliament, a post as director general of a ministry, governor, bank director, political party chief, or chairman of a professional association would only succeed with Bambung's recommendation.

These rumors swirled around Bambung, the prime lobbyist. And now he wanted to borrow Lasi. The bastard.

Handarbeni roused himself from his stupor and paced the room. He scratched his head and wiped his brow. He felt incensed and insulted. Son of a bitch. His eye caught the telephone and he stopped. Mrs. Lanting. That old hag of a pimp who enjoyed dating young men was the perfect person to consult about Bambung's insane intentions.

At first Handarbeni found it difficult to talk about the phone call that had knocked the wind out of him. He stuttered while opening the conversation, but the more he talked, the easier it became, until in the end, everything gushed out like water from a broken pipe.

"What should I do in this situation? Must I give up my bekisar, even though he says he only wants to borrow her? What should I do?"

"Hold on, Pak Han. You're chattering like a conductor who's missed his bus. Tell me, who is it that wants to borrow Lasi? There are many lobbyists in Jakarta."

"Please, don't pretend. Only one has the reputation of being the best and you certainly know who he is. He's the craziest of the lot."

The line went silent for a moment.

"Is… is he the one who officiated at the opening of that exclusive restaurant… and also the school for orphans? The one who gave several thousand dollars to the Indonesian Red Cross?"

"That's the one."

Handarbeni heard Mrs. Lanting burst into laughter. He pictured her corpulent body shake.

"It's hardly surprising, is it? You know what he's like. That old ram is a maniac, and he's unbelievably horny and greedy outside his home. But at home, he doesn't dare budge from under the wing of his old, nagging first wife. Why are you so worked up? Don't you understand, or are you just pretending not to know what a womanizer he is?" Mrs. Lanting laughed again.

To Handarbeni, her words were harsh and hurtful. He snorted, angry that he had become the object of ridicule.

"Pak Han, where did he see your bekisar? How did he meet her?"

"At a Japanese restaurant."

"Here in the Cikini area?"

"Never mind. It doesn't matter where the old goat saw Lasi. I'm really sorry for bumping into him when I was with her. I truly regret it. What should I do?"

"Why ask me this kind of a question? Did you tell him that Lasi is your wife?"

"He said he knew Lasi was my wife. Yet he insisted."

"He knows the way you treat women: easy come, easy go. It's no secret you drool when you see a beautiful woman and don't care if she's someone else's wife. Now the tables have turned. It's only natural, isn't it?"

"Don't talk like that. I don't think of Lasi that way. She's my special bekisar."

"Yes, Pak Han, but I'm surprised your values suddenly have become those of a normal person. What has turned you old-fashioned? Just take it easy. If Bambung wants to borrow Lasi, you have two choices: keep her for yourself and risk having to face Bambung's lobbying power which means putting your job as director of Bagi-Bagi Niaga and your political career on the line, or hand over your bekisar and your position remains secure. It's that simple."

"Wait a minute. I'd hate to give up just like that. Besides, no matter how influential he is, he's not my superior."

Once again, Handarbeni heard Mrs. Lanting laughing.

"Pak Han, what's with you? What has made you so thick skulled? Even though Bambung no longer holds an official position, he's still Bambung. His lobbying network is solid and sophisticated. I know this very well. He is truly someone to reckon, he's brilliant. With his power, he can penetrate the bureaucracy above you, and his influence can affect your position. You don't believe me?"

Handarbeni drew a deep breath. He was about to speak when Mrs. Lanting resumed.

"Pak Han, please forgive me, but…"

"Yes?"

"Aside from Bambung being so great, there's something strange about you these days."

"How so?"

"You've given Lasi quite a bit of freedom, and allowed that bekisar of yours to find another man, as long as she stays quiet and remains married to you. Why are you all wound up because Bambung wants to borrow her?"

Handarbeni bit his lip. He frowned as perspiration filled the creases in his forehead. Damn it, Lasi had revealed their secret to that old Manila duck, Mrs. Lanting. "I should just submit to that lobbyist?" he asked after a long silence.

"I didn't say that. On one hand, you've given Lasi this freedom, even though I know she hasn't used it. On the other hand, you've become desperate when Bambung wants to borrow your bekisar. Why?"

Handarbeni found it difficult to answer the question and another silence ensued.

"Why are you so quiet, Pak Han?" Impatient, Mrs. Lanting prodded him. "Should I hang up?"

"Wait. I did give Lasi that freedom, if indeed she choses to use it. Rather than leave her unsatisfied with what I can give her and have her looking for it on the sly, I gave her the opportunity as long as she acts on my terms. I choose the man, the place, and the time. Of course, everything has to be done in the strictest confidentiality."

"What's the difference? In both instances you're still lending your bekisar."

"If that horny goat gets Lasi, he'll definitely play with my bekisar without my supervision. He will humiliate me everywhere, and I won't accept that. Even if I did agree, I'm faced with another problem."

"Which is?"

"Lasi is human. She's her own woman. She might refuse to be loaned out, and if that happens, my position becomes more precarious. Bambung will blame me for Lasi's refusal to go with him."

"That's certainly what will happen, Pak Han."

"Do you have any advice?"

Mrs. Lanting answered with a small cough.

"Oh, I see," Handarbeni said hastily. He remembered he was speaking with a high-level pimp, a sex broker, to be precise. "Of course there's a reward if you can tame that devil and keep him from disturbing my bekisar."

"But you just said that would be impossible because the consequences would be too dire. If she refuses, it's going to be doubly complicated for you."

Mrs. Lanting let the silence hang between them. She smiled to herself, the receiver pressed to her ear. Her hand was practically inside Handarbeni's pocket. "To be honest, Pak Han, I know the devil very well. He's going to make your life difficult when he doesn't get his way. Let him borrow your bekisar. That's the least amount of trouble you'll face. Besides, Pak Han, as much as you like your bekisar, you can always find another."

Handarbeni let out a long breath. "I'm still left with the problem of Lasi. Will you convince her?"

"I'm willing to try. Who knows, I might succeed. But you won't forget, will you?"

"I really am cursed. I have to loan my bekisar to another man, and I have to pay the broker too. Damn it. That bastard. Shit."

Mrs. Lanting laughed. "Come now, Pak Han, it's better than losing your job and political career. You can always find a new bekisar. Don't worry, I'll help. Do you want one with Chinese, Arab, Spanish, or Jewish blood? Or how about a Chinese-Papuan mix? The latter are today's fad."

"Don't add to my heartache. Just take care of Lasi and arrange the date with that bastard. I don't want to hear any more about it. Just tell me when everything is done. You only have until Saturday morning, which is four days away.

"Yes, boss. Just take it easy and go earn the money to buy a new bekisar. Bye-bye, Pak Han."

Handarbeni held the receiver to his ear after Mrs. Lanting had hung up. He seemed lost for a moment, and then wiped his forehead and put the receiver down. For no real reason, he pressed the small button on the side of his desk. A moment later, the door to his cool office opened and Oning, his secretary, came in.

"Yes, sir? What do you need?" she asked with a contrived smile. She had the face of an adolescent.

"Did I call you?"

Oning was confused. She stared at Handarbeni with genuine concern, fearing she had done something wrong. She had only been his secretary for a few weeks, replacing the previous one, who had gone into public relations at a hotel.

Handarbeni smiled. It was all he could do. He looked at Oning. Sweet, naïve, and still a child, her father, one of his comrades during the revolution, had put her under his care. Handarbeni found the situation funny: why would his old friend trust him with a girl as sweet as Oning?

"I may be old and weak at times, but I'm not impotent," Handarbeni had once blurted out to Mrs. Lanting.

Handarbeni preferred not to make a move on Oning. He enjoyed the distance between them that left Oning confused and scared. Oning, as pretty as she was, would never hold a candle to his bekisar. Or a more trivial reason: he didn't have the heart to touch a girl fresh from her childhood, and the daughter of a friend.

Handarbeni was often tempted by the thought that Oning had been presented to him. Her father could barely afford to raise eight children, and by giving him his eldest daughter, he might have hoped for an improvement in his household's cash flow.

"Pak?" Oning stammered after standing in confusion.

"Oh, sorry, On. Please call Min."

"Are you going out? It's lunchtime."

"No. Tell Min I need a massage. As for lunch, please take care of it. I'll eat here."

Oning left to call Min. She knew he was more than a driver. He was also Handarbeni's personal masseur.

When Min entered the office, Handarbeni lay face down on the couch with his shirt off and a sleeveless undershirt covering his fat upper body.

"You don't feel well, pak? Min asked.

"My neck is stiff and hurts. My forehead is heavy and my chest constricted."

"You might be catching a cold."

"It's just dizziness, and I have too many problems. Pak Min, why does life suddenly become mixed up? Has that ever happened to you?"

The question baffled Min. He began kneading the muscles in Handarbeni's back, neck, and shoulders.

Min came from Central Java, and although he had lived in Jakarta for decades and married a local woman, he clung to his Javanese ways. Min believed he was destined to be of no importance, and Handarbeni's question bothered him. Why would he have problems? What could he possibly want?

Min had known Handarbeni since he was a child. His father had served Handarbeni's father, a government official in charge of several sub-districts around the foot of Mount Merapi. Min knew his employer had lived in luxury from childhood. He believed his master was among those who had been pre-ordained to live in comfort.

In his younger days, Handarbeni had been undisciplined—from being a poor student to misconduct with the women who came to the market at dawn, and playing cards. There were rumors he had hid behind the line of fighting during the war for independence. Yet, fortune smiled on him and he was prosperous.

Min, who knew a little of Javanese mysticism, saw his employer as someone who had attained all the joys of life.

Handarbeni had everything he needed: power, wealth, many houses, more cars than his garage could hold, and, of course, women.

He had one official wife, and several others he had married on the sly. And that wasn't counting his mistresses. How could he be burdened with problems?

"Pak Min, answer my question."

"Ah, sorry. What was it you asked?"

"Why does a life so soft and breezy suddenly turn so hot it causes a headache?"

"Oh, that, pak. How can I ever answer?"

"I know you like to pretend to be stupid. I'm sure you can answer my question."

"Honestly, pak, I can't."

"Yes," Handarbeni insisted. "This isn't the first time I've asked you. Stop pretending."

Min continued massaging Handarbeni's back as he tried to think of something to say. He finally said, "Pak, I can only repeat the advice my late father gave me. It's from an old farmer who never stepped inside a classroom."

"What was the advice?"

"To live in peace, a man must be aware, take the good with the bad, and never indulge in his desires."

Unseen by Min, Handarbeni smiled.

"I've heard that before, and it's boring. I'm already aware. I'm not drunk, I'm not passed out, and I'm not asleep. That's being aware."

"Pak, you're pretending you don't know."

Handarbeni felt satisfied with goading Min. He knew what it meant to be aware, but had never been able to act accordingly. He would lose much of the joy in his life if he did. Meanwhile, Min found the courage to continue talking.

"My father once said that to be aware means having a connection with *Gusti Kang Murbeng Dumadi*, The God Who Precedes All Intentions."

Handarbeni pretended to be interested. "What about indulging in one's desires?"

"My father said a man must limit his desires to those things he truly needs."

"You're clever, Pak Min. Go on."

"A man who doesn't limit his wants to what he needs, and allows those wants to expand and become needs, will never be at peace. During his life he is pursued by his wants that keep growing without limit."

"Pak Min, a man has to have ambitions and desires. Men have to go after what they want, or what they dream about. If not, they're miserable and might as well die. A man without ambition and who accepts things as they are will never advance. Shall I give you an example?"

"Yes, pak," Min said.

"The example is yourself. Your father used to be a servant in my parents' home, and you're my driver. Will your child be my child's driver or servant?"

Min laughed.

"Why are you laughing?"

"I'm sorry, pak."

Min fell silent. Handarbeni made him think of Sabar, his eldest child. Even though his father was just a driver, Sabar had graduated from the Bandung Institute of Technology and received a scholarship to continue studying in Japan. Sabar would never work as a driver.

Min also thought of Handarbeni's children, who were just like their father when he was young—with the addition of drugs, pointing a gun at one of their father's employees, and bouncing checks. The daughter was just as reckless. If not for Wasis—Handarbeni's son from either his second or third wife, and a well adjusted doctor—who knew what would become of the wealthy family?

"Pak Min, you're quiet again."

"It's hard to say, pak. Let me put it like this: *kejawen* doesn't prohibit a person from having wants, as long as they're good, and *sakmadya* is so they don't go beyond need. Without limits in place, a want can very easily become a desire. I'm not saying you always indulge in your desires."

Handarbeni said with a laugh, "I've heard this sort of advice very, very often. And I understand. I also believe it, I truly do. Don't forget that I'm a Javanese nobleman."

"You believe in the importance of the kejawen sayings?"

"I'm Javanese nobility from head to toe. I believe in all the kejawen sayings, but a nobleman who believes in them doesn't have to live by them, does he?"

"What do you mean, pak?"

"Pak Min, those sayings are a talisman to Javanese noblemen like myself. A talisman, that's all. In reality, more noblemen flout the sayings than abide by them. Let's look at the five no's: no playing around with women, no gambling, no drugs, no drinking alcohol, and no stealing. As far as I know, stealing is the only thing a Javanese nobleman refrains from.

"Perhaps not. A nobleman like myself never steals from a neighbor, but from the country? Is taking public money wrong for a nobleman? Officials who are convinced they are noblemen run the state.

"Javanese noblemen gamble, drink, and play around with women. They also use opium if they can handle it. Only stealing ruins their reputation, and that's if it's done in a stupid and obvious way. If the theft is subtle, and better still, the money is stolen from the country, hahaha…"

"Is that how it is, pak?"

"Yes. The ones trusted to receive revelations of power are the noblemen and those who consider themselves noble. Noblemen believe they have a limitless right, justified by cultural beliefs, to control everything around them, including all available sources of wealth."

"Even for their personal interests?"

"Hahaha. If they want to, who can stop them? They are justified by cultural beliefs."

"That was before, when we lived in the time of kingdoms," Min said, his expression ingenuous. "Is it still like that today? We've been a republic for awhile. Even during the Dutch colonial times, the country's wealth was managed properly, with no room for misappropriation."

"Pak Min, you're a wise guy, but correct. It really was like that. We have to admit the colonial administration was much more orderly. It's a shame the spirit of our revolution burned down everything linked to the Dutch.

"That's how it is, Pak Min. Today many officials, whether a nobleman or not, have the same mentality as the feudal lords. This continues to thrive and is being revived.

"We've since long been a republic, shaped by the minds of the noblemen. I just dance to the beat of the drum. I'm proud of my nobleman's status and spirit even though I'm involved in the administration of a republic... which is actually a make-believe republic."

"And you believe the kejawen sayings are just a relic?"

"That's right. Most noblemen don't follow the sayings, no matter how precious."

"Then who are the sayings for?"

"The farmers and the little people like yourself," Handarbeni said with a loud laugh.

"If you believe in the sayings and don't live by them, what is the use? Knowledge or faith is only useful when it is the basis for one's behavior."

"Yes, I believe that wholeheartedly, and I treat it as a relic."

Min was caught in his employer's words. Of course, a Javanese nobleman like Handarbeni must know of kejawen. It befuddled Min that his employer preferred to flout rather than comply with the principles he knew so well and took such pride in. Was that hypocrisy?

"Pak," Min sounded doubtful. "I believe I've adressed your question to the best of my ability."

"What's your answer?"

"It's hard to put into words. To find peace, a man must be mindful or aware, be able to control himself, and not indulge in his desires. That's about it. You said yourself, that you know the principles but refuse to treat them as anything more than a relic. So be it. I can't say anything else."

Handarbeni quietly smiled. He lay face down with his eyes shut, but remained awake.

Min left quietly, and took with him Handarbeni's theory regarding Javanese cultural values.

After the driver left, Handarbeni sat up and stared at the floral-print rug. The image of three people moved into his vision.

First, there was Lasi, with her exotic eyes and the dimple in her cheek. The bekisar was truly worth owning. Then came Min, always calm and clear-headed because he abided the kejawen principles. Bambung, who had his eye on Lasi, followed them.

When he thought of Bambung as a Javanese noblemen like him, and equally hypocritical when it came to principles, Handarbeni felt a tingling in his stomach. He almost burst out laughing, but instead yelled curses. "Bastard. Son of a bitch."

Handarbeni decided to let things run their course. He was deeply disappointed and very tired. When he realized it was no use going up against Bambung's power and influence, he relaxed and steeled himself to act indifferent and apathetic. His breathing grew gentler, and he fell fast asleep. He missed Oning calling him on the intercom that lunch was ready.

***

Lasi restlessly waited for Mrs. Lanting on the terrace of her mansion in Slipi. The fat woman had called her earlier that morning. She was the only friend Lasi had and her visits were always enjoyable.

Despite having lived in Slipi for more than a year, Lasi had yet to talk with her neighbors. She had problems accepting the situation and often missed her life in Karangsoga. Everyone in the village knew each other; the bonds between them were so tight that not congregating was considered wrong.

What made things worse for Lasi was that after her marriage to Handarbeni, she wasn't truly his wife or part of Jakarta, her husband's world. She was merely an accessory to the rich man's life. She remained alone, unassimilated.

Lasi did enjoy the opulent lifestyle she never had imagined would be hers. The beautiful house had a swimming pool and came with everything imaginable. She had clothes and jewelry, and a car. She ate whatever she desired, bought whatever she fancied, and watched whatever movie she wanted to see at home. Mrs. Lanting was right when she said that to be Handarbeni's wife meant to live a good and comfortable life of prosperity. Lasi never had to lift a finger, except for her personal needs.

She lived in a make-believe world, while she knew there was a real world, the one she still looked for.

With Darsa, Lasi had a sense of purpose and an acute awareness of being present. She cooked for her husband and washed his clothes; she also was the one who cooked the nira and turned it into the sugar they sold. Lasi may have sweated at her work, but relished being in the real world. As hard as life was with her husband, they shared good times and bad, and celebrated their togetherness. Their life in Karangsoga was looked down on as one of misery, hunger, and sickness, but it felt more wholesome, understandable, transparent, and tangible.

Lasi had clearly understood her role and significance in the deep and beautiful quality of the home. That quality had vanished from the pampering that came with being an accessory in an obscenely rich house.

She tried hard to understand what Mrs. Lanting meant when she said that money was the most important. Only with money, Mrs. Lanting often said, could a person live well. It was nonsense to think anyone could live well without it.

To some degree, Lasi understood. Yet, the world of plenty remained unfamiliar; one she indulged in, but never fully adopted. She felt like the day she had escaped from Karangsoga, riding in a truck that sped toward an unknown destination and she was unable to get out. For Lasi, that was the best analogy. She was a stranger in her own life, like a passenger locked inside a speeding car, not knowing where she was being taken.

Lasi often asked herself: *Where will this lead me?*

That morning was a good example. After getting dressed up and looking at pictures in a magazine, she ate and drank her fill and talked with her husband on the telephone. She then wondered, *What else is there to do? Sleep? Shop? Eat in a restaurant?*

People had to work. Her mother, who had shaped her character, taught her that lesson. Working had always been a necessity when she was a child. Lasi found meaning and purpose by working. When she was idle, she felt like a burden, an empty cocoon that never hatched. But what work could she do?

Handarbeni told Lasi to banish her boredom by shopping and traveling. After all, everything to make this happen was already in place. For the first couple of times the advice worked like a charm. Rather than sit at home, Lasi went to the Sarinah department store and for a drive around the city. Soon boredom caught up with her again.

Lasi was happy when Mrs. Lanting telephoned her that morning. The fat woman who waddled like a duck was coming over. Whatever the purpose of the visit, Lasi would have the chance to talk and shake off her weariness.

She almost ran when Entang, her other driver, announced a taxi had pulled up outside the front gate. Mrs. Lanting stepped out of the vehicle and gave her a wide smile. The smile was filled with satisfaction for having transformed Lasi into Mrs. Handarbeni, and reminded Lasi of a large unpaid debt.

"I haven't seen you in two weeks and you've changed, Las," Mrs. Lanting said, walking toward her.

"I've changed, bu?"

"You've put on some weight. Be careful. It's okay that I'm fat but not you. Take care of your figure. I tell you, a woman's figure is extremely valuable these days. You can be a little ignorant as long as your legs, neck, and arms are beautiful. A shapely body can change a woman's destiny. With an attractive body, a woman can enjoy a lavish life. You really have to take care of yourself. Believe it or not, for women in this city, a beautiful body is everything."

Lasi smiled. She was uninterested in what Mrs. Lanting said. She stepped ahead of her to open the front door and invited Mrs. Lanting to have a seat.

Mrs. Lanting looked around the foyer and the living room and smiled. When she finally sat down, she continued to scrutinize the porcelain urns, Italian tiles, aquarium by the window filled with piranhas, small jade statues, and the new curtains that probably came from Belgium.

Lasi stayed quiet. She felt like a student who watched her teacher check her homework. Mrs. Lanting might criticize how she had arranged the items in the room, even though she had tried hard to replicate what she remembered from Mrs. Lanting's house. Lasi was relieved when she smiled again.

"What did I tell you? It's not hard being a rich man's wife, is it? Look, you've managed to arrange the decorations well. Some of it doesn't look quite right, but it'll do."

Lasi smiled at the compliment. She excused herself to fetch the drinks. There was liveliness in her step. Behind her, Mrs. Lanting's smile turned sour. She envied Lasi's beauty, something she would never have.

"Take good care of the house and your body, and your husband is bound to return to you every night," Mrs. Lanting said when Lasi returned. "He'll forget about his other wives." She laughed, and Lasi blushed.

Mrs. Lanting pulled out a thick envelope. "Las, do you know what's inside?" she asked, her eyes twinkling.

Lasi stared for a moment and then shook her head.

"Two plane tickets to Singapore for this afternoon. We've been cooling our heels in this crowded and traffic-clogged city for too long. Let's have a change of scenery. Get ready. I'll pick you up this afternoon and we'll go to the airport together."

Confusion and happiness spilled across Lasi's beautiful face. Her lips moved, but didn't make a sound.

"Don't worry, Las. I'll only take you if Pak Han allows it. Call him now."

Lasi went to call Handarbeni. She returned to the living room with a bright smile and a light in her eyes.

"He said yes?" Mrs. Lanting asked.

Lasi nodded, her smile bringing out the dimple in her left cheek.

"It felt like he was forced to agree. His voice was heavy."

"Maybe he's just very busy. It happens, Las. When a man's busy, he loses his warmth. But you need to get ready. It's ten now. I'll be back at twelve-thirty."

"Yes, bu."

"Las, bring a change of clothes. If you get tired, we can stay the night."

Mrs. Lanting was back at exactly twelve-thirty. She stayed in the taxi.

Lasi joined her, carrying a small bag. She was immediately struck by Mrs. Lanting's makeup, which looked overdone. Makeup was her vain attempt to stave off old age.

In the airplane, Mrs. Lanting's excitement was evident in her non-stop chatter. When the stewardess offered something, she responded with, "No, thank you. I need nothing."

Lasi remained quiet, and occasionally forced a smile at what Mrs. Lanting said.

"From the airport we'll go straight to the shopping center. I want to buy a Saint Laurent bag and a De Beers ring. Maybe also shoes or the newest watch from Lanvin or… What would you like, Las?"

"I don't know yet. I'll find something when we get to the shopping center."

"Are you scared your bank balance is going to shrink? Come on, that's how a country girl thinks. How about this, Las: you can buy whatever you want up to a hundred thousand US dollars, on my account. That's a pretty sweet deal, don't you think?"

"Oh, don't do that, bu. I still have plenty," Lasi tried to preserve her dignity. "I'll shop with you, but only with my money."

"Of course you have plenty. You're Mrs. Handarbeni, after all. Okay, then, we'll go shopping. After that, don't become jealous, okay?"

"Why should I be jealous?"

"I wouldn't be going to Singapore if I just wanted to shop. I plan to meet my boyfriend later. I may be old and fat, but I can still have fun. People say that because I missed dating when I was younger, I'm trying to make up for it now. So be it. I like going out with men even though I'm in my fifties. What can I say, it's good. I have a date today. And you, who is young and beautiful, are you jealous?"

Lasi feigned a smile.

"How's Pak Han? Has he recovered from his impotence or is it worse?"

"Oh…" Lasi blushed.

"Well, it's not easy to cure, especially for a man over sixty. Can you accept him the way he is?"

Lasi's froze at Mrs. Lanting's insistent line of questioning. *Does Mrs. Lanting know that I'm starting to feel lonely?* Lasi thought.

Mrs. Lanting tried to set Lasi at ease with a smile. Her attempts to pique Lasi's envy were cut short by the announcement that the plane would be landing soon. She stopped talking and busied herself with her seatbelt. Landings always made her anxious.

As they exited the arrival gate, a Chinese man held up a piece of cardboard with Mrs. Lanting's name.

"I'm Mrs. Lanting. Are you here to pick me up? Do you speak Malay?"

"Yes. You're expected at the Orchid Hotel," the man said in quite good Malay.

"You hear that, Las? My boyfriend's waiting for me at the hotel," Mrs. Lanting said as she nudged Lasi's arm. She smiled impishly, like a teenage girl.

"First take us to the shopping center."

"All right, bu. I'll inform him of the change of plans over the car phone."

Once at the exclusive shopping center, Mrs. Lanting quenched her thirst for spending. She bought everything she had mentioned on the plane.

Lasi became caught up in the shopping spree as well. She bought Italian shoes, a Cartier handbag, and a ring worth twenty thousand dollars. That was enough for her but Mrs. Lanting goaded, "Why come here if you're only going to get that? This isn't Pasar Rumput. This shopping center is for the wives of the richest men in all of Asia. Look at this diamond pendant. Mrs. Handarbeni deserves to wear a forty-thousand-dollar pendant."

Lasi's eyes lit up when she saw the De Beers pendant and gave in to Mrs. Lanting's persuasion.

When they were done, Mrs. Lanting took Lasi to a heavily guarded room with a discrete front. A guard asked to see Mrs. Lanting and Lasi's passports and made a note of them before escorting the women inside.

"I've brought you here to see a necklace that costs one-and-a-half million US dollars, which is I don't know how many billion rupiah. There it is."

Lasi looked at the small item inside a thick glass case.

Mrs. Lanting kept talking. "That one necklace could pay for every man and woman in your village to go on the Hajj. In Jakarta, all the wives and mistresses of the businessmen are wearing them. You could have one too, Las, if you wanted. If your husband won't buy it for you, I can arrange to make it yours. Do you believe me?"

Mrs. Lanting cackled, oblivious to the attention from the guards. Lasi was embarrassed, but she smiled, never taking her eyes off the necklace. She thought the price was exaggerated. When she turned, Mrs. Lanting was no longer in the room and Lasi saw her at the cashier's desk.

"It's done, Las. Your bill didn't even come to a hundred thousand dollars. I've taken care of it. Come on, let's go. The things we bought will be sent to the hotel."

Lasi was dumbstruck at being obliged to Mrs. Lanting. There was plenty of money in her bank account. Mrs. Lanting had no reason to pay.

"Come on, Las. Why do you look so troubled? It's like you don't know me."

Mrs. Lanting took Lasi by the hand and they walked out of the shopping center. The Chinese driver waited for them with the reverence of a valet to a grand madam. Soon the luxury car headed for the Orchid Hotel. They drove through clean and orderly streets. Even Lasi could tell the difference between Jakarta, with its filth and chaos, and Singapore, orderly and clean.

In the hotel lobby, a man about the same age as Handarbeni, but slimmer, waited for them. He looked athletic with a flat stomach and deep black eyes. His clothes, shoes, and tie were clearly of the best quality money could buy. What distinguished his appearance were his thick sideburns, which were white while the hair on his head was gray. The frames of his sunglasses accented the oval shape of his face, making him look strong. Ambition and a zest for life were folded in his gaze. Yet, when he smiled he looked like a calm and understanding man. For a moment, Lasi wanted to hold on to the smile of this man she assumed to be Mrs. Lanting's boyfriend.

Her guess was proven correct when Mrs. Lanting rushed toward him, embraced him, and kissed him on the cheek. "Let me introduce you to my boyfriend, Las. Don't say he's old, because I'm no spring chicken myself. What's important is that he's manly."

Lasi clasped the hand offered to her. "Mrs. Handarbeni," she said, but missed his name.

After a bit of small talk, they sat down.

"Las, this gentleman is truly generous. He arranged for the car at the airport, and everything we bought, Las, was charged to his account. Isn't he wonderful?"

Mrs. Lanting laughed as she dropped her head against the man's shoulder.

Lasi was perplexed. It troubled her to know that a man she had just met had paid for all the fine things she bought.

"Say thank you to Pak Bambung, Las."

Lasi was startled. What kind of a name was Bambung? She blinked. In the end, she followed Mrs. Lanting's instructions. In a low voice, and without looking at Bambung, she thanked him. A moment later, she had a pang in her heart. How could she be indebted to a man without knowing him? She didn't have time to think about it. Mrs. Lanting began talking again. "We'll stay here tonight, Las. Of course, you need to ask your husband for permission first, but you can call later."

Lasi simply nodded her head.

"We'll rest a bit. Come on, I'll take you to your room. I believe Pak Bambung has ordered a super luxurious room for you. What's Lasi's room number?"

"Suite D on the first floor," Bambung said evenly.

"A suite? Oh, well, a super luxurious room is clearly not enough for a woman as beautiful as you. Isn't that right, Pak Bambung? Come on."

When they entered the room Mrs. Lanting was still talking. Even when she retrieved snacks and drinks from the bar, she chattered. "I tell you, even though he's the same age as your husband, Pak Bambung has a lot going for him. He's more mature, more calm, and certainly, more manly. Those white sideburns make him look like a billy goat, and even more manly. Virile. Don't you think?"

Lasi stayed quiet. From her smile, Mrs. Lanting knew what she was thinking about.

"Who is he, bu?" Lasi asked, still smiling. Her expression softened and the exotic accents of her Japanese heritage surfaced.

"An important man, a very important man. He's one of the very top people."

"You really are great, aren't you?"

Mrs. Lanting laughed.

"Las, men are easy. The hard part is they're attracted to young, beautiful women with slim figures, like you. That doesn't mean a woman old and fat like me has to despair. A man's vision is easily flipped around: ugly becomes beautiful, and old becomes young. I'm proof of that. But who knows? I saw Pak Bambung stealing glances at you. Damned men."

"I know he's good, but he's still your boyfriend." Lasi felt guilty.

"He *is* good, and more important than your husband. And, yes, he's my boyfriend."

"Of course, bu."

"I'm off to see him. You can rest and take a bath. We'll meet later."

Lasi nodded and smiled. Mrs. Lanting kissed her on the cheeks before leaving. The fat woman waddled like a duck. Lasi smiled again, reflecting on Mrs. Lanting.

She was definitely over fifty. Everything about her was either fat or sagging, except her lust. *How can there possibly be a woman like that? She might be in better shape than me when I'm her age—and I'm not even thirty.*

Lasi grimaced. Mrs. Lanting's zest for meeting men reminded her of her own situation. Her nights were drier and emptier than usual. Retired Chief Handarbeni had lost most of his virility. He was unable to perform without the help of pills. Unfortunately, the pills had side effects. Handarbeni already suffered from high blood pressure and passed out one night while trying to demonstrate he still had something to give. Since then, Lasi didn't want him to take the medication.

Her mind continued to meander. She went back to Karangsoga, where she was the wife of a young palm tapper. Darsa had a wiry body and enthusiastic virility. One rainy afternoon they were asleep in their bamboo house. The smell of the pandan mat and the sound of raindrops trickled through the roof and a gush of water flowed through the bamboo rain gutters. Darsa's sweat had the sour smell of nira. The two of them melted into each other and blended perfectly. They achieved that perfect fusion whenever they wanted. It was a shame that such a tantalizing memory was tarnished by Darsa's betrayal.

Lasi preferred to dwell on her memories with Kanjat, who was a lecturer in Purwokerto and still single. Kanjat was two years younger. He was the only child in Karangsoga who had never taunted her by calling her "Lasi-pang." The sweet boy always defended her. During their adolescence, he often gave her a shy smile when she sold palm sugar to his father, Pak Tir.

Lasi remembered when Kanjat had come for her in Jakarta after she ran away from Karangsoga. She wanted to be rescued by her one-time playmate, to hide under his protection, and become his wife.

On empty lonely nights, Lasi dreamed of Kanjat. The dreams were warm and often exciting, as though he knocked at the door of her desire. With her body covered in sweat from the provocative dreams, Lasi stayed awake. Her passion was suppressed by the absence of Kanjat. Lying next to her was the old snoring ox, Handarbeni.

"Goodness gracious, haven't you bathed yet, Las?" Mrs. Lanting's voice jolted Lasi out of her reveries. She was surprised to see Bambung behind the fat woman.

"That's fine. Sit down for now. Pak Bambung and I need to talk to you."

The three of them shuffled to the adjacent luxurious living room. The lush carpet absorbed their footsteps.

"Listen, Las. We're in a bit of a bind. In three hours, Pak Bambung is scheduled to host a dinner at this hotel for his business partners and friends. The problem is that Pak Bambung doesn't have a consort for the evening. I may be his girlfriend but I know my place. The guests are businessmen from Japan, America, and Europe. Our ambassador will also be there. They're all going to bring beautiful women with them, which is why I say I know my place.

"Please help us out, Las. I'm asking you to stand in for me with Pak Bambung at tonight's dinner."

Lasi looked from Mrs. Lanting to Bambung. *Ah, those damned bushy white sideburns.* She stuttered, "Me, bu?"

"Yes. You often accompanied your husband at events in Jakarta. This is just like that. The only difference is that most of the guests are going to be foreigners."

"Why don't you go?"

"I already told you, I know my place. What if the ambassador sees the woman with Pak Bambung isn't his wife, but someone old and fat? Besides, you only need to stay with him for the dinner. After that, he goes back to being my boyfriend."

"But I'm not his wife either, bu."

"It's different, Las. You're young and so very, very suited to appear among other beautiful women. The ambassador and his wife will know you're not Pak Bambung's wife, but what are they going to do? You'll be the most beautiful of all the women who have been seen with Pak Bambung. The ambassador will smile and understand, being a man himself. All his wife can do is look at you in envy. What matters is that you're willing to do it."

Lasi's face reflected the conflict in her heart. She blinked rapidly. Worried about the attraction of his white sideburns, she avoided looking at Bambung.

"But I didn't bring anything appropriate to wear. I..."

Mrs. Lanting, sensing victory, cut her off. "Las, this is Singapore and Pak Bambung wants you by his side. Believe me, clothes won't be a problem.

"Within an hour, the best boutique in this city will deliver any dress you desire, with accessories. Don't fret and go take your shower. I have to see about your clothes. Isn't that right, Pak Bambung?"

Bambung smiled in agreement. Lasi saw the smile and the sideburns. She was about to speak but stopped when Mrs. Lanting turned to leave.

Mrs. Lanting paused in the doorway with Bambung to say she would be back in less than an hour. She added, "I want you bathed by that time."

Lasi was trapped in a mix of emotions. After thinking about her situation, she knew she had to answer Mrs. Lanting's plea. She wanted to help and there was no harm in aiding a friend. It was only for dinner, and damn, those white sideburns had a strong appeal. Lasi enjoyed them in her mind.

She walked to the bathroom. It had a shower, which was what she was used to instead of bathing in a tub. The soft spray of warm water swept over her body and refreshed her.

Wrapped in a towel, she stood at the bathroom mirror. The steam of the hot water had fogged the mirror. She wiped it with a tissue and her true reflection came into focus. A sigh escaped her lips.

Lasi looked at the woman in the mirror. *Mrs. Lanting may be right and I'm beautiful. Maybe the men are right, too. Their eyes light up and get narrow when they look at me.*

In the end, Lasi had to believe she was beautiful. She exuded a natural beauty that was extremely tempting.

She had served Darsa with all her heart. He took pleasure in her, just as she took pleasure in him. They pleasured each other in a fusion until neither could tell who was enjoying whom.

The telephone next to the toilet rang. Mrs. Lanting spoke hurriedly. "Las, I'm on my way. You need to be ready. I'm bringing a makeup artist with me. I took care of the clothes, and I have a surprise for you. Oh, I brought you some food."

Mrs. Lanting entered with a Chinese man carrying a large suitcase. He frequently glanced at his watch as if Mrs. Lanting had hired him by the hour.

Thirty minutes before the dinner, Lasi was ready. The dress clinging to her body was the finest she had ever worn, comfortable and exceedingly elegant. Her hair had been done up in a style that made her seem almost fully Japanese. What made her different were the exotic features of her face, particularly her eyes.

Lasi accepted the dress and accessories. Her surprise came when she saw the necklace worth billions of rupiah she had seen at the shopping center. Lasi was dumbstruck. *Was it real or an imitation?*

Mrs. Lanting said it was genuine and Lasi's lips trembled. She was proud that the necklace would circle her neck, and the main part studded with diamonds grace her chest. Mrs. Lanting said earlier that its value was enough for everyone in Karangsoga to go on the Hajj. Lasi bristled at the thought. She let the billion rupiah necklace be placed on her.

"What did I tell you, Las? Pak Bambung is great. No other man in Jakarta can match him for greatness, and he's turned his attention to you. It's true. He didn't buy this necklace for me; he bought it for you."

"But… But he's still your boyfriend."

"For now, but I don't know about the future. I told you he was stealing glances at you."

"Do you regret bringing me here?"

"Oh, Las, I'm an old woman with a lot of experience. I know what men are like. If Pak Bambung likes you, so be it. It's no loss to me. I already have his money. You'll see. When we're back home, I'm going to buy the latest Mercedes. With that car, the man wearing dark glasses will definitely want to take me everywhere. What more do I need?" Mrs. Lanting laughed long and hard.

The dinner began at seven. Bambung greeted his arriving guests with Lasi standing a little stiffly next to him. She had done this before with Handarbeni, and the experience gave her enough confidence. Everyone who shook Bambung's hand did so with tremendous respect, almost reverence. The Indonesian ambassador to Singapore was no exception. From the murmurs around her, Lasi gathered that the ambassador himself was among the top people.

"Is that Pak Bambung's new sidekick?" the ambassador's wife whispered in her husband's ear after they had shaken hands and moved on.

"Don't be nosy. You know what kind of man Pak Bambung is."

"Are you afraid he's going to recommend you be sent back to Jakarta?"

"Fine. The woman hanging on Pak Bambung's arm is the wife of the director of some state-owned company. She's half-Japanese."

"How do you know?" the ambassador's wife asked, her whisper tinged with suspicion.

"I even know her name," the ambassador said, not caring about his wife's thoughts. "Her name's Lasi."

"Did you notice her necklace?"

"How could I not? You'd have to be blind not to see the light from those hundreds of diamonds."

"I know how much it cost—one and a half million US dollars. How about that?"

The ambassador raised his eyebrows for a moment and flashed a smile. It may have been a diplomat's smile or that of an experienced man. It was obvious who was responsible for putting that necklace around Lasi's neck, and why. *If I were as powerful as Bambung, I wouldn't mind paying one and a half million dollars to have Lasi by my side*, the ambassador thought. He understood why Bambung took pride in standing or sitting next to Lasi. In the early 1960s, Bung Karno showed the same pride the first time he paraded Naoko Nemoto, the hostess he brought back from Tokyo, to the political elite in Jakarta.

Lasi stood next to Bambung for the simple reason of helping Mrs. Lanting. She still delighted in the dress and the necklace.

If only Mrs. Lanting had kept the cost to herself.... Lasi thought about her duty that night, one she enjoyed, which was to take Mrs. Lanting's place with Bambung. She had no clue she was in the middle of a group of people who met earlier that afternoon.

Bambung had called a meeting for dozens of businessmen from Indonesia and abroad to agree on the details for plans to exploit the forests of Sumatra and Kalimantan.

They planned to carve up millions of hectares of forest, as they would divide a parcel of inherited land. To ensure nothing would hinder them, they had money set aside to bribe politicians, silence journalists, and neutralize any environmental campaign. Considerable funds were allocated to generate a positive image for the companies clearing the forests, and toward religious activities, building arts centers, and sponsoring sports competitions. University students would be bought off with scholarships to study abroad.

Months earlier in New York, Bambung had organized a similar event. The only difference was that the participants were oilmen who had long coveted the billion barrels of oil beneath Indonesia's soil.

The fervently anti-capitalist Bung Karno had refused to open the door to them. When he fell in 1966, the oilmen offered to assist the new ruler, who certainly needed huge amounts of money. The offers from American oilmen were immediately accepted. The aid, which was really a debt, was paid off with mineral rights to the companies for exploiting Indonesia's oil under arrangements that heavily favored the foreigners.

With neither capital nor experience, and certainly no knowledge of modern oil technology, the new Indonesian government was in an exceedingly weak position to negotiate. Yet, the need for large amounts of oil money to shore up the New Order regime was urgent. The government agreed to sell Indonesia's oil through highly disadvantageous deals. Disguised as "production sharing," the strong exploited the weak.

The production sharing system left the foreign companies with the biggest share of the revenue, and what little was left went to the rulers of Indonesia under Bambung's control. The official state oil company had highly opaque financial management, with no single overseeing entity that knew what was happening inside. The politicians involved and those in parliament were disarmed or blinded with bribes. Along with extremely corrupt government officials and their cronies, these politicians also gorged on the oil money, so that only a pittance was left for development.

In the early 1970s, a veteran journalist sought to get at the bottom of the oil company's mess. He revealed through his newspaper the truth about what was happening to the country's immense wealth, and published an open letter in the candid *Batak* style to Suharto, who had recently been re-elected president in an election rife with fraud. He challenged the government to take the matter to court and prove his allegations false.

The valiant journalist lost.

Those in power and the oil companies put up money to silence him. The money went to the law enforcement agencies and the courts to look the other way, and took care of the opportunist politicians. Money flowed across the editorial boards of the tabloids for them to contest what the journalist wrote. In the end, the money changed public opinion to the view that there was no corruption at the state oil company. People were convinced the oil money would be used for the public good.

Admittedly, people enjoyed the economic growth, in part generated by the revenue of the oil money. Statistics showed per capita income had increased. The tangible proof was seen in the construction of roads, schools, hospitals, houses, factories, and hotels. But along with the growth came moral rot in the form of abandoning the principles of the Republic and the proliferation of corruption, collusion, and nepotism by state officials. The progress enjoyed by the people wasn't commensurate with the price to be paid: the forsaking of the Republic's democratic ideals. The advancements attributed to the government were merely numbers on a sheet of paper to cover up the ulcers underneath.

Lasi was one of over one hundred and seventy million people who never understood the high-level game in Indonesia, and that the man who stood beside her was the main player.

The dinner ended at ten. Bambung and Lasi stood together until the last guest, the ambassador, left the room. Lasi noticed how much respect the guests paid Bambung. She believed what Mrs. Lanting had said about him. He had a much higher position than her husband.

"Would you like to sit in the lobby or return to your suite?" Bambung asked with the airs of an old gentleman.

"Thank you, pak. I'd like to go back to my room." Lasi was flustered.

"Very well, I'll take you. What should I call you? Mrs. Handarbeni or…"

"I *am* Mrs. Handarbeni, but you're welcome to call me Lasi."

The moment she turned the doorknob, Lasi heard the telephone ring. She left Bambung by the door and hurried to pick up the receiver.

It was Mrs. Lanting. "Oh my God, I called you three times. What's going on? Are you done?"

"Yes, bu. We just finished."

"It was easy, wasn't it? All you had to do was accompany him to dinner for a gift worth billions. So how was the dinner? Is Pak Bambung pleased?"

"I don't know."

"Las, don't be shocked, but I've moved to the Sea View. It's another hotel."

"Are you there now?"

"Yes. While you were with Pak Bambung, I met…umm… a white rooster. You know what I always say about money being important. Well, it turned out I could buy that young white man. He's expensive, but that's okay because I haven't feasted on white meat in a while.

"Now that I have a new rooster, and a younger one, I'll leave Pak Bambung in your care. Please look after him. Do whatever he wants. You won't regret it. Trust me."

"But he… I mean…"

"No buts. He was my boyfriend until an hour ago. Not anymore. Like I said, I've found me a new rooster."

Lasi remained quiet. She had nothing to say to Mrs. Lanting.

"Hey, Las. Are you still with Pak Bambung?"

"Yes, he's here."

"Good. I'd like to talk to him.

Lasi looked behind her.

Bambung sat on the sofa. He walked to Lasi when she told him Mrs. Lanting wanted to speak with him.

"Yes, I'm here. What? You've moved to another hotel? Oh really? You've asked Lasi to do what?"

Bambung kept the receiver pressed to his ear. He looked disappointed when he hung up the phone and sat down with a sigh.

Lasi felt sorry for the old man. How could Mrs. Lanting do such a thing?

"I've struck out this time," Bambung lowered his head. "Mrs. Handarbeni, did you know that Mrs. Lanting moved to another hotel?"

"I know, pak. If saying my name is too much trouble, call me Lasi. Don't stand on ceremony."

"Very well, Lasi. I'm alone now. My friend had the heart to leave me."

Lasi stared ahead so as not to be affected by the attractive white sideburns. They still supported the notion of Bambung being a mature man.

Bambung rested his arms on his knees. He interlaced his fingers and stared at his shoes.

Lasi was curious about how he felt being left by Mrs. Lanting. She sat in silence with her head bowed, twiddling her fingers. Colorful beams of light radiated from the diamonds on the necklace spilled across her chest. Lasi was starting to like it. Before she knew, she was talking.

"Mrs. Lanting asked me to keep you company. I don't think I can."

Staring at the floor, Bambung smiled.

"If you want to, you can, and I would very much appreciate it. We can just have a chat and a drink. I understand if you don't want to. I'm not having much luck."

"Mrs. Lanting said you bought this necklace for me. Is that true?"

"It's a small gift because you agreed to join me at the dinner. Don't let it sway you. If you have reservations about looking after me as Mrs. Lanting asked, it's all right."

"About the necklace, pak, I'm truly grateful." Relieved to know the incredibly expensive necklace was really hers, Lasi took a deep breath.

Hers? She realized that she owed Bambung. It was like what Grandfather Mus in Karangsoga had said: "Only Allah gives without expecting something in return. As for humans? Even a mother, whether she knows it or not, demands loyalty from her child through words or actions in exchange for having carried it in her womb, suckled and cared for it."

Lasi was stunned.

Bambung said he didn't intend to influence her by giving her the necklace. In that case, a simple "thank you" to the nice gentleman should have sufficed, but her gratitude had to be backed up by something real.

"I'd better get changed. And, if I may, I'll return." Bambung's voice roused Lasi from her thoughts, and she raised her head. Their eyes met briefly. They smiled.

Lasi gave him a sincere smile to ease his disappointment for being abandoned by Mrs. Lanting. "Come back and we'll chat for a while." The words flowed automatically and a shadow of regret traveled across her face.

Bambung's face broke into a wide, warm smile. He walked away like a child whose parents promised to buy him a new kite.

Lasi pitied him.

She, too, wanted to change. She went into the bedroom to call Handarbeni and tell him she would be home the next day, or how, because of Mrs. Lanting's conduct, she was forced to keep the old cougar's boyfriend company. Lasi was unsure of how to tell him about the necklace, but this didn't matter because no one answered the telephone.

Lasi relaxed in her regular clothes and wandered lost in the luxurious surroundings. She moved awkwardly, like a fig being swept along on a river. She floated, fell into whirlpools, and smashed against rocks at the whim of the current.

She flung herself on the sofa and evaporated in the silence. *Mrs. Lanting is a tramp. Why did she switch hotels? Can't she have her tryst with her new boyfriend here?* The telephone rang.

Lasi got up happily, certain that it was Mrs. Lanting. "Where are you?"

"Oh, sorry, Las. I'm not Mrs. Lanting."

Lasi immediately recognized Bambung.

"I'll be there right away. You said I could come, didn't you?"

"Yes, pak. You're most welcome."

Lasi turned around before setting down the receiver. She wasn't ready for him, but she was a fig swept by the current and had to accept whatever came her way.

Bambung entered the room. Back home, he had several grandchildren, yet still looked dapper in his cream trousers and long sleeved ivory shirt. He wore yellow shoes and his hair looked neater than before. He appeared relaxed. Unlike Lasi, Bambung seemed very poised.

"Lasi, we've actually met before. I saw you and your husband at a restaurant, and to be honest, this old man has found it impossible to forget you. That probably sounds like the sweet talk of a corny old man, doesn't it?"

Lasi tried not to laugh. Bambung had spouted some cheap lines that she somehow enjoyed. Was it because of his candidness, or because women liked to be flattered, even when they knew the words were insincere?

"I was jealous of your husband. He's a very lucky man, but I'm lucky too. Just a little bit. I've had the chance to meet and talk with you, and you joined me at dinner. That qualifies me as lucky."

Lasi blushed at his new line of flirting. The man she met only a few hours ago kept plying her with sweet talk. Judging by his smile and the light in his eyes, it was clear where the conversation was headed.

Men. Whether it was Handarbeni or Bambung—when they wanted something, they were all smiles. They acted like little children begging from their mothers. Lasi had seen how, an hour earlier, Bambung appeared authoritative and self-confident in front of his foreign guests and the ambassador. Even though she was young, Lasi knew plenty about men. Their strength and authority crumbled at moments like this.

"Las, you know that I'm sad because my friend left me."

"I know, pak."

"You can help me get over my sadness. You will, won't you?"

"Yes. Didn't I say I was willing to chat?"

Bambung's eyes glowed. He moved to Lasi's left side and laid his right arm along the back of the sofa, almost circling her shoulders.

The red bekisar stiffened and her expression turned cold. Bambung's cologne, which had given off musky hints throughout the day, enveloped Lasi. "We'll just chat, right, pak?"

Bambung raised his eyebrows to send her the message of what he wanted, nothing more than what every man wanted when alone with a woman in a very private room.

Lasi responded with a cold stare to Bambung's advances. *Don't. I'm not like Mrs. Lanting.*

The intense dialogue conducted through facial expressions ended when Bambung drew a deep breath. He needed to control his feelings and be patient.

"Yes, we'll have a nice chat and a few drinks."

"What would you like? I'll get it."

"I don't really like drinking, or smoking. Drinking and smoking make a man older and worn out quicker. I want to stay healthy."

"You look pretty healthy."

"Thank you."

"You said you wanted a drink?"

"Yes, just to get over this confusion. Maybe it's because Mrs. Lanting left me, or being alone with you. Why do I feel young again? Please get me a Johnny Walker."

Bambung watched Lasi walk to the bar. He smiled to himself. There it was, the exposed nape of Lasi's neck, just like the Ginza girls in Tokyo, who always sparked the fire of his manhood. Frustration began to consume him. He imagined stroking the fine hairs along Lasi's cheek while whispering sweet nothings and looking into her exotic eyes.

His reveries were wild. Lasi was only willing to exchange some conversation. They had no agreement between them. He counted on the necklace to compel Lasi to do whatever he wanted. *If it doesn't, I might have to force her.*

That was a petty thought. Forcing himself on her would only bring satisfaction to one side.

In his long history of conquests, Bambung had occasionally forced himself on his partners like a young, virile rooster—impatient, pursuing and crashing into its mate to couple. The body would be sated, but not the soul. In the end, he felt like a thief with nothing to gain except a jail sentence. It was truly pathetic.

Bastard. Bambung cursed himself. *No. I am Bambung, a man highly respected by the most important people in Jakarta—generals, ministers, politicians, bank directors, community leaders, and even the shamans. Why should I demand service through force? I want to enjoy a dish prepared with care, not a meal obtained by breaking into the cupboard. I want to see myself as the king enjoying the bodily offering of his newest concubine, who is beautiful and obliging.*

Bambung smiled. Every woman he bought had serviced him as if it were an offering. All the girls, artists, film stars, and working women he used were compliant after he paid them.

Bambung smiled again. One could say the women gave themselves to him more than willingly. Each of them wanted to be the consort to this wealthy man. Bambung was certain many gave their full loyalty in hopes to become his umpteenth wife. Yes, but those girls and women were whores or semi-whores. Their compliance, no matter to what degree, was colored by commerce. Lasi was a simple young wife who took pains to guard her image. Her eyes, her face, and everything about her behavior said as much. Her charm was magnetic; its strength was apparent, but it was difficult to say where it came from.

If only Lasi consented, Bambung would truly feel like a king being pampered by his new concubine.

Lasi returned with the whiskey. Bambung studied her face. He hoped to find, no matter how small, the flash of a green light to indicate the fire inside. But he found nothing. Lasi's expression was as ordinary as could be. Her smile was one of obligation, and looked stiff. Even so, Bambung lit up when he saw the dimple in Lasi's left cheek.

During the next half hour, Bambung found fresh ways to flirt, leaving Lasi flattered and almost swept off her feet. This seemed effective, and he smiled and nervously moved closer to Lasi. When his words missed their target, he nursed his drink.

Bambung's chatter stopped flowing. He smiled more, drank more, and looked nervous. He gave Lasi meaningful looks, but unlike the other women Bambung had bought, she didn't respond. Her expression remained cold and even. It served as a tightly locked beautiful gate, and even a man as experienced as Bambung was afraid to try opening it.

Bambung was getting drunk and began to babble. He mumbled snatches of Javanese love songs, and "*Sepasang Mata Bola.*" He shook his head while smiling with passion and satisfaction, like a mother taking pride in the beauty of the child in her lap.

Bambung's babbling became progressively worse. In his drunken state, he thought he was Rusman, the legendary *wayang orang* actor who played the role of Gatotkaca. Bambung never forgot the scene in which Gatotkaca tried to seduce Pergiwa.

He performed Gatotkaca's love dance. He was good. He sang a love song off-tune: "Oh, surrender, my beautiful."

With moves worthy of the real Rusman, Bambung embraced and lifted Lasi. The red bekisar had no chance to refuse and Bambung rocked her in his arms.

Reading the wild look in his eyes, Lasi knew she was in danger. "Stop, pak. I don't want this."

Bambung held Lasi so close their foreheads almost touched. His eyes narrowed. His smile dripped with lust. Then, as if under a spell, he put Lasi back down on the sofa.

"Oh, beautiful one, you don't want me? Well, that's all right. Gatotkaca never forced Pergiwa. He only enjoyed her when she was willing. Gatotkaca was right. Forcing one's way never brought satisfaction. We'll just chat."

Lasi smiled while her heart raced. Bambung babbled again, his head wobbling.

"If you give me what I want, I'll take care of you. I'll spoil you rotten. You can ask for anything. Would you like to be a bank commissioner, or a member of parliament? Why not? I can arrange it; everything will be taken care of. Honestly.

"There are too many politicians in the parliament building. They're brokers and opportunists. I know who they really are.

"Las, parliament doesn't need just politicians. It needs beautiful women, cheeky beautiful women like you. Oh, brother, it's true.

"Parliament needs an ornament, a beautiful woman to gaze on. It's important to trigger people's passion so they stay enthusiastic and don't fall asleep. It's true, isn't it? That's how some snot-nosed girl became a member of parliament. She was a feast for the eyes. I arranged that. The arrangement was approved by acclamation after the other members met her.

"Do you want to be in parliament, Las? It's easy, all you have to do is sit there and look pretty. You don't have to do any thinking, and the pay is big. Oh, beautiful one, let me take care of you…"

Bambung flopped on the sofa and hung his head.

Lasi was at a loss. She giggled. Even if Bambung had been sober, Lasi wouldn't have understood what he was talking about.

The ridiculous, pitiful, man who according to Mrs. Lanting was very influential, sat slumped over. Gone was the veneer of his authority. Even the white sideburns that were the hallmark of his manliness were of no help. Before her was a man struck down by liquor and doubts of getting what he desired by consent, and the possibility of heeding his lust to take it.

Save for Bambung passing out and Lasi obliged to take care of him, nothing else happened that night. Lasi peeled off his vomit-stained clothes, dressed him in hotel pajamas, and brought him a pillow. She had the same compassion for Bambung as any human being rendered helpless.

Bambung felt dizzy when he woke at eight the next morning. It was as though he had woken in another world until he quickly regained full consciousness. He guessed at what happened, and Lasi had changed his clothes.

He walked to the bedroom door and tried turning the doorknob. The door was unlocked.

Bambung found Lasi fast asleep. She had her own way of sleeping, turning off the air-conditioning and lying on top of the covers with her legs spread apart.

Bambung narrowed his eyes. He hesitated. He had worked hard to borrow Lasi. Desire made him feel like a lion ready to pounce on his prey. And she was sprawled before his eyes.

He squeezed his fingers. His breathing quickened and perspiration broke through his palms. The moment had arrived to do what he planned when he arranged to have Lasi brought here. His face went hard. He started to loosen the string of the pajamas when the thought that he was about to rape Lasi flashed through his mind.

Bastard. No, it's shameful. What am I? Who am I? I'm Bambung, I have to make Lasi serve me willingly. I have to. If I can't take her now, I'll wait for another time.

The words echoed in his ears, and prompted him to back down. His heartbeat slowed and became regular.

Bambung stared at Lasi as she dreamed. The expression on her face was blank, serene. She looked elegant and innocent, as fresh as the clear, cool water of a mountain spring.

As he stepped back, the telephone rang. He waited for Lasi to wake and answer it, but she remained motionless. There was no sign that she would wake up.

Bambung picked up the receiver. The call was for him, not Lasi, a short message from Jakarta. The most important person in the city requested Bambung's immediate return through his assistant.

"Damn it. How did he know where I was?" Bambung fumed after putting the receiver down. "Bastard."

He had to wake Lasi. He gently touched her cheek. When she opened her eyes, he asked her calmly to get up.

"Las, we have to return to Jakarta right away. I have an urgent matter to attend to. Get ready; someone is waiting for me. We'll take the first flight."

Chapter 8

After Bambung dropped her at home, Lasi found the house in Slipi quiet. Entang, the spare driver, told her Handarbeni had been away. Lasi felt uneasy for having spent the night with another man and wanted to talk with her husband. When she telephoned his office, his secretary said, "He's not in."

Weary and sleepy after having gone to bed at three in the morning, Lasi went into her bedroom. She took a bath, changed her clothes, and went to bed to fall asleep immediately.

The next day she received a telephone call from Mrs. Lanting. Lasi was alarmed when Mrs. Lanting started the conversation agitated.

"Las, Pak Bambung called me. You didn't give him anything the other night."

"Give? What do you mean?"

"What is it with you? Don't you understand what a man wants when he's alone with a woman? I told you, do everything he wants."

"But I'm Mas Han's wife. How could I?"

"You really are a country girl. Why not after accepting the necklace? For that price, the next seven generations of your descendants will live in comfort. Why not give Pak Bambung something?"

Lasi remained silent. Indeed, the necklace had started to demand payment. Lasi regretted her acceptance, even though she really liked the jewelry.

"Las, Pak Bambung had a lot to say, but he didn't ask for the necklace back. He didn't even bring it up. He's still interested in you and he'll wait until you come around to the idea. You're lucky he's being patient. He usually he just takes what he wants."

"How can I, bu? I still have a husband."

"Listen, Las. I've also spoken with Handarbeni. He decided to let you go with Pak Bambung. A divorce certificate from Pak Han and a marriage certificate from Pak Bambung can be issued as quickly as you want."

"Mas Han has divorced me?" Lasi asked naively.

"Yes, he has. Ask him yourself. He's in his office."

Lasi froze when she heard Mrs. Lanting laugh. She felt like a piece of trash that had been thrown into the bin. "So be it. I'm only a woman."

"That's right, and it's best you hear it straight from Pak Han. Go on, talk to him."

Lasi hung up the phone hesitantly to call Handarbeni.

"Yes, Mrs. Lanting is right," Handarbeni said in a strained voice. "I divorce you. You can keep the house in Slipi and everything in it. You can also keep the driver, but not Pak Min. Sorry."

Lasi felt weightless, floating. Her hand trembled as she put down the receiver. Her life was a void. She attributed the floating not to having lost Handarbeni, but to being broken. *Why is the path of my life so obscure that I lose my way and my men so easily? My God, what must I go through next?*

She was still gripped by doubt when Mrs. Lanting called again.

"I was right, wasn't I?"

Lasi sniffled.

"This is how big people are. Don't blame Pak Han. He just lost his most prized, beloved bekisar, which is you.

"Pak Bambung says he'll be compensated by becoming the director of a large shipping company. He might even be a minister. Now do you understand?

"You now belong to Pak Bambung, so don't try to avoid him. It's dangerous. I repeat: it's dangerous. Accept him and enjoy his wealth and power. It'll be easy and comfortable, and believe me, you'll stand out even more. Congratulations, Las."

The moment Mrs. Lanting stopped talking, Lasi felt as though she was in a dimly lit room. A bee flapped its wings in her ear. She felt a cold draft across the back of her neck. It was difficult to digest and understand Mrs. Lanting's words. *I've been let go by Mas Han and now I belong to Pak Bambung. How can that be?*

Lasi suddenly had the urge to urinate. In a hoarse voice, she told Mrs. Lanting she needed to hang up, but the pressure below her stomach disappeared the moment she shut the bathroom door. She stood alone inside the room with white marble walls. Tears welled up and she couldn't control them.

Crying, Lasi pressed her hands to her chest, where she felt a sudden acute pain. Mrs. Lanting's last words rang in her ears. Lasi shut her eyes and clenched her teeth to resist the pain tearing at her heart.

Her feelings in a jumble, she heard the wind blow through the leaves of the bamboo grove towering over her little house in Karangsoga, where the storks returned to their nest at twilight. She heard the prayer drum from Grandfather Mus' surau. In her blurred vision, she saw Kanjat pass in front of the house. She wanted to reach out and stop him, but Kanjat vanished in an instant.

She also saw her mother, but the old woman cared nothing for her. Like Kanjat, she only remained in Lasi's vision for a moment.

Lasi's tears continued to fall. She knew Mrs. Lanting waited for her to call back, but she stood, not urinating, not knowing what to do.

She stepped in front of the mirror above the sink and saw the truth in Mrs. Lanting's praise; she was young and fresh, even with only tears as makeup. Lasi stared at herself. She was indeed young and beautiful.

What am I really like? With those simple words, Lasi questioned her existence, which had become increasingly unclear, especially her marital status. The day before she had been Mrs. Handarbeni, and now she belonged to Pak Bambung. *How can I understand all this?*

She heard a ringing in her ears amid her heartbeat. When she clenched her fists, she felt the sweat on her palms. A new vision played out before her, this time of a rainy afternoon in the small house in Karangsoga, when she was married to Darsa. It was quiet, save for the sounds of raindrops falling on the roof and a pair of frogs jumping together.

Only she and her husband—a village man, but complete in his manliness. Darsa. Lasi's blood quickened, her heart started to beat faster. Her palms sweat more. Something heated, churned, and lashed against the walls of her desire. Her arms and legs trembled. Lasi shut her eyes to subdue the emotions that sprang up.

Once she composed herself, Lasi stood in a daze and swallowed several times. As though propelled by an outside power, she left the bathroom and picked up the telephone. Once connected, she asked Mrs. Lanting to continue the conversation.

"This is where things stand, Las. You belong to Pak Bambung, and he'll come over tomorrow. He'll take you to a new house in Menteng, east of the Hotel Indonesia. It's near my house in Cikini. Don't you go anywhere tomorrow morning, is that clear?"

"Just a moment. What if I don't want to go, or return the necklace?"

"You can't do either. Pak Bambung is a very difficult man. He always gets what he wants. He will be insulted if you return the necklace. Don't play around with him. Even your Pak Han was powerless against him."

"Are you sure? He seemed nice enough the other day. He was funny and didn't seem to be mean at all."

"You don't understand, Las. Pak Bambung is a Javanese nobleman. His softness hides a hard edge, a vengefulness, and even cruelty. Follow my advice or you'll have a lot of trouble. Pak Bambung can have the police arrest you. I'm not joking."

Lasi trembled and turned pale. She put the telephone down and paced the room with her head bowed, biting her lip. She sat down, nervously. An unsettling feeling grew inside and depressed her. She wanted to escape what was closing in, and run and run. At the same time, she felt like a moth that had crashed into a spider's web and was trapped. She was more uncertain than ever.

Lasi ran to her bedroom, curled up on the bed, and cried again. Uncertainty and darkness combined to form a strange fear that dragged her into its vortex. Lasi wanted to grab on to something, to resist the strong pull. All she had was her growing apprehension; Bambung would come for her tomorrow. She shivered.

***

Lasi walked quickly from the house, carrying a small bag across her shoulder. As she walked down the porch steps, Entang, the driver, ran after her. "Are you going out, ibu? I don't have the car ready." He was startled at seeing the tension on Lasi's face.

"There's no need, Pak Entang. I'm going on my own." Lasi said, coldy.

"You don't want me to drive you? The master will get angry…"

"No."

Entang frowned and watched Lasi open the gate. A taxi pulled up without her flagging it down. Lasi got in and the taxi sped away. Entang knew how angry his employer would be when he found out the mistress had left.

"Where do you want to go, ibu?" asked the driver, a young man with shifty eyes. The taxi kept moving.

Lasi was silent.

"Where are we going, ibu?" he said as he sped up. He looked in his rearview mirror and saw a unique face with tears streaming down. He was being treated to a live show. Here was a beautiful young woman, alone and crying. He chuckled. His chest filled with hopes of being the knight who consoled the grieving princess in a fairy tale. His imagination took off, but the realization that he was only a taxi driver and his passenger was clearly of a much higher class, catapulted him back to earth. She might be a foreigner, Japanese perhaps.

"Miss, wer-yu-go?" he asked, hoping she might make sense of it. When she remained quiet, the driver made up his mind. He headed for the hotel on Thamrin Street where Japanese tourists and businessmen of Jakarta congregated. When they reached the hotel, the driver was surprised by Lasi's question.

"Driver, where are you taking me?"

Apparently, his passenger could talk. "This is the President Hotel. Many Japanese come here. You're Japanese, aren't you?"

"I didn't want to come here," Lasi said.

"Well, you didn't say anything when I asked."

"I'm sorry, pak."

"Where do you want to go?" The driver parked the taxi.

Lasi bit her lip and frowned.

The driver swiveled around in his seat, and looked straight at her, smiling.

"Do you want to drive around, maybe go to Ancol Beach? I'll keep you company, if you like. What do you say?"

Lasi detected the inappropriateness in his words. "Take me to Cikini," she snapped.

"To the Japanese restaurant? You *are* Japanese, aren't you?" He was more brazen than ever.

"I don't want to go to a restaurant. I'll tell you the address when we get there. And don't try anything."

"But you're Japanese, right?"

Lasi ignored the question. *Why did I ask to be taken to Cikini? Mrs. Lanting lives there.* "Driver, I'm not going to Cikini."

The driver braked abruptly and pulled over. He turned around and grinned. *Ah, she really is beautiful, but why so sad and confused?* "Why don't we see a movie? There's a good one playing nearby. How about it?"

Again, he spoke out of turn, and this irked Lasi. She needed to decide where she wanted to go. To Ibu Koneng's restaurant in Klender? She might find Pardi, Pak Tir's driver. Lasi wasn't in the mood to see the working girls, the one with large earrings and the other with chafed calves.

"Take me to Pasar Minggu," She'd gone there once when Min celebrated the circumcision of one of his sons.

"Please make up your mind," the driver whined.

"Pasar Minggu," Lasi ordered. When the cabbie continued to whine, Lasi grew more irritated. She stepped out of the taxi and ignored the driver's pleas to come back. Lasi paid the fare and walked off to another taxi.

In Pasar Minggu, in the south of Jakarta, Lasi left the taxi at the entrance to an alley. She walked down the narrow passage flanked by a gutter and a wall. A question hung between her eyebrows as the three o'clock sun seared her fair face. The stench of trash wafted from the open gutter. Lasi trudged on and broke into a smile when a woman in her fifties met her at the door of a simple house.

Mbok Min went into a tizzy at welcoming the wife of her husband's boss. "What a privilege to have you at our little shack. What brings you here? Pak Min's at work, isn't he? What's going on? You have me worried." Mbok Min babbled in her old Jakarta accent.

"There's nothing wrong, Mbok Min. Your husband is driving the boss, as usual."

Mbok Min tried to regain her composure. "What brings you here? Please come in, ibu. I'm embarrassed; my chairs are so shabby. Wah, I'm shocked to see you here. Did you bring a gift?"

Lasi sat on a plastic chair and ignored Mbok Min's joke. She looked around the small, bare front room. She smiled as she listened to Mbok Min babble. She was surprised to be in Pak Min's house. She hadn't planned to go there.

"I don't have anything to serve you, except sweet tea. Would you like bananas? I grow my own out back."

"Don't put yourself out. Sweet tea is enough. Besides, I only came here to, er…" Lasi stopped mid-sentence.

Even without asking, Mbok Min could tell the young mistress was in trouble; her behavior and expression said it all.

"Mbok Min, I'd like to rest here. I'm tired and I'd like to sleep a bit. May I? Do you have a room?"

"Oh mercy, my room is as messy as a pigsty. If you want, you can use the children's room, but it's also a pigsty. I'm so embarrassed."

Lasi nodded and stood.

Mbok Min was about to dash off to fix her children's room when Lasi grabbed her by the shoulder. "Mbok, what time does your husband come home?"

"Seven or eight at night. Do you want to wait for him?"

"Yes, I want to ask his opinion."

"What about? What can he do? You really want to wait for my husband? Have you eaten?"

Lasi smiled as she listened to Mbok Min's fussing. "I'd like something spicy. Is there anyone who sells *gado-gado* around here?"

"Gado-gado or spicy *rujak*? Wanting to eat spicy food is a good sign. Have you missed your period? Oh my, this is a good sign. Thank goodness…"

"Mbok Min," Lasi sharply interrupted. "It's not a pregnancy craving. I have a headache, and spicy gado-gado would help ease it. I'm not pregnant."

"You don't feel well? Would you like me to *kerok* your back? Or would you rather have a massage?"

"Would you massage me?"

"Kerok works better."

"No. Just a massage. My husband gets mad when he sees red marks on my back, more so on my neck."

"I forgot. It would be such a shame to leave marks on your fair skin. A massage it is. I'll tell one of the children to go buy gado-gado. Spicy, right?"

Lasi shook her head and followed Mbok Min into a cramped, stuffy room. Everything was different from her bedroom in Slipi. Here she smelled her childhood, the rooms and the bamboo furnishings she once owned in Karangsoga, the creased pillows and woven pandan mats.

Lasi lay down.

Mbok Min began massaging her. She was patient and gentle. Mbok Min marveled at Lasi's soft and fair skin. It felt like stroking a baby. After a while, Mbok Min almost asked Lasi what was going on, but she held her question because she knew nothing about Handarbeni's affairs. Besides, Lasi's breathing was soft and regular and soon she closed her eyes, and transported to another world.

In her dream, Lasi walked a footpath that climbed a limestone hill. She kept going until her feet were sore from stepping on the small, sharp rocks. To either side were shrubs and dried reeds. The sharp leaves brushed against her arms and calves.

At times, the footpath ran alongside a high rock face topped by large boulders that looked as though they would fall at any moment and crush her. She saw a spider's web, a dead bird, a snake's shedded skin, and bones.

Lasi stopped when a millipede crawled near her foot. She shuddered. Her legs trembled as she turned away, only to be confronted by a valley with deep ravines blanketed in clouds.

She stood at the top of a boulder that jutted out and pierced the sky. Far below, she saw her mother wave her hand, signaling to come down. Lasi wanted to go and hug her mother, but being so high up made her scared. She cried and shivered with a fear she never felt before. Her breathing grew ragged and she gasped for air. The rocky outcrop began to shake. It was about to crumble. She screamed in fear and shouted for help. She felt her body float in the air, and hurtle toward the bottom of the ravine below. Lasi shouted for her mother.

"Are you dreaming?" Mbok Min shook Lasi's leg.

She jolted awake. Her face had turned unusually pale. She sweated and her eyes were filled with an unbridled fear. She panted and let out a long sigh.

"Yes, my mother… oh my mother…" Lasi shook her head.

"That's odd. I didn't think you were asleep, and yet you dreamed."

Lasi stood up. She wiped the sweat from her brow and asked for tea.

Mbok Min quickly fetched the drink. Along with the sweet tea, she brought a plate of gado-gado.

Lasi finished the tea, but was no longer hungry.

At four in the afternoon, Lasi took her leave. She told Mbok Min she wanted to go back to Slipi. She tried to smile, and concealed her worry with light conversation.

Mbok Min responded amiably, but wondered why the mistress looked so strained, as if she bore a heavy burden.

Lasi stood by the side of the road with empty eyes. She had no place to go but Slipi. A bus approached. The conductor called out, "Pulogadung. Pulogadung." Lasi waved and got on. The bus was packed. A young boy gave her his seat. There was still some chivalry left; either that or Lasi's beauty had compelled the boy.

She got off at Pulogadung Terminal and was swept into a constantly moving crowd. She found the platform for out-of-town buses. A ticket scalper asked where she was going. Lasi shook her head. Cirebon? Slawi? Solo? Not there, either. She lit up when the scalper named a town close to Karangsoga and followed him to the bus as it started to fill. Heat from the running engine filled the air with body odors.

The bus set off after sunset. Lasi took a deep breath. She bought a drink from a traveling vendor and gulped it down. The cold spread through her body. She rode the hot bus for some time before she fully realized she was speeding to Karangsoga. She had escaped from whatever was hunting her.

Lasi smiled when she thought of the cool village she had left. She hoped to see the blanket of ferns covering the walls of the ravine. The freshness of the leaves and the spiral of the tendrils were parts of a living painting she had memorized from her childhood. The painting became more beautiful when it was wet with morning dew or rain.

A mist blanketed the lowland in the south. Flocks of egrets often flew there, but the people in Karangsoga had to bow their heads to see them because the white birds were below their line of sight. There would be the splash of water in the fishpond when the kingfisher swooped in for its prey, the scent of nira about to caramelize, and the sounds of the children reciting their verses at Grandfather Mus' surau. The roar of the bus engine reminded Lasi of the students' chanting in Karangsoga.

The earth is moving—it's called an earthquake
People who don't pray shortchange themselves
Be careful as long as you live
Never be selfish, not even for a moment.

Lasi jerked to the present when the bus driver braked abruptly. She looked to her side. An elderly man sat next to her and kept falling asleep. He smelled of Java tobacco.

The bus drove on. A strong wind blew through the open window. The sound of the steadily humming engine lulled Lasi to sleep.

She dreamed about walking home from school. She followed the footpath beneath the shade of the bamboo thicket. The dried leaves crackled beneath her feet. She crossed the areca-palm footbridge, over the brook with crystal-clear water. The rock crabs chased each other along the creek bed. It was the same as before: the male crab with the large pincers defeated all the other crabs. Lasi wished she had large pincers to cut off Mrs. Lanting's head. As always, she was left disappointed because she had no such things attached to her hands.

She continued to walk. The branches of a *jambu* tree shook. Her favorite childhood friend, Kanjat, sat high on one of the branches. Lasi joined him without climbing; instead, she soared. The branch curved when she landed next to him and they held on to each other. They sat so close that she felt Kanjat's body heat. The branch continued to curve toward the ground. They both got down, happy. Lasi reached to pinch Kanjat's cheek, but stopped mid-motion. The child Kanjat became an adult, an engineer, and handsome.

The cold draft coming in from a crack in the window woke Lasi. The lights of the houses by the side of the road were quickly left behind. There was only the flat, monotonous hum of the engine.

At four thirty the next morning, the bus reached a road that passed through Karangsoga. It stopped at the intersection and Lasi got off. She stood for a moment to get her bearings, and walked toward the village. The air was cold, and the eastern sky filled with color. Lasi walked through the mist, accompanied by the sounds of her footsteps.

She walked for a long time without meeting anyone. There were signs of life in a few of the houses she passed: the sound of a hand pump, the crow of a rooster, the chirp of a fantail in a bamboo thicket, and the flash of a bat. Then came the beat of the prayer drum at Grandfather Mus' surau, followed by the call to prayer.

Feelings of awe and longing filled Lasi's heart and tears moistened her eyes. Her chest felt tight as she kept walking. A mouse squeaked in the ditch by the roadside, and dewdrops fell on dead leaves with a soft plop. The new day was peaceful and familiar, and embraced her with the freshness of her birthplace.

As a child, she was often taunted for being different from the others. Her skin was fairer and her eyes were narrower. Her father, a Japanese soldier, had left her exotic features no one else in Karangsoga had.

Despite the taunting she had suffered, Lasi believed the land of her birth was a benevolent mother who would welcome her to her bosom. She never turned away a child coming home, especially if the child was troubled. Karangsoga would accept her grievances and complaints, and cure the fears she brought from Jakarta.

Lasi wanted to be comforted by the soft stroke of her mother's hand. A simple greeting from Grandfather Mus would bring relief. The old man had the ability to understand anyone, especially those mired in difficulty. It was here she also secretly hoped to meet Kanjat.

Lasi continued to walk. In the dim light, an old man hobbled along. She heard the tap of his wooden cane against the road every other step. Shuffle-shuffle-tap, shuffle-shuffle-tap... The sound continued in the direction of the surau. He used all the strength he had early in the morning to heed the holy call Mukri recited. Amplified by loudspeakers, the call that had been such a natural part of the village's spiritual life had lost its gentleness.

Lasi found her parents' house quiet. The front door was locked. She walked around and entered through the back door. The house was empty. A glass of coffee left on the table was still warm. That meant her mother and stepfather were awake, and likely praying together at the surau.

Lasi wanted to pray too. It had been so long since she had done so. She walked through the quiet house to the bathroom, and then to the prayer room. Stillness descended over the house again. It was so quiet, Lasi could hear the praise chanted at the surau. The words penetrated her soul:

If you weigh yourself in terms of life, the scale will tip toward hardship
For life will pass through the gate of death.
If you live a sinful life, you will encounter suffering in the end.
Therefore, solicit Allah's mercy.
And listen to the drumbeat of the one who warns.
Remember it as long as you live in this world.
Seek knowledge, and the door to repentance will remain open.
So let us clear the way to Allah's compassion.
Move forward not with a machete,
But praise and awareness.

Still dressed in prayer robes, Lasi lay down on the prayer mat. The praises calmed her heart. Somehow, the chanting made Lasi feel she was understood and accepted by the land of her birth. The turmoil she had brought from Jakarta began to dissipate. Lasi had slept very little during the overnight journey in the packed bus from Jakarta. She was exhausted and soon fell fast asleep.

***

When the surau was orignally built nearly seventy years ago, it was a simple affair with a palm-thatched roof and walls of woven bamboo. The floor was made of split lengths of bamboo, raised half a meter above the ground. To the right of the hut were a pond and a natural spring where children and adults did their ablutions before entering for prayers and recitals.

The surau used to be the place where the children spent their evenings before going to bed. Kanjat, even though he was the son of the richest man in Karangsoga, was no exception.

The first time he slept away from the hut was when he was sent to a boarding house in town to continue his schooling. After their recitals, the children of Karangsoga played hide-and-seek, martial arts games, or night football.

Some of the naughty children climbed Grandfather Mus' mangosteen tree and picked the ripe fruits. They refused to be accused of stealing, and their reasoning was sound. According to Grandfather Mus' own teachings, it wasn't a sin to take something from someone who would have given it away. Who in Karangsoga doubted his generosity?

When they were tired of playing, the children bathed in the pond or spring next to the surau. Then they chose a place to sleep on the bamboo floor. Sarongs were used as blankets, arms were their pillows, and they stayed warm by huddling together. They slept soundly until they awoke the next morning when the sky in the east turned bright and it was time to pray.

Each day as the sun rose, the pond came alive. The children bathed in the frigid air while playing. The sound of their splashing mingled with the crowing of roosters and calls of the plaintive cuckoo. The cattle lowed, and there was a clacking of sandals and wooden sticks as the old people walked the path to pray together.

Grandfather Mus' surau was once part of the pulse and breath of every resident in Karangsoga, and the environment. The tiny hut was the umbrella of life that offered shade and welcome to everyone. And Grandfather Mus, who held the umbrella, had for decades been the provider of that shade.

Children no longer slept at the surau. The bamboo floor was transformed into concrete; first plastered red, then blue, before being replaced with green tiles. Electric light replaced the oil lamp. The previous year, Lasi had proposed the surau be rebuilt at a cost of tens of millions of rupiah: a new floor changed to a material of better quality, concrete walls, and a roof of factory-made tiles. Grandfather

Mus had disagreed, on the grounds the people of Karangsoga were used to the more humble building.

Even so, Grandfather Mus had failed to fend off having the surau fitted with loudspeakers.

"The chants from this small hut are the human heart and soul. The praise is for the All-Hearing. Why do we need loudspeakers?"

He understood that change was the order of the day, and his surau was markedly different. If one thing remained constant, it was Grandfather Mus, always friendly and soothing.

He looked frail, but the calm that radiated from his smile and his words remained a source of comfort for the people around him. The old man's role as comforter was hampered by his failing strength. He spent much of his time lying on the bamboo bed in his house not far from the surau. The duty of leading the prayers often fell to Mukri, who was still young. Fortunately, one of his granddaughters lived close by, so the old man was never alone.

Everyone in Karangsoga knew Grandfather Mus was in his final years. They took every opportunity to visit him, particularly in the evening. This included Kanjat, who had moved back with his parents several months earlier and often went to see Grandfather Mus after sunset.

That night, after he left the surau, Kanjat headed to his house. When he called out, the old man's visiting granddaughter responded. A mouse scurried away squeaking as Kanjat opened the front door. The granddaughter ushered him to her grandfather's room.

Kanjat pulled a chair up to the bed.

Grandfather Mus greeted him warmly, "Is that you, Kanjat, good man?" He tried to sit up.

"Yes, Grandfather, it's me."

"What a coincidence. I'm glad you came. I've been waiting for you since morning. I forgot you're working as what, a lecturer?"

"That's the story, Grandfather. I commute to work every day and when I get home I'm always a little tired."

"You go to town every day? These days that's easy. Besides, I heard your mother bought you a car."

"That's true, Grandfather. She wants me to live at home. I'm actually embarrassed. I'm a university lecturer, but here I am with a car from my mother."

"That's all right; she can afford it. Besides, it gives you more time to spend with her. Hey, do you know why I've been waiting to see you?"

"No, Grandfather."

"Lasi came last night..."

"She's here?"

"Yes, and staying at her parents' house. Lasi's been unlucky since she was little. I feel sorry for her."

"Why? She's married to a rich man."

"Are the rich exempt from problems?"

"I'm sorry, Grandfather. What problem does she have?"

"It seems her husband left her and another man has claimed her. Lasi is very confused. Last night she was here and crying.

"I gather that she's not only hurt, but also frightened. She asked me for help to free her of all complications, but I'm counting the days I have left. What can I do other than feel sorry for her and pray for things to get better?"

Kanjat waited for Grandfather Mus to continue.

The old man smiled. "You're an engineer now, and you've been Lasi's friend since the two of you were children. Can you come up with an idea to help her?"

Grandfather Mus spoke soft and clear, but his words left Kanjat tongue-tied. He bowed his head and took a deep breath.

Grandfather Mus chuckled. "Are you also confused, Jat?"

"It's true, Grandfather. I'm not ashamed to admit it, especially because Lasi's problem seems to be a personal issue."

"Yes, that much is clear, but what harm is there in asking her? She might speak to you openly."

"Should I see Lasi?"

"In this village, you're the only one who's educated, and who else in Karangsoga would dare to befriend her now that she's a wealthy city woman? The sooner you see Lasi, the better. She needs a friend."

Kanjat coughed. In the silence that followed, a pair of lizards chased each other along the top of the bamboo wall, tussled, and fell. Outside, a night bird sang. The mist became a screen on which Lasi's face was projected. Kanjat had never forgotten that face. He carried the picture of Lasi wearing the red kimono in his wallet.

Grandfather Mus laughed when he saw the young man's dazed expression.

"Jat, why are you worried? It's fine if you don't want to do it. What harm is there in calling on Lasi? You might be able to help her. At the very least, hear her out. That's all."

"I want to," Kanjat still looked doubtful.

"Thank goodness. Lasi will be relieved once she meets the right man to share her feelings with. So, please help her."

"I'm worried she might not want to talk." Kanjat stopped short, interrupted by Grandfather Mus laughing.

"You have a sharp perception and that's good. But look at it like this: I'm an old man. Even though Lasi only told me roughly what has happened, I know she needs someone to listen to her and share her feelings. Stop by Wiryaji's house to see Lasi on your way home from here."

"Yes, Grandfather," Kanjat said in a flat tone.

Grandfather Mus smiled. Relief settled on his weathered face. When Kanjat took his leave, the old man gave him a warm smile. The light in his eyes had dimmed, but still radiated a sense of calm.

***

The rain started with a drizzle as Kanjat left Grandfather Mus. He walked with an umbrella along one of the village's rocky footpaths flanked by shrubs. Pale lights came from the houses with electricity. Save for raindrops rolling off the leaves onto his umbrella and the sound of his footsteps, the night was quiet. The cold air and rain had driven everyone indoors, huddled around their televisions.

Wiryaji's house was quiet when Kanjat arrived. He called out and Wiryaji quickly opened the door to invite him in.

"I hear your step-daughter is home," Kanjat said after sitting down.

"That's right. She came yesterday morning, but she hasn't gone out, except to see Grandfather Mus."

"That's right." Mbok Wiryaji joined them in the front room. "I don't understand why, but she prefers to stay to herself."

"She's probably tired. I'd like to see her, if she doesn't mind."

"Very well. I'll ask." Mbok Wiryaji left the room.

Kanjat heard knocking and Mbok Wiryaji call Lasi's name. He smiled when he heard Lasi respond.

Wiryaji excused himself; Kanjat was there to see Lasi, not him. Mbok Wiryaji also left.

Lasi entered the front room with her face creased from sleep and her hair tousled. She stared at Kanjat, astonished, and smiled widely. "Wait a minute," she said as Kanjat stood to greet her. "I'm sorry, I'll get changed first. These clothes smell."

When Lasi reappeared, her hair was neater. She greeted Kanjat and sat down on the chaise longue. She looked refreshed, but a visible burden rested on her eyebrows. Her smile, awkward at first, soon radiated the magnetic strength that pulled at Kanjat's heart. She had cosmetic work done on her teeth, which were neat, white, and clean. Her eyes, which always had their own special appeal, were even more enchanting.

Jakarta has polished Lasi, Kanjat thought. How she moved was very different, and very pleasing to watch.

"What should I say?" Lasi let go of his hand. "Thank you for coming. How did you know I was here?"

Kanjat felt Lasi slightly tremble. "From Grandfather Mus," he said in a hoarse voice.

"Are you all right, Jat?"

"Yes, thanks be to God."

"Are you a… what is it? Lecturer?"

"What else can I do? Besides, I like the job."

"That's good. If you enjoy your job, it means you've found your place. As for me, my life has become more uncertain." Lasi stopped short and regretted what she had said.

"I thought you were living in Jakarta. You have a lot of money and look even more beautiful."

"Don't tease. The truth is that I'm older. I'm almost thirty, and two years older than you."

"No one would believe it. Anyone would think I'm older than you."

"It's because of your mustache. That's what makes you look older."

Lasi laughed, and again Kanjat was pulled in by the magnetism that radiated from the space between the corners of her mouth.

"A man with slightly darker skin and a mustache is considered handsome," Lasi went on, laughing lightly.

Kanjat felt he was being made fun of, but smiled. He started to speak, but instead pulled out a cigarette.

"You didn't smoke before."

"I don't know why, but I smoke now. It's because I often feel empty."

Lasi smiled and reached for his cigarette.

"What, you smoke too?"

"You're right. Emptiness can drive a person to smoking. You and I are proof."

"You also often feel empty?"

Lasi only laughed. "Mukri's wife came here this afternoon. She said you were single. You must have a girlfriend."

"Not yet. I just haven't met the right woman."

"That makes both of us single. The difference is that you're a bachelor and I'm twice divorced. All that matters is we're both free. It's important because I want to talk with you until morning. Would you like that?"

"I would, but only as long as possible, not until morning. You forget this is Karangsoga."

"Oh yes, sorry. The point is I want to talk. There's so much…"

"Then talk to your heart's content. I'm right here."

Lasi's expression changed. She bowed her head and fell silent. Kanjat waited, but she remained quiet except for her sniffles.

Mbok Wiryaji entered the room with drinks and banana chips. She offered Kanjat a drink and hurried away.

The rain fell heavier. By the side of the house, a tree frog croaked, hoarse and dry. A mouse darted through a gap beneath the door and squeaked as it raced along the foot of the wall. Kanjat stuck his foot out and the mouse bolted away, still squeaking.

"Jat, are you cold?"

"I forgot to bring a jacket."

"Sit with me if you want to get warm. When we played hide-and-seek you used to press yourself against my back," Lasi laughed.

Kanjat smiled as he sat beside Lasi and felt her warmth. He looked sideways, hoping to catch her smile.

She flashed her white teeth and the sensual dimple in her cheek appeared for a moment before her blank expression returned as she stared at the floor.

"Jat, I've changed my mind. I don't want to talk. I think you'd better go home. Thank you for your kindness in coming here."

"What's the matter, Las?" Kanjat was surprised. "You said you wanted to talk until morning. And now you want me to leave?"

"I'm sorry, Jat. I don't want to trouble you. At any moment, someone can come here and force me to go back to Jakarta, or worse. The police might arrest me. I'm accused of cheating someone. Go home so you won't get involved. They might come as early as tonight."

"The police? What is happening with you?" Kanjat eyed her intently.

Lasi sobbed. Her ragged breathing showed she wrestled with a serious problem. After she calmed down, she told Kanjat about her escape and the terribly expensive diamond necklace in her room.

When Lasi mentioned Bambung, Kanjat raised his eyebrows. Bambung's name appeared often in the newspapers. The faculty at the university believed him to be behind every important government decision.

"You could say I'm trying to escape Pak Bambung," Lasi said. "Maybe it's only going to last a moment, until tomorrow or the day after, who knows? Now you see why I asked you to go home."

"Yes, but I won't go." Kanjat walked around the room, and sat down again. A look of concern came over his face. He wiped his forehead and stubbed out his barely smoked cigarette in the ashtray. "Do you really want to get away from Pak Bambung?"

Lasi nodded.

"And you're divorced from your husband?"

Lasi nodded again, sobbing. "Apparently that's what Jakarta men are like, Jat. They discard their wives just like that. I was told I'd been given to Pak Bambung."

Kanjat fell deep in thought.

"Give me some time. I have to consider the possibility of marrying you. Being married to me might protect you from Pak Bambung. You want to, don't you?" Kanjat's lips trembled as he spoke. Clearly emotional, he lit another cigarette.

Lasi, who never thought she would hear him propose, sputtered, "You want to marry me? Don't. I'm telling you, don't."

"Are you refusing me, Las?"

"Don't misunderstand me. Oh, Jat, I still like you. I keep your photo with me. But don't say you want to marry me."

"Why not?"

"I'm unworthy of being your wife. Maybe I'm beautiful, but I'm twice divorced. You're clean, a bachelor. In the end, I'm the former wife of a tapper, and I was a rich man's plaything in Jakarta. What will the people in the village say if I became your wife? I don't want to make you an object of ridicule. I don't want to dirty your name. I…"

"Enough, Las."

Lasi's sniffles and the tree frog croaking filled the silence. The drizzle turned into rain. Water gushed from the downspout. The mouse appeared again in the gap under the door. Its squeal was the same as the moan of someone feeling cold.

"Las, I've been too hasty," Kanjat admitted. "Only a few minutes after seeing you I already talked about marriage."

"I don't want to be your wife because I know my place. Please forget about it. Take me to my Uncle Ngalwi if you really want to help. Since yesterday, I've been thinking about going to his house."

"Your Uncle Ngalwi?"

"He lives in a transmigrant area in Central Sulawesi. I want to hide there for a month or two. I just want to get away. You'll help me like you've always done, won't you?"

Kanjat took deep drags from his cigarette and exhaled to the side. "Very well, I'll take you. I can't go at the drop of a hat because I'm working. I have to arrange for time. And my offer still stands; give me time to figure out how to marry you."

"You'll take me to Uncle Ngalwi even if I refuse?"

Kanjat was lost for words. He looked as though his heart had snapped. He coughed and stubbed out his cigarette.

"I can't force the issue of marriage. When do you want to leave?"

"As quickly as possible. Even tonight."

"You know that can't be done. The soonest is Friday afternoon, because I have no classes on Saturday. It's only Wednesday today."

Lasi frowned and bit her lip.

"It seems too long, but I'll wait. Thank you for doing this."

"Thank you for giving me the chance. Now…"

Kanjat got up, but Lasi quickly took his arm and pulled him back to his seat.

"Don't go home just yet. I still want to talk."

"It's late, and weren't you the one who told me to go home, earlier?"

Lasi pinched his arm. "You've grown a mustache, haven't you? Ah, that mustache of yours."

She pushed closer against him, until they both leaned off to the side. The mouse darted into the room, this time with a friend. They scurried together nose to tail, like a truck and trailer. The two of them slipped behind the door.

Outside, the rain had let up. The gush of the water in the gutter lessened, but the sound of raindrops dropping on the leaves grew more distinct, as did the croaking of the tree frog.

"You're not angry with me for turning you down, are you?" Lasi asked. Her question filled the suffocating silence.

Kanjat shook his head and smiled petulantly.

"Are you truly willing to take me to my uncle's house?"

"I have a mustache, remember. I don't play with my words."

Lasi smiled and pinched his arm. "Let me see your eyes. A willing heart shows in the eyes."

Kanjat turned his head. They gazed at each other, smiling.

Lasi closely studied Kanjat. An unseen bond joined their hearts. The light in Lasi's eyes and the charm in her smile dazzled Kanjat.

"You can go home if you want," Lasi said.

"Where are your parents?"

Lasi went to look for them. She came back a moment later shaking her head. "It seems they're asleep."

"Well, it *is* late."

Lasi clung to Kanjat's arm as she walked him to the door. It still drizzled. Kanjat opened up his umbrella and stepped outside. The tree frog croaking by the side of the house welcomed him. Kanjat looked back at Lasi in the doorway.

As he walked home, his thoughts dwelled on Lasi. He saw her clearly, the country girl who had blossomed with the charming beauty of a young mother. She spoke more directly and openly. The way she walked and her row of straight, white teeth were such a pleasure to look at. That night, Kanjat was unable to fall asleep until past midnight. He woke up late and missed the morning prayer.

On Thursday, Kanjat left Karangsoga at six thirty in the morning as usual. He drove to the university and twice came close to grazing a cyclist. When he pulled into the campus entrance, he hit his side mirror on the gate. In the parking lot, he left his car door open until a student reminded him.

He drove home after his classes were over and realized too late he'd forgotten his bag at the campus. Since it would take too long to turn back, he kept going. He ran into a bigger problem when his car stalled. He'd forgotten to fill it up at the gas station. Fortunately, a nearby vendor sold gasoline by the bottle.

With his mind in turmoil, Kanjat set off for the sunset prayer at the surau. Grandfather Mus led the prayer that evening. After praying and meditating, Kanjat wanted to see Lasi right away, but the old man asked him to stop by his house. He also asked Mukri and Wiryaji to join them.

The four sat down in the sparsely furnished front room. The mood was a bit uncomfortable until Grandfather Mus spoke. "I'd like to talk a bit, especially to Kanjat. It might be important. I've heard from Wiryaji that you plan to take Lasi to Ngalwi's home in Sulawesi," he said without looking at Kanjat.

Kanjat forced a smile. Lasi had told Wiryaji her plan, and that was good. Kanjat would never leave without Lasi telling her parents.

"It's true, Grandfather," Kanjat said.

"That's all right. It wouldn't be good for Lasi to go by herself, especially since she's never been there before. Jat, do you know how long it takes to get to Ngalwi's house?"

Kanjat looked to Wiryaji and Mukri. He hoped they could answer the question. He had never been to the remote transmigrant area.

"If you take the boat from Surabaya to Palu, the whole trip lasts ten days." Mukri had visited Ngalwi a year ago.

Grandfather Mus frowned and grew pensive. "You have to spend several nights together on the way."

"They do, Grandfather," Mukri said, speaking for Kanjat.

Grandfather Mus frowned again. His clouded eyes were fixed on the table. He reached for his tobacco pouch, but refrained from rolling a cigarette. "That's why I wanted to see you. Do you think it's appropriate in the eyes of the Karangsoga people for a single man and a divorced woman to travel together for ten days?"

The question rose in the air and floated around the room.

Kanjat bowed his head, looking nervous.

Mukri coughed.

"What do you think, Wir?"

"It's hard to say, Grandfather. I think it's inappropriate, but that's me. It's really up to Lasi and Kanjat."

"And you, Mukri?"

"It's clearly inappropriate, Grandfather, unless there's another person with them, so they travel in a group of three."

"I agree. A line is being crossed if Lasi travels alone with Kanjat. We trust you, but a certain amount of decorum still applies in Karangsoga."

"I have no problem calling off the journey, Grandfather. It's really only a plan at this stage," Kanjat said in a low voice. "Maybe we can find a third person to go with us."

"Patience, Jat. Finding a third person won't be easy during the planting season. I want the two of you to go, but in a proper manner. In order to accomplish this, it's best that you and Lasi are married. Don't be shocked. This is important, but also simple. We're here to discuss this. Wiryaji, Mukri, what do you think?"

Wiryaji and Mukri were stunned. Kanjat tensed and quickly looked down, afraid that Grandfather Mus and the others noticed the sudden flush of joy on his face.

Grandfather Mus went on. "What I mean is, Kanjat and Lasi will be married in a purely religious ceremony before they leave to maintain their dignity and respect, as well as ours. They're young. With no marital ties, somewhere along the trip they might succumb to temptation, and I'll feel guilty.

"Once they get to Sulawesi," the old man said, "they can decide whether to continue the marriage. So much the better if they want to formalize it, but that will be up to them. They can dissolve the marriage if they both agree. That's what I wanted to put forward to all of you. Wiryaji, Mukri, and you too, Kanjat—do you agree?"

"I agree, Grandfather," Mukri said. "I also agree to Kanjat and Lasi getting married officially. It's better than her being taken away by someone we don't know."

"And you, Wir?"

Wiryaji looked hesitant. "Yes, I agree, but what if Lasi refuses? I also have to ask her mother's permission."

"Obviously this decision depends on Lasi and her mother. We'll have to find out. Kanjat, what's your opinion?"

He smiled and coughed, even though there was nothing wrong with his throat. "I'd like to, Grandfather. I'd really like to..." He smiled again.

"What about your mother?" Wiryaji cut in.

"I'll talk to her," Grandfather Mus said, smiling. He looked like he was about to speak, but paused. He thought of Mbok Tir. She often came to him complaining that Kanjat had yet to marry. "Here I am, getting old and sick. I want to see Kanjat married right away," she said every time she visited. "It's up to him who he chooses. All that matters is Kanjat likes her and she's willing to treat me like her own mother."

Mbok Tir's words echoed in the old man's ears, but he kept them to himself. "Okay, we all agree. Mukri, go get Lasi and her mother and bring them here. Tell them I need to see them, and nothing more."

Mukri left with a spring in his step. The three men listened to his footsteps recede into the night. He reappeared fifteen minutes later with Lasi and her mother.

Lasi became flustered when she saw the men gathered in Grandfather Mus' house. Her intuition told her they had been talking about her.

Grandfather Mus asked Lasi and her mother to sit on a bench at the other side of the table. He told them softly about the plan. "It's up to you and your mother, Las. Will you accept this marriage completely? Thank God if you do, because you will be respecting the traditional laws we observe in this village. It's fine if you don't, because even though it's only a religious ceremony, no one should feel forced into it."

"Wait, Grandfather," Kanjat cut in. "Please tell them this is all your idea and that I agree."

"Yes, that's how it is," Grandfather Mus said.

Lasi was stunned. She heard a sudden ringing in her ears. She swallowed several times, and looked flustered at Grandfather Mus, her mother, and Kanjat. Tears welled in her eyes and her lips quivered.

In the silent room, Lasi heard her own heart beat. She also heard the words she had said to Kanjat the day before. "What will the Karangsoga people say? You're a bachelor and I'm twice divorced."

Why did Grandfather Mus, Mukri, and her stepfather want her to marry Kanjat? Lasi wondered. Tears rolled down her cheeks and she kept her head down.

"What do you think, Mother?" Her voice was faint and hoarse.

Mbok Wiryaji twisted a corner of the wrap she wore. She coughed and looked like she was about to cry.

"The decision depends on Lasi and Kanjat. I've always trusted the good intentions of Grandfather Mus. To be honest, I'd be ashamed to face Kanjat's mother. No matter what the circumstances are, Lasi is the daughter of a poor woman. No one knows where her father is."

"Enough," Grandfather Mus interrupted her gently. "I already said I'll talk to Kanjat's mother. Answer my question: do you agree to Lasi marrying Kanjat?"

Mbok Wiryaji looked down and wiped her eyes. "Yes, I'll go along with whatever you say."

"There, your mother has agreed. You're the only one left now, Las. What will it be?" Grandfather Mus asked gently.

Lasi cried. Her palms were sweaty. She wanted to refuse, but Grandfather Mus, the most influential person in the village, had dismantled her reason.

"Las, we're waiting for your answer," Mukri reminded.

Lasi stayed quiet.

Grandfather Mus chuckled. He was used to reading all kinds of situations. He knew that Lasi disagreed with the offer, but neither would she refuse. Since he was unsure she would accept it wholeheartedly, Grandfather Mus looked for the smallest sign.

"The truth is that I've been meaning to get Kanjat and Lasi together for the longest time, ever since she and Darsa separated. My reason is simple: Lasi and Kanjat have gotten on well since they were children. My intuition tells me they like each other. So tell me, Lasi and Kanjat, am I mistaken?"

All eyes turned to Lasi. Feeling herself the center of attention, Lasi only smiled. She glanced at Kanjat. Grandfather Mus caught the smile and the soft glint in her eyes as she looked at Kanjat.

Those subtle signs were enough to convince Grandfather Mus that Lasi really did like Kanjat and would marry him of her own free will. Grandfather Mus smiled, relieved.

The gathering at the house grew quiet and solemn as the ceremony began. Mukri and Wiryaji served as the witnesses. Grandfather Mus took the place of the guardian marrying Lasi to Kanjat. There was a comical moment when, as the guardian, Grandfather Mus asked Lasi whether she was clean, whether she was having her period, and when was the last time she had lain with her previous husband.

"How long ago? A month?" he asked.

"Longer, Grandfather."

"Two months?"

"Longer."

"Three?"

"Even more." Everyone smiled.

"May Allah bless you both. Amen," Grandfather Mus said at the end of the prayer that marked the conclusion of the brief ceremony.

"Amen."

Mbok Wiryaji took a deep breath and wiped her eyes. She hugged and stroked Lasi like she was still a child. Wiryaji quietly lit a cigarette. Grandfather Mus smiled with satisfaction, as did Mukri. Kanjat felt as though his feet were no longer touching the ground. He looked at Lasi. She only glanced at him before looking down and wiping away her tears.

"Thanks be to God," Grandfather Mus said. "Something I have long wished for has finally happened, to see Kanjat and Lasi as man and wife. Thanks be to God."

With no preparation for the wedding repast, they had to do with cassava chips served by Grandfather Mus' granddaughter. Grandfather Mus announced the marriage later at the communal night prayer at the surau.

***

On their way to Central Sulawesi, Lasi and Kanjat stayed overnight in Surabaya. The boat to Palu would leave in three day's time. Lasi wanted to stay at a nice hotel; Kanjat thought it better to stay in a guesthouse.

"Las, Grandfather Mus was right," he said as he and Lasi entered the same room. "If we hadn't gotten married, we would break the rules."

"Why?" Lasi asked.

"Being with you like this, I'd never be able to control myself. I'm just an ordinary man."

"What do you want to do now?" Lasi asked with a smile.

"Since we're husband and wife, according to religion…"

"Is that true, Jat?" Lasi interjected. "You're really serious about our marriage?"

"I'm very serious. Before meeting with Grandfather Mus, you turned down my proposal. Are you still turning me down?"

"Jat, am I really your wife, and are you really my husband?"

"Yes."

Lasi started to cry. She cried so long that Kanjat wondered what to do. His confusion dissipated when Lasi whispered between sobs, "Jat, why have we waited to be together like this?"

It was close to midnight when Lasi awoke Kanjat gently by tickling his mustache.

"Jat, I'm hungry. I can hear the chicken satay vendor outside," she whispered in his ear.

"I'm not, but okay."

He turned on the light. He looked at Lasi on the bed in her nightdress. She smiled. Kanjat felt himself rise off the ground, as happened often in the two days since the wedding. The happiness he experienced made him feel he was soaring.

Kanjat watched Lasi eat her chicken satay with rice cakes. He brought her a glass of water when she was done, and a pair of slippers when she wanted to go to the bathroom. Kanjat went outside to pay the satay vendor, and came back and turned out the light.

"Las, how long will you stay at your uncle's house?"

"Until the people in Jakarta forget about me."

"Will it take weeks or months?"

"A month or two at the most. I have to stay out of Pak Bambung's reach."

"What about our marriage?"

"What do you want to do?"

"I haven't had any intention of dissolving it from the beginning. You're my wife and all we need to do to make it official is go to a religious affairs office. Don't stay too long at your uncle's house. Send me a letter when it's time and I'll come get you."

"Thank you, Jat. Oh, thank you."

Lasi cried again and hugged Kanjat with all her strength. "Will we live in Karangsoga? I don't want to. I'd be ashamed."

"You must. At least while your mother's still there. I have to stay and look after my mother because she's getting old."

"Are you sure your mother will accept me?"

"To be honest, I'm not. She'll come around when I tell her you're the only woman I'll ever marry. Besides, we have Grandfather Mus on our side. My mother's always thought highly of him."

"And then?"

"We'll have children."

"How many?"

Lasi held her answer, but Kanjat knew she wanted a family with all her heart. The room went quiet. From outside came the tapping of a blind man's cane and the shout of the satay vendor in his thick Madura accent: "Sat-t-t-t-tay!"

On the morning of the third day, Kanjat and Lasi were ready to go to the port. Kanjat packed their things soon after breakfast. He'd never been to Sulawesi, but imagined that during the journey they would have poor service, bad food, and hot weather. All of that vanished at the thought of traveling with Lasi. Kanjat was on a sweet, dream journey, and knew the dream was real.

He was enjoying the dream when there was a loud knock on the door. Kanjat finished tying his shoelaces. Lasi stopped painting her lips and looked at him nervously. They heard another, even louder knock. Kanjat ran to unlock the door and opened it. His mouth dropped half open.

Two brawny men with mean stares and a fat woman stood in front of him. One of the men wore a police uniform and announced the reason for their visit.

"I'm Major Brangas from the Jakarta Police. I have a warrant to bring in the ex-wife of Pak Handarbeni, by the name of Lasi, to my superior. Is the said ex-wife of Pak Handarbeni here?"

Kanjat was shocked into silence. The man in plainclothes pushed into the room, followed by the fat woman. Kanjat tried to stop them, but the man shoved him aside.

"There she is. Las, what are you doing in this dilapidated little room?" Mrs. Lanting grabbed Lasi by the shoulders. "I've been looking for you everywhere, at Ibu Koneng's restaurant, at Pak Min's house, at Karangsoga, only to find you here. What do you think you're doing? Let's go, we're going back to Jakarta."

Lasi shuddered seeing Mrs. Lanting with the policeman. She turned pale and her lips turned blue. Her limbs trembled. She dropped her lipstick.

"Wait." The sight of the woman pulling at Lasi incensed Kanjat. "You can't take her with you. She's my wife. We're married."

"You only had a village wedding," Mrs. Lanting said sharply. "I know everything from the people in Karangsoga. Don't dare say you're married to Lasi. You don't have the papers to prove it. Officer Brangas has a warrant to bring Lasi back to Jakarta. By force, if necessary."

"That's right. Don't try to stop me in the course of my duties," Major Brangas glared at Kanjat.

"Come on, Las. You've made Pak Bambung really angry. You have to return with us to Jakarta. If you do as we say, we promise you'll be treated the same as before. But if you act up, who knows what might happen. Officer Brangas has a pair of handcuffs for you. Rather than be dragged off to the police station, you'd better do as I say. Where's your bag? Hey, wait. Did you bring it with you?"

Lasi was baffled as she tried to understand what Mrs. Lanting said. She nodded, the tears streaming down her face.

"You're crazy," Mrs. Lanting hissed. "It's not insured. The papers are with Pak Bambung. You're lucky no one snatched it."

"I'll return the necklace, but I beg you, let me stay with Kanjat. Take the necklace for yourself and leave the two of us here. Please."

"Las, the necklace doesn't matter to Pak Bambung. Even I don't dare mess around with him. Enough talking. Come with us."

Kanjat froze. His hand quivered. He was enraged, a fire blazed in his eyes as he clenched his jaw. Major Brangas insulted him, treating him like a criminal suspect, taking down his name, address, and work details. He watched helplessly as Lasi was unable to resist the fat woman's demands. Her sobs broke his heart.

Kanjat wanted to fight them; he held himself back because he knew he was dealing with the police. The fat woman was right: he had no official proof Lasi was his wife.

Kanjat could do nothing except exchange looks with Lasi. In each other's eyes, they saw a dead end. When Mrs. Lanting pulled her arm, Lasi tried to speak to Kanjat. His attention was drawn from her by a harsh voice.

"We're very offended by your taking Ibu Lasi," Major Brangas told the defiant Kanjat. "There's no need to take you into custody just yet. I don't know about later. For now, this is enough."

A punch from a trained hand zoomed in on Kanjat in a straight line and slammed into his chin. It was lightning quick, and Kanjat, lacking any self-defense skills, walked into it. He was knocked over backward. He heard Lasi scream as he saw stars. When he got up, he couldn't see clearly and heard a car leave the guesthouse. The other occupants stayed where they were and looked on. No one moved to help Kanjat, who leaned unsteadily in the doorway to his room with a bleeding lip.

***

Lasi cried during the flight from Surabaya to Jakarta. Her eyelids and nose turned red. With her lips set in a tight line and cold eyes, she looked like a person who had lost her soul. She ignored the offered services on the flight and Mrs. Lanting. Repressed anger flared in her eyes, and each time she blinked, the anger hardened her heart.

Two cars waited for them at the Jakarta airport. Lasi burst into tears again. She had returned to being a fish inside a lavish aquarium, where everything was artificial. If she had to be a fish, she preferred living in the creek at the bottom of the ravine in Karangsoga. It was a simple life, but one to which she belonged, where she played an active role she understood.

Lasi kept crying. *Why did the policeman hit Kanjat? Why is he in the car with me? Cruel policeman. I will swear a thousand times that Kanjat is my husband.*

From the airport, the car headed to the Semanggi cloverleaf and turned left on Sudirman Avenue. It went around the traffic circle in front of the Hotel Indonesia before turning on Latuharhari Street. The car kept going east, turned right, cut across Imam Bonjol Avenue, and continued straight south until they reached a stately home in the shade of several large trees.

A security guard opened the gate and saluted. The car stopped in front of the porch. Major Brangas sat next to the driver and got out first, with Mrs. Lanting following. She turned and led a reluctant Lasi from the car.

"This is your new home, Las. If you only knew how lucky a woman is to receive a house on this street as a present. Your neighbors here are important people, and, of course, fabulously rich. Pak Han gave you luxury; Pak Bambung will give you two or three times as much."

Lasi ignored the chatter. She entered the house with her head bowed, steered by Mrs. Lanting. They went straight to the living room. Mrs. Lanting summoned the household staff: three male servants, two women, two gardeners, and three drivers.

"This is Ibu Lasi, but you should call her *Nyonya Muda,* the young mistress. If you want a salary raise from Pak Bambung, you better serve her very well."

The staff took Mrs. Lanting's words to heart. They were bewildered when, by the third day, they had yet to hear a peep from the young mistress. Lasi remained aloof and left her meals untouched.

On the afternoon of the first day, Mrs. Lanting found Lasi twisting a veil into a rope. She gasped at Lasi preparing to kill herself. She grabbed the rope and quickly tossed it out of reach. Mrs. Lanting decided it was in her best interest to watch over Lasi day and night, because she feared Lasi was brave enough to take her own life.

Mrs. Lanting asked Pak Bambung to restrain himself and not to see Lasi until the bekisar no longer felt under pressure.

"Pak, your bekisar is throwing a temper tantrum. Be patient for one or two months," Mrs. Lanting told him over the telephone. "She doesn't want to eat and only drinks. This morning she had a banana, a very good sign."

"Don't leave her alone. Take care of Lasi, and don't let her get sick from not eating. Do what you need to do. I trust you to handle this matter."

"Relax, pak. Just remember: this isn't part of the contract."

"I know, I know. My secretary has your bank account number. You'll get your extra pay."

"Thank you. I'll stay until your bekisar is singing. You have to be patient."

Bambung needed to be very patient. After a month, Lasi still pined for Kanjat. She lost weight. Her eyes were sorrowful and the color faded from her face. Mrs. Lanting became worried because she looked weak. She spent her time brooding and crying. What if she was depressed?

"Las, take care of yourself," Mrs. Lanting implored before dinner. "You're the mistress of this house, the consort of a rich and very powerful man. What greater fortune is there? Pak Bambung could have paid the police to throw you in jail for any reason, like you were on the run with a necklace worth billions and no papers. What would you rather have, to live well here or go to jail? The security guard outside is one of Major Brangas' men. You're always being watched."

Lasi turned pale and her lips quivered.

"You'd rather live here than go to jail, right?" Mrs. Lanting pressed on.

Lasi nodded.

"In that case you must eat."

"I'm not hungry."

"You're going to damage your body."

"So be it."

Mrs. Lanting thought for a moment. "Would you like to eat out? I can arrange it."

To Mrs. Lanting's surprise, Lasi reacted to the offer. The reaction was barely perceptible, but there. Lasi smiled weakly and swallowed. Mrs. Lanting pressed on, encouraged.

"How about the President Hotel? You might meet your father, because many Japanese people go there." Mrs. Lanting laughed. She stopped short when Lasi spoke.

"I'd like to have *laksa*, bu."

"What's that?" Mrs. Lanting asked, her eyes widening.

"You don't know what laksa is? It has noodles and coconut milk, and uses chilies…"

"Oh, now I know. It's a traditional Betawi dish."

"Maybe, I'm not sure."

"Lasi, ask for something nice, like shark fin soup or *teppanyaki*." Mrs. Lanting shook her head and frowned.

"I want laksa. There's a vendor near Ibu Koneng's restaurant in Klender. Can you take me?"

"We'll send one of the drivers."

"No. I have to eat sitting close to the vendor."

"Ah, you're a strange one. Let's go anyway."

After the dinner in Klender, Lasi ate more regularly, but only laksa. Soon she looked healthier and started to talk again. She knew what had happened to her, and with the knowledge came memories of her sweet experience with Kanjat.

Her two nights as Kanjat's wife meant more to Lasi than two years as Handarbeni's wife. Lasi had found herself, especially when she and Kanjat melded into one so completely. It had been a perfect fusion of body and soul, and the true meaning reached beyond the sky.

Those days and nights had united Lasi with a husband whose world was not foreign to her and she understood well. More than that, Kanjat had lived in her heart since they were children. The time spent with Kanjat took Lasi to the peak of her being.

Will I always feel the same?

She was shocked. The clamoring in her soul made her head dizzy. Lasi held her breath. She searched for something that had become evident in a short space of time. Her chest throbbed. She examined the subtle sensations of her whole body.

Lasi resumed breathing. *What am I really feeling when I'm certain something is happening in my body? Why am I dizzy and constantly salivating? Why haven't I had my period?*

Anxiety, joy, disbelief, and misery crossed her face.

Lasi was astonished. She felt a tremor going through her. A vision of Kanjat passed by and Lasi almost called out to him. The vision dissolved into the tears that welled in her eyes. Lasi touched her stomach. It felt normal, but she had to acknowledge the warmth that grew stronger inside her.

She was certain her period was late. She cried at night in her locked room, not because of her period or the sensation in her stomach. The thought she was pregnant came to her so quickly and definitely, she knew it came from deep within.

I'm pregnant, Lasi yearned to tell Kanjat. *In my womb grows the seed of your child, our child. We're going to have a child. You're happy, aren't you? If it's a boy, he'll be good like you. If it's a girl, she'll be beautiful like me. You once said I was beautiful, didn't you?*

The silence of the night swallowed Lasi's thoughts and questions without leaving a trace. She knew Kanjat couldn't hear her and grew pensive until suddenly joy appeared on her face. *How could I forget Kanjat giving me his name card? The telephone.*

Lasi dashed to the dressing table for her handbag. Her hands shook as she rummaged through its compartments for the slip of paper. She found it and dialed the number on Kanjat's card. It connected. She counted out the seconds: one, two, three... but there was no answer.

Lasi was chagrined; it was late at night and the number she had dialed was for Jenderal Soedirman University where Kanjat worked.

She lay back down and got lost in thought. The look on her face kept changing. She smiled, and then moved to near tears. Her mind drifted into the past when she was married to Darsa, the tapper.

Even though he was only a simple villager, Darsa was truly good when it came to fulfilling Lasi's physical needs. Lasi remembered her life with him. Back then she believed her life was easy. She gave herself fully to Darsa and prepared herself to be the field in which he planted his seed. A seedling did sprout, but it wilted and withered. Lasi had a miscarriage when she was four months' pregnant with Darsa's child.

Her thoughts switched to being Handarbeni's wife. For the nearly two years they were married, Lasi never opened herself up to be the field in which he planted his seed. Once or twice, she derived bodily pleasure while her heart remained closed. That prompted a question: *Is this the reason I never got pregnant from Mas Han?*

It was almost daybreak and Lasi was exhausted; her eyes closed. In her short sleep, she dreamed of eating lots of laksa, spicy and hot, fresh and cheery. The vendor was Kanjat.

Lasi awoke at five in the morning and rubbed her stomach. It felt the same as before. Lasi was certain something bloomed inside her womb, and she smiled.

Allah, thank you.

Allah had entrusted her with carrying a new life. This gave her more meaning as a woman.

She went to the servants' quarters, where everyone was awake, and asked to borrow prayer robes and a mat. *Allah, bless and grace my baby. I know, I want, and I must take care of it. But how, when I'm in a situation like this?*

"No matter what happens to you, take care and protect the sanctity of your womb."

Lasi was startled to hear the answer so clearly. She wanted to know who had spoken with such authority. Only silence surrounded her.

Her tears began falling as she was overcome with emotion. Lasi realized the voice had come from her own conscience. It reverberated in her soul, and solidified and strengthened her heart. Lasi steeled her resolve and made a decision: no matter what happened, the safety and sanctity of her womb was everything. She would die defending it. She shut her eyes as she felt stirring at the bottom of her soul. Her confidence slowly rose.

Once she had something to defend and chosen a truth to believe, Lasi was at peace. The tension and uncertainty that had gripped her during the past several days slowly faded. She smiled when Mrs. Lanting walked in as she was praying.

"That's it, pray. Some say prayer gives peace of mind. I say you can only be at peace when you have money. Which is true, Las?"

"You're right," Lasi smiled.

"I was just kidding, Las. Don't be offended."

"I was too, ibu."

"Joking only adds to my sins. I'm sorry. Just forget about it. Anyway, Pak Bambung called last night. He said he misses you. Will you see him?"

Lasi's face tensed. She looked down, wringing her hands and frowning. Her chest throbbed.

Kanjat appeared before her eyes. Lasi knew he was willing her to protect the sanctity of her womb, her own being, as she had pledged moments ago. Even though she could only tell him of her resolve over the telephone, Lasi had to protect the new life with hers.

How could she maintain her resolve in front of Bambung? *I have nails to scratch and teeth to bite. I have a mouth to scream if my womb is threatened.* Lasi swallowed. Calm and order spread through her heart.

"Why don't you speak?" Mrs. Lanting said. "Will you see Pak Bambung this evening?"

Lasi looked up and took a breath. She squared her shoulders and smiled coldly.

Mrs. Lanting was relieved. The fat woman took Lasi's cold smile as a good sign.

"There isn't anything I can do, bu. If Pak Bambung wants to come, I can't prevent it."

"You really are a sweet child, Las. What could be wrong with being the consort of an important man like Pak Bambung? If anything, you're very lucky. Life is..."

"All about money," Lasi cut in, laughing.

Surprised at the impertinence, Mrs. Lanting frowned for a moment, and then laughed. "You said it. I know you're joking, but what you said is true. The only thing that matters is money. If I were you, I'd live by these words: rather than suffer while resisting being raped, it's better to enjoy the rape. It sounds crazy, but you've seen it proven: no matter where you run you will never be out of Pak Bambung's reach. Why not enjoy a life where he pampers you with loads of money? It makes sense. Besides, Pak Bambung doesn't want to rape you."

Lasi was amused and smiled.

Mrs. Lanting misread the meaning of her smile. "I'll call him later. He'll come over to… Take a guess, Las."

Lasi stayed quiet.

"To pamper you, of course. Pak Bambung has everything to make you happy. You believe me, don't you? Go get ready."

A faint smile fluttered on Lasi's lips.

Mrs. Lanting waddled away like a duck as she always did. Her job with Lasi was almost done. This meant more money in the bank.

The next morning, Lasi sat before the telephone at five minutes before eight. Her fingers were sweaty and her face was tense. Lasi's heart thumped when the line connected. One, two, three, and no mistaking it: Kanjat's voice.

"Jat, it's Lasi," she choked.

"Where are you?" Kanjat was tense.

Lasi felt like something was stuck in her throat.

"I'm… I'm in Jakarta, Jat. In a house, I don't know where. Mrs. Lanting, the fat woman, says it's Pak Bambung's house."

"You have to get out…"

"Patience, Jat. I haven't seen him yet. You're all right, aren't you?"

"Tell me first, where is the house?"

"I can see the Hotel Indonesia to the west. It's nice. There's a guard post, and the fence is painted white with a green gate."

"Yes, yes, but I'm getting muddled. I can't wait to see you. I'm worried. What should I do?"

"You have to stay calm. Because—listen to me, Jat—I'm late…"
Lasi heard Kanjat's breathing over the telephone.

On his end, Kanjat heard Lasi's sniffling. "You're pregnant?"

Lasi swallowed. She nodded as though Kanjat was nearby.

Kanjat asked her again. His hand holding the receiver shook.

"Yes. I'm certain of it. It's your child." Lasi cried over the telephone. Her whole body trembled as she waited for him.

"Of course, it's my child."

"Jat," Lasi said with joy. She fell silent, save for her deep sobs.

"Calm down, Las." This time Kanjat soothed Lasi. "Tell me what to do. I'm ashamed to ask, but to be honest, I'm lost."

"The house is guarded. I can't escape, and you can't get inside."

"What then?"

"I'll take the very best care of your child. I'm asking you to trust me. Your child and I will remain pure. Forgive me, Jat, I have to hang up. I hear Mrs. Lanting."

The line died. Kanjat felt like his own breath had been cut off. He gasped. He brooded until he returned to his senses. *Lasi's right and I must stay calm. Calm?*

***

Bambung showed up wearing a fatherly smile, and with a serving of hot laksa that Lasi had to accept. His white sideburns as thick as before, he was courteous, warm, and full of understanding. He looked like a better man than the one who ordered Major Brangas to go after her, the savage Brangas who had destroyed the most beautiful moment of her life.

Lasi appeared ready for him. She exuded calm and confidence that gave her dignity. Her persona shone through clearly, even though she had dressed down and wore no makeup.

"We meet again. How are you, Lasi?" Bambung was friendly. He shook her hand firmly and leaned in to kiss her cheek.

Lasi bowed her head. "I'm fine, thank you, pak," she said evenly, and showed Bambung to a seat.

"I trust you're content here. Tell Mrs. Lanting if anything is missing, or call me directly."

"Everyone working here is very good."

"They're under orders to be like that."

They chatted in the living room until nine, a mix of small talk and jokes that made Lasi laugh. In between, they enjoyed the laksa, which served to lighten the mood.

Bambung was an experienced hunter and Lasi was the beautiful bekisar he was after. They ran out of things to talk about and their conversation sputtered. Bambung stood and took Lasi by the hand. With a smile and a wink, he showed he wanted to take her to the bedroom.

She pulled her hand away, and rejected his advances with a smile of her own. "I'm sorry, pak, I'd like to keep talking. Besides, I have a question for you."

"Yes. What do you want to ask?"

"It's just this, pak. What did you expect when you had me brought here?"

"Look here, Las. From the moment you came here you were the mistress of this house."

"You mean I'll be your wife?"

"Yes," Bambung said with a confident smile. His eyes glimmered.

"Wait," Lasi's face was blank. "You need to know my condition. I'm pregnant. So I can't…"

Bambung pressed his lips into a thin line as he stared at Lasi. She was eager to see how he would respond. When he stayed silent, she continued to talk.

"I'm carrying the child of Kanjat, my husband. Do you still want me to live here? Please, tell me."

Bambung's first reaction was an ironic smile. An unexpected situation had presented itself. The flame of desire that burned in his chest died down and was on the verge of extinguishing. "Remain here until I decide otherwise. As for your pregnancy, that's a matter for the doctor," Bambung said, stiff and flat.

"What do you mean?"

"The doctor will tell me whether you're pregnant or not. He will determine the possibility of an abortion."

"No," Lasi said quickly, calm and confidently.

Bambung was surprised Lasi had dared to interrupt him.

"If you want a doctor to confirm I'm pregnant, that's fine. I'd be very grateful, but I will never consent to an abortion. I'm pregnant and will look after my child as best as I can. This is what I want. I've waited many years for a child."

A stony look spread across Bambung's face, and his jaw muscles tightened. "I don't want to hear anything more about this damned situation. Mrs. Lanting will take care of it. That's all that needs to be said." Bambung abruptly stood.

"Wait. I haven't finished…"

Bambung stormed out, slamming the door behind him.

Lasi cried from relief that Bambung had gone. For a moment, fear took over. She was surprised at her courage to speak so directly to him and soon regained her composure.

At home, Bambung went into his study and telephoned Mrs. Lanting in Cikini. "Bitch. Why didn't you tell me that Lasi was pregnant?"

"She didn't say anything to me. How would I know?"

"Listen to me. I don't like pregnant women. You got that?" The tension in his voice threatened to explode the telephone receiver. "You want to know why?" Bambung yelled.

"Um… Yes," Mrs. Lanting stammered.

"When I was a child, my mother was constantly pregnant. You could say she always had a baby inside her. I had fourteen brothers and sisters. The smell of the herbal concoctions she drank made me sick. That's why I don't like pregnant women. My passion goes down when I see a pregnant woman. Do you understand? Bitch."

Mrs. Lanting laughed heartily. "Hold on. Even if she's pregnant, Lasi looks normal. She hasn't changed at all."

"She said she was pregnant. That was enough to kill my mood. You talk too much. Bitch."

"Don't be angry. Your blood pressure will go up."

"It's already up because of you."

"Okay, fine. Take it out on me so you can get over it quicker."

"You really are a bitch, and a crappy agent."

The line went dead. Mrs. Lanting imagined Bambung's flushed face. It didn't matter he called her a crappy agent. She knew she was the best in her business of supplying women to the elite. She was also very experienced when it came to handling a man's basic nature. She dialed Bambung's number. "Pak, given the situation, what should I do?"

"You bitch. Take her to a doctor and check whether she's really pregnant."

"And if she is?"

"Then have it aborted, bitch."

"What if Lasi refuses?"

"You should be able to handle her, unless you're completely worthless."

The line went dead again. Mrs. Lanting gulped. She rubbed her forehead and dialed Lasi's number.

"I just had a call from Pak Bambung," she said in a sharp voice. "So you're pregnant? Answer me: are you pregnant?"

"Yes, with my husband's child."

"Tomorrow morning I'm taking you to the doctor. Be ready at eight."

"I'll be ready, bu. Did Pak Bambung mention an abortion?"

"Yes. If it's true, he wants you to have an abortion."

"I don't want to."

"And what if you're forced?"

"You know what a woman will do when she's desperate."

Mrs. Lanting fell silent. She pondered Lasi's words. She remembered her first day in the new house, when Lasi made a rope from a veil. Committing suicide was easy. Ropes, pesticides, razor blades, and even walls could be used to cause death. Just the other day, near her home, a young girl had taken her life by sticking her metal hair clip into an electric outlet. Was Lasi that desperate?

"Las, the doctor can abort the baby without you feeling a thing. He'll give you something to breathe and you'll fall asleep. By the time you wake up he'll be done. It couldn't be easier than that. Your baby's very young, and who knows, maybe swallowing a pill can abort it. That's easy, right?"

"You don't understand. I'm not against the abortion because of pain. I'm against it because I want this child. We're women. Have you never felt like this?" Lasi said calmly.

Mrs. Lanting frowned.

"All right, Las. I understand. The problem is Pak Bambung is capable of violence. Yesterday on television, the police found the remains of a beautiful woman chopped up and dumped at a bus stop. My gut tells me the woman was killed because of an illicit affair with someone powerful. I don't want that to happen to you."

"What's the point of living if I lose the child I've wanted for so long?"

Mrs. Lanting hung up. She stood lost in thought by the telephone. It occurred to her to go ahead with the abortion without Lasi's permission. She knew the procedure would be easy for the doctor. After thinking it through, she realized Lasi might go through with her threat when she found out.

Mrs. Lanting called Bambung the next day. After having her call transferred several times, she was finally put through. "I'm sorry, pak. Call me worthless or crappy all you want, but Lasi stands firm that she won't get an abortion."

"Why can't you force her?"

"To be honest, I think she'd turn self-destructive. If anything happened to Lasi, would you be prepared to deal with the trouble?"

"I've never had trouble with women and I don't want any. Why should I?"

"Please hear me out. It's a middle road, pak. You don't like pregnant women, but as you saw for yourself, Lasi remains exotic and beautiful. As long as her pregnancy doesn't show you can use her as your play doll. For the next few months, you can take her anywhere—the golf course, racetrack, concerts, or fishing at sea. Believe me, pak, having Lasi by your side will make your friends drool."

"And then?"

"Once her stomach gets big, leave her to me. A month or two after giving birth, Lasi will be back to being beautiful. She'll have the beauty of a full-grown woman, and serve you with a smile. That's what you want, isn't it?"

"You really are a bitch. The damnedest thing is that what you say makes sense."

"You'll go along?"

"Yes. But don't ever bring me a pregnant woman again."

Mrs. Lanting smiled as she pressed the receiver to her ear. She was more convinced than ever that she was the best high-class pimp.

An hour later, she visited Lasi and told her about the conversation with Bambung. Lasi was all ears. Her eyes sparkled when she learned Bambung had changed his mind and no longer insisted on an abortion.

"Wait, ibu. There's one other thing I have to protect."

"What now, Las? Why are you so demanding?"

"I want to preserve the sanctity of my womb. I'll accompany Pak Bambung anywhere, but if he wants that one thing, I'll refuse."

Mrs. Lanting smiled and Lasi started to worry.

"Well, it's doubtful whether Pak Bambung will be able to control himself when he's alone with you. From what I know, he's a bit of a horny goat, but Pak Bambung has made it clear he feels no desire for pregnant women."

Mrs. Lanting related the story of Bambung's mother, and Lasi had to smile.

"One more thing, bu," Lasi said when she was done laughing. "What happens after my child is born? Will I still live in this house?"

"From my experience, important men get bored rather quickly of their mistresses. They have a lot of money, so they always look for a new toy. Look at Pak Han. He handed you over to Pak Bambung when he was offered a shipping company and a post as minister.

"For Pak Bambung, I'll bet that he'll get bored of you once he sees your stomach grow. Think about what you can do now. What happens after can wait until later. It's easier that way."

Chapter 9

In Karangsoga, Kanjat only told Lasi's parents, Grandfather Mus, and Mukri how Mrs. Lanting and the police had taken Lasi to Jakarta. He apologized repeatedly to Lasi's mother, but the guilt continued to weigh on his heart. For several days after returning from Surabaya, he was unable to sleep or eat.

When he received the telephone call from Lasi, Kanjat was relieved despite her being almost a prisoner. The news of her pregnancy made Kanjat happy and despondent, and he knew he owed her. It saddened him that he was unable to prove his intentions to Lasi and the child. He felt stupid and crippled. He told no one else about Lasi's pregnancy.

Kanjat thought of turning to the law to bring her home to Karangsoga. Courts, police stations, prosecutors, and lawyers were everywhere. The idea vanished when he remembered the police had dragged Lasi to Jakarta. The most important man in the country was said to be afraid to take Bambung to court; how could he?

Lasi refused to give him her phone number. She said it was for his safety. Kanjat could only wait. Meanwhile, he was consumed by deep sorrow and shame.

During the second call, Kanjat heard Lasi had taken the role of Bambung's consort. He felt ready to explode. He clenched his jaw, balled his fist, and listened thunderstruck as Lasi told him in a light and airy voice about the events.

253

"Jat, I go everywhere with Pak Bambung. We eat out, have parties at white people's homes, watch boxing matches, listen to Dutch music at… er, what's it called? Concerts?"

"Yes, concerts," Kanjat said in a tired voice.

"Yes. We watch the horse races. Did you know Pak Bambung owns many horses? They're not ordinary horses. His horses are huge."

"Yes, I saw it in the newspapers."

"Most people think I'm Japanese. It makes Pak Bambung proud, so I often wear a kimono. The maid who helps me dress is real Japanese."

"Enough, Las. I only want to hear about you and the baby," Kanjat barked.

"Forgive me. I'm healthy and the baby's fine. You don't have to worry about the sanctity of my womb. Our child is still pure. Jat, I've something else to tell you."

"It's not about Bambung, is it?"

"It is, but it has to do with our security. Not everything Mrs. Lanting said about Pak Bambung is true. She said he was a horny old goat and enjoyed having women outside, but was powerless when facing his nagging, tough wife. This last bit is true, but the rest isn't."

"It's not?"

"Pak Bambung is like any other man. He might even be unfortunate. Everyone is in awe of him, but at home he gets no respect from his coarse and controlling wife."

"How do you know this?"

"Pak Bambung told me himself."

"How does he treat you?"

"He's a man, Jat, so he has habits and requests. You know how that goes. He often kisses me on the cheek in front of his friends."

Kanjat's jaw muscles tightened and his eyes turned red.

"I've never let him have me," Lasi went on. "Besides, he's never asked. He never sleeps here. He says all he needs is my gentleness beside him. He's tormented by his wife's violence. It's odd that a man who is publicly so respected has no say in his own home."

"Las, tell me when or how you can get out of there. Or do you intend to stay with Bambung?"

Kanjat resented it when Lasi was slow to answer him. She repeated what Mrs. Lanting said and which couldn't be guaranteed: Bambung would tire of her once her pregnancy started to show.

The stories Lasi told Kanjat over the phone increased his frustration. His heart shrank when the question sprang into his mind: *Can I trust Lasi? If I can't restrain myself when alone in a room with Lasi, what about Bambung, the horny old goat?*

Kanjat shared his worries with Grandfather Mus. The old man was always willing to listen wholeheartedly.

"You feel like Rama after losing Sita?" Grandfather Mus asked Kanjat as they sat together one night. His light voice and welcoming smile eased some of the turmoil in Kanjat's heart.

"In terms of losing a wife, yes. The difference is that Rama was a king with magical powers who won his wife back in the end. But me? I can't do anything."

"That's called a limit, and everyone has one. The man who wrenched Lasi from your arms has one too. Only Allah is without limits."

"Yes, Grandfather. I'm aware of my limits, but isn't there anything I can do to help Lasi? I'm ashamed."

"You should be," Grandfather Mus chuckled. "You also know what you can do."

"What is it, Grandfather?"

"If you still believe, pray with all your heart and soul."

"I often feel that God doesn't hear my prayers."

Grandfather Mus chuckled again. "How do you know your prayers aren't being heard?"

"That's how I feel, Grandfather."

"Banish those feelings and your prayers will calm your heart. It's not easy because the matter that draws on your deepest feelings. I understand your reluctance to pray, and why you're so agitated."

"Very well, Grandfather. I'll pray, even though I doubt my prayers will be heard."

"Good. Other than praying, recite '*khasbunallah wanikmal wakil.*' The verse is for strengthening the heart of anyone who feels helpless.

You need God to stand in for you during this trying time. God willing, you will feel at peace and everything will be easier."

The next telephone call Kanjat received from Lasi came when his office was about to close for the day. She spoke casually, only for much longer.

"Jat, I've extra work. It's quite easy and pays well. Mrs. Lanting gives me letters for Pak Bambung when he comes over."

"What kind of letters?"

"She says they're from people who want an elpee... er..."

"LP. A logging permit," Kanjat explained.

"Yes, that sort of thing. There's also a letter from someone who wants to drill for oil off the coast. Oil comes from drilling?"

"Yes."

"Mrs. Lanting says there are letters from people who want to be chairman of political parties, members of the House, and ministers, who want to set up banks, who want to be something dir..."

"You mean dir-gen, for director general."

"Something like that. Mrs. Lanting says that people who want to win in court can also ask for a rec... rec... er..."

"Recommendation," Kanjat said in a flat voice.

"Yes, that's it. With every letter, Mrs. Lanting brings a receipt showing money has been deposited in my account. How much? It can be a few millions, tens of millions, even hundreds of millions. That's a lot, isn't it, Jat?"

Kanjat felt his face burning. His ears were hot. "What does this have to do with you?" He frowned.

"I give Pak Bambung the letters when he comes over. Mrs. Lanting says that when he gets the letters from me, he reads them immediately and gives rec... rec... what was that word again?"

"Recommendations?"

"Yes, anyone who gets a rec... rec... from Pak Bambung can be what they want."

"And you're involved because you give the letters to Bambung."

"I am, aren't I? I'm a country girl who knows nothing, and here I am playing a part in important matters. It's funny when you think about it."

"I don't like these stories. Just tell me where you live in Jakarta. When you can't take anymore, I'll come for you."

"I told you before, the house is near the Hotel Indonesia. That's the only landmark I recognize. I beg you, please don't come for me. The house is heavily guarded. Be patient. I know we'll see each other again. You have to believe that as long as I call you, my womb is pure. Have you ever doubted my loyalty?"

Kanjat's face went slack when he heard Lasi cry. If he succumbed to the fire of his ego, he would always have a burning in his chest. Lasi remained the same; her candid way of speaking was enough proof.

When she telephoned in the fifth month of her pregnancy, Lasi said her condition was quite noticeable. Her waist had filled out and her breasts were fuller. Mrs. Lanting said her face looked more radiant, even with the weight.

"Jat, I pray that Mrs. Lanting is right and Pak Bambung will throw me out when he sees my big stomach. I'll come home right away. We'll seal our marriage and I'll live with you in Karangsoga."

"Why?"

"I want to hear the chime of the tappers' pongkors and smell the nira as it boils. I want to watch the rock crabs in the clear water beneath the areca palm bridge. Our child will run across that bridge. He'll learn the Qur'an at Grandfather Mus' surau."

"What else?"

"The valley to the south. Is it still covered by mist in the morning and do the egrets fly just below our line of sight in the evening?"

"Yes, everything is the same, except there are fewer egrets."

"We'll buy a nice car and a telephone and have a swimming pool, and anything to make our child happy. We'll turn the surau into a big mosque…"

Kanjat coughed.

"You have a lot of money and a very expensive necklace. All of that belongs to you, but I'd be ashamed to enjoy that wealth. Don't set your sights too high. I'm just a lecturer. I don't make that much.

"And about the mosque, Grandfather Mus says that a glorious mosque is one that spreads faith and compassion. According to him, the glory of a mosque isn't its size and shape, but its spirit."

"I'm sorry, Jat, I forgot. I know you've been sensitive since you were a child. In that case, forget what I said. Jat, your child is moving."

At one end of the line, tears streamed down Lasi's face. At the other end, Kanjat swallowed. He felt his responsibility as a husband to Lasi and a father to the child she carried. His chest felt full. The feeling turned into an unspeakably heavy burden when Kanjat realized again he was paralyzed to help Lasi. He was ashamed.

***

During the first five months of Lasi's pregnancy, the constant waiting and uncertainty tormented Kanjat. He frequently felt as though the moment he reunited with Lasi would never come. *What if Lasi grew to enjoy her growing wealth and luxurious lifestyle? What if Bambung wanted to keep Lasi?*

The long period of uncertainty was even more tortuous when, quite by accident, one day Kanjat heard a foreign radio broadcast. The announcer said that in Jakarta, there was a closed but fierce struggle among those at the peak of power. According to the announcer, a high-level lobbyist believed to be very close to the ruler was being driven out because he had crossed the line. This lobbyist wielded tremendous power within and beyond his official domain, and it was feared he would become a competitor for the highest seat of power.

The long explanation from the foreign radio station also gave background on the cultural aspect of the struggle. In the Javanese concept of power, there could never be twin suns, or two seats of power. The system of government in Indonesia followed the Javanese power system, so the lobbyist with undue influence had to be removed.

Kanjat told his fellow lecturers at the university what he had heard, eliciting a variety of responses.

"Kanjat, you're behind the times. I already heard it from an acquaintance in Jakarta, long before that foreign broadcast," said Cablaka, the lecturer in economics. "A group of foreign and domestic investors see this high-level lobbyist Bambung as a problem. He's one of the reasons for the high inflation, which they don't like. That's why they want to bypass him. They want to arrange their investments directly with the official center of power. So they agitated. One way they used was giving material to foreign radio stations to discredit Bambung. They can easily do it because they've worked with him for a long time and know all his secrets."

"That doesn't make sense," said Martacarub, who taught criminal law. "My brother works at the State Secretariat, and he said the man at the center of power thought it was time to prove he's the only person in the number one position. Having a power broker like Bambung so close made him look weak and incapable as a leader. He's getting rid of the brokers, one by one. Bambung is no exception."

Laughter broke out from the back of the group. "You're all wrong and just pretend to know," said Santamin, the fisheries lecturer. He often spoke of his pursuit of supernatural powers and talked like a sage. "It's like this: among those of us who appreciate mysticism, Bambung isn't just anybody. He's very gifted in the ways of the mystical. His inner strength is unmatchable. We believe his influence extends to the realm of the jinn. He truly is a master in the world of spiritualism. That's why he's been held in such high esteem by the ruler for so long. He's a kind of spiritual teacher.

"But on the other hand, Bambung is also an ordinary man, and like most important men, he caught the common disease called greed. He's made many formidable enemies, even among his own kind, the shamans. It isn't just one, but a whole battalion. A conflict of interests has caused a spiritual clash, pitting one side against the other.

"The first side comprises Bambung and his followers. The other side comprises those who want to replace Bambung at the side of the ruler."

"Didn't you just say that when it came to this sort of stuff, Bambung was unmatchable? How could he lose?" Cablaka asked with a smirk.

"I can't answer that question. The fact is that Bambung and his followers are losing. Someone said the other group has managed to get the *Setan Kober kris*, the legendary dagger with extraordinary powers from the Pajang Kingdom. Among those who believe, the kris is the symbol of the highest power, and it periodically demands the blood and lives of dozens or hundreds of people."

"Where is this Setan Kober kris?" Kanjat asked.

"Why do you ask?" Santamin shot back, cocksure as ever. "The second group of shamans have presented the kris to the ruler, the most important man in the country. His vitality depends on the number of lives offered to the Setan Kober. After an offering is made, through an airplane or train accident, the ruler appears fresh and healthy. Of course, the shamans demand something in return of very high value, and that's a position close to the ruler, which is now occupied by Bambung. Because the shamans are already defeating Bambung, the ruler has no issues in confronting him. Rather than face an inconvenience, it was easier to get rid of him. This is what seems to be happening."

Nonsense, Kanjat thought. The speculation of his fellow lecturers was nothing more than idle talk. They might be scholars, but not one could prove what they were saying with facts and numbers. It was shameful, especially that nonsense about the Setan Kober kris. Should a normal engineer, especially Kanjat, believe in such a thing?

The next day, every newspaper in the country reported the story of Bambung. An influential daily reported the attorney general investigating possible corruption had arrested him.

Another daily said the attorney general had summoned everyone in Bambung's circle of influence. It was the same for officials in the central and regional governments who acquired their posts through his influence. Even his prized mistresses, the paper went on, were being investigated. They were barred from leaving the country and their bank accounts were frozen. A fringe newspaper blared across its front page that Bambung's influence in the government was being purged from the top down.

Kanjat reeled. He knew Lasi was one of Bambung's mistresses. *Will the prosecutors or the police investigate her? What if they mistreat her?*

He pictured Lasi, naïve, uneducated, and pregnant, turning pale and stammering as she answered the questions posed by prosecutors and police officers. She didn't understand legal jargon. He wondered if she had a lawyer.

As his worry mounted, Kanjat yearned for news from Lasi. He waited several days without a call from her. *Is she detained?*

You have an obligation to go to Jakarta and find Lasi, Kanjat told himself. *Don't be such a shameful weakling, just waiting and doing nothing. Go right away. Find Lasi and bring her to Karangsoga. She's your wife and carrying your child.*

Kanjat immediately drove home from the university where he had been reading the newspaper. On the twelve-kilometer trip, he remembered Pardi, the truck driver who took sugar to Jakarta. The moment he got out of his car, he called for Pardi. Kanjat was tense, but when the driver showed up, he was grinning with a cigarette glued to his lips.

"What is it, Mas Kanjat?"

"Come with me to Jakarta."

"I'm taking a load of sugar, leaving tonight."

"We'll go in my car. Find someone else to drive the truck."

"Your father's going to get mad at me. If the shipment is late, it'll ruin business."

"I said, find another driver, and do it now. We're going to look for Lasi in Jakarta and bring her home. This is urgent, so don't waste time talking."

"Why, what happened?"

"I said, don't waste time. You'll find out later."

"Your car won't get us far since the radiator's shot. We'll take my truck."

Kanjat gave in to Pardi; they'd pick up Lasi with a truck full of sugar.

The men left after sunset, in the same truck that had helped Lasi escape from Karangsoga.

Pardi paused at the turnoff to the main road until the traffic cleared. "We'll look for Lasi once we drop off the sugar. Do you have an address?"

Kanjat grew nervous. "Yes, but it's incomplete. She said it's not far from Hotel Indonesia. She can see it to the west. I know roughly what the house looks like, but I don't have the exact address."

"That's going to be difficult. Will we check door to door?"

"You're just an inexperienced driver. We'll drive the roads to the east of Hotel Indonesia until we find a house that matches Lasi's description. That's easy enough."

"Looking around is easy for a driver. The problem is, how long are we going to search in an unfamiliar area?"

"That can't be helped. I'm going to keep searching until I find Lasi. Let's go."

The sugar truck turned left onto the main road and trundled toward Jakarta. By four the next morning it was parked outside a warehouse in West Jakarta. While they waited for the cargo to be unloaded, Pardi took Kanjat to a restaurant where Kanjat could bathe, change his clothes, and pray. Pardi stretched out on a bench and fell asleep. Kanjat felt his own eyelids drooping, but the thoughts racing through his mind kept him awake.

They had breakfast at seven. On Pardi's recommendation, they rented a car to look for Lasi. A seasoned driver who had driven the Karangsoga–Jakarta route for years helped Pardi to quickly find a car. They circled the roundabout and turned east. From that point on, Kanjat and Pardi kept their eyes peeled for a house with a guard post, a white fence, and a green gate. They went up one road and down another for almost an hour, until they found the house.

Pardi pulled over and Kanjat got out. The gate was shut and the guard post was empty. Kanjat tried to look into the yard. Pardi joined him. Their presence at the gate drew the attention of a police officer sitting on the terrace, unseen from the road. The young officer got up and walked toward the gate.

"Good morning, pak," Kanjat called out.

"Morning," the officer said, crisp and formal. "What do you want?"

"We'd like to see Ibu Lasi. Is she home?"

The policeman remained indifferent.

"You see, Ibu Lasi and us, we come from the same village," Pardi chimed in. "We wanted to see how she's doing."

"Is the Ibu Lasi you're talking about the mistress of this house?" the policeman asked.

"Probably," Kanjat said, hazarding a guess.

"This house has been empty for the past two days. I was only posted here earlier this morning."

"In that case, do you know where the mistress is now?" Kanjat's anxiety was mounting.

"I heard she was being investigated. She might be at the police station, or the prosecutor's office. Maybe you can find her there."

Kanjat turned away, frowning. Pardi also looked downcast. They barely spoke on the way to the police headquarters near the Semanggi cloverleaf, and continued to blow clouds of cigarette smoke.

"Are you sure Lasi is inside?" Pardi asked when they reached the headquarters.

"Anything's possible. Who knows?"

"Wait," Pardi cut him off. He eyed a traffic police officer at the entrance of the building. "I know him. We should ask for help."

"Who is he?"

"He's a traffic officer and I'm a truck driver. Do I need to say more?"

Kanjat smiled as Pardi rushed after the officer. He watched Pardi engage him in conversation. The officer seemed reluctant, but Pardi kept after him until he succeeded. They looked like they were in a serious discussion. Five minutes later, Pardi returned more cheerful.

"Wait here. He's going to find out if Lasi is here. No matter what information he comes back with, we have to be ready."

"Money?"

Pardi grinned. Kanjat had to admit that when it came to dealing with the police, a driver like Pardi knew much more than he.

The officer emerged fifteen minutes later and took Pardi and Kanjat to the edge of the parking lot to talk. Lasi was being detained pending an investigation. So far, she was being treated as a possible witness. Kanjat had a sudden pain in his chest.

"Do you want to see her?"

"Of course. We came from our village far away. Please help us, pak. Try to get us inside."

"I don't know if it's possible. She's being held in connection with a high-level corruption case."

"I'm sure you can find a way."

"Seeing a detainee is difficult, and there are many requirements. I'm not the one who decides. That's the job of the senior officer."

"We know, pak, that's why we ask for your help. We've known each other a long time on the road, so we know…"

"You good-for-nothing. All right, I'll try. Wait here."

Kanjat and Pardi went back to waiting. It took longer this time, and in the meantime, Pardi asked Kanjat to prepare an envelope. They had to use the money for renting the car and Pardi dipped into his own pocket too.

Almost at midday, Kanjat and Pardi were finally allowed to see Lasi. Kanjat and Lasi were bewildered when they met each other in the visitors' room. Kanjat, who seemed more composed, looked at Lasi. She was plumper and her tummy showed, and she was more beautiful than ever. Kanjat's heart raced.

Lasi's mouth dropped open. She raised her arms and ran across the room to hug Kanjat tight. She shook. Her sobs rang out, punctuated by deep breaths, and she broke into a cold sweat.

Kanjat felt her warm tears on his shoulder.

Pardi, who was usually full of jokes, only bowed his head and lit a cigarette.

"Finally… Finally we're together, Jat," Lasi said between sobs. "Jat, it's so good that you came. Who would stay with me if not you? I have no one in Jakarta." She kept crying, her embrace growing tighter.

"Yes. Calm down."

"You're the only one who'd stay with me. Oh, thank you for coming. How did you know I was here?"

"From the newspapers," Kanjat tried to keep the answer simple.

"You know I'm being detained?" Lasi almost started sobbing again.

"It's only temporary. They want to hear your statement as a possible witness. You'll be free as soon as the questioning is done."

"They'll let me go? I won't be jailed?"

"Hopefully not."

"Why are they holding me? What have I done wrong?"

"The fact is you're only a witness. I'm sure you won't be here too long."

"Don't be too sure, Mas Kanjat," Pardi cut in. "Everything depends on how we approach these people. I'll bet that even if they're done with Lasi, they won't let her go without an understanding from us. I'm afraid that will be in the form of a very thick envelope."

"Not so loud."

"Jat…"

"Las, address him properly as your husband," Pardi said. "You're his wife, aren't you?"

Lasi blushed.

Kanjat tried to speak, but instead took a drag on his cigarette.

"Las, your tummy is big now. Take good care of yourself and the baby. I won't go home until your case is over. I should find a lawyer."

Lasi asked what a lawyer was for, and Kanjat explained.

"You're right. I know many of the food vendors around here. As long as we pay them, they'll bring Lasi meals every day," Pardi said.

"Will I have to stay here for long? Jat, I mean, *Kang* Kanjat, I can't take it anymore. I want to go home."

"That's why I'm going to call a law office this afternoon and get you out of here as quickly as possible. A man I went to university with in Purwokerto practices law here. I'm sure he'll help for a small fee. The problem is that I don't know where his office is."

"Yes, Jat, er… yes, Kang, hopefully it works out. Promise you won't go back to Karangsoga without me."

Kanjat nodded sincerely. At the same time, an officer called out their visiting time was over. Kanjat kissed Lasi on the forehead.

Sobbing, Lasi wanted to keep him in her embrace. She finally let go, and waved as Kanjat and Pardi left.

After making several telephone calls to people in Purwokerto as well as Jakarta, Kanjat found his university friend, the lawyer. By two that afternoon, he sat in Blakasuta's law office.

"We haven't seen each other in so long, and here I am, bringing you nothing but problems," Kanjat said. "I desperately need help."

"Jat, it's written all over your face. It must be serious. Have a seat and calm down. What's the problem?"

Kanjat told Blakasuta about Lasi, and showed his apprehension.

Blakasuta listened with clenched jaws. His eyes occasionally widened. The young lawyer was surprised that Lasi, whose name was linked to Bambung in the newspapers and under investigation by the prosecutor, was a Karangsoga woman. He was even more shocked to hear Kanjat say Lasi was his wife and pregnant.

"She's carrying my child. You must know how I feel right now."

"I truly understand, that's why I'm willing to help. Let's prepare the papers so we can start working. I'll take the papers to your wife this very afternoon to sign."

The weight on Kanjat's heart eased a little when he knew Lasi would have a lawyer at her side. Pardi was great too, even if he was just a driver. He found a vendor to bring Lasi her meals.

During the next fifteen days, Kanjat shuttled between Jakarta and Purwokerto, which conflicted with his teaching schedule. He suppressed his relief at being able to see Lasi until the investigation was finished.

The sixteenth day was a big day. The police declared they were finished questioning Lasi. They released her, thanks in part to Blakasuta vouching that she would come in for questioning if needed in future. Lasi's belly also elicited compassion, making the police and prosecutors reluctant to hold her any longer.

"It's a shame I can't make her joy complete," Blakasuta said as he escorted Lasi and Kanjat from the police headquarters to his car.

"What do you mean?"

"The prosecutor has seized her house in Slipi, along with the necklace worth billions. Her bank account with hundreds of millions has been blocked too. I'll keep trying. Who knows, maybe as the case develops they'll return her property. That's my challenge."

Lasi listened to Blakasuta's explanation and managed a tired smile. "I never really owned it, kang," she said when she sat with Kanjat in the back seat.

Blakasuta turned on the engine and drove to the exit of the police station. He was about to enter the main road when a fat woman jumped in front of the car.

"Stop, stop. Lasi, get out. Are you running away again? Pak Bambung may be in jail, but there are other old men—lobbyists, officials, politicians, and businessmen—who are lusting after you. Jakarta has many rising stars with plenty of money. Let's wring them for all they're worth. Come on, Lasi, get out."

"Oh, not her again. Las, isn't she the one who came after us in Surabaya?"

"Yes, it's her."

"Who is she?" Blakasuta asked.

"Mrs. Lanting. She knows many people high up. Did you hear what she said?"

Blakasuta raised his eyebrows and smiled wryly. "Well, this is Jakarta."

"Get out," Mrs. Lanting shouted. She kept blocking their way.

Lasi drew closer to Kanjat and leaned her head on his shoulder. She asked Blakasuta not to pay any heed to the fat cow. The car jerked forward. Mrs. Lanting jumped aside, swearing. "You stupid country girl. You'll never understand that in this life the most important thing is money. Stupid."

"Let's go home to Karangsoga, kang. What should I call you?" Lasi sighed. She ignored Mrs. Lanting's ramblings.

"I like being called kang."

"Kang Engineer or Kang Lecturer or Kang Kanjat?"

"That last one sounds the best."

"Even though I'm older and twice divorced?"

"Yes. All that matters is you, not your age or your past."

They talked quietly in the back seat.

Blakasuta felt left out. "Hey, get intimate all you want, but where am I taking you?"

"Sorry, Mr. Lawyer. Please take us to the truck stop. We'll look for Pardi, my parents' sugar truck driver. He's bound to be there today."

"You're going back to Karangsoga in a sugar truck?"

"I came here in the same truck. Besides, my parents own it and I'm used to the ride."

Blakasuta shook his head and drove in the direction Kanjat had requested.

That night, a truck left Jakarta, heading east toward Karangsoga. As they passed the Klender area, Lasi looked out the window for Ibu Koneng's restaurant. It was there she had stayed before falling into Mrs. Lanting's hands and fed to Handarbeni. Lasi caught a glimpse of it. She saw the woman with big earrings and the one with chafed calves, and fleetingly saw the laksa vendor.

The truck kept going east. Kanjat, Lasi, and Pardi sat together in the cab. Three years earlier, Lasi had run away in the same truck. The difference between that journey and the one she was on was strikingly real.

The first time she felt she was inside a locked metal box that hurtled toward an unknown destination. This time, the truck was still a metal box, but it felt like riding in a carriage, gliding and swaying to a familiar and beautiful destination: home. Ah, to be home and oneself again and walk the earth of Karangsoga with Kanjat.

"We're going home, kang," Lasi whispered. Her words were almost drowned out by the roar of the truck.

"Yes, we're finally going home."

As he heard the word "home" exchanged between Kanjat and Lasi, Pardi sung a verse from a Banyumasan song in a teasing voice: "*Eling-eling, wong eling balio maning...* You who have settled the unrest in your souls, go home." Pardi laughed after singing the line, and lit a cigarette. Lasi massaged Kanjat's shoulder, and he joined in the laughter. The cool night air seemed to heat inside the cab.

The truck continued to drive Kanjat and Lasi home. Lasi grew drowsy as she leaned against Kanjat. She felt the truck hit a rough patch of road when Pardi braked hard. But for much of the time between waking and sleep, she was already in Karangsoga, cradling her baby in the shade of the bamboo grove behind her house. She heard the clanking of the tappers' pongkors and inhaled the smell of nira about to caramelize into sugar. She heard her mother's voice and saw Grandfather Mus walk to his surau, accompanied by the flat and regular tap of his cane. Lasi talked in her sleep and sighed, "Mother, mother… I'm home."

Notes

Chapter 1

Sengon tree: *Paraserianthes falcataria*, a soft wood with short harvesting age.

Jambe rowe: *Areca catechu*, also known as Indian nut, Pinang palm, and betel tree, its fruit is often chewed with betel leaves.

Nira: Coconut flower sap, used in the making of coconut sugar.

Pongkor: Small pail made of bamboo section with looped handle, used to collect sap from flowers at the top of coconut palms.

Surau: A privately owned place of worship for Muslims.

Azar prayer time: Muslim afternoon praying time.

Kebaya: Traditional combination blouse and dress worn by Indonesian women.

Pak: Respectful term of address for an older man, meaning "father."

Pandan: *Pandanus utilis,* also known as padanu, its young leaves used for handicrafts.

Mbok: Respectful term of address for an older woman, meaning "mother."

Snake-fruit tree: *Salacca zalacca*, sometimes known as salak; outer skin of the fruit is scaly with tiny spikes when fresh.

Tokay gecko: Colorful nocturnal tree-dwelling reptile.

Chapter 2

Gambang: Known also as *gambang kayu*, a wooden musical instrument of seventeen to twenty-one keys played with long slender mallets, similar to the xylophone.

Sinom: Also known as *srinata*, poetic verse form of eighteen-line stanzas.

Dhandhanggula: Poetic verse form of ten-line stanzas; each line has a predetermined number of syllables and ends in a vowel.

Puyengan: *Lantana camara*, also known as big sage in Malaysia, perennial plant with small tubular-shaped flowers.

Ibu: Respectful term of address for a woman, similar to *mbok*. Diminutive form, "bu," is more friendly and casual.

Chapter 3

Logondang: Local dialect for *Ficus benghalensis*, known as the banyan tree.

Sujud: Muslim position of prayer with forehead, nose, palms, knees, toes, but not arms, touching the floor or ground.

Wali: Arabic for "trusted one," the nine saints who introduced Islam to Indonesia.

"…suweng ireng digadhekna, wis kadhung meteng dikapakna.": Literal translation is "When you've pawned your black earrings, what can you do when she's pregnant?"

Gouramis: *Osphronemus goramy*, freshwater fish capable of breathing air for short periods.

Serunai: Wind musical instrument with quadruple reed made from a rice stalk, played by using circular breathing.

Chapter 4

Bekisar: A fine crossbreed between junglefowl and domestic chicken that often adorns the houses of the wealthy.

Mas: Friendly term of address among males of the same age group, meaning "brother."

Chapter 5

Sayur bening: Clear spinach and corn soup with chilies

Sambal trassi: Chili paste.

"...certificate of domicile...": Document required by Indonesia's Directorate General of Taxation to show proof of residence.

Rendang Padang: Beef and coconut milk curry.

Ayam kalasan: Chicken boiled in shallots, garlic, palm sugar, and coconut milk, and fried.

Lebaran or *Idul Fitri*: The end of the Muslim fasting month Ramadhan

Oman: In local dialect, a stalk of rice.

Iman: Follower of the six articles of faith in the Islamic religion, Belief in God, Belief in the Angels, Belief in Divine Books, Belief in the Prophets, Belief in the Day of Judgment, and Belief in God's Predestination.

Slawatan: Arabic for "song of praise," a traditional Islamic hymn accompanied by percussion instruments.

Suluk sisiringan: Muslim verses of praise recited before saying the *subuh* (before sunrise), *maghrib* (sunset) and *isha* (night time) prayers.

Albizia trees: *Albizia julibrissin*, also known as silk trees.

Peci: Black brimless felt hat worn by Muslim men for celebrations and formal occasions.

Kalimantan: Indonesian part of Borneo, dominating seventy-three percent of the island.

Irian Jaya: Indonesian province covering the western peninsula of New Guinea Island, its name changed to Papua in 2007.

Soga: *Peltophorum pterocarpum*, also known as yellow flame tree.

Chapter 6

Wayang: Shadow play, originally from Java.

Chapter 7

Kejawen: Javanese religious tradition that combines the beliefs and practices of Islam, animism, Buddhism, and Sufism.

Sakmadya: Principle of Javanese philosophy that says people should want only what they need or can afford, and not have too high expectations.

Pasar Rumput: Traditional market in Jakarta.

"…candid *Batak* style…": Batak people live in north Sumatra and are known for being straightforward, unlike the Javanese who are known for being sly.

Sepasang Mata Bola: A well-known *keroncong* song, an old-fashioned slow, crooning music style; Indonesian for "A Pair of Eyes."

Wayang orang: Highly formalized theater style based on the *wayang*, or shadow play.

Chapter 8

Gado-gado: Blanched vegetable salad with sauce made of ground peanuts, palm sugar, dried prawn paste, and chilies.

Rujak: Fruit salad made with palm sugar, tamarind juice, and chilies.

Kerok: Indonesian cold remedy where Tiger Balm or eucalyptus oil is rubbed along the muscle lines on the back, neck, and chest, and a coin is used to scrape the skin along the lines.

Jambu tree: *Syzygium cumini,* also known as Java plum.

Laksa: Spicy prawn or chicken noodle-based dish made with chilies and coconut milk.

Teppanyaki: Meat or seafood cooked on an iron griddle using soybean oil.

Chapter 9

"…Rama after losing Sita…": Characters from the Hindu epic, the *Ramayana*.

Khasbunallah wanikmal wakil: Allah (alone) is sufficient for us, and He is the best disposer of affairs (for us). Qur'an 3:173.

Kris: Ceremonial Javanese dagger with a wavy blade.

Kang: Also known as kangmas, meaning "elder brother."

About the Author

Award-winning and acclaimed Indonesian author Ahmad Tohari has written numerous novels and short story collections. He is the recipient of the South East Asian Writers Award and of a fellowship to the International Writing Program of Iowa City, Iowa. He is also a respected journalist for the Central Java newspaper, *Suara Merdeka*, and *Tempo*, the Indonesian weekly.

Ahmad is best known for his trilogy, *Ronggeng Dukuh Paruk* (*The Dancing Girl of Paruk Village*), published by Gramedia in 2011. The novels have been translated into Dutch, English, German, and Japanese, and adapted into the film, *The Dancer*, directed by Ifa Isfansyah. Ahmad is also held in high regard for his knowledge of Javanese art. He currently lives near Purwokerto, where he runs an Islamic school with his family and is consultant for the regional office of the Indonesian Ministry of Culture and Education.

*More Storytellers from
Dalang Publishing*

Only a Girl
Lian Gouw

Three generations of Chinese women struggle for identity against a political backdrop of the World Depression, World War II, and the Indonesian Revolution. Nanna, the matriarch of the family, strives to preserve the family's traditional Chinese values while her children are eager to assimilate into Dutch colonial society. Carolien, Nanna's youngest daughter, is fixated on the advantages to be gained by adopting a western lifestyle. Jenny's western upbringing puts her at a disadvantage in the new independent Indonesian, where Dutch culture is no longer revered. The unique ways in which Nanna, Carolien, and Jenny face their own challenges reveal the complexity of Chinese society in Indonesia between 1930 and 1952.

Price: $17.95
Paperback: 298 pages
ISBN: 978-0-9836273-7-1

My Name is Mata Hari
Remy Sylado
Translated from the Indonesian by Dewi Anggraeni

My Name is Mata Hari tells the story of Margaretha Geertruida Zelle, a young
Dutch woman married to an older military officer assigned to the Dutch East
Indies. Claiming her mother's Javanese ancestry, she changed her name to Mata
Hari, Malay for "eye of the day."
As Mata Hari, she danced on stages across Europe and the Middle East, and took
many high-ranking military and government officials as her lovers. Convicted of
espionage during World War I, she said at the end of her tumultuous life, "I am a
genuine courtesan. And I am a dancer in the true sense."

Price: $17.95
Paperback: 334 pages
ISBN: 978-0-9836273-0-2

Potions and Paper Cranes
Lan Fang
Translated from the Indonesian by Elisabet Titik Murtisari

In Lan Fang's award-winning novel, Sulis is a young woman selling potions
in Surabaya's harbor district. She meets Sujono, a day laborer with dreams of
becoming a freedom fighter, and whose passion for Matsumi, a geisha called to
Java by a Japanese general, is destined to ruin all of them. Each tells the story
of their lives during the Japanese occupation of Java and Indonesia's transition
from a Dutch colony to an independent republic.

Price: $17.95
Paperback: 252 pages
ISBN: 978-0-9836273-3-3

Kei
Erni Aladjai
Translated from the Indonesian by Nurhayat Indriyatno Mohamed

At the end of Suharto's New Order, the Kei people hold on to their traditions
as they flee the violence that divides Muslim from Christian and destroys the
villages. Namria, a Muslim girl, works as a volunteer in a refugee camp when
she meets Sala, a young Protestant man. Grounded in the islander's belief of
"We drink from the same spring and eat from the same land, the land of Kei,"
the two fall in love amid the chaos that will soon separate them.

Price: $17.95
Paperback: 224 pages
ISBN: 978-0-9836273-6-4

Daughters of Papua
Anindita Siswanto Thayf
Translated from the Indonesian by Stefanny Irawan

Seven-year-old Leksi lives in modern-day Papua with her grandmother Mabel
and her mother, Mace. Pum, an old dog of unknown ancestory, and Kwee, a
pig, along with Leksi, look back at the past as they face an uncertain future. In
Daughters of Papua, the present is marked by a contentious election, with the
gold company that wants to rob Papuans of their heritage the only winner.

Price: $17.95
Paperback: 224 pages
ISBN: 978-0-9836273-9-5